LAND OF THE MORNING CALM

PREQUEL TO *EAST OF THE SIN*

HEIRS OF FREEDOM SERIES

ENDORSEMENTS

In *Land of the Morning Calm*, Rebecca Price Janney provides a well-crafted historical novel reflecting on faith and purpose amid cross-cultural encounter, telling the story with historical care and spiritual attentiveness.
—**Kevin J. Brown**, PhD, President, Asbury University

Dr. Rebecca Price Janney has done it again, creating a powerful story that transforms time and spans cultures. Through complex, relatable characters and rich, vivid details, *Land of the Morning Calm* brings to life the great harvest and its individual impact as Christianity spread in Korea in the early 1900s. The story shows that the need to forgive others, surrender arrogance and find love knows no boundaries between east and west—a great read.
—**Jane Hampton Cook**, author of *Stories of Faith and Courage from the Revolutionary War.*

Deep and fascinating as always.
—**Jason W. Karpf**, author, *Brimstone 1, The Deliverer, Honor System*

What a delight! Readers are sure to enjoy *Land of the Morning Calm*, Rebecca Price Janney's prequel to her popular *East of the Sun*. The richness of historical detail against the backdrop of war, education, and spiritual crisis spanning from the East Coast of the United States to Korea is sure to draw the reader in as her characters wrestle with questions of faith, faithfulness, and revival. Don't miss this story of growth, culture, and the power of personal relationships in the first decade of the 1900s.
—**Marlo Schalesky**, award-winning author of *Women of the Bible Speak Out*

One of the greatest cultural and religious shifts in the Twentieth Century was the massive acceptance of Christianity by the people of Korea. Though only marginally noticed by the media, this revival has given biblical Christianity a strong base for reaching the rest of Asia in our day. In her book, *Land of the Morning Calm*, Rebecca Price Janney tells the story of the beginnings of this world-changing move of God through the stories of simple Korean disciples and American missionaries who obeyed the call of Jesus to "Go ye into all the world," and by doing so, sowed the seeds that would reap this miraculous harvest. Janney is a master historical writer and in this tale she reveals another way God is at work in the world today through humble servants of Jesus Christ.
—**Dr. Craig von Buseck**, award-winning author and speaker

Christians are crying out for a mighty move of God upon our nation. Anyone who prays for revival will want to read *Land of the Morning Calm* in which Rebecca Price Janney takes the reader back to the 1907 Korean revival. This was a period when the Holy Spirit also moved through southern California, Wales, and other parts of the world. The leaders and members at Pyongyang's Central Presbyterian Church gathered to cry out to the Lord to move upon their church and nation, and God answered their prayers with a mighty move of His Spirit. Even people who opposed this visitation experienced their own meeting with Him on the Damascus Road. Today, God calls us to redig these wells of revival from long ago. Read this book and be encouraged.
—**Wendy Wirsch**, President of the William Tennent House Association

LAND OF THE MORNING CALM

PREQUEL TO *EAST OF THE SIN*
HEIRS OF FREEDOM SERIES

REBECCA PRICE JANNEY

A Christian Company

COPYRIGHT NOTICE

Cover and Interior Design: Kelly Artieri, Deb Haggerty
Editor(s): Cristel Phelps, Deb Haggerty
Author Represented by David Fessenden: WordWise Media

PUBLISHED BY: Elk Lake Publishing, Inc., 35 Dogwood Drive, Plymouth, MA 02360, 2026

Library Cataloging Data

Names: Price Janney, Rebecca (Rebecca Price Janney)
Land of the Morning Calm / Rebecca Price Janney

408 p. 23cm × 15cm (9in × 6 in.)
ISBN-13: 9798891345195 (paperback) | 9798891345201 (trade paperback) | 9798891345218 (e-book)

Key Words: Christian historical romance Korea early 1900s; Inspirational friendship story wartime sacrifice; Heartfelt historical fiction America Korea pastors; Religious men bond women love historical Jesus; Danger duty romance historical fiction Christian; Christian war historical inspirational romance God; Christian fiction relationship culture clash 1900s

Library of Congress Control Number: 2026934906 Fiction

ACKNOWLEDGMENTS

Many people have shared their expertise and insights with me, and I'm thankful to each of them for contributing to this novel's authenticity: David Stewart, Westminster Theological Seminary Librarian; Ana Ramirez Luhrs, Co-director, Special Collections and College Archives, Beth Sica, David Bishop Skillman Library, Lafayette College; Allison Graham, Reference Librarian, Princeton Theological Seminary; Sharon Gothard, director of the Marx Room, Easton Area Public Library; Wendy and Dave Wandersee, First United Church of Christ historians, Easton, PA.

I also owe a debt of gratitude to the following works by and about those who labored in Korea during the great harvest: The Correspondence of Samuel Austin Moffett from Princeton Seminary's Moffett Korea Collection; *The Christian's Secret of a Happy Life,* Hannah Whitall Smith, 1942 Spire Edition, pages 34, 76-77; The memoir of William N. Blair and his son-in-law Bruce F. Hunt, *The Korean Pentecost and the Sufferings Which Followed*, 1977, Banner of Truth Trust, Edinburgh, Scotland.

I'm deeply grateful to my fellow historian and dear friend Jane Hampton Cook for being a first reader. Her insightful comments and encouragement about the characters and the story's development were as "iron sharpening iron." She blesses me in so many ways.

One of the happiest privileges I've known was studying under Dr. Samuel Hugh Moffett at Princeton Seminary. An elegant, kind, gracious man in whom the Christian faith ran deep, he was the son of Samuel Austin Moffett, who in 1890 began laying the foundation for the Presbyterian Church in Korea. "My" Dr. Moffett and his radiant wife Eileen introduced me to the Korean people, establishing my lifelong admiration and affection for them. The Moffetts, my Korean friends, and the seminary students I once taught, blessed me with their cheerful resilience and dedication to Jesus, for whom there is no east or west.

I hope you will enjoy this "prequel" to *East of the Sun*.

Hananim chukbokhaseyo.

Rebecca Price Janney

DEDICATION

For Samuel Hugh Moffett and Eileen Flower Moffett.

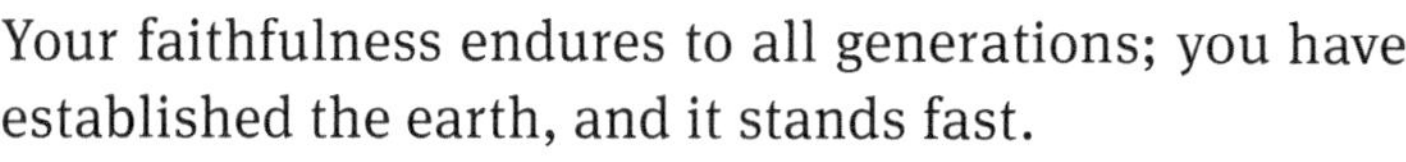

Your faithfulness endures to all generations; you have established the earth, and it stands fast.

(Psalm 119:90 ESV)

CHAPTER ONE

JANUARY 28, 1903
EASTON, PENNSYLVANIA

The sound of his frat brothers bantering in the hallway receded as Jacob Kichline recited his speech to the mirror. Delta Kappa Epsilon's Mastiff, ironically known as Minnie, eyed him with a tail wag, which he accepted as approval.

"Welcome brothers and sisters of Christian Endeavor to the First Reformed Church of Easton. We're delighted to host this regional meeting with schools across the Lehigh Valley, and I pray this event will bless you abundantly, beyond what you expect."

Frowning, he paused to adjust his uneven part to create a precise line across his scalp. The new chap at Tony's Tonsorial Parlor had done a fine job with Jacob's copious blond hair which had inspired his classmates' rather unfortunate nickname, "Haystack." He much preferred the other moniker they'd bestowed upon him, "Billy," a nod to his admiration for baseball player-turned-evangelist, Billy Sunday. Jacob had considered using a funny story or joke from his arsenal of mirth to loosen everyone up; however, while Pastor Kieffer was no killjoy, one never knew about the other college's representatives.

"We are standing on the threshold of a new century with endless possibilities to reach distant shores with the gospel in ways never before seen."

The sound of sniggering brought Jacob up short, and he spun around to see his roommate clutching his sides.

"Don't stop, Billy, you are such an inspiration."

His face aflame, Jacob lobbed a slipper at Fred Horn, catching him on the side of the head. "How long have you been crouching there like a baboon?"

"Long enough to watch you preen." He slapped a thigh, tears streaming down his face. "Isn't he killer, Minnie?" Fred gave the dog a vigorous scratch behind her ears, and she moaned in delight. "I don't know why you involve yourself with a bunch of holy rollers."

The thing about fraternity brothers was they always had your back. Unfortunately, they sometimes could stab the very same back.

"You could do with some holy rolling, you miserable cur."

"I get enough mandatory religion in class and at chapel."

Jacob winked at his nemesis. "There will be coeds there."

"And what would I want with a hallelujah lassie?" Fred lit his pipe and tossed the spent match on the floor. "Besides, I'm going to see the Four Cohans tonight."

This caught his attention. "I didn't realize they were playing in Easton. Where?"

"The Able Opera House."

He leaned against his chest of drawers. "Just think, you'll be able to sing and dance your way into Heaven."

"Why not arrive singing and dancing?"

"I doubt anyone destined for the other place will be enjoying themselves."

They all jumped at the sound of crashing glass, Minnie growling. When a burst of guffaws accompanied whatever accident had taken place, Jacob's heart rate settled down.

Fred released a small puff of smoke, no bigger than a man's hand. "Since everyone goes to Heaven, I don't know why you and your friend Harry, and those other guys get all fired up about soul winning and saintliness."

They'd had this conversation before. Wasn't he listening?

"As I've told you many times, orthodox Christians don't believe in universal salvation."

"Well, Billy Sunday, I happen to find my family's Unitarianism far more agreeable. Just skidoo, will you? You're annoying me." He gestured to the door.

Jacob gave a good-natured laugh. "Believe me, the feeling is mutual."

When Harry Flory met him outside DKE, Jacob frowned. "Where is everyone?"

"They went ahead to help Pastor Kieffer get the church ready. I stopped by yesterday to update you on our plans, but you were at a baseball meeting. I left word with Fred about the change."

Jacob raised his eyes to the pinking sky. "He didn't tell me."

"Oh. Well, we all figured since you're giving the speech representing Lafayette and emceeing, you shouldn't have to set up tables and chairs."

He clapped his friend's back. "That was nice of you. Thanks."

"So, are you ready?"

He briefly considered his practice run, as well as Fred's rude interruption. "Yes, I think so."

"I've heard you give at least half a dozen speeches, and you're good. I'll bet you don't even get nervous."

"Thanks, Harry. I do get some jitters, but I try to make the energy work for me."

They ambled down bucolic Sullivan Road in the direction of the old church on North Third Street, a twelve-minute walk. Snow piles on either side had reduced by half since Jacob had walked this route a week ago.

"How many guys are coming from Lafayette?"

"At last count, there were fourteen of us, including you and me," Harry said.

"Not bad." Out of the college's twenty-five-member Christian Endeavor group, this was a good showing for the Day of Prayer for Colleges.

Jacob wondered how many students might be attending from Lehigh, Moravian, Muhlenberg, Moravian Female Seminary, and Allentown College for Women. He'd told his mother to prepare refreshments for seventy-five to a hundred, but the women's circle had insisted on baking cakes and cookies for at least a hundred. He'd objected at the overkill, but his mother stood as firm as Mt. Parnasus along the Delaware River. No one would ever accuse this German church of sending people away hungry.

He filled his lungs with the soft spring air on March's lamb-like breeze. The lion part of the month had included flooding from heavy rains and melting snow, but now Bushkill Creek at the base of the road flowed placidly within its banks. He often tried to picture what this very scene had looked like a hundred and fifty years ago when his ancestor Colonel Peter Kichline operated mills on either side.

Just before they crossed over Bushkill Street and onto North Third, Harry suggested they pray together.

"Yes, let's. Would you lead us?"

"I'll be glad to."

They paused along the side of the quiet street and asked God's blessing over the rally Harry concluding, "May all we say and do, including our conversations over refreshments, honor your great name. May you equip us to do your kingdom work now and into the future. Amen."

"Amen."

At North Third Street, they encountered the lamp lighter at work in the gathering dusk and raised their hands in greeting.

"Hello, Mr. Cherry. What a fine night we have," Jacob said.

The middle-aged man doffed his cap. "Good evening, Mr. Kichline, Mr. Flory." Holding the lighting stick in the other hand, he gazed heavenward. "This is indeed a fine night. I hear there are big doings at the church."

"Today's the Day of Prayer for Colleges, and Christian Endeavor groups from area schools will be coming."

"Well, God bless you. The world needs more of your kind."

As they passed Spring Garden Street, Jacob glanced eastward to his family residence at the end of the block. He would have liked to pop in to say hello to his father and siblings, but judging from the gas lamps' spreading light, there wouldn't be time.

The army of Lafayette students and church members had transformed the Revolutionary War-era church. His buddies greeted him with grins and back slapping. Between them and the church women, the Session Room appeared ready for a wedding reception with gleaming silver and trays arrayed with cold salads, hearty sandwiches, cookies, and cakes. Candlelight illuminated glass punch bowls with ice chunks cooling the colorful drinks.

"Mother, you've outdone yourself." Jacob bent down and hugged her plump shoulders.

"We wanted to make sure our guests feel welcome."

"Oh, I'm sure they will."

He saw her eyes look to someone behind him, and he turned to face his minister.

"There you are, Jacob." Pastor Kieffer's white hair shone with a peculiar halo effect as he ushered over a young woman.

His lips parted at the sight of the prettiest face he'd ever seen outside an art gallery.

"Miss Pearl Smith, I'd like you to meet Mr. Jacob Kichline. He's a member of this church as well as tonight's Lafayette College representative and emcee. This is his mother, Mrs. Helen Kichline."

She smiled as she extended her hand first to Jacob's mother, then to him. "I am happy to meet you both."

"Miss Smith comes from Allentown College for Women," Pastor Kieffer said. "She tells me this marks the occasion of her first speech. Perhaps you can offer some encouragement, Jacob."

When nothing came out of his mouth, Jacob nearly let an "ooph" escape when his mother performed an unsubtle rib jab.

"My son will be the perfect host, I assure you, Miss Smith. If there is anything I can do, please let me know."

"Thank you, Mrs. Kichline. I've always heard about this church's history and couldn't wait to see inside."

Pastor Kieffer took charge. “And Jacob is just the person to tell you its secrets. Now then, come with me.” He led them to a quieter corner in the narthex. “As the other schools’ leaders arrive, I’ll direct them to this spot, so you can all coordinate. At seven sharp, I’ll open the evening with a small welcoming speech, then Jacob will take over. The schools will be represented in alphabetical order, and I suggest no one talks for over ten minutes—closer to five is ideal.” He winked at Pearl. “I know from experience how much some people enjoy the sound of their own voices. Well then, I shall leave you two while I keep the processes flowing.”

When Pearl smiled, Jacob’s breath hitched. Everything about her appearance exuded a refreshing pleasantness.

“How long have you attended this church, Mr. Kichline?”

“Uh, since I was born. I live, that is my family lives, on the next street over.” Her brown eyes seemed to welcome him into her space—or were they blue? He couldn’t quite tell and didn’t want to ogle.

“My church is only ten years old, and while I love going there, this place has such depth of history, and I do love history.”

Hungry for details about her life he asked, “What church do you go to?”

“The Presbyterian church in Bethlehem, where I’m from.”

She’s local.

“Just how old is this church?” she asked, glancing this way and that.

“The congregation began in the early 1740s not too far from this site. After a courthouse was built in 1766, the people worshiped there until this church was constructed right around the time of the Revolution.”

"How exciting! Was your family here way back then?"

He squared his shoulders. "They've pretty much been part of the German Reformed Church from the start, and my ancestor loaned the money for this building."

She gawked as if this were St. Peter's Basilica. "I am amazed. Oh, I just love this place."

The church was so familiar to him Jacob forgot its legacy until someone reminded him. Then he was fascinated and thankful all over again.

"So, uh, Miss Smith, you'll be speaking right after me. Although your school is first alphabetically, the committee decided the host school and church should open the program. I hope you're comfortable with the arrangement."

"Yes, of course." She smoothed a flyaway hair along her right ear, causing Jacob to study her dark tresses. She opened her beaded purse and pulled out a piece of paper. "I have everything written down. The other girls from ACW had me practice before them so many times I've memorized the speech. Of course, I'm liable to forget once I realize everyone is looking at me."

"I'm sure you'll do just fine. Would you like to see where we'll be speaking?"

She rubbed her chin. "I would, but what if the others come, and we aren't waiting for them?"

"I'll just take a few minutes, and then we'll come right back."

Pearl had been correct. While they were in the sanctuary, students from the four other schools had arrived and were milling around in the narthex like sheep without a shepherd. Greeters had just positioned themselves at the Third Street entrance and were gesturing at Jacob, who wasn't looking in their direction. When Pearl touched his forearm, he startled.

"Excuse me, Mr. Kichline, but I think we should return to our post."

He gazed at her before interrupting his train of thought. "Yes, right. Let's go."

He greeted the other students with handshakes and began providing details for the evening's program, trying to focus on the matters at hand. He was glad when Harry inched next to him with a suggestion.

"Maybe you'd like to write down everyone's name and school to make introductions flow smoothly."

His friend was brilliant. Truly, the only name Jacob would be able to remember tonight was "Pearl Smith."

She'd been the first college leader to arrive, and she was the last to depart. Jacob walked her and her friends to the door where their horse-drawn carriage awaited them in the lamplit evening.

"Thank you so much for coming, Miss Smith. I enjoyed meeting all of you, and again, your speech hit just the right notes."

She awarded him with a smile. "You and your church have been so kind, and I loved every minute. What a grand evening this has been."

He wondered when the next time Christian Endeavor would host a regional meeting, realizing no time could be soon enough.

Just before she walked down the steps to street level, Pearl made an offer. "You are such a fine speaker. I wonder if you would consider coming to my school and giving the same talk?"

There was no hiding his spreading grin. "I would enjoy that very much."

She hastily scribbled on an edge of the night's printed program and tore off the section. "Drop me a line, and I'll be in touch about a date."

Harry nudged Jacob. "Oh, right. Let me give you my address as well."

When they'd finished exchanging the information, he waved Pearl and her friends into the night.

"I'd say everything went very well." Harry was grinning to beat the band.

"I couldn't agree with you more."

CHAPTER TWO

Spring 1903
Pyongyang, Korea

Soon-hee Oh laid down his pen and rolled his tight shoulders after translating a Bible passage from Greek to English. He became aware the other four scholars had already turned in their exams and left the wood-scented room. He scanned his work one last time before presenting the fruit of his labor to Mr. Moffett.

The lanky American smiled. "And how did you find this assignment, Mr. Oh?" He spoke to Soon-hee in English, the language the missionaries and staff used privately. In public teaching and preaching, however, Korean was mainly spoken.

He rubbed a finger across the top of his lip. "This was most challenging."

"Why do you say so?"

"There is a rather fine point in the text I wanted to make sure I interpreted correctly."

"Were you adequately prepared?" Moffett raised an eyebrow.

"I believe so."

"Then I expect to be pleased with your efforts." The missionary-scholar rose from his desk. "You are aware of how we missionaries provide training, and when Koreans are ready to step up, they become teachers and pastors."

"Yes."

"In my role overseeing the academy and seminary, as well as Central Presbyterian Church, I've not yet encountered a scholar as promising as you are."

Soon-hee's cheeks flushed, and he gave a slight bow. "You honor me, Mr. Moffett. I must work hard when I hope to become a pastor like my father and a scholar like yourself."

"Your father has a keen mind, Mr. Oh. If he had been trained in his youth as you are, I think he could have been a professor. As matters stand, he is a fine elder and a close brother in the faith. Both he and I have strong hopes for your future labors in the Kingdom of God. Before long, you'll be teaching." He started gathering test papers into a neat stack. "Speaking of teaching, how is the catechumen class coming along? I believe you and Mr. Bernheisel conducted the first one just last week. I regret I've been away since then and unable to check in with you both."

The missionaries referred to people seeking church membership as catechumens, and the classes prepared them for baptism and exercising their spiritual gifts.

Soon-hee straightened his shoulders. "A great many men came from the city as well as the nearby countryside. They hung on the words of his Bible teaching."

"Excellent. And what did Mr. Bernheisel give you to do?"

"I spoke of my journey to the Christian faith when I was a boy, then mingled among the catechumens to answer some of their questions."

"And how did you find the experience?" Moffett crossed his arms.

"I enjoy working with Mr. Bernheisel and am most grateful for the opportunity."

"And you, my friend, are ready for this challenge. You have a strong aptitude for languages and a heart for the Lord Jesus. These fellows are hungry for the gospel and need to be steeped in the faith before making a public profession. How many men would you say attended last week?"

Soon-hee looked upward. "I believe there were fifty."

Moffett compressed his lips before responding. "Don't be surprised if the number doubles this week. Once the word spreads, our classes all seem to burgeon."

"Burgeon?"

"Yes. This word means to multiply."

Moving their conversation outside, Soon-hee filled his lungs with the lilting air. Spring was his favorite season, a time of promise and rebirth after Korea's cruel winters.

Moffett stretched, his long arms extended skyward. "I believe you have enough time for lunch before your class with Mr. Bernheisel. Will you join me and Mrs. Moffett?"

Normally, he would have jumped at the chance to be with them. If only he'd not forgotten his teaching materials at home. There wouldn't be time to dine with them, run back to the house, then hurry to the classroom. He wasn't one to do things in a rush.

"I would like nothing more, but this morning in my haste, I forgot my notes."

Moffett laughed and clapped his shoulder. "You already have the makings of an absent-minded professor. We are known for thinking such lofty thoughts we forget to tie our shoes."

Soon-hee grinned. What higher praise could there be than to have a trait in common with his favorite teacher?

"Perhaps we can share a different meal together soon? Mrs. Dr. Moffett has been asking for you."

"She is so very kind. Please let her know I will gladly come whenever she wishes." He paused. "I believe my mother will be assisting at her clinic today or tomorrow."

"Yes, they have one planned at the academy's infirmary. Your mother is a blessing to my wife as your father is one to me. Good day, Mr. Oh."

Soon-hee always benefited from lingering in the Moffetts' presence, their words like apples of gold in settings of silver. In the future, he would try not to be so scattered in his ways as to miss such opportunities.

He entered his home, eager to tell his parents how his test had gone, until he encountered a noisy and unsettled atmosphere inside.

"You must not neglect your wifely duties." His red-faced father clearly had worked himself into a lather. "I am happy to have you assist Mrs. Swallen, but if you cannot have my meals ready on time, I will rethink the arrangement."

His mother mouthed apologies while she and their daughter Sora whirled about the kitchen.

"Am I not a generous husband?" Mr. Oh asked. "Yet you treat me this way in return."

Jeongsook, his mother's women's ministry assistant, caught Soon-hee's eye. He wished he could shut off his father's running mouth. Despite the domestic vortex, Jeongsook calmly carried a tea pot to the table. This was just one of the many things he admired about her. Their families had come to the Christian faith at the same time eight years ago when Samuel Moffett first told them about the Christ. Kyung Oh, Soon-hee's father, and Jeongsook's father, were two of the first men Moffett had baptized and since then, the families had labored together in ministry. Lately, when Soon-hee's head wasn't stuck in a book, he liked to imagine a day when he and Jeongsook might have their own home and their own ministries. She'd never given him a reason not to believe.

He ducked into his small room to collect the Bible class materials he'd left behind and although his stomach growled, the domestic disruption put him off the notion of eating here. As for telling his parents about his test, he would have to wait for a more agreeable time.

"Soon-hee!"

He wheeled around from the door to face his mother. "Yes, *Eomeoni*?"

"I did not see you come in." She paused and waved to her daughter. "Sora, you must give your father a larger portion of rice."

"I arrived a few minutes ago."

"I am happy to see you."

He brightened. Maybe she hadn't forgotten his exam after all.

"As you can see, we are frantic here. Jeongsook and I will be helping Mrs. Swallen in the country today, and your brother is home sick."

He glanced over his shoulder and saw his younger sibling on his mat. *Again.* He tried to dismiss the uncharitable thought.

"You will need to pick up his teacher's assignments."

Soon-hee's back stiffened.

"He is ill with the headache, and I must leave shortly."

"I have no time either, *Eomeoni*. My catechumens will be waiting." He checked the time on the American watch Mr. and Mrs. Moffett had gifted him for his twentieth birthday.

There was just enough time for a quick bite in the dining hall before helping Mr. Bernheisel set up the classroom.

"He needs to complete his work this afternoon, Soon-hee. Go now, and you will be on time for your class." She grimaced when her husband started shouting at their daughter.

Soon-hee caught himself in the act of smoldering, which surely must be a sin. She didn't seem to care what a great honor her son had to teach alongside Mr. Bernheisel, only that he cater to his chronically indisposed brother. And did his father have to tyrannize his mother and sister, in front of Jeongsook no less?

He followed his mother back to the main room without catching Jeongsook's sympathetic expression. He did, however, hear her.

"Mrs. Oh, I will be happy to get Yong-bin's classwork."

"You are helping me today. After serving lunch to my husband, we must leave for our classes."

"Could not Sora do this errand?"

"She assists us. Soon-hee will do as I ask."

His stomach wasn't the only part of him grumbling when he left the house. He'd taken several adrenaline-laced steps when he heard Jeongsook call his name.

"Here, Soon-hee." She thrust a cloth-wrapped package at him.

"What is this?"

"You must not go without food. Here are some rice cakes and dried fish."

He balanced his books while accepting her offering, allowing his fingers to touch hers for a brief shining moment. "How kind you are, Jeongsook. Thank you."

She bowed, her dark eyes twinkling. "How was your test this morning? I said a prayer for you."

She remembered. "While I found it demanding, I believe I will earn a strong grade."

"I am sure you will." She glanced back at the house. "I must see to your mother. May the Lord bless your class."

"And may he bless you also."

He watched her walk in the opposite direction, admiring the way her sleek hair draped over her *Hanbok*. Then he raced to the Boys Academy building to find his brother's teacher, procure the necessary materials, and hurry back to the house.

Mr. Bernheisel met him in the teaming classroom. "Mr. Oh, thank the Lord you are here. There are so many more men coming this time, and I began to fear something had happened to you." He looked the young man up and down. "You seem breathless. Are you well?"

"I am very sorry to be so late." He wanted to pour out his frustration, but this was neither the time nor the place to vent. "My family detained me."

"I see. Well, then, would you please make sure everyone has a Bible?" The American teacher lowered his voice. "I don't believe we're going to have enough to go around."

"How many did you bring?" Soon-hee asked.

"Seventy-five. This rooms holds a hundred, and we're already beyond capacity. I suppose the men will just have to double-up today."

Soon-hee had been so distracted by his test and disquieting family interactions his spirit wasn't up to teaching the men today. He would have liked to repair to the chapel at the Boys Academy and pour out his thoughts to the Lord. Instead, he acted his part until the joy of being with these spiritually hungry souls purged his vexation.

Mr. Bernheisel spoke of the nature of sin and God's redemptive plan, a message Soon-hee had heard many times since boyhood when Mr. Moffett had come to Pyongyang. In those days, the Ohs had offered their hospitality to the tall American and not only became good friends with him, but they had also surrendered their lives to the Lord. After Mr. Moffett had examined each family member and was satisfied they understood the gospel and sincerely desired to be Christians, he baptized Mr. and Mrs. Oh, Soon-hee, and Sora. Yong-bin was judged too young to enter church membership but made a profession of faith five years later. Mr. Oh had become one of the first ordained Korean elders and was now a Pastor's Assistant while Mrs. Oh was a Bible Woman charged with teaching classes to females in the countryside surrounding Pyongyang. In addition, she often assisted Dr. Alice Moffett at clinics the missionary doctor conducted for women in and around the city. Tenderhearted Sora often served as a helper. As for Yong-bin ...

Soon-hee perked up when Mr. Bernheisel began explaining the concept of forgiveness.

"You see, men, our Savior put no limit on forgiveness. Let me show you. Please open your Bibles to Matthew, the eighteenth chapter, the twenty-first verse."

Soon-hee quickly opened to the passage.

"Mr. Oh, would you read verses twenty-one and twenty-two?"

He rose and began to speak, the words searing his conscience.

"Then Peter came to him and said, 'Lord, how often shall my brother sin against me, and I forgive him? Up to seven times?' Jesus saith unto him, I say not unto thee,

Until seven times: but, Until seventy times seven." He softly released his breath.

"Thank you, Mr. Oh." The teacher paced at the front of the classroom. "So, men, forgiveness is without limit. When the Lord Jesus forgives us, he doesn't say you only have one chance. If you fall back into sin after choosing to follow him, he doesn't abandon you. He forgives you when you come to him and repent of the evil you have done." He came to a halt. "Likewise, when someone sins against you, you must also offer forgiveness. In this way, your character becomes even more like the Savior's."

Soon-hee retreated to his thoughts, and a silent prayer. "Lord, I have forgiven my brother many times. I must do so yet again. I also forgive my mother for not seeming to care about what concerns me, and my father for being harsh with her and Sora. Help me not to sin against Thee or against them as I try to live among them as Thou wouldst."

The last of the talkative students had left, and Soon-hee helped the teacher straighten desks and collect Bibles. They completed their task in less than ten minutes, and Mr. Bernheisel invited him to tea at his home.

"My wife is with the other women in the village today, but I make a good brew."

"Thank you. I am happy to accept your kind invitation."

In the comfortable domicile featuring a blend of American and Korean furnishings, Bernheisel asked which kind of tea his guest would like to drink. "I can make British or Korean," he said.

Soon-hee enjoyed the Westerners' hardy black blends and took every advantage of opportunities to drink them. "Thank you, I would like your style."

Moments later, they took their beverages to what the Americans called a "parlor," settling onto a puffy sofa. The conversation consisted mostly of reviewing the class before Bernheisel became personal.

"You seemed out of sorts when you arrived, Mr. Oh. Was anything the matter, anything you'd care to talk about?"

He rubbed the edge of the china cup, breathing out. How much did he wish to disclose? He knew the teacher was trustworthy, and Soon-hee might do well to unburden himself, but to what extent? Mr. Bernheisel had only been in Korea three months, and there was still a professional distance between them.

"I thank you for your concern," Soon-hee finally said. "You see, my brother was too ill to go to his class, and my mother asked me to obtain his schoolwork so he could be engaged this afternoon."

Bernheisel frowned. "I'm sorry to hear about your brother. What seems to be the problem? Is it serious?"

He sipped the tea, finding its robustness bracing.

"You see, Yong-bin was very sickly as a baby. In fact, he came close to death a few times. As he has grown, he suffers much from encumbering pain in his head."

"Sounds like a migraine," the teacher said.

"Is this the word you use?"

"Yes. The condition can be incapacitating. I have an aunt who suffers in the same way."

When Soon-hee remained silent, Bernheisel peered at him.

"This must burden you and your family."

"Yes." He couldn't bring himself to say what he was really thinking.

CHAPTER THREE

Maybe the calendar didn't mark this as such but today had been a red-letter day for Jacob. As the locomotive chugged away from Princeton Junction, Pearl's high color and animated gestures seemed to reflect his joy. Even normally taciturn Harry Flory hadn't stopped grinning since the Lehigh Valley's Christian Endeavor contingent had arrived in Princeton early in the morning.

Jacob preferred what he was reliving in his mind's eye to the passing landscape until Pearl interrupted his daydream.

"What did he say to you, Jacob?"

After he'd spoken at her school three weeks earlier, they'd been on a first-name basis, a welcome development.

He blinked. "Excuse me?"

"What did Dr. Warfield say to you? I couldn't believe you actually got to talk to him."

He couldn't either. After the renowned theologian had addressed the CE convocation, Jacob had stood in line hoping to at least shake the great man's hand. He somehow needed to seal the trumpet call B.B. Warfield had roused in Jacob's soul.

"Was he nice?" Pearl's friend leaned forward.

"Oh, yes." He rubbed his right palm, the sensation of the man's large hand lingering.

"I'm so glad," Pearl said. "I would hate to think a man who'd stirred us the way he did could turn out to be pompous one-on-one."

"He seemed to have a lot to say to you," Harry said.

"Yes, I was surprised he took so much time talking to me."

Could he speak of their encounter when he was still processing what had transpired? He decided at least to provide a rough sketch.

"Do you remember how he spoke of the need for young Christians to bring biblical authority into the twentieth century?"

His friends bobbed their heads.

"I liked how he encouraged us to not abandon God's never-changing Word to modernism," Harry said.

"Oh, I did too." Pearl's eyes sparkled. "When so much is changing around us, knowing God never does reassures me."

Jacob received their hopeful expressions, six sets of eyes on him. "He asked me about my future plans." He avoided looking at Pearl. "I told him I was still considering my options and he, uh, said, 'Son, the fields are white unto harvest.'"

"I wonder what he meant." Pearl's friend knit her brow.

Harry offered his opinion. "I think he was encouraging you to become part of what God is doing in our time. Is that how you took what he said?"

Jacob's thoughts kept time with the train's rhythm. "Yes, I would say so."

At the time, Warfield's mysterious comment and the look he'd bestowed upon Jacob had seemed like a Mount

Sinai moment. His friends began talking about their own experiences on the venerable Princeton Seminary campus, leaving Jacob to his own thoughts, which became a prayer. *Lord, was Dr. Warfield pointing to my becoming a minister? You know this past year I've been considering different paths, and I just haven't known which one to take. Father tells me the silk mill needs more management, and I know a job there would be solid, just as my brother Robert has found since he graduated from Lafayette three years ago.* He opened his eyes and gazed at Pearl, his throat catching. Might she be part of his future, this pretty woman who combined keen intelligence with an even higher devotion to Jesus Christ? *I had the strong impression today at Princeton I somehow belonged there, Lord. What a joy it would be to study under Dr. Warfield, to prepare for the ministry under spiritual giants like him.* When the train lurched, his spirit shifted, the moment shimmering like the sunset glimmering against the window. *Lord, you want me to go into the ministry, don't you?*

As if in answer, the sun burst before dipping past the horizon.

Dr. Kieffer met him with a smile and handshake at the manse's front door. "Come in, Jacob. My wife left molasses cookies and tea for us in my office while she's entertaining the church women next door."

Jacob followed the only man he'd ever called "Pastor" into his book-laden study where two chairs awaited them at a small but overloaded table. He sniffed the scent of wildflowers in a vase, his mouth watering as he imagined the first bite of Mrs. Kieffer's toffee-like cookies. Unlike some heavier-handed bakers in town, her treats offered tantalizing hints of ginger, cinnamon, and cloves, rather than beating one's taste buds into submission.

Dr. Kieffer had begun his ministry at the First Reformed Church of Easton when Jacob was two years old, and they had bonded quickly. He had loved talking to the amiable minister, who always made time for his boyish questions, things like, "Where did Cain and Abel find wives?" and "If God knows how many hairs are on our heads, what about bald men?" Kieffer had always demonstrated patience and kindness in his responses. Now he was about to raise one of the most meaningful subjects of his life.

After two cups of tea, a handful of cookies, small talk about the church, and Jacob's recent sojourn, he sensed an opening.

"Dr. Kieffer, something became clear to me a week ago on the train coming home from Princeton." He rubbed his fingernails, searching for words.

The amiable shepherd angled his head.

"As you know I've been considering what comes after graduation. Pop has offered me a job at the silk mill." He paused, recalling his father's anticipation of having two sons working under his guidance and moving up the ladder of success as he had. Jacob had considered sharing his news about the ministry with him first but had decided to confide in his minister instead. He continued.

"I always knew I might end up at the mill, but this past year I've been thinking about possibly entering the ministry. Of course, you often tell us all Christians are ministers who can serve God in any profession." He sighed, staring at the wallpaper next to one of the copious bookshelves with its haphazardly stacked volumes.

Kieffer's cat rubbed against Jacob's legs.

"I can remove her if she's bothering you."

"No, thanks, I'm fine." He stroked her head, and she commenced purring. "I, uh, wonder if you think I'm a fit candidate."

The minister's eyes shone. "I was wondering when you might be coming to see me about this."

Jacob's teacup jangled in the saucer, and he placed them on the table. "You have?"

"I've long had a sense you might have a ministerial calling."

"I'm surprised to hear this."

"I don't know if you remember the story I'm about to tell you," Kieffer said, "but I can still recall it as if it were yesterday. You were five or six years old, and after church your parents were in the Session Room talking to various people. I suppose you became bored with the adult jabber and broke away. When they realized you weren't there, they found me and asked if I'd seen you. After some anxious moments, we were stopped short at the sight of you at the front of the sanctuary."

Jacob laughed out loud, recalling the incident. "And there I was trying to baptize a stray cat I'd found sitting on the front steps of the church."

They both slapped their thighs and carried on until Jacob's sides ached.

"Oh, you were quite the whippersnapper," the pastor said.

"My parents were furious." He wiped his eyes with the back of his right hand.

"I assured them you weren't in danger of becoming a pagan high priest. Instead, I saw something quite revealing in your act, a young man with a heart for the precious things of God."

He grinned. "I wonder what ever became of that cat."

"As far as I know, he never came near the church again."

They shared more laughter until the emotion ran down, and they picked up the reins of the conversation.

"Pastor Kieffer, with all due respect, I wonder why you never said anything to me about becoming a minister."

He spread his hands. "One must wait for the right timing, to be sure the Lord is planting the seed. You looked up to me so much, and I didn't want you to follow the path I had taken unless this was truly to be yours. Now, I will tell you that in my opinion you are as fit a candidate as any man I've ever known." His face clouded, and he looked out a window to busy North Third Street.

Jacob wondered what had caused the abrupt change. "Are you all right, Pastor?"

Kieffer closed his eyes and blew out a breath. "There is something I can trust you with, something only my wife and I have discussed between us."

The back of his neck prickled. Was he ill? Was Mrs. Kieffer ill?

"I've been in Easton nearly twenty years, and as you sense the Lord moving you toward pastoral ministry, he seems to be telling me the time has come for us to move on."

Jacob squeezed his eyes shut. How could Pastor Kieffer even think such a possibility? Jacob just assumed he would always be there, part of his life. He immediately recognized the immaturity of his perspective, but the shock was like receiving word of an unexpected death in the family.

"I hardly know what to say."

"You must keep this to yourself until I make my intentions known to the church's elders."

"You have my word." He swallowed hard. "Where will you go? Easton is your home."

"Yes, and I love this place. Still, another church has called me, and I think they may have greater need of my services. Someone else can build on the foundation I've laid here."

The streetcar rolled past the manse.

"Now then, Jacob, I can help you start the process of coming under the church's direction, which is part of going to seminary. They will oversee your progress and provide support and guidance along the way."

Kieffer's mind had been made up. He truly was leaving.

"Have you given thought to where you'd like to study?"

Jacob's emotions changed again as he smiled. "Princeton." Just as quickly, his posture stiffened at the sight of his pastor grimacing.

"Of course, Princeton is a grand seminary, but you're German Reformed, not Presbyterian."

He rankled at the pushback. "They're just a different kind of Reformed in terms of their organization. Theologically, they're similar."

"Perhaps on broader matters of the faith, but there are differences in church governance, nuances you must learn about. The Reformed Theological Seminary in Lancaster is our denomination's preferred training ground for pastors, and after you graduate, you'll be better placed to serve one of our congregations."

He didn't want to go to Reformed, he wanted to go to Princeton. A sour taste removed the last pleasant traces of the cookies he'd just enjoyed. He'd never doubted or crossed his pastor before and didn't know what to say now, or even to think.

"Have you told your parents?"

"No, sir. I wanted to pass this by you first."

"I think they'll be pleased." He put his napkin on the table and scooted out of his chair. "I suggest we get on our knees before the Lord."

I just hope the Lord is a Princeton man.

Jacob delivered another warm-up pitch to his catcher, hitting his stride. A few more throws, and he'd be ready for his last game on this postcard-perfect May day, curiously against the Princeton Tigers. In his previous appearance against Cornell, he and the opponent's ace had gone eight innings before his counterpart gave up a three-run homer. Shaken, he'd yielded two more runs in the ninth. Lafayette ended up winning by a score of six-to-two, giving Jacob a seasonal record of nine wins and one loss.

Now his catcher rose and walked the ball to Jacob. "You're in fine form today, Kich. Let's do your Billy Sunday proud, eh?

He grinned. "I'll certainly try, Willis."

His friend gestured to the bleachers. "You have your own peanut gallery there!"

Jacob shaded his eyes against the sun and tried to make out the spectators. Sure enough, there were his parents, four siblings, assorted aunts, uncles, cousins from both sides, and Dr. and Mrs. Kieffer. He did a doubletake at the sight of his pastor and his wife. Kieffer caught his eye and smiled, a gesture communicating to Jacob all was well. His heart swelled to know, like his father, they'd accepted his decision to go to Princeton Seminary. Squinting for a closer look, he also saw his dark-haired sweetheart, who waved her handkerchief at him. He broke into a grin when they all began whistling, cheering, and fluttering maroon and white Lafayette pennants. He would like to have had a few words with them, but Coach was signaling his players into the dugout. Jacob tipped his ball cap to his family and friends before joining the other players. This was the first time Pearl had come to one of his games, and all at once his stomach clenched. Sure, he was the team's star pitcher, consistent and reliable, but what if he faltered today? The coach's voice shook him loose.

"Gather around, men. There you go. I couldn't be prouder of you with the season we've had. Fourteen wins and twelve losses. Let's go out there today and give our fans even more to cheer about."

The players slapped each other on the back, shouting, "Hoo we! Hoo we! Lafayette Naughty-Three!"

"Let's have our prayer before we take the field. Kichline, will you lead us?"

"Yes, sir," Jacob said. "Let's bow our heads."

Everyone removed their caps.

"Heavenly Father, we thank thee for the blessings of this day, including the beautiful weather. We are grateful for strong bodies and minds and the pleasure of sports. May we behave as Christian gentleman in all aspects of this game, and may we glorify thee whether we win or lose. Through Christ our Lord, amen."

"Son, that was your best performance yet. I'm so proud of you." Sam Kichline squeezed his son's shoulder.

"Thanks, Pop. I'm happy you were able to be here."

He winked. "What good is being a manager if you can't take off a few hours on a day as important as this one?"

Robert pumped Jacob's hand. "A shut-out, little brother. You did great out there."

The compliments flew as quickly as his fastball, and now his mother was hugging him, his pastor grinning beside her. Jacob searched with his eyes for Pearl, finding her standing quietly with the freckled girl he recognized from Christian Endeavor. He admired the way she never seemed to feel a need to put herself forward. When at last he was face-to-face with her, he took her hands in his.

"You did a wonderful job, Jacob."

"I'm glad you enjoyed the game." Her eyes intrigued him, one the color of chocolate, the other light green, unlike any he'd ever seen. He forced himself to look away. "I really appreciate you coming."

He wished he didn't have to leave them, but he needed to attend a party for the players. He expressed his regrets.

"Please don't worry," she said. "Enjoy your teammates. I'll see you this weekend."

He watched as she took her leave.

His catcher sidled up behind him. "Hey, Kich, we best get going." Willis looked in Pearl's direction. "Nice gal."

"The best."

Jacob breathed in the scent of violets in Pearl's hair, the two of their heads bent over his newly-minted copy of Lafayette's yearbook, the *Melange*. Fred had just delivered them to Delta Kappa Epsilon, and the brothers had scattered throughout the common area, their noses stuck in the volumes. Occasional sputters broke out accompanied by loud horse laughs and knee-slapping.

"Let's find your picture," Pearl said, her eyes glowing.

He began leafing through the book, unable to resist teasing her. “You’ve already seen my class picture. In fact, I gave you one.”

“Silly, I want to see what they wrote about you.”

He jerked the book away, grinning. “If you don’t mind, I’d like to read it myself first.” He worried what embarrassing thing the editor might have written for a caption, knowing the fellow was a notorious jokester.

When he located his senior photo, Pearl dipped back into his space and after jockeying for position, read aloud. “Jacob Samuel Kichline. ‘Billy Sunday.’ Classical. Strong in athletics, brilliant in social circles, high in scholarship, marked in ‘college spirit.’ Delta Kappa Epsilon. Christian Endeavor and YMCA. Baseball and football teams. Franklin Literary Society. Plans to attend Princeton Theological Seminary.”

She sat back and chuckled. “I always thought you were an impressive fellow, but ‘brilliant in social circles?’”

His cheeks coloring, he closed the yearbook, rose, and extended his hand. “Let’s go for a walk.”

“But I’d like to see how many other photos of you are in here,” she said.

“Later. There’s something else I’d like to share with you today.” He guided Pearl into the early June afternoon replete with scampering rabbits and warbling finches.

“I’m glad we’ll get to spend the summer together before I leave for Princeton,” he said as they walked behind Pardee Hall to the Quad.

“Oh, me too. Of course, you’ll be working, and I’ll be volunteering at the YWCA.”

“And leading the men’s Bible study at church.” He paused. “Don’t worry. I’ll make lots of time for outings with you.”

"Like going to Island Park?"

He'd loved the amusement venue place since childhood and took every opportunity to go there. "Yes, we can go to Island Park."

"And picnics and buggy rides."

"Those too."

"And visit each other's churches."

He led her to a bench, and they sat, his body tensing. "Pearl, there's something I'd like to say to you."

He noted her tinted cheeks and the parting of her lips.

"As you know, I have three years of seminary ahead, and you have a year left of college. I'm not ready for a long-term commitment, but I would like to see you exclusively. I, uh, wonder how you feel about that." He could barely bring himself to look at her.

"I couldn't agree with you more." She squeezed his hand.

He exhaled as he dug into his coat pocket and produced his fraternity pin. "That being said, I wonder if you would accept this."

She broke into a smile. "Yes, Jacob, I will."

He gently pinned the emblem onto her sweater then kissed her cheek. Life was grand just now. Pastor Kieffer had finally acquiesced to Jacob's attending Princeton Seminary, and he'd been admitted to the prestigious school. All that, and he'd won the heart of the fairest of maidens. His cup overflowed.

CHAPTER FOUR

Soon-hee always enjoyed visiting the Moffett residence on campus, and today they'd invited him for tea to celebrate the end of the spring semester. They also planned to talk over an upcoming sojourn to some churches in the outer villages. He was glad he'd brought his appetite. His professor's wife, Dr. Alice Fish Moffett, had just put a plate of some sort of cakes on their Asian-style table. Soon-hee held her in the highest esteem, a lovely, tall woman who'd come to Korea as a medical missionary five years earlier. She and his professor had been married for the last four years now.

"I hope you don't mind drinking American tea today, Mr. Oh."

"I was hoping you might serve some," he said.

She clapped her hands together like a young bride. Soon-hee didn't know exactly how old she was but he considered her remarkable, a woman who sometimes baked cakes and other times, treated tuberculosis and leprosy without flinching. How opposite she was from the majority of Korean women who went about their grim lives in servitude. He gazed into her kind face, allowing himself to relax for the first time since his arduous last exam.

After Samuel Moffett prayed, his wife poured tea into Soon-hee's cup, its tannic scent like a bracing hug.

"I forget whether you take sugar, Mr. Oh," she said.

"I like my tea black as you say."

"As do I. Today I'm serving scones, a British tea cake. Let me show you how to prepare one." She went through the motions of slicing one in half, then applying clotted cream and jam. "Some people prefer to put the jam on first, then the cream, so you can experiment."

He looked to Mr. Moffett. "How do you like yours?"

The professor's blue-grey eyes shone. "I used to mix them together until my wife broke me of the barbaric habit."

They enjoyed a laugh then commenced eating. When Soon-hee bit into the treat, he closed his eyes. "Dr. Moffett, this is delicious."

"I'm so happy you like the scone. I have little time to bake and cook, so when I'm provided the opportunity, I enjoy myself in the kitchen."

Her husband winked. "I like it too."

Soon-hee withheld himself from staring at this attractive American couple. His father liked to tell the story of his first encounter with Samuel Austin Moffett some eight years earlier. The American had recently arrived in Korea, heralding great excitement in the insular city. With his light-hair, lofty stature, great nose, and narrow trousers, Moffett's appearance in Pyongyang was like the arrival of a mythological creature. Other missionaries had been there before, but none had stayed. News about a crazy foreigner's presence spread throughout the city. Once he had chosen and settled into a home, Moffett often found Koreans blocking the road in front of the house, as well as boys pressing against the paper windows, all for a better look at the new comer.

Among the stories Soon-hee most enjoyed was his father's, a man who'd kept a saloon in the city and who often went to visit Moffett. At first, he'd gone to extract stories from the American to share with his patrons, but as the weeks spent themselves, Kyung Oh's spirit stirred within him. Soon-hee was twelve years old when his father became a Christian and closed the public house. Not everyone had been as welcoming as his father.

When Mr. Moffett opened a church, the Pyongyang magistrate tried to stop him.

"You cannot bring this religion here," he'd said. Then he told the Koreans, "If you worship according to the foreigner's religion, you will be unable to properly worship your ancestors' spirits come New Year."

His father had stood strong with Mr. Moffett and the other believers, each prepared to make great sacrifices for the sake of Jesus who had died for their sins. Soon-hee had witnessed his father's arrest, the beatings of other believers, and a mob stoning the American missionary. As if from God's hand itself, Chinese descended upon the city from the north carrying yellow dragon-emblazoned banners, clashing with a Japanese army from the south. Soon-hee and his family had fled with their father and Moffett into the mountains, where during their exile they introduced more Koreans to Jesus.

When the American received instructions from his mission board to go to Seoul, Soon-hee's family accompanied him, and there they stayed until the battle for Pyongyang ended. When they returned with other believers and additional missionaries, the warring armies had burnt the city to the ground, and dead Chinese lay uncovered in the streets. Other Christians began to return, and the fire that had destroyed the city fanned into flame the Christian faith, spreading as far as the rice plains by the sea, and into the mountain valleys.

Kyung Oh had gone with Moffett and other missionaries from America and Canada into the countryside where they organized and instructed the new believers. Churches sprang up across the peninsula—Moffett dedicated to training Korea's native sons and daughters so they could one day lead. Soon-hee had attended his father and mother on many of the arduous journeys. Before long he received his own call from God to enter the ministry; he wanted to become just like his mentor.

He also wanted to have a marriage like the Moffetts enjoyed, one marked by respect and kindness. Although his parents benefited from a strong commitment to each other, there wasn't any light-heartedness or glimmers of admiration. This was, however, the way of traditional Korean marriages.

At the end of their repast, Sam Moffett spread his hands on the table his wife had begun clearing. "Mr. Oh, I'd like to discuss this summer with you."

"Keep your cup in case you'd like more tea," his wife said.

"Thank you, Dr. Moffett. I enjoyed these scones very much." He looked at his professor, waiting for him to continue.

Do you have any plans?" Moffett asked.

"My mother has asked me to create Bible material for her women's ministry. I would also like to continue teaching Sabbath school to the boys. Do you approve?"

"Both are certainly worthy endeavors. Isn't your father helping her, though?" He narrowed his eyes.

Soon-hee jiggled his right foot. "My father is much absorbed with his ministry." He didn't wish to say anything negative, wondering if the missionary was aware of Kyung Oh's dismissal of women's work in general.

He was silent for a moment, then blew out a breath. "Well, I have something in mind, and if you find you can't keep up, I'll assign someone to help your mother. Would that be all right?"

"Oh, yes." He bent forward, waiting for his mentor to continue. He didn't know if his mother would object, but then again, she hardly noticed him these days except when she needed his assistance with something.

"There are two things I have in mind for you. The first is some translation work Mr. Blair and I are working on, which would be helped by your facility with languages."

Outside, children newly-sprung from school galivanted with laughter and calling to one another on the nearby athletic fields.

"One of our initiatives is publishing classic devotional works into Korean, and our first effort is a book called *The Christian's Secret of a Happy Life*."

"I like this title."

"You'll like what's inside even more." He grinned. "This is one of my and my wife's favorite books on the Christian life, and millions of English-speaking readers have benefited from its wisdom."

"Who is the author?"

"Hannah Whitall Smith, a Quaker woman who is widely known in holiness circles. She wrote the book over twenty-five years ago." He tilted his head, smiling. "What is it, Mr. Oh?"

"I marvel at your openness to the ministry of women, who have such rich talents. As you know, women are not treated so in my culture."

"Jesus is the liberator of all souls, and the Holy Spirit knows neither male nor female in dispersing his gifts."

He had come to believe this in his own heart. "I would like to help you with this translation," Soon-hee said.

"Good. There's another aspect to this work. Our Mr. Swallen is creating Christian literature in Korean for use in the villages, something we call 'tracts.' They're short bits of information about walking in the faith. We wonder if you could translate these into your language as well."

This was going to be a busy, profitable summer. "Yes, I would be honored to support him."

He wondered if those were the two things Mr. Moffett had to share with him and waited for him to continue.

"Now then, Mr. Oh, after prayerful consideration and the advice of my very sage wife, I have yet another proposition for you."

Soon-hee detected a smile but couldn't be sure.

"You've proven yourself in many ways to be an upstanding and godly man, as eager to be of service as you are to learn. Would you consider becoming my assistant?"

Soon-hee's mouth dropped open.

Moffett raised his index finger. "You wouldn't replace your father but would instead relieve him of his work here at the schools. I need him just now to be in an oversight role with missions to the villages, and that leaves me scrambling here."

He felt like joining the children outside, shouting at the top of his lungs. "I am so deeply honored, Mr. Moffett, by your confidence in me and my work."

"Do you need some time to think about all of this?"

Nothing in his life had ever felt more right, aside from his acceptance of the Savior's gift of forgiveness for his sins.

"I do not. I am exceedingly happy to become your assistant here."

Moffett reached across the table and grasped Soon-hee's hand, breaking into spontaneous prayer. "Gracious heavenly Father, I thank Thee for providing Mr. Oh as a laborer with me in Thy vineyard. Grant him Thy wisdom, imagination, and love as he seeks to fulfill these important duties. Anoint him with Thy Holy Spirit that he may be used in ways pleasing to Thee. Through Christ our Lord, amen."

"Amen."

Without missing a beat, Moffett leaned back and crossed his arms. "Are you ready for our trip into the villages next week?"

"Oh, yes, I have been greatly anticipating it."

"We'll be plenty busy for several days, so we'll get to work on the projects I've just spoken about when we return. Of course, you should take some time off to refresh yourself first."

Dr. Moffett returned from the kitchen. "By the way, Mr. Oh, a new medical missionary arrived not a week ago and will be going with us. She's delightful, and I look forward to introducing you to her."

"I will be happy to meet her."

"Her name is Clara Story."

"Is she also a physician?"

"She has had advanced nurse's training but is not a medical doctor."

After a last cup of tea and general conversation about the weather, Soon-hee left, swinging his arms as he walked home.

On his way across the compound, he noticed Mr. Hamilton waving at him from a distance.

"Mr. Oh, am I ever happy to see you! I've been looking for you." The young teacher's face flushed.

Soon-hee bowed. “Good day, Mr. Hamilton.”

“Good day. Your brother missed several of my classes this past term and needs some remedial work this summer. I’m wondering if you’ll tutor him.”

His throat tightened. Yong-bin was a smart young man, too smart to be behind even with his infirmity. When he did feel well, Soon-hee’s brother spent most of his time goofing off with his friends instead of studying.

“Well, what do you say?”

He drew himself up. “Mr. Moffett has just assigned me to translation work this summer, and I am to become one of his assistants.”

Hamilton’s eyes narrowed. “I doubt this will take much of your time. I mean, the two of you live in the same house.”

Soon-hee couldn’t remember ever turning down a missionary’s request. “Perhaps one of my classmates may be looking for summer employment.”

“I thought you would want to help your brother. How hard can it be to work with him for a few minutes a day when he’s so often ill?”

Before Soon-hee could respond, Hamilton was speaking again.

“I’ll just have a word with Mr. Moffett. Maybe he can free you up a bit.”

“Please, Mr. Hamilton, do not trouble yourself. My assignment is already established.”

“We’ll see.”

The day before his trip, Soon-hee glared at his Sabbath school pupils. Clearly, his lesson on the Parable of the Sower was falling on deaf ears. Three-quarters of the students looked back and forth between him and their peers who whispered and jabbed each other with fingers and pencils, goaded by his younger brother. When their voices were the only ones carrying in the church's classroom, one-by-one they fell into guilty-faced snickers. His brother smirked at him, and Soon-hee wrestled a flash of anger. No Korean teacher would tolerate such behavior, but his brother seemed to enjoy putting his sibling to the test.

"Now then, if you young men would turn your attention to your Bibles, we can continue with Jesus's story." He faced his brother. "Yong-bin, perhaps you would read for us."

Slumping in his chair he murmured, "I do not have a Bible."

When his friends broke into a new round of sniggers, Soon-hee raised his voice. "I am sure one of your classmates will loan you his."

An earnest fellow behind Yong-bin handed over his copy, but Yong-bin feigned illness. "I am sorry, Mr. Oh, but I am not feeling well." He pulled a long, pathetic face.

One of his buddies raised his hand. "I will be happy to take him home."

"I am sure you would." Soon-hee grimaced. "Very well, go."

If Mr. Hamilton thinks I am going to tutor Yong-bin, he is very much mistaken. Taking a deep breath, he closed his eyes. Was he becoming as insubordinate as his brother?

The Oh's household pulsated with last-minute preparations for the excursion into the villages, his parents shouting directions to their house help while Jeongsook packed medical supplies into wooden crates and Sora served soup to their brother. Soon-hee gazed at him, wondering if Yong-bin's drawn expression was a result of true illness or more pretending. He had difficulty believing the previous day's Sabbath school escapades had been carried out by a chronically sick young man. He breathed easier, however, knowing Sora would be staying behind to care for Yong-bin rather than himself. When Mr. Moffett caught Soon-hee's eye, he wondered if his teacher could read his thoughts. The American's presence had brought a measure of stability to the household as he oversaw the logistics of a dozen people planning a long-distance trek by foot.

Mrs. Dr. Moffett had brought her newest protégé', Clara Story, a sturdy American woman from the physician's hometown. Soon-hee had taken an immediate liking to her open-faced warmth and eagerness to learn about Korea and its people. All at once, the activity stopped as an old woman entered the home.

Mrs. Oh led the wrinkled woman to a place of honor among them.

"You must not cease in your labors for me," Kim Gang said. "I am certain there is much to do."

Nevertheless, Jeongsook brought the woman a cup of tea and rice cakes. After each person had paid his respects, the work continued. Kim Gang, who was also called Dorcas, smiled at Soon-hee.

"Good day to you, *Halmeoni*." He bowed. "I am happy to see you. Are you well?"

"Each day is a gift from Jesus, and this gives me joy." She smiled as Mrs. Dr. Moffett brought the new American to meet her. "Mrs. Doctor, who is this fine young woman?"

Alice Moffett bowed. "*Halmeoni*, I would like to present Miss Clara Story. She has just arrived from the United States to assist with my medical ministry."

Soon-hee watched Clara bow as if she'd done so a thousand times. "I am very happy to meet you."

"Perhaps, you will share your story with Miss Story."

Kim Gang smiled at the play on words. "I like this name. Please, sit next to me."

Clara did as she was told, and Soon-hee lingered nearby. He was mostly packed and wished to hear Kim Gang's account again.

Mrs. Dr. Moffett began the tale. "In the past, male missionaries were prohibited from speaking with Korean women, nor could they gain access to what is called the *anbang*, a private room for women in the home. Missionary wives began to minister to the women, and God raised up Korean female evangelists, who were known as 'Bible women.' They helped spread Christianity in the early years of Protestant missions here, and Kim Gang was one of these." She nodded her head at the lady. "You may have noticed we address her as '*Halmeoni.*' This means 'Grandmother' and shows how highly we regard her."

"How lovely," Clara Story said.

"Most of us had been neglected by our husbands. You see, in Korea men rule over their wives and households much more than in your America," Kim Gang said. She paused for a sip of tea and continued. "The day that Jesus Christ was preached in Korea began the emancipation of women from the bondage of thousands of years. I first heard the name of Jesus at the age of fifty, and I was taught in the faith, baptized, and received into full church membership."

She smiled, revealing teeth in various stages of decay. Nevertheless, Soon-hee considered this wrinkled woman to possess true beauty.

"My baptism was the happiest day of my life. Until then, in our Confucian society, a woman was never called by her name. She was known by the name of her father, husband, or son. When freedom came to me in Christ, I received a New Testament name, 'Dorcas.' I resolved to live up to this name, and I was given a preaching circuit of many hundreds of miles of mountainous territory. There were times when people verbally attacked me and refused me food. One time, I was imprisoned."

Mrs. Dr. Moffett touched the woman's hand. "Nevertheless, our Dorcas continued to evangelize Korea, and she will be going into the villages with us again."

Soon-hee could not wait to be out among the people himself, sharing the name above all names.

CHAPTER FIVE

SEPTEMBER 1903
PRINCETON, NJ

If Lafayette College had been impressive, Princeton was in another league—the Ivy League to be exact. Unlike industrially-oriented Easton, Princeton exuded gentry, old money, and very blue blood. Jacob stood before Brown Hall inhaling the scent of flawlessly mowed lawns while gray squirrels vied with each other on the quadrangle for the season's first acorns. His class of thirty men had been carefully selected from the East's best colleges, and he considered himself blessed indeed to be numbered among them. He surveyed the students moving trunks and suitcases inside the dormitory, speculating as to which of them might be his roommate.

Inside the brownstone building with its marble flooring, an upperclassman sat behind a desk checking in the new arrivals. Some of them wore crisp new suits and shirts, others more threadbare togs. Jacob smiled to himself. *Those of us in new gear probably don't have the deep pockets of the less smartly dressed.* At least, this had been the case among his Lafayette fraternity brothers.

The guy behind him extended his hand. "I'm Rand Ainslie, and you are?"

"Jacob Kichline."

"I'm glad to meet you, Jacob. Where do you come from?"

The fellow with dark hair and eyes to match had a grip as firm as his jaw, which didn't seem to move much when he spoke. His was not among the newer suits of clothes.

"Easton, Pennsylvania."

"A college town if I'm not mistaken."

"That's right, Lafayette. I'm a graduate. What about yourself?"

"I'm a Yale man out of Locust Valley, New York."

"I'm happy to meet you," Jacob said.

"Name please."

"I think he means you." Rand gestured to the desk.

He turned to address the fellow. "Jacob Kichline."

The bespectacled upperclassman peered at him. "I was wondering how to pronounce your last name."

"Kish-line."

He grimaced as if running the information through a mental filter then ran a finger down the list. "You're on the second floor about midway down the hall."

Jacob took the key offered to him.

"If you lose that, you'll have to pay a dollar for a replacement."

He wanted to ask about his roommate, but the attendant was looking past him. Instead, Jacob returned Rand's small salute and went in search of his quarters.

Jacob hefted his suitcase onto the unmade bed, then dragged his trunk from the hall into the spacious room smelling of fresh paint. His colleague had already claimed the space on the right and was filling his chest of drawers with monogramed shirts. Jacob squinted for a better look at what appeared to be some sort of flask on top of the bureau.

"Here, let me help you with that." The young man took one end of the wood-framed trunk and helped position the behemoth at the foot of the bed.

"Thanks. I don't know how, but this steamer seemed to get heavier with each passing hour."

He gave a chuckle. "They do have a way of doing that."

"Jacob Kichline."

He took the guy's hand, which seemed as outsized as his height. At five feet eleven, Jacob was often the tallest man in any room. This fellow, however, topped him by at least four inches. He couldn't see the top of his head but suspected some serious thinning was going on up there.

"Charles Winthrop Brown," he said. "Everyone calls me Win."

Jacob tilted his head, grinning. "And here you are in Brown Hall." When Win didn't return the levity, asked, "Might there be a connection?"

"Actually, there is."

He sat on the edge of his bed inviting the rest of the story, grateful for the chance to rest for a second before unloading his belongings.

"My great-grandmother Isabella McLanahan Brown gifted this building to Princeton."

"What was her relationship to the school?"

"My great-grandfather's investment firm provided financial guidance to the seminary, of which he thought highly."

Jacob didn't know what to say so he set to work unpacking and setting up his new living arrangement as if he were used to rooming with heirs. When he crowned his efforts with photos of his family and Pearl, Win took notice.

"Is she your sweetheart?"

Jacob had the feeling of becoming taller. "Her name is Pearl."

"She's lovely."

"Thank you." He pointed at Win's photos. "Do you have a romantic interest?"

"As a matter of fact, I do, although we're not exclusive." He waved to the array he was setting up. "Those are my family."

Jacob leaned in for a closer look, noticing the backdrop of an enormous mansion in one of the pictures.

An hour later, Rand poked his head in their open door as other students passed behind him in the hallway.

"Would you blokes care to dine with me? That is, were you also invited to the Benham Club?"

Jacob had been looking forward to the possibility of joining this brotherhood since he'd heard about the dining and social club during his campus tour.

Win smiled. "My father advised me to join."

"Smart man. What say you, Mr. Kichline?"

Would joining the Benham be this easy? "Yes, thank you. Rand, have you met my roommate?"

"Can't say as I have." He entered and shook Win's hand. "Rand Ainslie."

"Win Brown. Might you be connected to the Oyster Bay Ainslies?"

"One and the same."

They smiled as if they'd known each other all their lives.

"How do you know Jacob?"

"We just met downstairs," Rand said.

Win peered at Jacob as if he were taking stock.

The three of them set off for the Benham, where white-coated waiters hovered over them. During the first course,

Jacob learned Win was from Boston and had gone to Harvard College, which led to playful jibes from Rand, an "Eli." Both of their families appeared on the social registers while Jacob disclosed his father's far more pedestrian occupation as a silk mill manager. At least, he could say his mother was a member of the Daughters of the American Revolution. Fortunately, neither of his new friends seemed repulsed by his humbler circumstances.

"What brought you to Princeton?" he asked Rand over their soup course.

"I suppose the ministry is in my blood."

"How do you mean?"

"You've heard of Jonathan Edwards?"

"Of course." Jacob reminded himself not to slurp. This was no frat house.

"He's my third great-grandfather."

Jacob suppressed a boyish *wow*. "That's quite a connection."

"Like him, I sensed an early calling to the ministry," Rand said. "I was about thirteen. What about you, Jacob?"

"I've been active in my church, the YMCA, and Christian Endeavor for several years," he said. "I got the call during my final semester at Lafayette, after coming to Princeton for a regional CE event."

Rand turned to Win. "And you, my fine fellow?"

He shrugged his shoulders. "I've never received such a call, as you say."

Jacob blurted, "Then why are you here?"

"To study Church history and theology, my friend. I plan to become a professor."

As one, Jacob and Rand said, "Oh."

September 21, 1903
Princeton, NJ

Dear Pearl,

I hope this letter finds you well as you commence your senior year at ACW. Do tell me what courses you're taking and if you got the professors you desired. How is your family? You had mentioned before I left Easton that your mother was afflicted by toothache. Functioning normally with a throbbing tooth is vexing, and I have been praying for her relief.

I find it difficult to believe I'm already into my third week at the seminary as the time appears to have gone by on winged feet. By this point, I know my way around and am falling into an agreeable routine, including taking long walks through the adjoining university campus where the trees are putting on a dazzling show.

Do you recall how much more difficult college was than high school? I am finding this to be the case with seminary. For example, in one of my first classes, the professor referred to some unfamiliar theological terms, including "JDP" and "form criticism." I stole a glance at my classmates to see any signs of confusion on their part, but they all appeared at home with the terminology. Afterward, I bared myself to my new friend Rand. He said he'd learned about these concepts from German theology while he was at Yale. I can't say I'm happy about these teachings which challenge the very fabric of our belief in biblical authority. I don't know if my professor believes these things or is simply teaching us about them, which I find unsettling. Truly, I'm surprised to find such teaching here—that is, a progressive school of thought about how we interpret Scripture. That group regards the Bible as if it were no different from any other ancient text, to be understood within its historical context. Like you, I maintain the Bible is the inspired Word of God, unlike any other human writing.

> Fortunately, Dr. Warfield is of the old school, firm as Gibraltar on the veracity of Scripture. Just listen to me, using such a word. I guess this is to be expected when one is studying theology. When I sit under his teaching, I'm far more at ease in my spirit. I wonder if my professors at Lafayette, or if Dr. Kieffer, were aware of those German theologians. Have you ever heard of them?

Jacob looked up when Win blew in the door, his face ruddier than usual. "My good man, what are you doing?"

"Taking a break from Hebrew to write to Pearl."

"No one should be studying when there's a great football game at hand."

"Football?" He perked up.

"Yes, you know the game, right?"

"I most certainly do. I played at Lafayette." He grinned. "Mind you, I was much better at baseball."

"Well, then, Princeton is going at Harvard today."

"No wonder you're excited."

"Some of my cousins have come down for the game, and my uncle is hosting a party afterward."

"Is this the uncle who's a professor at the university? Is he coming to the game?"

"The very same, and he'll be sitting with his cronies. He gave me some tickets at the fifty-yard line." His blue eyes glinted. "Finish your letter and forget about Hebrew for the rest of the day. Rand's coming too."

"Okay. Thanks."

"Don't mention it." He rummaged through his chest of drawers muttering to himself. "I need to find my Harvard muffler."

Jacob picked up his pen.

> Pearl, my roommate just invited me to attend the Princeton football game with our friend Rand and some of Win's family. I think I mentioned earlier his uncle

teaches history at the university and Win often visits his home on Mercer Street. Sometimes, I can hardly believe an ordinary guy like me is breathing such rarified air. I'll write again soon and let you know all about the game and the party, both of which would be much more enjoyable if you were here.

With love,
Jacob

They met Win's cousin at University Field where introductions carried on the breeze and general buzz of excited fans.

"Jacob, Rand, I'd like to present my cousin Ted, who goes to Groton and is an aspiring Harvard man."

Jacob squinted as he received a firm handshake. "I'm happy to meet you." *He looks familiar, but I know I haven't met him before this.*

The young man winked at his cousin while addressing Jacob and Rand. "The fam have me marked for Harvard, which is why I'm wearing the colors today. So, which one of you has the misfortune of sharing a tenement with my cousin?"

"That would be me," Jacob said, noting the strong New York accent.

Ted raised his hand to shield his response. "Don't let him throw you. He can be a pompous ass sometimes, but he's a good fellow overall. Not exactly ministerial material, but he'll make a good prof."

Jacob grinned. "Thanks for the warning."

Win peered at Jacob, a smile arching his upper lip. "Don't believe a word this little miscreant has to say."

Ted clapped Win on the back, and they settled into their seats for the game.

He told himself to close his mouth when Win and Ted ushered Jacob and Rand into their uncle's home. The place oozed old money and sophistication from the foyer's Tiffany chandelier to the maid to the gilt-framed portraits of stalwart ancestors. Before Jacob could lose himself in the ambiance, Win led his friends into a paneled drawing room where a genial fire glowed.

A man rose and walked to them. "Win, Ted, you're back. What a game, wasn't it? And our Princeton Tigers still undefeated." He looked at Jacob and Rand. "Who are your friends?"

"Uncle Louis, this is my roommate, Jacob Kichline, and our fellow friend and seminarian Rand Ainslie."

"I am happy to meet you, sir," Jacob said shaking his hand.

"Where are you from?"

"Easton, Pennsylvania."

"Lafayette grad?"

"Yes, sir."

The professor cuffed his shoulder and turned to Rand. "Ainslie. Are you from Locust Valley by any chance?"

"Yes, Professor."

"I know your family." He clapped his hands. "Welcome to my home. This is my dear wife, Ophelia."

Jacob gave a slight bow and smiled at the perfumed and powdered lady.

"Rand, dear," she said, "I know your mother from DAR gatherings. Lovely woman."

"Thank you, Mrs. Winthrop."

She turned to Jacob. "Is your mother by any chance a member?"

"Yes, ma'am," he said. "She's quite active in the organization."

Was it his imagination or did she seem friendlier?

"And this is Ted's sister and my beloved niece, Alice, who went shopping with me today rather than attend a football game."

When she held out her hand to Jacob, he mentally scratched his head. Why were both she and her brother so recognizable? All at once he failed to breathe. *Ted and Alice—Roosevelt—the President of the United States's two eldest children.*

CHAPTER SIX

FEBRUARY 9, 1904

Something was in the air besides unyielding cold and snow. Soon-hee sat with corded neck muscles, alert not only to Mr. Moffett's brilliant interpretation of the Sermon on the Mount, but to a rising tension. When a near-distant bugle call sounded, he followed his professor and the other students to the windows. His lips parted at the sight of Japanese soldiers moving in ranked columns from the Pekin Road into Pyongyang's main thoroughfare.

"What is happening?" a classmate asked.

Moffett grimaced. "Gentlemen, I believe the Russo-Japanese War has reached Pyongyang."

A collective gasp arose, and several students chorused, "What does this mean?"

Moffett provided an explanation. "For many decades, the Russian Empire has sought to expand its interests in China. Over the years, the Chinese government has become steadily weaker while the Japanese have increased in strength."

Soon-hee well knew how Japan had consolidated its power after modernizing its military forces. Not so long ago, they had marched in these very streets and taken over China's governance of Korea.

"There's been a good deal of saber-rattling between the Russians and Japanese," Moffett said. "I suspect what we're seeing now is an outbreak of open warfare."

The other men began speaking all at once in a cacophony of fear, but Soon-hee resorted to silent prayer. He lifted his head when a breathless Mr. Blair entered the classroom patting his hand over his heart.

"I was hoping to find you here, Mr. Moffett." He stepped aside to reveal a brusque Japanese officer. "This is Colonel Ohnishi." Blair swept his hand in the direction of his missionary colleague. "This is Dr. Samuel Moffett, whom you wished to see."

Soon-hee held his breath as his mentor crossed the room, standing over a head taller than the grim man. Shadows slithered into this place of light.

Moffett offered a customary bow. "How may I be of service?"

Eschewing niceties, the man got right to the point.

"The Japanese Imperial Army has taken possession of Pyongyang in our fight against the Russian aggressors. By order of the Imperial Government, all missionaries are confined to this city until further notice. You are not to leave or to receive anyone from outside these limits under penalty of death. Do you understand?"

"Yes."

When the officer eyed the students, the hair on Soon-hee's nape rose. He finally relaxed when the fellow turned brusquely on his heels and departed. He watched Mr. Blair follow Ohnishi while casting a raised-eyebrows look back at Moffett.

"Gentlemen, I suggest we end today's session."

"Can we go to see if our families are all right?" one of them asked.

"Unless they are close by, I think we should all stay within the compound until we have further details. Those of you from the villages should keep to your rooms on campus." He paused, sober. "Most importantly, we must pray. Let's do so now."

The men formed a circle and bowed their heads.

"Heavenly Father, we do not understand all that is happening just now, but none of this surprises thee. We beseech thee to watch over all of us at the mission and our families, some who are near and some who are in distant villages. May thy angels keep charge over us to guide and protect us as we seek to be a blessing to thee in this perilous time. May thy will be done on earth as it is in Heaven. Through Christ our Lord, amen."

"Amen," they said as one.

Everyone but Soon-hee departed in haste against the backdrop of Japanese soldiers streaming through the city.

"What would you like me to do, Mr. Moffett?"

He rubbed his chin. "Go to your family. They'll want to see you and be assured of your safety. Then as soon as you're able, come back to the church and bring your father with you."

As Soon-hee moved to the door, Moffett spoke again. "Try not to call any attention to yourself."

He understood.

He met his brother on the way home, Yong-bin's eyes wide, his breath halting. All around them, Koreans and missionaries moved in a daze, grabbing on to one another as if for dear life.

"What does this mean, Soon-hee?"

His recent annoyance with the youth lessened when he took note of Yong-bin's shaking hands.

"I do not know all the implications." Why did his brother think he would know?

"What should we do?" Yong-bin stumbled, seeming to struggle to keep up with Soon-hee's longer strides.

"We will check on our family and support them."

"But how? The worst may be happening."

Soon-hee stopped moving, and Yong-bin bumped into him. "Even when the worst happens, our God is still on his throne. You must remember and rely upon this truth, my brother." He peered at the enlarged brown eyes. "And you must rise to the occasion like a man."

The Adam's apple moved on Yong-bin's throat. "Y-yes, of c-course."

His ashen-faced mother received them both with outstretched arms and a deep sigh. Soon-hee's eyes swept the interior. His father stood close to her, gripping her shoulders.

"Where is Sora?"

She responded with a trembling voice. "She is still at school."

"School has been dismissed," Yong-bin said.

She clutched Soon-hee's forearm. "You must go and find her."

He closed his eyes in silent prayer then faced his mother. "Mr. Moffett has asked me to bring *Abeoji* to the church for an emergency meeting. I will look for her on the way there, but perhaps Yong-bin can search for her. I am confident she is safe with her teacher."

Mr. Oh reached for his Bible and hat, joining Soon-hee at the door.

His mother's voice rose. "Yong-bin cannot do such a thing."

Soon-hee watched as his brother stepped closer to her.

"Yes, I can."

"First of all, my brothers, we must look to the Lord for guidance, remembering how he has delivered us from many past dangers."

"You were here ten years ago," Mr. Blair said. "Tell us what happened then."

Moffett leaned against the back of a chair in momentary silence before sharing the oft-repeated story to Blair, Swallen, and Bernheisel.

"Mr. Oh and Soon-hee can attest to my story. In their mighty clash for power, the Japanese met the Chinese here in the city. Another war, however, was waging for the souls of men. We had taken a firm stance against the worship of ancestors, trying to teach how Koreans can honor their parents without engaging in idolatry. The authorities began arresting Christians, beating some, and threatening to kill them." He pinched his lips together.

Kyung Oh spoke. "A mob attacked Mr. Moffett in the streets, hurling stones to kill him. As this was taking place, the Chinese army descended upon Pyongyang from the north while the Japanese poured into the city from the south, much like today. The crowd went away."

Soon-hee worked his knuckles as the other men listened, openmouthed. He had been eleven years old, the sight of the warring armies indelibly inscribed on his memory.

"Tell us, when did the Christians return?" Mr. Bernheisel asked.

"As soon as we got word to them of our reappearance in Pyongyang," Moffett said.

Soon-hee considered those terrible days and what this new invasion must be doing to his mother's sister. After what a gang of rogue Japanese soldiers had done to her, she had opted never to leave her father's house next door to theirs again.

Outside, soldiers marched, their commanding officers' voices carrying on the wind.

Soon-hee focused on Samuel Moffett as he spoke to the small gathering.

"I assure you, we will get through this. We will prevail just as we did ten years ago. Mr. Blair, perhaps you would share with us what you've recently been writing about those days."

The American cleared his throat. "I'll be glad to. Let me just gather my thoughts. Well, then, have you ever seen a fire smoldering in the ashes on a still day? Suddenly, a little whirlwind comes down, raises the embers, and scatters them all around, so that here and there other fires begin burning. This is just what happened in Korea in those days. The fire that God's Spirit had kindled burned in Pyongyang. Then, suddenly the whirlwind of the war came down and lifted up and scattered the fire for hundreds of miles in every direction. Everywhere those living embers fell, whether near the sea or in deep-set mountain valleys, other fires began to blaze and spread. Soon, the fire of the gospel was burning throughout the whole length and breadth of the peninsula."

Moffett's eyes shone. "Mr. Blair, you've captured beautifully what happened back then. I recall, the field was so white unto harvest we had to appeal to the mission boards with great urgency to supply laborers. That's when you came to us in answer to our Macedonian Cry."

Blair dipped his chin.

"So, you see, my brothers, the dispersed believers were able to bring forth a great harvest of souls. While hiding in those remote places, they spread the glorious gospel message." He paused. "The Lord always has the final word."

In the initial days of the war, Japanese officials not only required the missionaries to remain in the city but to offer their homes for the billeting of soldiers. Soon-hee had been able to persuade them to use his parents' home instead of his aunt's, citing her fragility. Fortunately, they had acquiesced and while his father kept a close watch on his household, Yong-bin had gone to stay with his aunt. Soon-hee rejoiced at his brother's rising to the needs of others, rather than just focusing on his own.

Japanese troops moved daily in and out of Pyongyang, storing their baggage on the mission's campus and making little fuss in the homes they occupied. Soon-hee suspected the mission's American identity offered a large degree of protection.

Several weeks passed when Mr. Blair went to see Moffett about his deep concern for his country churches. Soon-hee happened to be present.

"Do you think the authorities would allow me to visit them?"

Moffett took a moment before responding. "Perhaps you could ask the Japanese Resident here in the city for permission."

He sat up straighter. "I would like to accompany Mr. Blair with your blessing."

"Let's first see what the Resident says."

The following day, Blair returned to Moffett's office to share the outcome of his meeting. "I have their consent." He produced a document. "This passport is written in Japanese and English and enables me to go to three of my churches to preach. I'm to be allowed passage without interference."

"This is good news," Moffett said.

Soon-hee spoke up. "What about me?"

"I asked if I could bring a Korean assistant, and although you aren't mentioned in the paperwork, I have a tacit understanding about bringing you along."

Moffett turned to Soon-hee. "There are no guarantees for your safety. Are you still willing to go with Mr. Blair?"

He stood tall. "Yes, Mr. Moffett."

"Then we shall cover you both with prayer while you're gone."

They reached the small city of Anju on the second evening of their journey to find the gates closed and guarded by Japanese soldiers. A group of Koreans quickly joined Soon-hee and Blair, speaking all at once and with considerable agitation.Blair stepped closer to his companions. "Mr. Oh, would you please interpret? I can't keep up with them."

"They say several hundred Russian Cossacks arrived yesterday, cutting telegraph wires and firing upon Anju. The residents were able to telegraph news to Sook Chun, and that city's company arrived a short time ago. The Japanese have armed the Korean residents and told them not to worry if they could not hit anything, just shoot and make a lot of noise. They are badly outnumbered, but the Russians seem unaware of this."

"Do you hear that?" Blair looked first this way, then the next.

A Korean man cried out, and Soon-hee explained to his companion, "He says the Russians are coming again, and we must take shelter. He says to follow him."

They were led to a largely hidden area outside the village wall and watched as a brief battle ensued. An undermanned company of Japanese soldiers charged straight up a nearby hill at the Russians, who turned and fled. The entire affair was over in a matter of minutes. In the aftermath, a middle-aged Korean man approached Blair and Soon-hee speaking rapidly, accompanied by much gesturing.

Soon-hee spoke above the pounding in his chest and ears. "He says the Christians inside the wall are expecting a service tonight."

"How in the world are we going to get inside? The gates are still shut."

Soon-hee spoke to the Korean man, then turned to Blair. "He will guide us over a breach."

"Very well. Lead on!"

They followed the man making as little noise as possible, crawling on hands and knees up broken passes halfway between the gates. When they got inside, dusty and sweating, a group of Christians surrounded them with cheers and hugs. They immediately took the missionaries straight to the church where Blair delivered the sermon they longed for. Soon-hee might have been exhausted except for the exhilaration in his spirit. The following day, he and Blair learned everyone had fled the city except for the Japanese and Christians. The man who had led them through the gate the night before told them the bottom had fallen out of the housing market, which might prove beneficial. At first, Soon-hee didn't know what he was talking about.

"You see, we have outgrown this church and need a new one. One of the best houses in Anju is for sale and would be perfect for our needs."

"How much is it, and how much do you have?" Blair asked.

"We have taken up a collection and have secured half the funds."

Soon-hee watched Blair as he sat and thought. He knew the American missionaries could make up the difference, but there were rules against using American money to build Korean churches. In bearing such burdens alone, the Koreans always grew stronger.

"Has everyone been asked for a contribution?" Blair asked.

"Yes." The man bowed his head.

"Not everyone."

The men turned to face an old Korean woman who had stepped forward.

"I am Choi-si, a widow. While I have no money to offer, I do have some property to sell. We must have this house for a church, and if you agree, I will give proceeds from the sale of my land to make up what is lacking. In return, I ask to live in one room of the church as its keeper."

Twenty-four hours later, Soon-hee witnessed the official purchase of Anju's new church building.

CHAPTER SEVEN

MARCH 1904
PRINCETON, NJ

"Hey there! Wait up, Jacob."

He turned to his friend's distinctive voice before crossing Alexander Street.

"Hey there, Rand."

"Heading into town, are you?"

"I need some things from Nassau Pharmacy."

"I have a bit of shopping to do as well. Mind if I tag along?"

"Not at all. I could use a couple of new shirts, and the only stores I know here are the drug and university bookstores."

"I'm actually heading to Hiltons for an appointment with a salesman." Rand tugged at his threadbare coat, which still managed to convey a certain élan. "I'm sure they can fix you up as well."

Jacob smelled the word "expensive." His parents had just given him a new suit, but he welcomed the opportunity to bring the rest of his wardrobe more in line with his affluent classmates. That is, if he could afford doing so.

Once they reached the university campus they began discussing a recent theology exam.

"I think I did all right," Rand said. "How about you?"

"I think so, although, well, I'm not sure ..." His throat constricted.

"Something bothering you?"

They nodded a silent greeting as they passed two university students, then Jacob ran a finger under his collar. "Sometimes, I feel confused."

"Oh?"

He grappled to articulate the silent drama he'd been playing out since late fall. Might Rand be able to understand? He knew Win wouldn't.

"I don't know what to make of our professor. On the one hand, he seems orthodox, affirming the doctrines of our faith. On the other, he's sounding a different trumpet than, say, Dr. Warfield."

Rand shot straight. "He's a theological liberal, and you're right. Some of his beliefs align with sound teaching, but he emphasizes reason and experience over scriptural authority. He's one of the modernists who want us to engage theology critically and form our own beliefs."

Jacob pictured himself on a rowboat with no oars.

"Do you think he's trustworthy, Rand?" He found it hard to believe such a teacher could expound such undermining beliefs at Princeton. There had to be something important in the professor's ideas or he wouldn't be allowed on the faculty.

"In what sense?" They paused at the curb until several carriages passed by them on Nassau Street.

"I, uh, supposed everyone here would be rock solid in their faith, and I could be confident in their teaching without reservation. Like I did at Lafayette, and with my old pastor."

Rand closed his eyes for a moment. "I see what you mean. From what I've been able to figure out, Princeton used to be that way and mostly still is, but theological liberalism and modernism are making inroads."

"How do you know this?"

"My pastor went here years ago and has stayed close to the seminary. He told me to be aware of these trends and how subtle they can be."

"By modernism, do you mean evolution?"

"Evolution is part of the modernist package." Rand spread his hands. "There's also historical criticism and the social gospel."

"I've been trying to wrap my mind around those concepts," he said, smoothing back a lock of hair loosened by the wind. He took a deep breath before daring to get more personal. "Does any of this ever disorient you?"

"Fortunately, I'm close to my pastor and follow the professors who maintain a strong orthodoxy. I try to avoid the one or two others."

Jacob wondered why these trends hadn't been discussed in his Lafayette religion classes. He also wished he could have remained under Pastor Kieffer's care but wondered if he would understand what was happening at Princeton. What kind of exposure had the quaint minister ever had to modernists?

Rand continued. "I think at its heart, modernism is about replacing scriptural authority with human understanding. In other words, just another version of what took place in the Garden of Eden."

"How so?"

"Remember when the serpent asked Eve, 'Did God really say?'" Rand waved his right hand. "There's nothing new under the sun."

At least for the moment, Jacob's fog seemed to lift.

When they entered the elegant establishment catering to Princeton's gentry, Jacob sucked in his breath. This gilt-accented place of rich woods, marble flooring, curated artwork, and furniture befitting a private men's club contained men's furnishings he'd feel like a million bucks wearing. Unfortunately, his budget was more suited to Laubach's of Easton. His parents were as generous with his allowance as they could afford, and his church covered Jacob's room and board, so he had no complaints or unmet needs. Nevertheless, an Ainslie or Brown he was not.

"Mister Ainslie, how nice to see you." An impeccably dressed and groomed salesman approached them across the carpeted store.

"Hello, Mr. Vickers. You're looking well. I'd like you to meet my good friend Jacob Kichline."

He shook hands with the clerk, who gave him a once-over.

"My mother told me to hie myself here and stop disgracing the family name."

"One must always heed one's mother. Well, then, I see you require some new tweeds." He added, "And perhaps a visit to the tonsorial parlor."

"I need the works. Even my collars and cuffs are fraying."

"We can take care of you." He turned to Jacob. "And how about you, Mr. Kichline? What do you need today?"

Deeper pockets.

By the time they finished their sojourn at Hiltons, Jacob had just enough money left for some necessary toiletries. He'd purchased two custom shirts and a first-rate top hat. The knowledge he wouldn't be able to pay for a ticket to see Pearl until his next allotment in three weeks laid heavily on his conscience. The hat his father had loaned him still had plenty of wear left, but then again, wouldn't she be impressed with his more sophisticated appearance?

Before returning to their dorm rooms, they checked their mailboxes. A heavy vellum envelope lacking a postmark stood out among the handful of letters addressed to Jacob. On the back, a wax seal bore the initials BBW. Curious, he opened the envelope and extracted a note card featuring the same monogram.

Rand glanced over Jacob's shoulder. "I see you got one too." He read aloud. "'Dr. and Mrs. Benjamin Breckinridge Warfield request the honor of your presence at their home for light refreshments and conversation. Monday, March 28, 1904, Two O'clock in the Afternoon.'"

Jacob grinned. "This is incredible."

"What is?" Win appeared, ducking into his mailbox.

"Dr. Warfield has invited us to his home on the 28th," Rand said. "You probably got one too."

Win sorted through his correspondence and waved his own invitation. "I see the old boy is entertaining again."

Jacob winced at his roommate's disrespectful attitude. "What do you mean?"

"He used to have students over all the time." Win looked about and lowered his voice. "His wife isn't well." Then he circled the side of his head with his forefinger.

Rand appeared not to have heard or seen Win. "I know exactly what I'll be wearing—one of my two new suits. The tailor will have them ready a few days before the soiree."

Despite his small regret at being a waster, Jacob at least took pleasure in knowing he also would be well dressed for the important gathering.

A maid ushered him and the other first-year seminarians into the foyer, Jacob noting the usual ancestor portraits lining the wallpapered stairwell. Gleaming hardwood floors peeking from underneath Aubusson carpets. Classic Princeton. Rather than the ambience of class, power, and old money at Win's uncle's home; however, the Warfield domicile seemed more to Jacob like the inside of a church—peaceful, holy. Dr. and Mrs. Warfield received their guests in their gaslit dining room against a backdrop of several dozen plants and an array of artistically prepared sandwiches and confections. On the table, Villeroy and Boch china, gleaming cut crystal glasses, and silverware caught Jacob's attention.

The young men filled their plates and took them into a cozy parlor where a fire crackled. Photos rested on a burnished grand piano, but none included children, and Jacob guessed the couple didn't have any. Mrs. Warfield seemed fine to him, if a mite delicate, and after seeing to her guests, excused herself. The tender way Dr. Warfield squeezed her hand and gazed at her moved Jacob.

In addition to the delectable food, he filled himself on the professor's vibrant conversation, drawn to the Bible's centrality in his life. Various verses and passages rolled off his tongue as if they were part of his very being, the man living and breathing Scripture. If only he could stay close to him, Jacob figured, the slings and arrows of the modernists wouldn't be able to touch him.

At the end of their visit, Warfield's eyes twinkled. "Before you go, gentlemen, you are in for a surprise, especially Mr. Kichline, our resident baseball expert. A certain, shall we say unconventional Presbyterian minister will be preaching in chapel next Wednesday." He scanned the room, smiling underneath his signature beard until his eyes rested on Jacob.

"Who is it, Dr. Warfield?" Rand asked.

"The Reverend Billy Sunday."

Jacob shot out of his chair. "Billy Sunday! Here?"

The professor chuckled. "I'll wait to provide details until our friend sits back down."

Jacob did as he was told.

"I thought all of you might benefit from hearing a different kind of preaching than you get from our usual starched crowd." He laughed. "I include myself of course."

Jacob hadn't felt this giddy since he was eight years old and watching the circus come to town. *I wonder if I'll get to meet him.*

"I'm having difficulty understanding why in the world this wag was invited to speak at such a place of cultivated learning as Princeton." Win failed to chew and swallow first before sharing his unsought opinion with Rand and Jacob. "Do you know he actually put his foot on top of a pulpit while haranguing one of his audiences?" His eyes flashed. "Just let him try that stunt here."

"Being exposed to him will be good for us stuffed shirts," Rand said.

Jacob stifled a laugh, causing a mouthful of water to geyser up his nose. He started choking, but Win seemed not to notice.

"This is a largely uneducated and vulgar man, and he stops at nothing when it comes to theatrics." His nostrils splayed. "He makes George Whitefield look like B.B. Warfield.

I half expect him to slide across the chancel as if he's at a baseball game."

"Who knows," Jacob said, "he might just throw a chair at the devil." He winked in Rand's direction, both of them sniggering.

Rand leaned back in his chair, arms crossed. "I guess you'll be sitting out tomorrow's chapel in protest then."

Win snorted. "And miss such a performance? Not a chance."

Jacob had volunteered to usher at the service, handing out bulletins and helping townspeople find seats once the seminarians had filled their assigned pews. A dozen university professors showed up including Win's uncle, who seemed more than a little smug as he shook Jacob's hand.

"I couldn't pass up the opportunity to see this snake oil salesman," he said.

Jacob grimaced, his assessment of the man coming down several notches. He went on to show a contingent of newspaper reporters to the balcony, and a half-hour before the service, Jacob was scrambling to set up extra chairs—first in the aisles, then in the narthex. For his labors he received a coveted front-row seat.

Miller Chapel's hallowed setting had always confined itself to quiet contemplation before worship, but today's mood was more was like New York City's Grand Central Station the day before Christmas. Noisy conversations cloaked the organist's prelude.

At precisely ten o'clock, Professor Woodrow entered the chancel from the side followed by B.B. Warfield, Professor Browne, and the Reverend Billy Sunday. Jacob's heart raced at the sight of his boyhood hero, in a Geneva gown no less. He'd never seen the man in anything but a suit or baseball uniform.

Professor Brown went to the lectern and raised his arms. "Let us stand and worship God."

In response, a swooshing sound filled the chapel as people rose to worship.

"God was in Christ reconciling the world to himself, not counting their sins against them, and has commissioned us with the message of reconciliation. Praise the Lord."

The people thundered back, "The Lord's name be praised!"

"Please remain standing for the opening hymn, 'All People That on Earth Do Dwell,' number twenty-four in the hymnbook."

Jacob had heard some powerful singing in Miller Chapel, but this rendition of the "Old One-Hundredth," the beloved singing of Psalm 100, fairly lifted him off the ground. After the hymn came the prayers of confession and pardon, New and Old Testament readings, and the Apostles' Creed.

Warfield went to the pulpit and addressed the congregation.

"Our preacher this morning is well-known to us all, a successful baseball player who left the game he loved to follow Jesus Christ, whom he loved far more, into the work of evangelism. Just last year, the Presbytery of Chicago ordained him, and I am pleased to welcome the Reverend Billy Sunday to Miller Chapel." He turned to his side. "Mr. Sunday."

The forty-one-year-old hopped to his feet and shook the esteemed professor's hand before entering the pulpit. Jacob wondered if he'd be his usual boisterous self or tone down his sermon for this refined crowd.

"Did you know," Sunday began, "there are vast multitudes in this enlightened land of ours who are in open rebellion against God? 'We will not have this man, Jesus Christ, reign over us,' is the heartless cry that winds its flight from office, shop, store, factory, home, college, and the busy mart of trade. Lots of people are willing, my friends, to accept whatever they want from the Bible. They would like to codify it. They would like to sit down and eliminate that which isn't pleasant to them and which they don't like to adjust their lives to and insert something they would like instead."

Jacob grinned at the plainspoken words, imaging Win's blood at a simmer two pews behind him. He hoped Sunday would continue being himself because anything less would be, well, less.

"You take it as it is given, and if you don't, you will go to hell. God almighty won't adjust his principles to suit the opinions of anybody."

The congregation collectively gasped, but Jacob smiled to himself.

"They say they will give us the Sermon on the Mount, or the Decalogue, minus the things that they don't like. They say, 'We have no king but self,' and the only law that multitudes of people recognize is the law of their own desires and ambitions. And so our Lord is now rejected, and by the world disowned. By the many still neglected, but by the few enthroned."

Sunday marched to the side of the sleek pulpit, removing and casting his tie to the ground. He began pacing back and forth.

"Out in a western state four years ago, a report was made that there were three hundred churches of this denomination in that state. They spent $300,000 for current expenses, they held 46,000 meetings, and during the year there were just eighty-seven men and women who were converted and received on confession of faith. I suppose that is this safe and sane evangelism that I hear so much about."

Sunday paused and punched his right fist. "It wouldn't take the world long to get into hell if that is all there is to it! In Chicago just a few years ago, the Presbyterian churches there published a report. There was an average of five who joined each congregation by a confession of faith. And this last year of 7,500 churches from all denominations that made reports, there was not one person who joined any of those churches in that year by a confession of faith."

Jacob squirmed at the pathetic statistics.

The preacher shook his head and spread his hands. "All right, look at it! Just face the conditions, and you will see why probably I talk in a way that grates on your nerves, but you will realize that I am only telling you the truth. Now, what is lacking? Why these meager results? Why the expenditure of so much energy, time, and money? It is because there is not a definite effort put forth to persuade a definite person to accept a definite Savior at a definite time?"

He pounded the side of the pulpit so hard Jacob wondered if the structure would survive the assault.

"That time is now! That is the whole thing in a nutshell, boiled down to one sentence. That is why we are not making headway."

A sound of feet shuffling in the aisle began a few rows back. A handful of seminarians, including Win, were getting up and leaving. Sunday seemed unfazed, charging ahead.

"A while back, an evangelist preached a series of revival sermons in a church, and night after night, there was but one response when he asked people to raise a hand if they wanted to follow the Lord. An adolescent boy was the only one lifting his hand. Finally, the preacher shouted ..." Sunday raised his voice. "What you need in this town is an undertaker not an evangelist. You are the deadest crowd that I have ever seen. And if God or anybody else had told me that there was such a dead, indifferent membership on earth, I wouldn't have believed it."

He went on filling out the story of just one boy who said "yes" to Christ.

"After he was baptized, the boy went to his grandfather, a reprobate who for sixty years had rejected God and followed after all the modern nonsense you're probably filling your minds with here."

Jacob saw Warfield lower his head and grin, the other professors' mouths swinging open as on gates.

"But the earnest boy convinced the old man to go hear the evangelist. The sinner came to his senses and asked God to remove his guilt. The next day, the little fellow sought out his father at the miserable saloon he operated. The dad told him to leave—this was no place for a boy. But that fellow persisted, I tell you."

Sunday cavorted, waving his hands, the Geneva gown like a bullfighter's cape until he seemed to have had enough and yanked off the restrictive garment. Several more people left in protest.

"The Holy Spirit got hold of that saloon keeper until he got down on his knees and repented." Sunday sank to his own. "And as the blood of Jesus cleansed him, he went forth and broke every bottle of booze in his establishment, letting them run into the sewer right where they belonged."

He rose and returned to the pulpit leaning over so far Jacob half expected Sunday to land in his lap.

"It all started with that little boy." His look pierced the audience. "You've got as much sense as the boy, haven't you? Go do likewise—that is my message."

The final hymn seemed flat after Sunday's electrifying presentation. After the benediction, Jacob's heart raced when the former ballplayer, though surrounded by the curious, strode over to him. Grasping his hand and gazing into his eyes, Sunday said, "Don't let these fellows get you down." He gave Jacob a wink before the crowd engulfed him.

Chapter Eight

Late Summer 1904
Pyongyang, Korea

Soon-hee's eyes glowed at the sight of Jeongsook as they met near the Moffett's home, from which she was coming and he was going. They hadn't seen each other often since the outbreak of war, her parents keeping her close to home.

"I understand you have had a full summer," she said after their initial greetings.

"Yes, I have. I am happy to see you out and about. Do you have time to sit and talk? I have a few minutes before Mr. Moffett is expecting me." Soon-hee motioned to a bench under an oak tree whose spreading branches promised a respite from the late-morning heat.

"Oh, yes."

After they settled in, they observed some summer school students crossing the grounds.

"This has been for me a productive time, but I regret not having had more time to visit with you." He hoped she detected his deeper meaning.

She looked down at her hands. "I have felt the same."

He might have taken wing had his feet not been firmly set on the ground.

"What work have you been doing with Mrs. Dr. Moffett?"

"Now that the danger of a Russian invasion has passed, she has been preparing visits to the outlying churches. Your mother and I have helped her and Miss Story secure and organize supplies. I have also worked on a simple Bible study for the children."

He smiled at her. "You have a fine gift."

"Thank you. I so love God's Word and the children. Are you planning to travel with Mr. Blair's group?"

Soon-hee and the missionary had decided to check on the Anju church in Blair's charge but not about who would accompany them.

"Yes, I will be going."

Jeongsook toyed with her basket's handle. "I wish I could, but as you know, only the American women have been permitted to leave the compound. It is not safe for us with so many Japanese soldiers in our midst."

This he could understand since those men could not be counted upon to act honorably toward Korean women. About to change the subject, he scuffed his right foot on the hard ground, wondering when the last time they'd had rain.

"My translation project is nearing completion, and I will have a couple of weeks until fall classes begin." He searched her face. "Perhaps before I leave we can—"

"Soon-hee! There you are."

His face tightened at the sound of his brother's voice. Yong-bin approached them, clasping his hands together. "Oh, hello, Jeongsook."

"Hello."

"I must speak with you at once," the young man said. "The matter is urgent."

She rose and bowed. "I will leave the two of you. Soon-hee, I look forward to talking with you again."

He wanted to reach for her hand and beg her to stay but instead growled at his brother after she left. "What is the problem?" With Yong-bin, there always seemed to be one lurking somewhere.

He flopped onto the bench uninvited. "I have a test tomorrow for my Old Testament class, and I am in danger of failing."

"Why are you in this danger? Have you not studied?"

Yong-bin fidgeted. "Yes, but the Hebrew translation is so difficult. I cannot seem to understand the language while grappling with my headaches."

"I will be willing to tutor you, to help you prepare."

"Oh, but my headache is too strong, and I must pass. Mother and father expect me to do well."

Soon-hee's hands clenched.

"When you took the exam, you got the highest grade ever recorded here. Professor Bernheisel told us. If you will just share the answers with me—"

"I most certainly will not." He rose from the seat, glaring.

"Just this once. What will Mother and Father say if I do not pass?"

"They will make excuses for you, just as they always do." *On the other hand, if I were to fail a class, they would exhibit no such understanding.* "You should have thought about the consequences when you were cavorting with your friends."

Yong-bin rose and came to within an inch of his brother's face. "I cannot believe you refuse to help me, and you a Christian leader. You are heartless." He made a face and kicked up a small dust cloud as he stormed away.

This was not how he wanted to leave his family as he made final preparations for the Anju sojourn. Although he was slow to anger, he teetered on the verge.

"I do not understand how you could deny your brother help." His mother dabbed her tears. "You know how he suffers."

Sora watched, wide-eyed and twisting the front of her dress.

"And now you have upset your mother." His father scowled at Soon-hee.

Their glaring expressions immobilized him. He glanced at Yong-bin with his dejected face knowing a smirk lay just underneath.

He took a deep breath to steady himself. "I offered to help him. He refused."

A vein popped on Mrs. Oh's face. "How could you lie to me, Soon-hee?"

"I am not the one lying. I told him I would tutor him, and he would not let me. He ..." Could he tell them what had really happened? Would letting his family know Yong-bin wanted to cheat do any good? Would they even believe him? Soon-hee sincerely doubted they would take his word over his brother's. Yong-bin seemed to be holding his breath. Soon-hee decided to save his.

He reached for the belongings he had packed for his trip, his parents hovering on the sidelines silently accusing, shaming. At the door, he gave his crying sister a slight smile of affection and left his parents drowning in their outrage.

On the walk to Anju, there was plenty of time for reflection, and Soon-hee had sunk into subterranean thoughts about his home situation. Walking alongside the ox cart in which Mrs. Dr. Moffett and Clara Story conversed with each other, he barely noticed the passing scenery or realized he was grinding his teeth. When William Blair sidled next to him, they matched each other's strides and engaged in light chit-chat. Then the missionary started probing.

"You have been unusually quiet, Mr. Oh. Are you all right?"

Have I been so obvious? He knew a response was required, but he didn't know what, or how much, to say. Fortunately, Blair seemed comfortable with Soon-hee's need for some time before answering. The sound of the ox cart trudging on the dirt path filled the pause.

"I have been struggling with a situation at home."

"Would you care to discuss the matter?"

He smiled into the face of the kind American. Perhaps if he shared some of the circumstances, he might be able to unload their weightiness and not be encumbered during this important mission.

"There is much tension between my brother and myself." He looked straight ahead where the rest of their company walked and conversed. Mrs. Dr. Moffett was laughing.

"Your brother is often sick, isn't he?" Blair's brow wrinkled.

"He was not expected to survive infancy and was frequently compromised as he grew. He has terrible headaches." Soon-hee didn't know what else he could comfortably say.

"I can imagine your parents try hard to protect him."

"Yes."

"Perhaps they try a little too hard?"

Blair had given voice to what Soon-hee often thought. "Yes."

"You have a discerning spirit, Mr. Oh, one keen to anything not of the Lord. This is a wonderful gift, but when you see a truth that others can't, tension can result."

His eyes brimmed.

When the Anju Christians met their party at the city gates, Soon-hee noticed circles under their eyes and their stooped posture. A small contingent of Japanese soldiers lingered around the edges, curious. The children encircled Mrs. Dr. Moffett, their faces upturned as they gave and received hugs, staring at the tall American woman with her.

"Why the long faces?" Blair asked. He lowered his voice. "Have the Japanese been treating you harshly?"

"They have not been much trouble," the leading elder said. "Because of a certain, uh, situation, they have kept their distance from us."

The missionary pushed his lower lip out. "I'm afraid I don't understand."

A shrieking female brought the conversation to a stunned stop, Soon-hee's neck hair bristling. The ranking Japanese officer strode over to William Blair.

"See if you cannot do something about this. Short of locking her up, we are limited." He scowled. "I know what I would like to do with her."

"Who is she?" he asked the church's chief elder, Mr. Ko.

"She is the stepsister of Choi-si."

Blair grimaced. "Isn't she the woman who sold some land to buy the new church?"

"Yes, Mr. Blair. She now lives in one room and takes care of it."

By now Choi-si's relative was foaming at the mouth, reminding Soon-hee of a rabid dog.

"People of Jesus, we want nothing to do with you!" She screeched and tore her hair.

Leading Ko aside, Blair motioned for Soon-hee and the American physician to join the conversation.

"Tell me more about this situation."

"Her name is Chun-si, and for thirty years, she and Choi-si lived together as very close sisters," the elderly man said. "When Choi-si became a Christian last year, a sword seemed to pierce her sister's very soul. The Lord Jesus had come between them, and Chun-si refused to put her faith in him. She harangued her sister so much, I suspect the reason Choi-si desired to live in one room in the church was because this was better than sharing an entire house with a contentious woman."

"I see."

"Shortly after Choi-si moved, her sister followed her. There has been no peace between them or for the believers when we meet. Chun-si is driven as if by demons into a frenzy at the sound of our prayers and singing. We have been at our wits' end to know what to do, awaiting your intervention."

Soon-hee pondered how family relationships can be the blessing or bane of one's life. His heart moved with pity for Choi-si who could not escape her sister's wrath.

"I will have a word with her," Blair said.

He didn't have long to wait. As he led the missionaries to the church, Chun-si hissed and sputtered at them. Blair stopped, locking eyes with her.

"Chun-si, by the authority vested in me by the Lord Jesus Christ, I command you to quiet yourself or leave this church. Your behavior will no longer be tolerated."

A crowd gawked at the scene. Even the soldiers ceased what they were doing to watch the latest show in town.

The woman gnashed her teeth, her eyes slits, but she remained silent. Soon-hee watched as she uncoiled her considerable energy and slunk away in silence, the Christians parting to let her through. Choi-si emerged from the church and looking around seemed to understand some of what had happened. She grasped Blair's hands and heaved a sigh.

Someone was knocking at Elder Ko's door, the men packed inside for Mr. Blair's Bible class. As he spoke, the missionary looked to Soon-hee and leaned his head at the entrance. Soon-hee rose to answer the summons.

His eyes widened at the red-faced nurse. "Miss Story."

"Is Mr. Blair available?"

"He is teaching. May I be of service?"

As her pale lips parted, Soon-hee's ears pricked at the sounds of distress emanating from the nearby church.

"Chun-si is in a perfect frenzy." Clara hands were trembling. "She's screaming and pulling her hair, and the women in our Bible class are frozen with apoplexy, at least those who haven't fled. Choi-si is in tears."

Anger and apprehension stirred the contents of his stomach. "Where is Mrs. Dr. Moffett?"

"She got called away to deliver a baby. Mrs. Ko and I are at our wits' end."

"Wait right here. We will sort this out."

Soon-hee reentered the house and whispered the news to Blair, whose countenance tightened.

The missionary rose, every curious eye on him. "Gentlemen, I must leave for a little while. Mr. Ko can continue our lesson until I return." He nodded at Soon-hee. "I'd like you to come with me."

Chun-si's maniacal tirade reached them before they opened the church door. Inside, Soon-hee went cold all over, sensing the presence of evil in the sacred space. Blair arrested his and everyone else's attention when he stepped forward and stood like a colossus before the raving woman.

"Chun-si, you must cease this at once!"

The woman stopped in mid-abusive comment and stared hard at Blair. Deathly quiet replaced the dissonance.

"You have behaved outrageously, and now you must leave this place. You must go immediately."

Soon-hee's heart pounded, wondering if the crazed woman would comply.

"Very well," she said. "I will go."

Chun-si stomped over to the apartment she shared with her sister and several minutes later took herself and a bound bundle out of the church. As she left, she resumed shouting.

"You will be sorry you did this to me, you despicable Christians. I loathe you. You will not get away with turning a poor old woman from her home."

The door slammed behind her.

The following morning the men were at prayer in the church while the women gathered on the other side of the sanctuary. Soon-hee was in mid-utterance when the door opened without warning. He peeked out of one eye to see what was happening and sat motionless at the sight of Chun-si rushing into the church.

Not again.

He was about to pray for her to be bound in the Spirit when a remarkable scene unfolded. Chun-si cast herself on the floor before the altar crying out, *"Kedo-hapsata!"*

When no one responded to her, she repeated the request for prayer several times, on her hands and knees crying out to the Lord.

Mrs. Dr. Moffett crossed the aisle, and Soon-hee heard her ask Blair, "Do you think she's pretending?"

The missionary pulled his chin. "I'll go see."

Soon-hee watched as Blair fell to his knees next to Chun-si, who began weeping as she leaned into his strong shoulders.

That night Chun-si spoke to the missionaries assembled at the evening meal. The force of her personality, once a vicious gale, was now a gentle breeze.

"Last night I was alone on the edge of the village, bitter and lonely," she said. "And then Jesus came to me, and he opened my eyes. I confessed my hatred for him, and he poured a great love into me. I wish to live with my sister again and share his name with all who will listen."

Soon-hee slowly released his breath.

When they left Anju three days later, the Christians assembled at the gate to send them off. Among their numbers Soon-hee grinned at the sight of Chun-si, the once blasphemer, now radiant with Christ's beauty. All her hard lines were gone. The sisters stood side-by-side in harmony.

I wonder if there might be such a hope for my brother and me.

CHAPTER NINE

JUNE 1904
PRINCETON, NJ

Jacob wondered if anyone was really listening to Professor Woodrow. With the fragrances of summer and freedom wafting through the Stuart Hall classroom's windows, who could pay attention to this droning? The only thing keeping Jacob from entering the land of nod was finding out his final grade in Greek.

Woodrow finally finished his lecture and perched on the edge of his desk, peering over his pince-nez. "Now then, gentlemen, before you come up for your marks, I have two items of business. The first is to commend you for applying yourselves so effectively this term. With one or two exceptions, I find your work most satisfactory."

Jacob tried not to look in the direction of the two students he thought might have come up short. For him, this Greek class had been a review exercise at best.

"I also would ask you to remember in your prayers our Presbyterian Board of Missions' laborers in Korea. I have just had word from one of them, Mr. William Blair, of the astonishing work of God in that land. This is despite the presence of Russian and Japanese armies vying for supremacy and using Korea as a battlefield."

Woodrow swatted a fly and managed to knock off his eyepiece, amusing himself and his students as he recovered and readjusted it.

"Flies are no respecters of persons. As I was saying, the Lord is powerfully using our denomination's missionaries in Korea, including Mr. Blair and Mr. Samuel Moffett, along with his physician wife, Mrs. Alice Moffett. Please keep them in your prayers this summer, that the Lord would use even the present circumstances for his glory and their good." He cleared his throat and retrieved a pile of cards from his desk. "Please come up when I call your name beginning with Mr. Avery."

Jacob waited through the first part of the alphabet until his turn came. The professor handed over the report card and inclined forward whispering, "Mr. Kichline, I'd like a word with you before you go."

"Yes, sir." He returned to his seat mentally scratching his head.

Moments later, Woodrow dismissed the students, followed by the scraping of chairs on the hard wood floors. Jacob guessed they'd all be checking their grades out in the hall.

"Are you coming?" Win asked.

"In a minute. I'll catch up with you outside."

His roommate glanced from Jacob to Woodrow. "Very well."

When they were alone, the professor said, "Mr. Kichline, I can see your thought process at work. I have nothing to tell you of an unpleasant nature." He signaled with his right hand. "Go ahead, take a look at your grade."

He glanced from the paper to Woodrow. "You gave me an A."

"You earned an A. You are the best Greek student I have taught in recent memory, and I have a proposition for you." He folded his arms. "How would you like to be a Greek tutor next term?"

Before Jacob could respond, Woodrow added, "You would of course receive a stipend."

"Why, Professor, I would be honored. Thank you."

"You will work under me, and I will make sure the load is light enough not to interfere with your own studies." He paused for a moment. "Your other teachers tell me you excel in their classes as well."

He remained silent, not wishing to call undue attention to his achievements.

"Do you think you could arrive two or three days ahead of the others before the fall semester starts?"

"Yes. I can come early."

"Very well. And what will you be doing this summer?"

"I plan to work in my father's silk mill and do some preaching around my hometown."

"Working with one's hands is fine preparation for the ministry, Mr. Kichline. We tend to dwell too much in our ivory towers and forget what life is like for most people."

He couldn't imagine this slightly-built man ever having employed brawn over brains.

"Yes, sir." He waited to be dismissed.

"And might there be a young lady waiting for you?'

His cheeks flushed. "Yes."

"Well, then, don't let me detain you. Have a wonderful summer, and I'll see you in the fall."

Jacob sat on the floor sorting out his books. He'd acquired two shelves' worth of volumes during this first year at

Princeton, and he didn't relish dragging suitcases and heavy boxes of books to the train. Fortunately, seminary officials had informed Brown Hall's inhabitants that they could keep up to two cartons of personal belongings in a storage room earmarked for them. Jacob was deciding which books to take home for the summer and which to leave behind. Naturally, he wanted his Bible with him, and he selected a commentary and Calvin's *Institutes*. He glanced at Win's side of their space, marveling at the military precision with which he'd arranged his effects.

He picked up a slender, vaguely familiar hardcover and read the title—*The Christian's Secret of a Happy Life*—and opened the cover. Inside, an inscription read, "To Jacob. I look forward to sharing this book with you across the miles. May its message encourage and inspire us. Yours, Pearl." He rubbed his upper lip with the back of his hand. He'd totally forgotten their mutual pledge to read a chapter every week then write to each other about what they'd learned. *Ah, so that's what she's been referring to in her letters.* Pearl had spoken about dealing with fearfulness and temptation, as well as holding onto one's self rather than yielding to Christ in every aspect of life. He'd rejoiced in her spiritual discoveries but had overlooked their source as well as his end of the bargain.

Jacob hefted a sigh as he read the author's name, Hannah Whitall Smith. This was certainly not a German theologian or spawn of the great Archibald Alexander or Charles Hodge. What could a mid-nineteenth century Quaker woman have to say to a twentieth-century Princeton scholar? He was about to consign the book to the rubbish when he realized how such an action would hurt Pearl. Instead he tossed the volume into his take-home stack. *I'll tell her I was too busy reading other things for classwork, and we can discuss it over the summer.*

Win entered the room and plopped onto his bed, the springs creaking under his bulk.

"I don't know how you've finished packing already," Jacob said. "We both have similar commitments and the same numbers of hours in a day."

He offered a smug laugh. "I have taught myself the secret of organization."

Win certainly hasn't learned the secret of a Christian's happy life. Otherwise he would be humbler.

"Are you nearly finished?"

"Just about," Jacob said.

Win picked up a devotional book Jacob had loved at Lafayette. "*The Imitation of Christ*." He scoffed as he tossed it onto the pile.

Bristling, he put the beloved copy on his take-home pile.

"My uncle and aunt are having a gathering tonight to bid me a summer adieu, just a few choice people. They'd like you to come along."

Jacob brightened. The Winthrops always had interesting guests, lively conversation, and fantastic eats. Who knew, maybe one of President Roosevelt's children might even show up again. Such an invitation covered a multitude of Win's sins.

"Thanks. Sure. I'd love to come."

"Knock, knock." Jacob turned to the door to see Rand. "Hello, fellow inmates. How's everyone?"

"Just dandy," Win said.

"If you fellows aren't doing anything tonight, a few of us will be gathering for a prayer meeting at Miller Chapel in support of our missionaries abroad."

Jacob caught Win's jaundiced eye.

"Oh, goodie. Just what I want to do before going home tomorrow."

Rand scowled.

"What a great idea," Jacob said. "Thanks for asking me but ..."

"He's going with me to my uncle's tonight," Win said. He didn't add, "And you're not invited." He didn't have to.

Jacob went to his other friend's defense. "What time is the prayer meeting?"

"Seven-thirty." He perked up. "We'll be there for a few hours at least."

Without looking at Win, Jacob declared his own intentions. "Maybe I'll stop by later, if that's okay."

"More than okay." Rand turned on his heels and disappeared into the bustling hallway.

He readjusted his collar in the searing June heat, grateful for Island Park's cool breezes and shade trees. In the near distance, the calliope pumped a jaunty tune as he shifted his weight from one side to the other awaiting the arrival of Pearl's trolley. He hadn't seen her since Easter and while lying awake the previous night imagined their reunion, trying on various scenarios. He'd considered greeting her in his new and best suit but thought the Princeton purchase might be overdone for an Easton amusement park. Instead, he donned the one he'd bought at Ziegenhorn's on South Third Street before going off to seminary.

The clanging of the trolley bell quickened his pulse and soon the vehicle hove into view, revelers packing the car. He scanned them for a glimpse of Pearl. When the vehicle crossed the trestle and shuttered to a stop, he waited near the main door for her, and there she was, appearing as if she lived among daffodils. The brightness of her yellow dress and hat set off her creamy complexion. She broke into a smile when he caught her eye, and they walked over each other as if no one else was around.

"Pearl."

"Hello, Jacob." She lifted her crochet-gloved hand to him. "How nice to see you again."

He fell into her unusual eyes, the green one and its sister all-brown orb. She exuded femininity, sweetness, and joy. He had a fleeting image of Alice Roosevelt at Win's uncle's house just days before, smoking a cigarette and telling racy jokes which he thought detracted from her refined appearance and upbringing. He wondered what her father thought of her risque conduct.

"You're looking especially lovely today." He couldn't recall ever seeing this particular dress before. Maybe she'd bought the garment for just this occasion.

"Thank you. You're looking well yourself."

"Shall we?" He offered his arm, and they entered the park's midway.

"Are you settled in yet?" she asked.

"I am. I'm enjoying being home again."

"Was your first year at Princeton what you thought it would be?"

He paused, not expecting such a question, but Pearl did tend to plumb the depths.

"In some ways, yes; in other ways, no."

She lifted her face to his. "I do apologize for being so serious. You can tell me more now or later."

"Later," Jacob said. "Tell me, how did your finals go?"

Her cheeks flushed. "Very well."

"I'm not a bit surprised." He swept his right arm as if presenting Island Park to her as a gift. "What would you like to do first m'lady? May I escort you to the genteel merry-go-round or ferris wheel? Or perhaps the Toboggan roller coaster appeals to your sense of adventure?" He liked the way she giggled. "Then again, we could go to the shooting gallery, go canoeing, or have our picture taken for a postcard. I also understand Alligator Jim is here today. Of course, we can dance under the electric nights later on. What is your pleasure?"

"All of the above." She sighed. "Except for the dancing. I can only stay until five o'clock."

He lowered his chin. "Oh, how sad. Why must you leave then?"

A child ran past them, banging into Jacob with his father chasing after the boy.

"My parents decided to visit my father's sister in upstate New York, and we'll be leaving tomorrow."

"Oh." He paused. "How long will you be away?"

"Two weeks. Don't worry—I'll be back in time to hear you preach at your church. I made sure of that. Then, we'll have the rest of the summer together."

"For which I am grateful."

"As for today, I want to do all of Island Park, except for swimming in the pool." She shuddered.

"Not your cup of tea?"

"Definitely not."

"Have you had lunch?"

"No. I'm embarrassed to say I packed one for us and left the basket on the kitchen table."

Jacob laughed at her absent-mindedness. "And I left my wallet near the kitchen sink. Fortunately, my mother saw what I'd done and caught up with me a block from the house. Thus, I am able to treat you to Island Park's best fare."

After riding the figure-eight roller coaster, they rented a canoe and absorbed the tranquility of birdsong and the splashing of their oars against the water. Several other couples seemed to have had the same notion, but for Jacob there was only him and Pearl. They'd talked all day long, mostly about their families, friends, and activities. When she mentioned a personally meaningful passage from *The Christian's Secret of a Happy Life* about discouragement, he looked away.

Pearl tilted her head to the side. "You didn't read that part, did you? I know you didn't respond when I commented on the book."

He detected no condemnation, just curiosity. He spoke after pulling an oar to avoid colliding with another boater. "I'm sorry, Pearl. I read the first few chapters before I got bogged down by classwork. Seminary is far more intense than college."

"I understand."

"You do?"

"Of course. You have a lot of important, difficult concepts to wrestle with to become an effective pastor."

He didn't say, "Yes, and there's no room for the scribblings of a female Holiness writer."

"I suppose my idea about reading a book together was wrong."

"Not wrong, not at all, and ours was a mutual decision. I didn't mean to let you down. How about if I read the book this summer?"

She brightened. "You'll have to catch up with me, you know."

He enjoyed her spunkiness. "I will try."

Jacob stood with her at the trolley depot.

"I so look forward to your first sermon. Have you chosen a text?"

"Yes. I'll be preaching from Luke 10 on the Parable of the Good Samaritan."

"That's one of my favorite New Testament passages." She paused. "I'll be praying for your preparation."

Some children riding the roller coaster began shrieking. Jacob chuckled. "Hopefully, I won't send the people screaming into the streets."

"Even if you did, I would stand by you.

He glanced at the bulletin for the tenth time enjoying the appearance of his name in print: "Mr. Jacob Kichline, Candidate for the Christian Ministry." He almost missed his cue at the end of the second hymn, but a quick glance from Interim Pastor Bowman roused him. Jacob took himself and his notes to the heavy pulpit in the chancel's exact center. His mouth dry, he swallowed hard to alleviate the discomfort, quietly clearing his throat. Placing his sermon notes on top, he lifted the Bible and assumed the pulpit voice he'd been practicing at home for many days.

"My sermon text this morning is from Luke 10, beginning at verse twenty-five." When he finished reading the familiar passage, Jacob lifted the Bible and said, "This is the Word of the Lord."

The congregation responded, "Thanks be to God."

Gripping either side of the pulpit, he glanced at the first line of his sermon notes, distrusting his current ability to conjure what he'd memorized. He briefly looked up to see his parents and four siblings and behind them, Pearl seated next to his Lafayette pal Harry Flory. His throat tightened, and he jiggled his right leg, grateful for the pulpit's cover.

"This reading is well-known to us all and one of our Lord's most cherished teachings. As I exegeted this pericope, I endeavored to search out some aspects we might have been missing. When we study the Scriptures, we need to have the right hermeneutical understanding in order to grasp their essence."

For the next twenty minutes, Jacob used a booming voice and more half dollar words to expound upon the historical rift between the Jews and Samaritans, exploring the meaning of various Greek words and phrases. He missed his grandfather's quiet snoring and his grandmother's grim-faced prods. When Jacob finished, Pastor Bowman rose and nodded in his direction without making eye contact.

"Thank you, Mr. Kichline, for your interesting message. Let us all stand for our last hymn, 'Ye Servants of God.'"

After the benediction, Jacob walked with the interim minister down the center aisle and stood in the open doorway to greet the congregation. He'd shaken about a dozen hands when his Lafayette pal appeared wearing a puzzled expression.

"Harry, how nice to see you."

"Phew, I am glad you're still you."

Jacob grimaced. "What do you mean?"

"I thought Princeton had changed your voice for good."

He tucked his arms at the sides. "Uh, not exactly."

"I'm glad you'll be around town this summer. Maybe you can join the Christian Endeavor at our Fourth of July picnic."

"Uh, maybe." Jacob noticed the line backing up. "I'll be in touch."

The Old Lamplighter came into view, the sight of him brightening Jacob's face. "How are you, Mr. Cherry?"

Dressed in his Sunday best, the humble fellow scratched his temple. "I am well. I liked your message."

"Thank you."

"I didn't understand the half of what you said, but you said it very well."

CHAPTER TEN

LATE FALL 1904
PYONGYANG, KOREA

After consulting his watch, Soon-hee relaxed his shoulders knowing he didn't need to rush to his next class. He enjoyed the sensation of standing still for a rare moment and drawing in the autumnal air, his face to the sun. He could almost taste his mother's hot apple cider. Students, young and older, hustled to the academic buildings while a group of adolescent boys laughed and flung dry leaves at each other. His heart thumped when Jeongsook came into view bearing an armload of what appeared to be Bibles. They hadn't seen much of each other recently, and he realized anew how her presence enriched his life.

He walked up to her. "Good morning, Jeongsook. Is this not a glorious day?"

"Oh, good morning." She failed to meet his eyes.

Soon-hee frowned at her flat tone. Come to think of it, she'd seemed distracted for some weeks, but he had attributed this to her busyness. Now, however, there could be no mistaking something decidedly chilly in her behavior.

"Is something the matter?"

She glanced at him for a second before abruptly turning away. "There is nothing I wish to discuss."

Jeongsook performed an obligatory bow and scurried off, leaving him in a state of utter astonishment. When two young women joined her, and Jeongsook began laughing, Soon-hee's heart seemed to freeze. *What just happened? Why was she so cold with me?*

After his class, he sat outside on a bench trying to concentrate on the Scripture passage they had just explored, as well as to put his thoughts aright. The earlier incident with Jeongsook had shaken him, making focusing on anything else challenging. When his sister came into view, she appeared as a kind of life raft, and he called out to her.

"I am glad to see you," he said when she came to his side.

"Hello, Soon-hee. You seem troubled. Is anything the matter?"

"Yes. I wonder, do you have any idea why Jeongsook may be acting strangely to me?"

Sora looked away as if she were deciding what to disclose.

"Are you reluctant to tell me?" he asked after a long moment. He noticed she was rubbing her fingertips.

"I fear the trouble your knowing might cause."

He shivered, like the time he'd come upon a coiled snake as a boy and his father had beaten the viper away with a staff.

"Is there anything you can say to help me understand her unexpected behavior?"

She let out a heavy sigh. "Soon-hee, I also carry a heavy burden about this. At times, I cannot eat or sleep." She met his eyes. "Perhaps we should share it."

He was in a state of high alertness, waiting for her to continue, the echoes of their vibrant campus fading.

"A few weeks ago, when I was talking about you to Jeongsook, she became extremely sad. When I asked her what was wrong, she told me she had discovered you did not care for her as she had thought you did. She has distanced herself to ease her pain."

Soon-hee flinched. "What? I cannot imagine why she would reach such a conclusion. I have never given her a reason to think in such a way. I have said nothing of the sort to her."

Sora paused before she whispered, "No, you did not."

His voice rose. "Then who did?" Realizing he'd upset his sister, he reached for her hand and said, "I am sorry. I should not have raised my voice." He shuddered to think he was becoming like his father.

"I know." She briefly bit her lower lip. "This is what I understand upset Jeongsook. Someone told her you were especially happy that Clara Story has come to the mission. In addition to her medical skills, you think she is a better teacher than Jeongsook. She believes you have a low view of her and no longer care to be involved with her as a man to a woman."

He fisted his hands, trying not to detonate. Furious as he was, he reminded himself his sister was not to blame as the bearer of tidings he'd practically begged her to share. How Jeongsook could have believed such a thing further agitated him. *She knows me better than that.*

Sora asked, "You did not say this, did you, Brother?"

"I would never say something I do not believe." He growled under his breath as his emotions internally collided. "How could she believe such lies, and who would dare tell her these things?"

She put her head in her hands.

"Sora?" If there was any peace to be had, he must know who was plotting to keep him and Jeongsook apart. Although he had no reason to think so, might there be a jealous suitor in their midst? He had no other explanation.

Tears ran down her cheeks. "You must not tell, Soon-hee. Promise me!"

"I cannot make such a pledge."

"How can I disclose this person then? I fear you might do something harmful to him."

He temporarily laid aside his outrage, this misjudgment of his character. "'Him'? Who, Sora? Who told Jeongsook these falsehoods?"

She sobbed her response. "Yong-bin."

"How have you gentleman handled this intriguing passage from Mark 16?" Samuel Moffett's gaze took in his small class of seminarians. "Mr. Lee?"

The young man averted his eyes as he spoke. "I have wondered if the handling of snakes was part of the original translation and also struggled to know how to apply this message to my own ministry."

"This is a good observation. You pose important questions about not only the text but the harder sayings of Jesus and how to understand them in light of our present work." He shifted his attention to Soon-hee. "Mr. Oh, what are your thoughts about this portion of Mark's Gospel?" When he didn't respond, the professor spoke up. "Mr. Oh, are you with us?"

The heat of shame stained Soon-hee's cheeks. He had been so preoccupied he had failed to heed his professor's teaching, something that had never happened before. "Please excuse me, Mr. Moffett."

"I see." The American stared at him before engaging a different student.

The truth was Soon-hee had been replaying yet again the ugly situation with his brother while a cauldron of anger and guilt simmered inside. As a Christian, wasn't he required to turn the other cheek, to forgive, to show mercy to his offender? Why then, could he not forgive Yong-bin? What must be lacking in him as a man and a follower of the Lord Jesus?

When class ended, Moffett asked to have a word with Soon-hee. Watching his associates file out of the room, he had the feeling of being eight years old and remaining after school for not knowing his lesson. Moffett jammed his notes and books into a leather satchel and secured its two straps.

"I wonder, Mr. Oh, if you have time to walk back to my house with me for tea."

This was unexpected. "Yes, of course."

As they walked across the vibrant campus, they made small talk about the weather, then went on to discuss the impact of the ongoing Russo-Japanese War on the mission. Japanese forces were still imposing martial law and surveilling the citizenry for any signs of opposition. Korea remained a nearly helpless bystander in the struggle between those two other nations and while most of its people acquiesced out of a sense of helplessness, resistance was also growing. Soon-hee welcomed the opportunity to think about something other than his own personal problems.

No one was at home when they reached the house, and Moffett went about the homey ritual of making tea. Then, they sat at opposite ends of the couch in the main room, the English-style beverage bracing Soon-hee.

“I am concerned about you, my friend,” Moffett finally said. “Are you getting enough sleep? You appear to have lost some weight.”

His mentor had always been a sensitive, discerning person.

“I have had some difficulty sleeping.” *And eating, especially at the same table as my devious brother.* He wondered how far Moffett was going to probe and how much Soon-hee was willing to divulge.

“What has happened to trouble you so?”

His eyes fell upon a neat pile of American books on the table, choosing to focus on them as he spoke. “Someone close has betrayed me.”

Moffett’s expression was unhurried, inviting.

“My brother and I have quarreled.”

Some moments passed. “Please feel free to tell me as much or as little as you want.”

Soon-hee couldn’t seem to find the right words.

“Have you tried to fix the problem?” Moffett asked.

Yes, he had, just a few days earlier. He could still see the smirk on Yong-bin’s face when he’d said, “You should have helped me when I needed you. Now you must reap what you have sown.”

Soon-hee raised his eyes to Moffett’s. “I spoke to him, and he was unrepentant.”

“I gather he did something to hurt you.”

“Yes. Deeply. I know I must forgive him, Mr. Moffett.” His voice carried a plea. “I am trying to conduct myself in a manner worthy of the gospel of Jesus Christ, who was longsuffering with sinners.” He swallowed hard. “My anger is so very difficult to overcome.”

He didn’t mention how his ire roiled inside. He wouldn’t allow himself to do physical harm to Yong-bin, although in weaker moments he did imagine giving his brother a good thrashing.

Moffett sat quietly, a clock ticking on a side table. "All of us struggle to overcome ourselves, Mr. Oh. I often consider the Apostle Paul's cry of desolation in Romans seven where he refers to himself as a wretched man who does what he doesn't want to and doesn't do what he should. You are not unique or alone in your anger. I've had my own challenges with this particular emotion. God knows we will wrestle. What we must do is not allow our emotions to cause us to sin."

His burden seemed to shift. If Samuel Austin Moffett struggled with anger, there was hope for Soon-hee Oh.

"Would you like me to speak with Yong-bin?"

"No!" Surprised at his vehement response, Soon-hee reined himself in. "I mean, I do not believe you need to." He didn't want Moffett to know the intimate nature of the quarrel.

"Very well." He fell quiet for a moment before saying, "I imagine being under the same roof is especially trying."

"Yes." He could barely stand the sight of Yong-bin or stomach how his parents indulged him.

"As you know, our new YMCA needs a resident house manager. I think you may be just the right person for the job. I doubt the easy work load would interfere with your studies, and your translation work is lighter during the academic terms. Would such an arrangement appeal to you?"

He had the peculiar feeling of floating. "Oh yes, I think I would like this very much." Just as quickly he thudded back to reality. "I do not know what my parents will say."

Moffett moved closer. "I can understand your desire to please them, but you are at twenty-one—an adult, Mr. Oh.

You have your own choices to make about your life. If it would help, I would be happy to speak to them."

"Yes, Mr. Moffett, I think hearing the news from you would be a good thing."

He liked the way his teacher thought, how Americans pursued their individual independence as they grew older. Perhaps he too could move away from the family home without showing his mother and father any disrespect. Hope kindled.

Sam Moffett was no stranger to the Oh's home, yet each visit was still quite the occasion. Mrs. Oh and Sora brewed tea for their visitor while the men gathered around the low table having a friendly discussion. Soon-hee sat as far away from his brother as possible, avoiding looking at Yong-bin as if by doing so he could render the young man invisible.

For twenty minutes, his father shared details of his ministry as Moffett's pastoral assistant. This included a detailed report about a leak in the church's roof and a pressing need for more hymnbooks.

"The war has created a delay in obtaining materials for the repair," Moffett said, "but I learned yesterday we might expect them in about two weeks. I've also asked the Board of Foreign Missions to send additional hymnbooks." He smiled at Mr. Oh. "Despite the war's ongoing challenges, just look at how the church continues to grow in numbers and in faith. The lack of hymnbooks is, therefore, a happy problem to have."

Everyone expressed their agreement with him, including Yong-bin, who seemed to be putting on a good show for the American and for his parents. Soon-hee's stomach soured.

"And how are the women's Bible studies coming along?" Moffett asked Mrs. Oh.

“We also have increasing numbers,” she said. “Sora has become one of their favorite teachers. Sometimes, we cannot find enough space to accommodate everyone who comes to study with us.”

The missionary smiled at the young woman. “I have heard good reports of the way in which you bring Bible stories to life and how the children love to listen to you.”

Sora’s face flushed. “Thank you, Mr. Moffett. Teaching them brings me great joy.”

Soon-hee’s neck muscles tightened, sensing the subject was about to change to the matter for which Moffett had come.

“As for the problem of enough space, now that we have the YMCA building, there are more classrooms and meeting areas available. I will help you find more adequate meeting places.” He folded his hands on his lap. “Speaking of which, there is a great need for someone to live at the YMCA and supervise the residents. I would like Soon-hee to fill that position.”

Incredulous stares fixed on Moffett. Soon-hee’s heart raced.

“You are saying our son would need to move away?” Mr. Oh frowned.

I will not be moving to New York City.

“Yes, he would need to live in this new dormitory. Soon-hee is my top candidate for the job, and it also will come with a small stipend.”

Mrs. Oh extended her hands. “But who will take care of Yong-bin?”

Soon-hee winced. *How like my mother to put Yong-bin’s perceived needs above mine. I am more like a servant to her than a son. She does not consider how this position would benefit me.* He immediately repented his harsh thoughts.

"I was not aware Yong-bin needed such supervision," Moffett said.

"Oh, yes, he has terrible pain in his head and must be looked after. I cannot always manage, and I require Sora's assistance with my ministry. Of course, Mr. Oh also is very occupied at the church. Soon-hee has always looked after his brother."

The missionary leaned back, gazing at Mrs. Oh as if he were assessing the situation. "Soon-hee is no doubt a capable helper, but indeed, he is a man now with his own call to ministry. Don't be concerned about Yong-bin. I will take care of this matter."

"How?" she asked.

"I will find an aide who can provide for his needs while not hampering any of your work." He smiled at each person in turn as if to seal the deal.

Soon-hee suppressed an urge to laugh. He'd never known Samuel Austin Moffett to interfere in the life of a Korean family. However, the Ohs were vitally important to the Pyongyang mission, except for Yong-bin, who was a steady drain on their efforts. In his thoughts, Soon-hee was already packing his bag.

CHAPTER ELEVEN

PRINCETON, NJ

May 14, 1905

Dear Jacob,

How are you coming along in these last weeks of the semester? I imagine like me, you're in the throes of final examinations and papers. I just completed my geography course work and thought I'd take a tea break before tackling an English Lit essay. If these come out well, I hope to make the dean's list again. This greatly pleases my parents and would be a nice way to finish my college career. Please do not think me boastful in this.

Jacob looked up from her monogramed stationery, happy for Pearl's success until a Win-like thought overrode his gladness. *Just how demanding could Allentown College for Women be?* He shook the unkind impulse and continued reading.

How I look forward to lazy summer days again. My family and I plan to make our annual trek to our upstate New York relatives for two weeks, and I do enjoy their sprawling farm, helping with chores, and sitting under a stately oak reading. There's a pile of books just waiting for me. Once I'm back home, I plan to volunteer at the

> Women's Christian Temperance Union and teach Sunday School. I'll also remain active in my Christian Endeavor group. Lest I fail to mention what is obvious to me, I mostly look forward to being with you, taking long walks, sharing meals, engaging in our deep conversations. I also hope we can go to Island Park again—and stay for the dancing. What will your summer look like this year? I'm confident you'll be filling pulpits again, but will you do any other work?

Jacob gazed out the dorm room window onto the quadrangle where students came and went. Yes, he would be doing other work. Most churches paid him more to preach one service than he would make at the silk mill in a week. He daydreamed about being in such demand with local congregations he wouldn't have to engage in menial labor. He didn't readily admit to himself that despite his athleticism, he disliked getting his hands dirty. Besides, he wasn't fond of mixing with the working class, whose lives he couldn't begin to understand. Unhappy with those unpleasant personal assessments, he read the last part of Pearl's letter.

> Before I go, I want to tell you something astonishing. Rhian is a young woman who cleans our dormitory, and she and some of her family recently immigrated from Wales to live in Wilkes-Barre. This week she told me about a fascinating movement of God in her home country, how tens of thousands of Welshmen are being saved. Rhian told me her father, whom she described as a rather uncouth miner still living in Wales, is now leading a Bible study for other miners as well as singing in their church's choir!

Jacob tried to digest the idea of how such a gritty fellow without proper training could be leading a Bible study. Even so, something in his spirit swelled at the idea.

Rhian also informed me this movement has reached all the way across the ocean to the Welsh community in Wilkes-Barre. Her aunt and uncle, with whom she recently lived, have been caught up in the fervor transforming their community. The men who used to frequent the gin mills after work are now singing in the church and sharing the gospel on the city's streets. I hardly know what to make of this, but I thrill at the thought of God moving like this in our modern times. I imagine you must be delighted as well.

Oh my, I hadn't noticed the time. I must end this letter now, sending you my deepest affection and the assurance of my prayers.

Yours,
Pearl

Revival? Common people doing the work of pastors? How could something so first century happen at the dawn of the twentieth when humans had progressed from swords and spears to Gatling guns, from bark canoes to steamships? Hadn't such activities ended with the apostolic age? Part of his heart's desire was to believe, but the other side scoffed. He wondered what Professor Warfield might have to say about this phenomenon.

Jacob sprinted the short distance between Brown and Stuart Halls in a driving rain. The past week of near-summer weather had given way to prematurely hot temperatures and downpours. He dragged himself up the grand staircase to the classroom where his colleagues steamed like clams in the sweltering room. Win was fanning himself with a book, his forehead glistening.

"I opened two windows only to be doused along with the first row of desks," Rand said, his hair and clothes sopping.

Jacob sniffed at the scent of what reminded him of his dog after being caught in a rainstorm.

B.B. Warfield entered the room as wet and bedraggled as his students. He brushed raindrops from his beard and cape then set his old-fashioned top hat on the desk nearest the ancient lectern.

"Good morning, gentlemen." He began arranging his Bible and class notes. When he looked at his suffering class, he smiled. "Just this once, I would invite you to remove your coats. Otherwise, you will be lulled into a heavy sleep from which I may not be able to revive you."

The men did as they were told.

"This being one of our last two classes, I have some news to share with you about an interesting phenomenon happening in the Church. You may be hearing of it when you return to your home congregations. I have been receiving reports from our missions Professor Dennis Cullen, in addition to overseas missionaries, about what is being called revival." He wiped off and repositioned his pince-nez on his nose. "Perhaps you also have heard some of these accounts."

Jacob wondered if what Pearl had told him about the Welsh situation might have anything to do with this.

"In February, a rather unusual and astonishing thing happened at a Wesleyan college in Kentucky," the instructor said. "For several days, the usual campus activities came to a halt, not because of a blizzard, but when a prayer meeting in the men's dormitory spilled across the campus and into the town. For two weeks, people prayed and worshipped around the clock, experiencing personal conviction of sin. There were reports of many conversions."

When he paused, Rand raised his hand. "Sir, I've heard of this too. Isn't the college near Cane Ridge?"

"You are correct, Mr. Ainslie. Mr. Cullen pointed out to me that this Asbury College is not far from the place where the Second Great Awakening began, I might add under the leadership of a Presbyterian minister." He grinned under his generous beard.

Win huffed. "Asbury? I never heard of the place."

"Well, Mr. Brown, I am certain Asbury has never heard of you either."

Warfield's warm eyes twinkled, and the seminarians sniggered.

"The school was founded a short time ago in the bluegrass part of eastern Kentucky." He paused. "Yes, Mr. Ainslie."

"Isn't it strange, sir, how God would move in such a way at such a young school? Why wouldn't he choose established and well-respected Princeton?"

"Think about what you just said, Mr. Ainslie. Recall the impact of our Lord's teachings among the Scribes and Pharisees."

Rand's face colored. "I see what you mean, Mr. Warfield."

"Now then, gentlemen, there have been further accounts from another place. Beginning last year, also in February, there has been significant spiritual activity in Wales. As far as anyone knows, it began when a girl gave her testimony at a young people's meeting. I am told her words were simple and few, basically a statement that she loved Jesus with all her heart and how he had died for her. Even so, this became a spark that lit the young people's spirits, and they began sharing this basic message in neighboring churches. One pastor has said a spirit of prayer and testimony fell on his church in a marvelous manner. Several times, he would end a service only to have the testimonies and prayers break out again. Many went forward seeking the full assurance of faith."

Jacob's scalp tingled. *I wonder if this could be true, a genuine move of God's Spirit*. He thrilled at the very idea.

Warfield continued. "I have also read about the minister at the center of this manifestation, Mr. Evan Roberts. For the past year, he and his team have been going the length and breadth of Wales preaching the gospel. As a result of these and other preachers' efforts, the country is being transformed. Not only so, but Welshmen living in the United States are experiencing a similar outpouring."

A buzz broke out among Jacob's classmates including questions about legitimacy. One student asked Warfield if these accounts might be counterfeits at worst or exaggerations at best.

"You are right to question, Mr. Martin. Like the people of Berea whom Paul speaks of in Acts 17, we should seek to discover whether any spiritual occurrence is of man or of God."

"What do you think, Mr. Warfield?" Jacob asked.

Win spoke before the professor could respond. "Surely, you can't believe stories from largely unlearned people."

The professor fixed his eyes on Jacob's roommate. "Mr. Brown, might I remind you whom God chose to be the parents of our Savior or what village they came from or under what conditions Jesus was born?"

Win gazed at the floorboards.

"I have been reading reports from the most trustworthy sources about both Kentucky and Wales and will share two with you now. The first is from the British Bible teacher and pastor, Dr. G. Campbell Morgan."

He readjusted his eye piece.

"He writes, 'This is no mere piece of imagination, and it certainly is not a piece of exaggeration. 'I will pour forth of

My Spirit upon all flesh, and your sons and your daughters shall prophesy' is the promise now evidently fulfilled in Wales.' And this statement is from acclaimed journalist W.T. Stead, 'There does not seem to have been any organized effort anywhere. If Mr. Evan Roberts is spoken of as the center, it this is only because he happens to be one of the few conspicuous figures in a movement which he neither organized nor controls.'"

Warfield leaned on the lectern. "There are countless stories of lives being transformed in both places. In fact, life in Wales has so profoundly gone from the profane to the secular that the horses have become confused."

Jacob looked over at Rand, and they both laughed.

"How so, Mr. Warfield?" Jacob asked.

"It would seem their owners used to prompt them with swearing and cussing to get them to do their work. Now that the men's tongues utter only what is worthy to be spoken, the horses don't understand the new commands."

Everyone laughed except for Win, who raised his hand, again.

"Yes, Mr. Brown?"

"With all due respect, are you believing these stories yourself? I understood you to say you are a cessationist."

The professor stroked his beard, Jacob's ears perking up so as not to miss a word of Warfield's response. He'd been wondering the same thing.

"You are correct, Mr. Brown, that I have long sided with John Calvin on this matter. Namely, I maintain that some of the Holy Spirit's gifts to the first century church ceased with the passing of the Apostles. Nevertheless, I do believe in the veracity of some revivals as they aid in the gospel's spread."

"Such as what's happening in Wales and in Kentucky?" Rand asked.

"Yes, such as these, Mr. Ainslie. This is my advice to you gentlemen—test the spirits to know whether they are of God, and do not hinder the Holy Spirit, who blows wherever and however he chooses."

LATE JULY
EASTON, PA

Harry Flory gave him a hard stare after they boarded the trolley to Bethlehem. One of the best aspects of this summer for Jacob was spending time with his fellow Lafayette classmate and friend. Since graduation, Harry had been teaching math at the high school and leading their old Christian Endeavor group. After the trolley picked up the rest of the passengers, Jacob detected Harry's puckered brow.

"Is something wrong?" His hand automatically went to his tie.

"I see you paid Tony the barber a visit."

The vehicle began rumbling along the tracks to Bethlehem.

"I know, I look like a sheep at the shearing, but I was getting tired of having all those silk fibers sticking to my hair."

"So, how's the job going?"

"In a word, I'd rather earn my way preaching."

"That hard?"

"I don't know how those women and children work there day in, day out, week after week. The bad smells, stubbed fingers, and back aches are temporary for me, but for them, there seems to be no way to a better life."

"Do you think they mind their lot?"

He shrugged his shoulders. "I don't know. We don't talk much. They don't exactly trust me."

"Because you're the manager's son?"

"Right."

"Maybe you could lead a Bible study for them this summer. I'm sure they could use the encouragement, and I could help you out."

"How could I possibly relate to them?"

He didn't see his friend grimace.

Harry had just called everyone to order.

"What a pleasure to be with all of you on this fine summer day. My good friend Jacob and I are honored by your invitation to bring a message at your summer picnic."

Jacob glanced at Pearl, sitting in the front row of the Christian Endeavor gathering with her closest friend Lucy Rowe. When she smiled at him, the grass appeared greener, the assorted wildflowers flowers in the church's courtyard more striking.

"Most of you know Jacob Kichline, and since he just completed his second year of ministerial studies at Princeton Seminary, I took the liberty to ask him to speak today. Now, now, I realize you must be terribly disappointed not to hear from me as originally planned. Then again, how can we not benefit from the insights of such an earnest Christian and scholar?" He turned slightly to Jacob, grinning. "The sight of all those picnic hampers makes me appeal to you to keep your message short my friend."

Jacob laughed as he rose to applause and shook Harry's hand. Then he smiled at a glowing Pearl and cleared his throat to assume his pulpit voice.

"It is indeed an honor to address you today." He swatted at a gnat buzzing around his ear. "At seminary I've come to imbibe deeply of some of the world's greatest thinkers, ones you may not have heard of. At Princeton, I have come to realize there is so much that most of us never get to learn about, so I've decided to draw my brief talk today from the writings of a Danish philosopher, Soren Kierkegaard."

He wasn't surprised by their puzzled expressions. They had no way of realizing they were in for a treat.

"Kierkegaard was born in 1813, and although he only lived to age forty-two, his writings have contributed a great deal to European Protestant thought. He's considered the founder of a movement called existentialism, and he's influenced thinkers in the phenomenological and existentialist traditions. A Lutheran, Kierkegaard emphasized the importance of Christian behavior and good works above the systematic formalizing of doctrine."

Jacob began quoting Kierkegaard, hardly noticing when several listeners barely concealed their yawns. One young woman fell asleep outright, her head back, mouth hung open as if welcoming the gnat horde droning around her. When he noticed Pearl's wide eyes and pinched lips, he shifted his weight and began to end his discourse.

"Well, as Harry said earlier, our picnic baskets are waiting, so I'll conclude now. I realize a lot of what I've said is probably over your heads, but we do need to stretch our intellects as we progress in the faith. After all, when we become Christians, we are not called to leave our brains behind." He was alone in laughing at his small joke. "Well, then, thank you again for inviting me."

He frowned at Harry who was gesturing at him amidst weak applause, wondering what his friend was trying to tell him. At last, he caught on.

"Oh, I, uh, well, let's pray. Lord God, we thank Thee for this gathering and for the food we are about to receive. Amen."

He waited at his post for anyone to come forward to chat with him, as folks normally did after he preached. No one did. At last, Harry wandered over and gave Jacob a long look.

"What?"

"Kierkegaard? I thought you were going to give them a word of encouragement, not a thesis."

Jacob's shoulders tensed. "I wanted to give them more than the usual pablum."

"Pablum? Do you think that's what Christian Endeavor is?"

He decided not to respond.

"I don't know, Jacob, but maybe your great learning is driving you mad."

"Or maybe these ignorant people need to climb out of their comfortable beliefs."

When he caught Pearl gaping at him as she approached them, he dismissed her silent censure. What did she know?

CHAPTER TWELVE

PYONGYANG, KOREA
EARLY SPRING 1906

These days in the war's aftermath, Soon-hee strained to keep the young men in his Bible class on track. More than discussing the Scriptures, several of them wanted to talk about the political situation. The victorious Japanese had laid claim to Korea, and one of their first acts was to demand the return of Korea's foreign envoys. By this action, they had rendered Korea null and void as a sovereign nation. Many young men, including a few in Soon-hee's group, rode on a wave of intense patriotism, their slogan, "Korea should be for the Koreans!"

He too chafed at being treated as an inferior Japanese underling. On the other hand, he aligned himself with the missionaries who found themselves in great difficulty. As some Korean men called for an open show of being either for or against the Japanese, the Americans maintained a strict noninterference stance. They dearly loved Korea and its people and understood their anxiety. However, the missionaries' stated primary goal was winning souls to Jesus Christ without regard to their nationality.

Despite Soon-hee's quiet distaste for the Japanese, his throat caught during a Wednesday night service when Mr. Moffett baptized one of them. Truly, this was what the kingdom of God looked like, no Jew or Greek, Korean or Japanese. All who were in Christ Jesus, according to St. Paul, were heirs according to the promise. Soon-hee had seen his professor turn the other cheek when some Koreans had hurled insults, and not a few objects, at him. They objected to his welcoming the Japanese with the right hand of Christian fellowship and not standing with the zealots. Since Moffett had forgiven them, Soon-hee determined he would do his best to follow his example.

As he led this day's Bible class, he prayed for the strength to do so.

"I would like us to return to our study in First Corinthians. Now then, what do you think Paul meant when he said, 'But the natural man receiveth not the things of the Spirit of God: for they are foolishness unto him: neither can he know them, because they are spiritually discerned?'"

When they remained silent, he surveyed their blank faces. "Have you nothing to say? Have you not read this passage?"

One of them raised his hand. "We have had a great deal on our minds beside our studies."

"I see. And what exactly is on your mind, Mr. Chun?"

Soon-hee regretted the words as soon as they'd sprung from his mouth, knowing there would be no chance of continuing the Bible discourse. An increasingly familiar burning in his gut returned.

Chun's eyes flashed. "How can we study, Mr. Oh, when our nation is in turmoil?"

Two of his classmates muttered their agreement while the others looked down at their desks.

The student continued. "The nations of the world have betrayed us, including these Americans who say they are Korea's friends. Will we stand by as sheep to the slaughter, or fight for what is right?"

His stomach churning, Soon-hee silently prayed to speak in a manner worthy of the gospel. "And what do you propose to do about this situation, Mr. Chun?"

"We must fight for Korea! We must vindicate those who have been sent to prison, tortured, and killed. The Christian church is the only powerful organization left in the country. If we unite, we can throw off the Japanese oppressors."

A chill ran down Soon-hee's spine. He'd heard talk like this before at church meetings that had gotten way out of hand. When zealots made no headway with the missionaries, several had organized into armed bands where they met in secret while hiding in the mountains. No Japanese dared travel alone away from the cities because of them. The last thing Soon-hee wanted was to have any of his young men join vindictive mobs.

"What about you, Mr. Oh?" Chun asked. "Are you for or against the Japanese?"

Bile rose in his throat. He hated being put on the spot like this. Nevertheless, he could not do otherwise than speak truth, no matter how unpopular.

"I believe the missionaries are right. We must pledge our primary allegiance to the Lord Jesus, who taught us love and forbearance, even for our most bitter enemies."

On a personal level, hadn't he been taking the same message to heart in his relationship with his sinful brother? Only with the help of the Holy Spirit was he finding such a thing remotely possible.

"Is it not better to die than to live as slaves?"

He gazed at the youth. "Mr. Chun, I do not believe we have to have warm feelings for those who oppress us or to be happy about our situation. But we must, if we go by the name Christian, follow our Lord's example when he forgave those who betrayed and killed him."

Chun's eyes were flinty. He stood in a show of disrespect, resulting in a collective gasp.

"I will leave you to your precious Americans." He gazed at the others. "Is anyone else with me?"

One of his comrades joined Chun as they blew out of the classroom.

Soon-hee needed a moment to collect himself, and when he found his voice, he called the rest of the students to prayer.

He lined up in front of the Central Church after the graduation ceremony on a day of bountiful sunshine. Mr. Blair fiddled with his camera while his wife organized the seminary graduates for a photoshoot, first with each other, then with their proud families. Soon-hee had the honor of having finished at the top of his small class. While the other students were going to be ordained to pastor outlying churches, he had chosen a different path. He was going to pursue graduate studies under Samuel Moffett's tutelage with a goal to being a scholar as well as a pastor. Kyung Oh had frowned when his son shared the news two weeks earlier, having thought Soon-hee was going to lead a church. When he explained he would, but also have teaching responsibilities, Kyung Oh had given his blessing. Mrs. Oh's response had been another story.

"Your studies have made you drawn and thin. You may make yourself sicker if you continue along such a path."

"I assure you, *Eomeoni,* my books give me tremendous joy." He would not tell her the unresolved conflict with his brother seemed a more likely cause of Soon-hee's stomach trouble.

When their turn came for the family photo, he spotted Sora heading to them, her face flushed.

"Where is Yong-bin?" their mother asked.

"He says he is too ill to stay."

Kyung Oh's lips pressed together, his wife's jaw set. Soon-hee got the distinct impression she was irritated with Yong-bin. He'd never known her to be anything but solicitous to the sickly young man.

"He should be here. This is a special occasion and an opportunity to have our photograph taken."

"I know, *Eomeoni.*" Sora hung her head. "I tried so hard." She appeared on the verge of tears.

"Do not worry," Soon-hee said. "This is not your fault."

As Mrs. Blair lined up Soon-hee and his family for the portrait, he allowed himself a slow smile.

He'd gone home to retrieve a Bible commentary and to pay a brief visit to his mother where he'd found her alone making rice cakes. Their conversation had been pleasant until she waded into muddy waters.

"Now that you are a seminary graduate, will you be thinking of taking a wife?"

When he gulped, he nearly spluttered the hot beverage. "I still have a few years of schooling."

She peered at him. "Why cannot you do both?"

"One needs first to find a wife, *Eomeoni.*"

"But I thought you had."

As if on cue, Jeongsook arrived at the Oh's home, Soon-hee amazed at the timing.

"Have I intruded?" She looked from him to his mother.

"Not at all," Mrs. Oh said.

"I cannot stay but just brought the Bible school notes you requested."

Jeongsook handed them to her after Mrs. Oh wiped her hands on her apron.

"Thank you. I am looking forward to the next class." She turned to Soon-hee. "Jeongsook does a marvelous job teaching our younger girls."

He smiled at the object of his affections. "She is wonderfully gifted."

Jeongsook's lips parted as she looked directly at him. "Well, I must go. Please excuse me for interrupting."

Without thinking, Soon-hee sprang from his chair. "I was also about to return to the YMCA. May I walk with you?" His hearted thudded.

"Why, yes, of course."

Soon-hee bade his mother goodbye. If he'd wondered whether she'd be upset at his abrupt departure, he need not have worried.

"Where are you heading?" he asked Jeongsook when they went outside.

"I am going to the library, to study the passage I will teach tomorrow."

"I had the impression you had completed this work."

"I never feel comfortable until I have done thorough research into the Scriptures. We must handle the precious Word of God correctly."

He wondered if she was being diligent, insecure, or a little of both. Either way, he found her completely charming.

"This is something for which I strive," he said.

As they walked, Jeongsook tripped over a protruding tree root, and he steadied her with his hand, her softness melting his heart.

"Are you hurt?"

She laughed. "No, thank you, but I am clumsy."

"No, you are not. You are poised and lovely." What was he saying?

Jeongsook's eyes opened wide. "But I thought ..."

They had both stopped and were facing each other.

"What did you think?" His voice was as gentle as the summer breeze.

"That you did not believe in my abilities, or my ..."

"Did not my sister tell you what you heard was false?" He met the thing between them head-on.

She closed her eyes. "Yes, she told me the first time, but I have not known what, or whom, to believe. I have been so, so very hurt."

"The first time?" His legs turned to water. "He has told you more than the one abominable thing?"

Jeongsook grimaced, and he dared take her right hand. When she looked into his eyes, he saw a flicker of something like hope, which swirled in him along with a rising tide of fury.

"I never said what my brother told you about Miss Story. He was angry with me for not ..." He paused, wondering how much needed to be said. "He asked me to do something for him that I could not in good conscience carry out. Telling you what he did was his revenge, along with anything else he has fabricated since then."

She gazed at him. "I am so very happy to hear you say this. Do you ... think I am an adequate teacher?"

"No, Jeongsook, I think you are an excellent teacher."

"And do you think Miss Story is a good replacement for me?"

"I think Miss Story is blessed to have you by her side."

The world started turning again.

"Can we pick up where we left off?"

"I will try to shed my hurt," she said.

Her cautionary note gave him reason to believe they might still have a chance, so why was his stomach lurching?

"What did my fine wife say, Mr. Oh?"

"She believes her regimen is having a positive effect," he told Sam Moffett in his crate-filled office.

"You don't appear as thin as you were a month ago."

"I have been able to eat more normally."

The professor grinned. "How are you managing without *kimchi*?"

"I do miss spicy Korean foods."

He seemed to perform his own examination on Soon-hee. "My wife believes physical complaints are often manifestations of emotional upset. Do you think there could be a connection in your case?"

"I have no doubt."

Moffett rested his arms on his desk. "Ah, yes, the situation with your brother. Has being at the YMCA helped?"

"Very much. I am happy there." He listened to the passing conversation of a few men moving along the hallway before speaking again, head down. "I am ashamed of my feelings regarding Yong-bin."

Moffett's brow puckered. "In what way?"

"I struggle to forgive him for trying to ruin an important part of my life. He is unrepentant, unwilling even to discuss the situation with me. I know the Lord Jesus said we must forgive our brothers seventy-times seven, but I have not been able to forgive him even once." He twisted his hands. "I am striving to attain this goal."

"We will continue to ask the Lord to help you in this regard, something I have faith he will answer in ways you can't even imagine just now."

"Have you ever wrestled to forgive someone, Mr. Moffett?"

"Oh, my goodness, yes. While the Lord requires us to forgive, we need his power to do so." Moffett peered at Soon-hee. "I can tell you want to do the right thing. As long as you don't let a root of bitterness grow, the devil won't be able to gain a foothold. Even if you do stumble, God will restore and forgive you even as he helps you forgive your brother." He added, "And when you don't want to, he can help you with that as well."

He spoke quietly. "Then I am not a failure as a Christian?"

"No, indeed. We all wrestle with this business of forgiveness. Just don't nurture hatred for Yong-bin." Moffett leaned closer. "I see you as a maturing man after God's own heart."

Soon-hee choked up. "I wish you did not have to leave, Mr. Moffett."

He dreaded the thought of his mentor, wife, and their small son Jamie leaving in just two days for a year's furlough. He had come to depend on the elder Christian and wondered how he would manage without his godly guidance, including with his post-graduate studies.

"In a way, I also regret leaving." He paused, his gaze fixing on the windows. "You see, however, there is so much of our work to oversee other than in Pyongyang and the countryside."

"How do you mean?"

"On the way to America, I must stop in Hawaii to assess the need for spiritual oversight of their Korean Presbyterians. Then, there are the Korean immigrants laboring in California who require a plan for their nurture in the faith. I also will be speaking at various conventions and churches about the work here, to encourage the people as well as to gain their support for our mission."

"I have been selfish to wish you to stay here then."

Moffett smiled at him. "None of us enjoys being parted from those we hold closest. I will miss you as well, my friend. Now then, I've developed a plan for your studies while I'm away."

He produced a rather thick file which he laid between them on the desk. Soon-hee considered finding any one item there a wonder, so jammed was the top with papers, boxes, files, and letters.

"You will find academic assignments to cover my year abroad, as well as ministry goals for you. I'm hoping you will be able not only to do your translation work but begin assisting with the Helpers course for our budding Korean leaders. These men require training as their exams have been far from satisfactory."

"I would be honored to do this."

He paused, stroking his chin. "I fear this work may be too heavy a load. Still, you'll find doctoral coursework different from your graduate studies. There's a more measured pace to them."

"I accept these new responsibilities gladly and will do my best to stay organized."

"I know you will. And if you need to let something go, we can always regroup when I return." He paused. "By the way, how have the young men been in your Bible class lately? Do you believe they're ready to become church members?"

"Yes, they are exceptional young men," Soon-hee said.

"And what about the Japanese situation?"

"They are much more in agreement now with the position the missionaries have taken."

"Have you lost any of them?"

"Just two." He named them, and Moffett nodded his head as if he wasn't surprised.

"I don't expect more trouble from rabble-rousers here, but we must be vigilant because anti-Japanese feelings seem here to stay. One of my goals to is create a Japanese church for the growing number of believers among them. Who knows what the Lord can do between people who are enemies?"

"I also see a need for such a congregation, especially since they do not speak Korean and find our services difficult to follow." Soon-hee didn't add, and because not everyone wants to worship with them.

Moffett seemed to have read his mind.

"Some among our church would rather they not be there."

"Do you think there may come a time when we can worship as brothers in Christ?"

"While we sew the seed, we need to depend upon the Lord to raise up a harvest," Moffett said.

"I understand."

"As for your path while I'm abroad, Mr. Blair will step in for me. He's promised to meet with you weekly for instruction and support in whatever way you require."

"Thank you, Mr. Moffett. He will be a blessing to me."

"As you are to him. He regards you very highly and is looking forward to working with you."

They shared a smile.

"Now then, shall we have a look at my plan?"

A lump formed in Soon-hee's throat. "I am ready." He hoped.

CHAPTER THIRTEEN

EASTON, PA AND PRINCETON, NJ
SPRING 1906

He waited in the shadow of the Soldiers and Sailors Monument for Pearl's arrival on the Bethlehem trolley, almost regretting their breakfast date. She hadn't been able to be at the Kichline's Easter dinner the day before because her New York State relatives had been in town. When she'd informed him of her plans, Jacob had breathed easier. If he could have simply told her he had to return to Princeton early Monday morning, he could have avoided her altogether. As a man of his word, he could not.

Eastonians flowed around Centre Square, the mourning doves pecking for their daily bread. Pearl wouldn't be here for another ten minutes, and the letter he carried in his coat pocket begged to be reread.

> April 13, 1906
>
> Dear Mr. Kichline:
>
> As chairman of the St. Luke's Richlandtown Reformed Church search committee, I am writing to inform you of our decision regarding your candidacy for our vacant pulpit. We deeply appreciate the opportunity to interview

> you and hear your candidating sermon. As the committee met afterwards, we were of nearly one mind about our decision.

The warm sunshine contrasted with his inner shadows.

> There is no doubt among us that you are a highly learned young man, and we believe you to have a bright future in the Christian ministry. However, we do not consider your scholarly style well-suited to our congregation of plain-speaking farmers and tradesmen. Perhaps one of the more urban churches would be better suited to your abilities.
>
> We enjoyed getting to know you and thank you again for your interest in St. Luke's. We wish you all the best in your ministry.
>
> Sincerely yours,
>
> Mr. Albert O. Umbehendin
> Chairman, St. Luke's Reformed Church, Richlandtown, Penn.[Letter block ends]

With rising shame, he folded the letter he'd shown to no one over the weekend, not even Pastor Leinbach or his parents. When Harry Flory had asked him about his prospects after the Easter service, Jacob had been evasive.

"Nothing has been settled yet."

He'd turned the conversation back to his best friend, asking about Harry's teaching duties. Jacob had also provided oblique responses to the church elders and members who'd inquired about his post-graduation plans, his chest tightening with each prickly encounter. He could've accepted St. Luke's negative response if only one of the other churches had invited him to be their pastor. In fact, they had been his last choice, a backup when the other nine had fallen through. Nothing was turning out as he had planned—as he and Pearl had intended for their future. Sure, he could try for a more sophisticated parish closer to New York or Philadelphia where people might appreciate his so-called scholarly manner, but she'd made clear to him a desire to stick close to her family.

At the rumble of the approaching trolley, he rose to meet her. Whenever he'd caught sight of her before, his hands had tingled. Now, he was clenching them.

"Good morning, Pearl."

"Good morning, Jacob." She wore his favorite yellow outfit. "What a glorious day this is! I'm so happy you could see me before going back to Princeton."

He spoke around the lump in his throat. "Did you have a nice Easter?"

"Oh, I did. My family went to church, which was packed, and then we visited for hours around the table. How was your holiday?"

"Good. It was good." He practically choked on the words. "Um, would you like to get a cup of tea?"

"Not just yet," she said. "I'd enjoy a walk after being crammed in the trolley."

She took hold of his outstretched arm, and he led her down North Third Street to the Bushkill Creek. He let her do most of the talking along the two-block stretch before they settled on a bench near the babbling waterside. Being here always reminded him of his ancestor Colonel Peter Kichline. Jacob had grown up wanting to be a man after his own heart and service, of use to the world as he had been. What would his illustrious forebear think of him now?

"So, did you hear back from St. Luke's?" Pearl asked.

His stomach soured. "Yes, I had a letter."

Her smile went south. "Oh. They turned you down, didn't they?"

"Uh-huh."

She looked away for a long pause. "What will you do now?"

The question was like fingernails on a chalkboard. "I don't know." When he noticed her jaw tighten, he became defensive. "Something appears to be on your mind."

"What was their reason?"

He assumed the aspect of the elder who'd written the letter. "They are a community of farmers and tradesmen, and my scholarly style wasn't suitable."

"Jacob, they weren't the only ones to say such a thing."

His eyes narrowed. "What do you mean by that?"

"Don't you understand?" She gripped his hands. "You're not reaching the average person. Your sermons are more like seminary lectures." She quickly added, "It's not that they aren't excellent, because they are, but ..."

"But what?" He jerked his hands from her.

"You've become so learned and sophisticated that few can relate to you or your messages."

He glared at her, watching her wither under his scrutiny. "And what about you? Are you able to relate to me?"

Her response was so quiet he strained to hear.

"I used to, when we first met. I loved that Jacob Kichline. Since you went to Princeton, I've watched you become someone else, someone I can't pretend to know anymore."

He knew if he had given her an engagement ring, this would be the moment she'd be taking it off.

He waited for Dr. Armstrong in the professor's tobacco and leather-scented office, ruminating on his friends' successes in stark contrast to his abysmal failures. He struggled to rejoice with Rand's call to a Connecticut pastorate and Win's Harvard Fellowship, when a stack of rejection letters and a break with Pearl were his own lot. What had happened to his golden future? When he'd graduated from Lafayette, he'd seen only vast possibilities for personal and vocational fulfillment. Princeton was supposed to be a gateway to spiritual formation and an effective pastoral ministry. Now, what did he have to show for three years' worth of hard labor? A heap of rejection letters, a break with his girl, and no foreseeable prospects. Harry was already three years into his teaching career. Jacob's brother was climbing the ladder of success at the mill after working there straight out of college. Not only were they much further along in their lives, but their faith was intact, unlike his own. Maybe he should've just gone to Pastor Kieffer's seminary instead of being dazzled by Princeton's lofty reputation.

Armstrong returned after conversing with another student in the hallway, this time closing the door behind him. If the man weren't his academic advisor and this meeting mandatory, Jacob would have preferred to be elsewhere on this rainy May afternoon.

The New Testament professor looked at him. "I do apologize for the interruption. Where were we?"

"We were discussing my, uh, future."

"Ah yes. I was sorry to hear about the rejection letters. I know you were counting on one of those calls to come through."

His face colored. Was he the only graduating student in this situation? All he'd been hearing in the hallways and the Benham Club were shouting and applause when another church had snatched up one of their numbers. Jacob had kept his own suffering to himself mostly. While he'd revealed his dilemma to Win and Rand, he told everyone else he was still waiting on pulpit committees' decisions. After the Richlandtown church's rejection, however, he'd begun avoiding most social contact because lying had never suited him.

"I hope you don't mind," Armstrong said, "but I took the liberty to contact a handful of those search committee chairmen."

Jacob's lips parted, but nothing came out.

"I assure you I did this with complete discretion. Now then, I found a common thread running through their responses."

"Oh." He braced himself for more bad news.

"They each spoke of having a sense of detachment from you. Their congregations felt that you were talking mostly down to them in your trial sermons and meetings with committees and members." He leaned across the desk. "Jacob, you mustn't think yourself unique or a failure. You can't imagine how many times I've seen this sort of thing happen."

The tension in his jaw loosened. "You have?"

"Oh my, yes, and it's no wonder. We cram your minds full of ancient languages and systematic theology in one of the most sophisticated places in the country. Then we turn you loose and expect you to somehow relate to everyday people. Well, to me it's a wonder any church accepts our graduates."

"I had no idea."

"You haven't heard, then, about the handful of your colleagues who are in similar positions?"

"No, Professor Armstrong. I just assumed I was the only one."

"Indeed you are not. I suspect all of you are embarrassed to tell others about your struggles."

He was right about that.

"You remind me so much of another young scholar with whom I am well acquainted. Did you ever get to meet Gresham Machen during your junior year?"

Jacob found his old sense of humor. "I think I'd remember a name that sounds like the German word for a girl."

"You catch on quickly. The words are pronounced the same, but this fellow's name is spelled M-a-c-h-e-n." He grinned. "His close friends call him 'Das.'"

Now Jacob laughed outright. "As in 'Das Mädchen.'"

"Precisely."

"Actually, I do remember him from the Benham Club, but he didn't associate much with us younger members."

He didn't know how long the lightness of spirit would last, but he savored it for the time being. That was another thing about Princeton. He'd become so serious he'd shed his former lighthearted ways like a too-small garment. Jacob had begun to believe he couldn't be both learned and cheerful.

"He is my dear friend, currently studying in Germany, and like yourself he is also trying to figure things out. I can see the way plainly for him, but his clouds haven't parted yet." He clapped his palms on the desk. "Well, then, back to yourself. The question remains, what shall you be doing about this situation?"

"I must admit, I have no idea. I'd still like to become a minister. I mean, I think I heard God correctly before, but now I'm not so sure." He twisted his fingers.

"How would you describe the current state of your faith, Jacob?"

He looked down at his polished shoes, noticing a few rain droplets clinging to the tips. "I admit I don't know how to express myself."

"Let me put it this way, are you closer to the Lord now than you were when you came here three years ago?"

He blurted "No" before he could be more circumspect.

"Do you still believe the fundamentals of our faith?"

Sensing no condemnation in Professor Armstrong, Jacob decided to be honest with him, and himself.

"I believe so."

"And yet?"

Jacob breathed deeply. "My faith is mostly intact, but I've been exposed to a more modern and sophisticated way of approaching Christianity."

"All of us who profess Christ must come to terms with the modernists, Jacob." He paused. "What has given you the most trouble?"

When he spread his hands, Jacob saw they were trembling.

"I mostly wonder if miracles can be real. I mean, did God really part the Red Sea? Was Jonah really swallowed by a whale?"

"Was there really a virgin birth?"

He raised his eyebrows.

"Jacob, some men come through Princeton, hear about modernism, and leave unscathed. Others like yourself, are wounded in spirit by the new teachings, which really aren't new at all when put within the framework of biblical history. A divided mind and spirit, as well as confusion are the result."

"Yes."

"I've seen men's faith shattered, but I've also seen others develop stronger spiritual muscles." He looked into Jacob's eyes. "I believe you are going to get through this."

He teared up despite his efforts at self-control. After a long moment, he whispered, "I don't know what to do."

Armstrong remained silent for several moments. "There's

a possibility I'd like you to consider. I'm aware of your excellent proficiency in languages. If I'm not mistaken, you earned the highest average in the senior class in Greek and Hebrew. I know you've been an instructor's aide in those departments."

"Yes, that's correct." Maybe he wasn't such a failure after all.

"You're fluent in German and Latin, are you not?"

"Yes, Professor Armstrong."

Again, the silence, the closed eyes, followed by a question. "I believe you know Professor Cullen."

"I had a class with him." Why was he mentioning the mission's instructor?

"In a few months, he and his wife will be going to Korea. Some of our best and brightest Presbyterian leaders are laboring in an amazing harvest there."

Jacob wondered where this was going, a fluttery feeling in his stomach.

"There's a great need there for translators. Professor Cullen has been praying for the right people to help with this critical part of the Korean missionary work." He leaned forward. "Jacob, perhaps this is what you are meant to do at this time in your life."

His mouth went dry. "Korea? Halfway around the world?" He gave a laugh. "I thought I'd be working in Pennsylvania and enjoying my homecoming."

"I've learned never to underestimate God's much larger vision for our lives." He paused. "I urge you to consider this."

"Would it matter that I'm still unsure about some things regarding my faith?"

"Personally, I think the experience would give you an even broader spiritual perspective. It would allow you to see how God is transforming people's lives in ways you can't even imagine just now. You would need to be honest with the board about your current state, but if you're open to having God work in your spirit, I think they would accept you. Besides, you wouldn't be a missionary, teacher, or preacher but a translator."

He threw up another barrier, part of him hoping to see it torn down, the other wishing it to remain fixed. "I don't know the Korean language—or the customs."

"Neither did Professor Cullen when he first went there five years ago. I'll tell you what, let's go to prayer about this now. Then I'll give you, say, three days to go to your own prayer closet and seek God's answer. We'll come together again afterward to further discuss this. Will that be agreeable?"

"Yes, Professor Armstrong." Jacob wasn't at all certain, but he seemed to be catching the notes of a still, small voice behind him saying, 'This is the way, go in it.'" To himself he said, *I believe. Help my unbelief.*

CHAPTER FOURTEEN

LATE SPRING 1906
PYONGYANG, KOREA

Soon-hee missed Samuel and Mrs. Dr. Moffett far more than he'd anticipated. He knew only Jesus could fill his soul's deepest needs, however, and was learning to depend even more on the only one who never leaves. He walked across the compound to the West Gate Church, considering another possible benefit from Moffett's absence. Soon-hee and his father were growing closer. They'd been preparing for and were now teaching a Bible-study class for a week-long session vital to the Korean missionary work. These trainings, run at various times and places, entailed setting aside all work so attendees could dedicate themselves to prayer and studying Scripture. The result of this system was ongoing renewal in the churches. Soon-hee's father, Kyung Oh, had charge of the West Gate Church's Bible-study class, the two of them working together.

On this sparkling Tuesday morning with the dew still clinging to the grass, Soon-hee imagined in what way the Holy Spirit might be moving among them today. The first of the classes had ended with dozens of men's hearts revived and not a few relationships restored. He wondered whether he and his brother could reach such a place, whether he would ever be able to stop holding Yong-bin's sins against him.

Lord, this will not do. Thou knowest how I struggle to forgive him. One day, I think I have managed to do so, the next, I am clenching my teeth at the thought of him. I am so like Paul when he cried out to thee as a wretched man needing to be freed from besetting sins. I beg thee to set me and my brother free.

He reached the church twenty minutes early and stored his gloomy thoughts in the back of his mind. The pews were nearly filled with men eager to know the Savior more intimately, and Soon-hee stopped to greet several of them on his way down a side aisle before joining his father on the platform.

"Good morning, Soon-hee." Kyung Oh looked up from his notes spread over the lectern and smiled at his oldest son.

"Good morning, *Abeoji*. I see you are hard at work. When did you arrive?"

"About three hours ago. I have been in prayer."

I should have been up earlier today to join him. I will not make this mistake again.

Seeing no condemnation in his father's expression, Soon-hee said, "I apologize for not joining you. Although our time is short, may we go aside to pray now?"

Kyung Oh waved him into a side room where they sought the Lord's favor upon the meeting.

An hour before the midday meal break, Pastor Oh was teaching from the book of Acts about the early Church.

"We see from this passage how the apostles responded to the jailer when the angel of the Lord freed them. In his writings, Mr. Moffett has commented on the grace Paul and Silas showed to their enemy."

Soon-hee nearly jumped out of his seat when two young men stood and shouted his father down. All heads turned toward the middle of the church where the fellows brayed for attention.

"Mr. Oh, do not you think those Christians should have allowed the jailer to take his life?"

Gasps like the striking of dozens of matches electrified the church. Soon-hee's pulse raced. *How dare he challenge Abeoji.* Simultaneously, he broke into a sweat. *What if this turns into a mob scene?* One of the Bible-study weeks in Kaesong had broken up after miscreants disrupted those proceedings.

Oh, Lord, hear my prayer. Let thy Spirit seize control before this gets out of hand.

With a chin high, Kyung Oh leaned over the pulpit. "Who is asking such a question?"

The taller of the two thrust out his chest. "I am, Pastor Oh."

"And who are you?"

"I am Choi Sung, recently arrived from America. I do not think you should rely on the teachings of an American missionary to understand the Word of God."

A rumble began in the back of the church before giving way to silence.

Kyung Oh's mouth turned down. "What right do you have to speak in such a way against Mr. Moffett?"

"Americans are a dissipated people. I have witnessed first-hand their ungodly, drunken ways and immoral behavior. I say the Americans, even more than the Japanese, are responsible for our country's deplorable status."

"It would seem you have learned their rudeness as well," Kyung Oh said.

The congregation erupted in what appeared to be nervous laughter. Soon-hee stared in amazement at his father, appreciating his diffusive humor.

Choi Sung fisted his hands. "I do not believe these American missionaries, these foreigners, have a right to lead the Korean church."

"They have helped us build our churches and bring us to faith in Christ." Kyung Oh spoke with authority. "They have labored side-by-side with us not as lords but as brothers, and soon, they will be turning over their authority to us Koreans."

All eyes turned back to the young man, whose companion spoke next.

"This may be so, Pastor Oh, but Americans who were our friends have followed Great Britain's example in recognizing Japan's control over us. They have betrayed us."

Kyung Oh stepped into the hush after the troublemaker's words. "I would ask you two young men to leave."

When they hesitated, Soon-hee spoke up. "Would the elders come forward and escort them outside?" For a horrible moment, he couldn't breathe, wondering which way this tide would be turning.

A half-dozen men rose and encircled the two who continued to shout as they were led outside the church. The disruption continued for several minutes.

Soon-hee watched his father with a growing admiration for his coolness under fire and his ability to seize control of the class.

I thank thee, Lord, for prevailing here this morning.

Kyung Oh completed the lesson in ten minutes and dismissed the assembly with a prayer over the midday meal.

The men streamed outside the sanctuary, and Soon-hee spotted Mr. Blair making his way down the center aisle against the flow. When the American reached him and his father, Soon-hee noted his breathlessness.

Blair clapped his right hand against his chest. "I got here just as fast as I could. Are you all right, Mr. Oh? Someone came to my office and told me what was happening."

The pastor wavered for a moment then sat down hard on one of the wooden chairs. "Yes, I am fine. Thank you for coming."

Soon-hee wondered where Miss Story could be found if needed.

"Let's all have a seat." Blair situated himself across from Kyung, and Soon-hee took the chair to his father's right. "Suppose you tell me what happened."

Soon-hee provided an account for the missionary, whose face turned grim.

"You both handled this volatile situation admirably," Blair said. "These troublemakers aren't numerous, thank the Lord, but they make a good deal of noise." He gazed upward. "I know how disappointed mostly everyone is about the American government's decision. Still, men who are not right with God can become twisted, and a few of them can do no end of damage."

"Is Elder Oh all right?" a student called from the front pew.

"Yes, yes." Kyung Oh responded for himself. "I am fine. Go have your meal, and we will commence as usual afterward."

They turned down the center aisle.

"*Abeoji*, are you sure?" Soon-hee asked.

"I will have some tea and kimchi, and I will be in fine form. You do not think a little commotion would stop me?"

Soon-hee appealed to Blair with his eyes.

"Nevertheless, Mr. Oh, you have withstood a shock. If you would like to hand over part of the afternoon's teaching and prayer, Soon-hee and I can assist you."

The fifty-one-year-old elder closed his eyes, moving his head from side to side. "Thank you. The Lord will strengthen me."

Blair remained silent for a short time. Then he said, "I have nothing pressing this afternoon and would like to attend the meeting."

Gathering courage, Soon-hee added his plans to the mix. "I will bring back food so we may eat here in quiet. Then, I would like to teach and leave the prayers to you, if you are amenable."

His father sniffed. "We are all stubborn men. As you wish."

Soon-hee's spirit briefly nosedived on the way to pick up the dinner the women had prepared for the class. Not only had he been wrestling with his animosity for his brother and struggling to see the occupying Japanese in a manner worthy of the gospel, now he had a group of ruffians to resent. Was there no end to his internal war against bitterness? Mr. Moffett had urged him not to let such things take root in him, but just when Soon-hee dug up one of the seeds, another started to sprout.

Lord, I must decide what kind of person I am to be, what kind of soil I will till for the growing of my faith. Help me choose thy ways when my spirit leads me otherwise.

Soon-hee wasn't far from the only struggling Christian in Pyongyang. By August, the situation had become grave, the mission surrounded by ravenous wolves, and dividing from within. One day a messenger brought a note from Mr. Blair to Soon-hee's room at the YMCA. He perched on the side of his chair and opened the envelope.

> My Dear Mr. Oh,
>
> The missionaries have decided to devote a week to nothing but Bible study and prayer in order to know God's will in the present situation. Dr. Hardy of Wonsan will be coming to Pyongyang to lead us as we seek the Lord in our time of need. We have reached a place where we dare not go forward without the Lord's abiding presence.
>
> Will you please join us? I will be happy to give you a dispensation for your school and translation work. Your father will be among our numbers.
>
> Yours in Christian Service,
> W. N. Blair

Soon-hee rested the letter on his knees, bowing his head. How humbling to be included among these esteemed missionaries. How unworthy he was.

Something about the missionary's face drew Soon-hee to him, perhaps a combination of qualities. A Canadian physician who'd become a Methodist evangelist, Dr. R. A. Hardie had been at the forefront of a revival in Wonsan three years ago. He shared his story with the gathering of missionaries at the Central Church, the heat of the day losing its impact among the delegates.

"You've honored me by your invitation to lead you in Bible study and prayer during this critical juncture." He looked over the assembly with a placid, friendly expression. "You are correct to look to God's Word and seek him in prayer because there's no other path forward that will result in his good will. So often learned men and women fall back upon their own devices before getting on their knees, where they should have been all along."

Mr. Blair, sitting with him on the platform, spoke. "Dr. Hardie, please tell us what it was like in Wonsan before the revival there."

"I can assure you, circumstances weren't ideal from any human standpoint. In addition to stress over the Japanese situation, there were several strained relationships between church officials."

"What was the turning point? What Bible studies and prayers resulted in thousands of Korean conversions?"

The forty-one-year-old evangelist closed his eyes for a minute. "There was no method, Mr. Blair. I was perfectly frank with my congregation about my own spiritual failings. Although I was plenty ashamed, I confessed my pride, hardness of heart, and lack of faith. I was astonished when the Holy Spirit came upon us in great power when I'd half expected the sky to fall. Since then, I've seen this same thing happen in other places. I've come to believe the path to personal and corporate revival lies in complete candor before our holy God. That's when we align ourselves with our position—we are the created, and he is the Creator." He paused. "I'm guessing you've heard about great movements across the world, how God has been transforming lives in Los Angeles, California, in Wales, in India. Raw honesty has been at the forefront in all those places too."

This wasn't what Soon-hee had expected to hear. He thought Dr. Hardie would reveal a certain Bible study process or form of prayer that had led to the Spirit's movement. Something about baring oneself to God exhilarated, as well as intimidated, him.

"In fact," Hardie continued, "I strongly suggest that at this juncture you seek God with your whole hearts, baring them to him."

Blair seemed as vulnerable as a child as he asked his next question. "And how will you guide us into such a place, Mr. Hardie?"

"I'd like to begin by searching the epistle of John with you. He taught us that 'God is love and he that abideth in love, abideth in God, and God in him.' John declared that everything in our lives depends upon authentic fellowship with the Almighty."

"What will this look like, practically speaking?"

Hardie grinned. "Let's start by spending time in corporate prayer, followed by delving into the Word of God, then breaking into smaller groups for prayer." He paused. "Now is a good time to begin. Would you open our meetings, Mr. Blair?"

"I'll be happy to." He lifted his voice to be heard across the sanctuary. "Let us pray."

On Thursday after Dr. Hardie led Soon-hee's small group, the missionary came over and sat with him after everyone had departed. At first, Soon-hee hadn't noticed the man's presence and jumped when Hardie spoke to him.

"Mr. Oh, you appear to have something on your mind." His smile was that of a benevolent uncle.

Soon-hee's eyes darted from the Canadian to the back of the wall. He couldn't find words.

A further surprise came when spontaneously, Hardie began to pray over him. "Dear Lord, I lift up to thee my brother, Mr. Oh, asking thee to have thy way with his spirit. Whatever is happening in him, please take charge and bring about thy will for thy name's sake and for his good. In thy Son's name we pray, amen."

Soon-hee spoke in a whisper. "Thank you. I feel unworthy of this work."

"What has you feeling this way?"

"I, I harbor resentment."

"Would you like to tell me what happened?"

"My brother did me a great wrong." Soon-hee recoiled over his inability to let go. "Also, I try to love the Japanese. I loathe their lordship over us and the great wrongs they have committed against Koreans, against my own family some years ago."

After a long pause, Hardie asked, "Is this all?"

"I am angry with those Koreans who stir up trouble in our midst." He sat on his hands to still their shaking.

"Have you spoken to your own brother?"

"I have tried, but he will not hear me."

"This may be a matter of confronting him in the presence of other witnesses."

Soon-hee gave a jump. "No. Oh, please no. This is a private matter." He knew he couldn't stand the shame if this became widely known.

"I see." He became thoughtful. "Since he won't be reconciled to you, and you seem to have done your part, I advise you to leave the matter to God to deal with. I also suggest you pray God will change your brother's heart and bless him."

He a felt a twinge of guilt, followed by a lightening of his spirit. *Perhaps this is a key to true forgiveness.*

"As for those in our land who foment distress, I understand your feelings."

"You do?"

"When Satan uses people to damage the Church, we should be disgruntled. However, if we take matters into our own hands, we create more distress. Our job is to relinquish our anger to him, trusting him to guide us as he works to bring about his good will. I'm expecting a great blessing to fall upon Korea and its people." He gazed at Soon-hee. "Have you been ill, Mr. Oh?"

Was nothing hidden from this unusually discerning man? "I have frequent stomach upset."

"Our bodies often reflect the state of our souls. Let's speak to the Lord about all these matters and allow him to redeem them."

The cold places in Soon-hee's heart seemed to be melting.

CHAPTER FIFTEEN

EARLY SEPTEMBER 1906
PRINCETON, NJ

At the end of his last Korean lesson before leaving the country, Jacob raked a hand through his hair, wondering if he'd ever be able to master this complex tongue. He just might be able to compliment a farmer about his oxen, however. Learning other languages had always come easily to him, but this one was in another category altogether.

Mr. Cullen's voice shifted from teaching to soothing. "Don't fret, Jacob. I've been where you are. I can assure you you're far more advanced than you seem to realize."

He took some comfort in the encouragement. "Tell me, how much time did you take before attaining fluency?"

The professor chuffed a laugh. "Don't kid yourself. I'm still working to get to that point."

"I never found Latin, Greek, or Hebrew this tough."

Rain spattering against the windows reflected his mood.

"Don't berate yourself for not grasping Korean as quickly as you anticipated. You're actually exceeding my expectations. This language is right at the top of the world's most difficult ones to learn because its pronunciation rules don't follow Western patterns. Then, there's its complex honorific system."

Jacob groaned. "I think that part has me the most concerned. There are all those rules about what words are appropriate in different situations and regarding social rank. I'm terrified of addressing someone incorrectly."

"I've done so on more than one occasion," Cullen said. "Fortunately, Koreans are gracious people. Most of them appreciate our stumbling attempts to use their complicated language."

"That's good to know." He paused. "What also baffles me is the unique word order Koreans follow in sentence structure and grammar. How will I get along if I can't communicate effectively?"

"But you will get along, Jacob, just as I have. Try not to take yourself too seriously. Be willing to have a laugh at your own expense when you trip up."

Ah, there was the rub. Before going to Princeton, Jacob had been known for his sense of humor. He wondered whether that person still existed, hoping he might find him again.

Cullen rose from the chair. "I'm confident you'll do very well."

"I appreciate your encouragement, Mr. Cullen."

"Just keep practicing. We'll have plenty of time to work on all these aspects of the language as we make our way to Korea in less than a week now."

Jacob mentally rehearsed the train traversing America, then arriving at the port of San Francisco, and finally boarding a steamer for the trip across the Pacific Ocean. He'd never been further from home than Niagara Falls to the north and Cape May, New Jersey, to the south as his mother kept reminding him on his most recent trip to Easton. She'd been filled with fears of the realistic as well as the unreasonable kind. Uppermost on her mind seemed to be whether Korean sanitation was up to American standards. He'd learned about the modern amenities the mission compound had, but in the more rural areas, they were deficient. Then again, how much time would he be on the outside of Pyongyang for his translation work?

"I think you should stay close to the American and Canadian missionaries," she'd said. "I shudder to think of the cannibals you might encounter."

"I assure you, Mother, Korea doesn't have cannibals."

"Well, maybe not," she'd admitted, "but they do have tigers and snakes."

He smiled at the memory as he marshalled his books and papers.

"As for our itinerary ..."

Jacob recited the first part of their trip from heart. "I'm to meet you and Mrs. Cullen at Broad Street Station on September 13th at eight-thirty in the morning."

"Yes. Will you have any difficulty getting there so early?"

"My father checked Easton's train schedule to Philadelphia, and the first one leaves at seven-ten. If all goes right, I'll get there in time." A baseball seemed to lodge in his throat.

"We'll just have to pray there are no delays."

"What if ...?"

He waggled a finger. "You're a Presbyterian, my friend. Our sovereign Lord will provide."

He managed a smile and left the classroom, heading down the rain-shrouded stairway. Although his mother's anxiety for his welfare bordered on the laughable, Jacob also worried about his reaction to Korea. Despite the theological confusion, life in Princeton had been such a joy to him, a refined environment and almost Southern in its gentility. Sometimes, even going back to grittier Easton jarred him. How might he respond to a truly backward place where all the sights and customs would be strange? What if he became sick with some unusual disease? What would a group of missionaries be able to do for him then? What if he ended up dying there, according to his mother's most extreme fears? Furthermore, would another year away from Pearl completely sever whatever bond remained between them? Although he hadn't spoken to her since their breakup, he hadn't put her out of his heart.

His palms turned sweaty, his heart racing as he left Stuart Hall and got pelted with raindrops. Before coming to Princeton, even up to his first year there, he would have turned to God with his unsettledness. He liked to think the Lord was listening and had the power to help him, but what if he wasn't?

Being at the Benham Club had always managed to cheer Jacob, a place where nothing bad could really happen. He didn't know who he'd find there at three-thirty in the afternoon before the start of the fall semester, but even if no one was there to banter with, he could at least take refuge in his surroundings.

The uniformed attendant greeted him. "Good day, Mr. Kichline. How are you keeping?"

"I'm well, and how are you, Wendell?"

He grinned. "Just fine. Any day this side of the grave is a good one."

Why can't I be more like him? Jacob smiled back before entering the main room, its gas lights shining against the day's sodden gloom. He saw one fellow, head bent over a book, his pen scratching on a notepad.

"Hello."

The man looked up and squinted. "Hello. Oh, it's you, Jacob."

"I don't mean to interrupt."

"I could use a break and some company. This place is quiet as a tomb, which is good for working but not socializing. Please, have a seat."

"Thanks." His spirit lifted at the thought of a conversation with Gresham Machen, Professor Armstrong's close friend. Although "Army" called him "Das," Jacob didn't think their recent acquaintance warranted such familiarity. "What are you working on?"

"I'm trying to get up to speed with my class notes for the fall semester."

"I imagine you must be eager to start teaching New Testament."

"Eager isn't the only word for how I feel." Machen chortled.

"Oh. Are you feeling apprehensive?" Jacob wondered if he might have found the perfect companion.

Machen's eyes twinkled. "Try scared to death." "I would have never guessed. You're so stalwart."

"So was the Apostle Paul. Never underestimate your emotions, my friend. They too are a gift from God. I wonder you're feeling not a little fear yourself, getting ready as you are to leave for Korea in, what, a few days?"

"Yes, on both counts. Two days from now I'll be going home to Easton for my commissioning service."

"Will there be an ordination then as well?"

Jacob bristled. “Um, no, not yet anyway.”

“I too am taking my time with that step. One shouldn’t enter into such a state carelessly.”

“You’ve been abroad—to Germany, right?”

“Basically, I’ve been all over Europe, but recently, I studied in Germany,” Machen said. “I’ve never been to the Orient, though. That’s a different world altogether.”

“My mother is convinced I’m going to meet a gruesome death at the hands of cannibals.”

Machen laughed. “Mothers are like that, Jacob. What about you?”

He’d hardly admitted some things to himself let alone share them with someone else.

The unexpected din when something metallic fell to the kitchen floor made them both jump ... and laugh.

His companion tilted back and crossed his arms. “What’s on your mind?”

“I, uh, wish I were going with, uh, the faith I had when I came to Princeton.”

Machen closed his eyes. “This place has a way of shaking the souls under her care.”

Jacob read between the lines of Machen’s earnest face. “Did you get shaken here too?”

“Not here exactly. My field of battle was in Germany studying under liberal theologians. One of them, Wilhelm Herrmann, taught that a person could be an earnest Christian without sticking to orthodox doctrine.” He rubbed the back of his neck. “Talk about being shaken.”

“Yet, here you are now, about to teach the New Testament. What happened?”

“If you’re like me, you had the great privilege of being nurtured in a Christian home.”

“I was.”

"Back then, we had the faith of wide-eyed children and believed without question. We were happy to accept what we learned at face value. As we matured, we started asking questions, which is a good thing. Our faith needs to be informed, not blind. But in a place like this, we also get challenged in unexpected ways. We didn't expect some people to openly doubt Jonah was swallowed by a whale and lived to tell about it or that Moses parted the Red Sea." He gave a laugh. "Or tell us its real name was the Sea of Reeds, as if to add insult to injury. Please don't misunderstand." He waved a hand. "As I said, intellectual labor is necessary. I also believe in the hard school of the struggles you and I have had, we can begin to substitute the unthinking faith of our childhoods with the profound convictions of full-grown men."

Jacob gently bit his lip as he took in the encouraging counsel. Machen appeared as one who'd been through the fire and come out like Shadrach, Meshach, and Abednego and in his experience, Jacob discovered a reason to hope he might too.

"To be perfectly frank," Machen said, "I'm still wrestling with some things, but my biggest hurdles are behind me now. I encourage you not to be discouraged or ashamed. Unless you're in rebellion against God, and I don't sense that you are, contend with him expecting him to guide you. You'll be amazed at the vital communion you'll have with our risen Lord even now. Then, when you're really convinced of the Christian message's truth, you'll be able to proclaim it before a world of enemies." He placed his hands behind his head and smiled. "We aren't alone, Jacob. The Church itself is in a battle for its life, and we can rejoice that God didn't place us in an easy age. He even uses people like us to wave his victorious banner."

A well of emotion prevented Jacob from responding.

Machen peered at him for a long moment, as if reading the contents of Jacob's soul. Then he said, "Believe me, you're going to come out of this a much stronger man."

Although he savored being home in cherished surroundings with beloved family and friends, Jacob chafed at the long goodbyes and questions about why he was being commissioned instead of ordained. Pastor Leinbach and most of the consistory had been fine with his decision, including his coming under the auspices of the Presbyterians. His church's leaders had even pledged financial support and encouraged him to take his time about ordination. Now, following his commissioning service at First Reformed Church, he'd given vague answers to others who'd asked why he was going to Korea instead of becoming a pastor according to his original plans. Most of the men had responded with a clap on the back, and the women promised to pray for him.

Another challenge came at the reception where the consistory presented him with a carton of hymnbooks for the Pyongyang mission and a new valise for his travels. Then Harry Flory stepped forward to give Jacob a gift from the Christian Endeavor—a Korean language Bible. That's when he'd first noticed Pearl, who lowered her chin when their eyes met.

Why is she here? Has she had a change of heart about me? His pulse quickened. Was there still hope for them? Did he want there to be despite their current differences?

Harry's speech brought him back to attention.

"Before I sit down, there's one more present. Someone in our group made a, well, I'm not sure what you call these things." He laughed as he handed Jacob a small-framed embroidery with Philippians 1:6, "He which hath begun a good work in you will perform it until the day of Jesus Christ."

Warmed by their gifts and their apparent forgiveness despite the way he'd insulted them, he accepted the items.

"Thank you, so much," he told the gathering. "Your gifts and support mean a great deal to me. I also want to thank Pastor Leinbach, the consistory, and everyone in the congregation for making my work in Korea possible." He cleared his throat. "I'll remember your generosity while I'm there, uh, missing all of you."

After the presentations, he greeted everyone in the fellowship hall personally. What in the world he'd say to Pearl, he hadn't a clue. Seeing her made him realize not only the strength of his feelings for her, but how her deep-seated faith was in an unexpected way drawing him back to her. How did she feel about him, though? Did she think of him as some sort of apostate?

He wandered over to her, his tightened stomach relaxing a little when she smiled.

"Hello, Jacob."

"Hello." He stared into those captivating, differently colored eyes, everyone else in the teaming room fading from his sight.

"I hope you don't mind that I came today. Your mother and Harry encouraged me to be here."

"Oh. Then, you didn't want to see me off?" *Smooth, Jacob, real smooth.*

"I'm sorry. That's not what I meant to say. Of course, I wanted to see you again before you left." She paused, twisting her handkerchief. "I just didn't know if you'd be glad to see me."

"I am, uh, very happy to see you." Sweat pooled under his collar.

"I made that embroidery for you."

His breath hitched. "You did? That was nice of you. I like it." *Great. I'm a Princeton Seminary graduate who can't manage more than one syllable words.*

"I believe that verse for you, Jacob." She gazed at him.

He surprised himself when he reached for her hand. "Thank you. I would like to write to you if that's okay."

"I don't want you to feel obligated. This will be an important year for you, and you don't need any distractions. Let's take this time to let God help us figure things out."

There were no promises, but there began to be peace.

CHAPTER SIXTEEN

LATE SEPTEMBER, 1906
PYONGYANG, KOREA

He regretted every bite he'd eaten of his mother's kimchi. These prayer meetings, which had begun after the August Bible study class, usually refreshed him, but not this afternoon. As they raised their petitions, Soon-hee was clutching his stomach against scorching pain. He'd gone to see his mother earlier in the day after a busy two-week absence, and she hadn't held back her assessment of his appearance.

"You are far too thin. You must not be eating enough."

She was half right. He was so absorbed in his duties he often forgot to take nourishment until his belly sounded an alarm. On the other hand, nothing seemed to agree with him lately, and he'd been subsisting mostly on a diet of rice and bland tofu.

"You must eat, or you will fade away, Soon-hee."

She'd gone straight to the kitchen and filled one bowl with *duk mandoo gok* soup and another with a hearty portion of kimchi. Although he'd regarded the food with not a little alarm, he'd been more concerned with offending or causing her undo worry by refusing the meal. He had choked down the food, thanked her, and hurried back to his quarters to take the antacid powder Mrs. Dr. Moffett had prescribed for him. The next-to-last bottle, he noted, was nearly gone.

Now, with Mr. Blair beginning to pray, Soon-hee restrained a rising moan. The American was always the last one to take a turn in these meetings, so relief was in sight. Soon-hee planned to return to his room and roll up on his bed in a fetal position. The only problem was Blair usually lost track of time when he prayed.

"Lord, thou knowest the condition of our hearts."

Soon-hee stifled a belch.

"Thou knowest how we've been filled with resentment for the Japanese rather than the love you call us to. Thou knowest how tepid we can be in our devotion to thee, which causes such hardness of heart when we are disconnected from thy mighty power. We appeal to thee to replace our hearts of stone with hearts of flesh."

Soon-hee broke out in a cold sweat when stomach acid geysered up to his throat. If this session didn't end soon, he might just deposit his unfortunate lunch all over his mat. He took a few deep breaths to calm himself and managed to get through the next ten minutes. As soon as Blair uttered "amen," Soon-hee rose with haste and fled from the church. He was about to make a run for his room when a feminine voice interrupted him.

"Mr. Oh, are you ill?"

He turned to the familiar face. "Miss Story. I, uh ..."

She stepped closer while a few of the missionaries began trickling out of the West Gate Church.

"I couldn't help but notice you appeared to be in some distress during the prayer meeting." Her warm brown eyes met his. "Is your digestion disturbing you again?"

He considered how lately he seemed to have become one with this pain. He closed his eyes and breathed out.

"Let's stop by the infirmary. Are you well enough to walk that far across the campus?"

He refused to believe he couldn't. "Yes, but I have much to attend to." He said this through clenched teeth.

"You're ill. Your work will have to wait."

"Very well."

Pain tore through his middle, and the nurse seized his arm to steady him. He feared Jeongsook might see them together just when the distance between them was beginning to narrow ever so slightly. Seeing no sign of her and wanting to leave before others could witness his misery, he acquiesced to Clara Story's assistance.

By the time they reached the infirmary, Soon-hee could barely stand. A man he'd never seen before helped him into a bed while Clara described the symptoms, as well as Mrs. Dr. Moffett's analysis and treatment. Soon-hee had never been reduced to tears over physical pain, but he could barely suppress them as the curly-haired young man came over and reached for his hand.

"I'd like you to meet Mr. Soon-hee Oh," Clara said. "He's one of the mission's best teachers and translators. He recently graduated from the seminary and is pursuing doctoral work with Mr. Moffett."

"I'm happy to meet you, Mr. Oh. I'm Andrew Walker from the Severance Hospital in Seoul. Dr. Allen has left for the States, so now I'm working under Dr. Avison."

He detected a kind of accent and wondered where the physician might be from in America. "I am happy to meet you."

"I'd like to perform an examination if you don't mind."

He consented to the uncomfortable prodding, then lay back in a sweat when Walker finally straightened.

"I definitely agree with Mrs. Dr. Moffett's diagnosis of a peptic ulcer, although your condition seems to have worsened." He turned to Clara. "What treatment did she prescribe?"

"Mostly antacid powders combined with belladonna alkaloids."

He looked at Soon-hee. "How has that course been working for you?"

"Mostly well."

Walker slanted his head to the right. "So, your symptoms have been under control? You've been watching your diet and getting sufficient sleep?"

"Yes, that is until the last two weeks." Soon-hee closed his eyes, shifting his weight on the cool white sheets. "I have been trying to follow these orders. Today, however, things went badly for me." He described the food his mother had pushed on him.

Walker gave a low whistle. "Doesn't she know about your condition?"

"I have not told my parents."

"I assume you don't want to worry them."

"This is correct." *I am not sure they would even believe me.*

"Well, Mr. Oh, I'm going to have to keep you here for several days for intensive treatments."

"B-but ..."

The young doctor raised his hand. "There can be no objections if you want to recover from this significant setback. I just happen to be here for a week."

Clara Story clapped her hands. "Your being here is no less than providential."

Soon-hee brushed aside her enthusiasm. "What about my studies and translation work, my Bible classes with the young men, the prayer meetings?"

"They're going to have to wait. I know this is difficult, but really, this is the only way if you ever want to be well again."

"Do you mean this could be permanent?" The acid in his stomach merged with a hefty dose of dread.

"We have to tackle this immediately to prevent such a thing from happening."

His parents were going to have to know. Everyone was going to have to know.

September 30, 1906
Pyongyang, Korea

Dear Mr. Moffett,

Greetings in the name of our Lord and Savior Jesus Christ from your student and fellow laborer. I trust that you, Mrs. Doctor, and son Jamie are in good health as you continue your year-long furlough. Mr. Blair has told me of your election to Moderator of the New Albany Presbytery in Indiana, and I send my heartfelt congratulations to you for such a distinct honor. Those ministers are surely blessed and will prosper under your godly leadership. The mission continues its work in your absence, which all of us feel keenly. Mr. Blair does a commendable job keeping the various components running smoothly for he is a good, competent, and godly man. Along with the Korean leaders, the Americans have continued the services, classes, country work, and discussions about adding to the Central Church's seating capacity. When you left, overall membership was just under 1600, and we have added fifty to those numbers since then. A few weeks ago, Mr. Underwood spoke to an open-air

> assembly of 2,000 souls to great effect. Rest assured, Mr. Blair also has enriched my doctoral studies and guided me in my translation duties.

He paused from writing to watch a group of boys playing at sword-fighting outside his window. When one of them waved, he lifted his hand and smiled, recalling such carefree days.

> Since we have been meeting for regular prayer to address our difficulties with the Japanese situation, a shift has been occurring. Dr. Hardie has urged us to continue our Spirit-led efforts to live according to the Apostle John's teachings about love, which include love for our enemies. We have been searching our hearts and allowing Jesus to deal with all unrighteousness, despite how uncomfortable this often feels. One remarkable result has been the acceptance of a former Japanese soldier into the West Gate Church's fellowship. At times, I have seen him break down with gratitude for the grace shown him, including when one of the loudest opponents of the Japanese offered him the right hand of fellowship. I also know of a few occasions when our praying missionaries and Koreans have quelled confrontations with those who strongly oppose the Japanese presence in our country. These instances have served to enlarge my own spirit.

He considered how much, if anything, to say about his own heart's condition. Since Mr. Hardie was encouraging him to be more transparent, he chose to follow his lead.

> You may be wondering how my relationship is with my brother. I am afraid Yong-bin still avoids me unless we are thrown together in our parents' home. Then, he is terse. I believe he wrestles with feelings of guilt over the injustice he showed me.

He thought about all the visitors who'd come to see him at the infirmary, including his mother and father, who'd been solicitous and kind, the way they had always treated his brother. This had been a balm to Soon-hee's spirit. He smiled when he pictured his mother's offering of a large container of kimchi, which Clara Story had confiscated on the spot. Sora had come as well, along with two young men from Soon-hee's Bible class who read and prayed with him. Best of all, Jeongsook had visited, quietly gracing his sickroom, chasing away some of the shadows between them. Yong-bin, however, had not come, excusing himself on account of his increasing headaches. Soon-hee had not been the least bit surprised.[Letter block resumes]

> In my heart, I have forgiven him, but I still remember what he did to me. Perhaps you can advise me as to the concept of forgetting an offense when we forgive those who trespass against us. I sometimes am distressed when I call to mind the transgressions, and I try quickly to put them away from me. I do wish when we forgave, we could altogether leave the sin behind us.

He sighed over his internal battle before writing about his recent physical condition.

> Personally, my health suffered a setback, and I am currently under the excellent care of Dr. Walker, a newcomer to the Severance Hospital, as well as Miss Story. I have been at the infirmary these past two weeks undergoing intensive treatment for my ulcerative condition and am feeling much better. Dr. Walker believes I shall make a full recovery. I am afraid my studies and work have been impaired, but he and Miss Story often remind me, had I not sought this cure, I might never be useful again. Thanks be to God for giving me ears to hear. You must not worry about me, Mr. Moffett, but I do ask you and Mrs. Dr. to pray for a complete healing. When I leave the infirmary, I must watch closely my diet and maintain a regular sleep schedule. Dr. Walker says I

> may slowly resume my studies and translation work. At first, I minded the thought of not finishing according to our original schedule. Now I am reconciled to this and believe you will understand.
>
> Please give my dearest regards to Mrs. Dr. and know that I pray for both of you not only daily but many times in a day. I would so enjoy hearing from you at your earliest opportunity, but I know how pressing are the demands upon your time. Until then I remain,
>
> Your humble son in the faith,
> Soon-hee Oh

The sound of heavy footsteps outside the room brought his attention to the doorway. Then Dr. Walker entered with a smile.

"You're looking well this morning, Mr. Oh."

"I feel well. How are you today?" He put the letter beside him on the bed.

Walker drew closer. "You're the only patient who asks me how I am. Thank you for being so caring."

"You are welcome." Soon-hee grinned. "So, how are you?"

"I'm well also. Did you have a good night's sleep?"

"Yes."

"How is the belly pain?"

His eyes glimmered. "What belly pain?"

"Good fellow! Your improvement is an answer to my prayers."

When Walker pressed around Soon-hee's stomach, he didn't wince at all. Then the doctor stood back, draping his stethoscope around his neck.

"Well, now, you're almost as good as new, Mr. Oh. I think you'll be able to return to your dormitory tomorrow, but only if you follow my instructions closely." He wagged a finger. "No more kimchi."

"I understand and will obey. When might I be able to eat Korean food again?"

"Let's not cross that bridge until we get to it. I know it won't be for a while, though, not until your digestive system is back to normal—and then only gradually." He smiled. "If you want me to talk to your mother about this, I'll be happy to do so."

"Thank you. I think she will understand or at least comply with your wishes."

"I'm glad I came to Pyongyang when I did so I could take care of you. I think our Lord wanted me to be here."

"I believe so as well."

"I'll be going back to Severance the day after tomorrow to resume my duties there."

His shoulders slumped. "I will miss you, Dr. Walker." He started worrying about having a setback without this man's watchful eye on him.

"Miss Story has instructions for your ongoing care, and I'll stay in close touch with her about your progress. Do you think you could come to Seoul in about two weeks to see me for a check-up?"

Soon-hee sat up straighter. "Do you think I will be up to such a journey by then?"

"I don't see why not. Now that there's a train connecting the two cities, the trip will be much easier."

"I would enjoy coming to Seoul to see you."

"Well then, Mr. Oh, I look forward to catching up one last time on my rounds tomorrow. I promised to go to Anju today to do a clinic, and your sister and mother are going to help me out. Don't worry, though. Miss Story will stay here with you."

"May I pray for you before you go?"

Walker grinned. "Yes, thank you very much."

"I thought I might find you here."

Soon-hee raised his head from a commentary on Galatians and smiled at Mr. Blair. "I find there is not so much traffic here in the library as in the YMCA."

"How right you are." The missionary gestured to a chair across from his student. "Mind if I sit?"

"Not at all." He pushed the book and his tablet to the side, sensing his teacher had something on his mind.

With a glance at the formidable Korean librarian, Blair lowered his voice. "You're looking so much better than when I saw you in the infirmary. How are you feeling?"

Warmth spread through his middle. "I am healthy again, thanks be to God."

"Do you have any restrictions, besides doing your work at a reduced speed and minding your diet?"

"I am free to go about life again, just more carefully."

Blair raised his right hand to his mouth and cleared his throat quietly. "I understand you're going to Seoul in a few days to see Dr. Walker."

"Yes, this is true."

"I have a favor to ask—that is, if you feel up to it." He seemed to hesitate.

"Please, Mr. Blair, do share your thoughts with me."

"A couple of missionaries will be arriving just then at Chemulpo. One of them, Dr. Cullen, has been here once before."

Soon-hee grinned. "I remember him. He always slipped American candy to me when my parents were unaware."

Blair laughed. "This time he's coming with a wife and a recent graduate of Princeton Theological Seminary. The

Board of Foreign Missions is sending him here for a year to assist with the translation work. I heard he's a wizard with languages."

Soon-hee's brow wrinkled. "A wizard?"

"I meant to say he's unusually gifted. Sometimes, I forget and use slang expressions. Anyway, there's also a new physician who'll be working at Severance Hospital. Miss Story will be going to meet him and his family at Chemulpo, then accompanying them to Seoul. They're all traveling together, and I'd like the two of you to meet them at the boat. Then, you can go to Severance to see Dr. Walker and return on the train with the Cullens and Mr. Kichline. That is, if you think you can manage."

Ah, but life felt good again. "I will be happy to do this, Mr. Blair."

"Wonderful. And of course, if you don't feel well during the trip, Miss Story will take good care of you. Let's hope, of course, that all goes smoothly." He breathed in, seeming satisfied. "Can you meet me in my office at teatime to discuss details?"

"I will be there."

CHAPTER SEVENTEEN

September - October 1906
Easton, Pennsylvania to Chempulo, Korea

The train bearing its native son away began its slow chug from Easton Station, Jacob's vision blurring as he waved to his family. He cast a final look at his church's iconic steeple, then glanced back to his mother who fluttered her white handkerchief as if in surrender. She'd promised not to cry when she saw him off, but even at a distance he could tell by her trembling chin what an effort she was making. His father tipped his hat to Jacob with one hand and held his wife close with the other while his two brothers seemed to be shouting, and his two sisters offered tear-streaked smiles. An urge to bolt from the crowded passenger car almost overtook him. A job at the silk mill might not be so bad after all, or he could do as several other Princeton seminary graduates and take a year of study in Germany or Scotland. At least he'd understand the language.

He closed his eyes and drew in a deep breath. His hand was to the plow, there was no turning back. He looked to the train platform one last time and saw Harry Flory signaling him and smiling as if to cheer him on. Jacob waved, replaying his best friend's last words to him, "I truly believe this is the right path for you, for now." Encouraged, he clung to the message like a faltering swimmer to a life raft. Besides, this stint was only going to be for a year. Someday, he'd be able to tell his grandchildren thrilling stories of his foreign adventures. He wondered whether they would be his and Pearl's.

His family, friend, and home slipped from his sight.

October 4, 1906

San Francisco, California

Dear Mother and Father, Robert, Grace, Mae, and Teddy, Greetings from your wandering nomad at the City by the Bay. I trust this finds you well. Dr. and Mrs. Cullen and I arrived late this morning following nearly five days of cross-country travel. I began writing to you on several occasions but constantly needed to abandon my efforts to gape outside the train windows. I felt as though I were living the words of "America the Beautiful" while beholding amber waves of grain, fruited plains, and purple mountain majesties. Dr. Cullen said he enjoyed the scenery too, but I could tell the panoramic views did not affect him as deeply as they did his wife and me. I took several rolls of film with the Folding Kodak you gave me and when I get the photos developed, you'll be receiving some in future letters. I so appreciate this gift, which is enabling me to capture what I'm experiencing first-hand.

We arrived in San Francisco just a few hours ago, and you can imagine how jarring the sight has been. The sparkling bay provides a vivid contrast to the ghostly shells of once-splendid buildings brought low by the earthquake and subsequent fires back in April. They remind me of photos I've seen from the Civil War. Eighty percent of the city was devastated by the disasters, and most of the survivors are living in makeshift shelters in small communities as they rebuild. The sound of hammers can be heard throughout the city providing a noisy but optimistic backdrop.

We were downcast to find most of the hotels are not yet operational, but relief came when we discovered one of them offering small-scale lodging with reduced services. My room has the feel of a dormitory and alas, there will be no fabled dining with gleaming crystal and dinnerware. Just to be still without the train rocking underneath me constantly is a luxury however, and we'll only be here for two days before catching the *SS America Maru* steamship.

As we anticipated, the young Methodist family I told you about has joined us here. Dr. Allen Davis is a physician assigned to Severance Hospital in Seoul. Imagine being his three-and-five-year-old children going off to such a strange land! The little boy's name is Harold, and I smiled when he asked me to call him "Harry." I told him my best friend shares the same name, and we have bonded quickly over this happy coincidence. His older sister is Iris, and she's as adorable as little girls come. I'm happy to have such marvelous companions for my voyage.

I'll write to you again once I'm at sea, as I understand the Pacific Steamship Mail Company allows passengers to send letters along the way to their destinations.
May God bless and keep you all. Please write and share all the little details of your lives with me, as well as news of Easton so I don't get too homesick.

Your devoted son and brother,

Jacob

He put down the pen, a gift from Harry, and flexed his fingers. Under normal circumstances he would have begun writing to Pearl, but these were definitely not normal circumstances. Just outside a young boy pulled a wagon, bumping over the wooden sidewalk, and Jacob considered what his life must be like. He related to the fellow, each of them on uncertain terrain, not knowing what would be happening next. His thoughts circled back to Pearl, to the sentiment she'd embroidered about God completing the work he'd begun. Somewhere beneath the rubble of his once-certain faith, he still believed. Maybe, like this little fellow, the time had come to rebuild.

"Beautiful, isn't it?"

Jacob turned his head in the direction of the familiar voice. "Good morning, Mr. Cullen. Yes, the ocean is so vast, so ... If I were an artist, I could attempt to paint what I'm seeing, but I'm not sure I'd be able to find the right colors to do this beautiful sight justice."

They lingered by the railing, the wind making a hash of their hair. At seven-thirty, the ship's daily routine was underway, its crew carrying out their work.

"The way the water foams as we pass through intrigues me," Jacob said. Then he turned to his companion. "How is Mrs. Cullen feeling this morning?"

"Much better. I was up at six and brought her some toast and weak tea, which she's been able to keep down."

"That's good."

"And what about you? You seemed a bit green around the gills yesterday."

Jacob grinned. "I felt a little seasick, but today I'm fine. I just ate breakfast and came here for some fresh air."

"Yesterday's heaving waves were no respecter of persons. I'm happy the sea is mostly calm today and hope it will stay this way."

His eyes turned from the boundless expanse to a group of chattering passengers setting up small blankets in one corner of the top deck. “What do you suppose those Orientals are doing?” Jacob asked.

Cullen watched them before giving his opinion. “I think they’re about to gamble at cards and dice, their way of passing the time.”

Jacob saw a dignified older man in a shiny black hat with a high crown, something like a small opera hat. His white silk coat featured enormously wide sleeves that fluttered as he passed by the group of men and settled into his own space. A few of the crew pointed to him, whispering and laughing, but he seemed to take no notice.

“I can tell by his clothing that man is Korean,” Cullen said. “Let’s go talk to him.”

Jacob wasn’t as gregarious as his companion but meeting his first Korean was going to be interesting to say the least.

“Good day, sir.”

The man looked up and gave a bow of his head.

Cullen spoke slowly. “We are American missionaries on our way to serve in Korea.”

The man frowned until the last word, Korea, which he repeated with a smile.

“Yes, and I’d like to introduce myself.” He pressed his right hand to his chest. “I’m Dennis Cullen, and this is Jacob Kichline.”

The man looked from one to the other, his face blank.

“Do you speak English?”

“Eng-lish?” His eyes widened, then he closed them and shook his head.

“Maybe I should try some Korean,” Cullen told Jacob. He repeated his greeting in the man’s language.

The fellow's eyes sparkled, and he began speaking rapidly, leaving Jacob dazed. When he and Cullen lifted their hands in resignation, the Korean closed his eyes and leaned back his head as if he understood. The Americans took their leave of him with resigned, though polite, smiles and bows.

At a safe distance, a sheepish Cullen turned to Jacob. "What do you think of your teacher's language skills now?"

He was quick to reassure the man. "If you couldn't understand him, I don't see how anyone could. He spoke so fast."

"Clearly, we both still have a lot of Korean to learn."

Three days later, they were strolling the deck with Mrs. Cullen, exclaiming over the sight of dolphins following the ship, when they encountered the same man. In the background, the never-ending card and dice games continued. Jacob followed the Cullens as they approached the Korean and offered a slowly spoken, simple greeting.

"*Annyeong haseyo.*"

"Ah, *annyeong haseyo.*"

"This is the man I was telling you about," Cullen said.

Eileen Cullen curtsied and smiled, and the man answered with a bob of his head.

A middle-aged Japanese passenger came over to them and bowed.

"Good day, gentlemen. I see you are trying to converse with this man. Perhaps I can help."

"Do you speak Korean?" Cullen asked. "I do, but not well enough to understand his rapid speech patterns."

"Yes, I do. What do you wish to communicate to him?"

"We are American missionaries on our way to Pyongyang to preach, teach, and do translation work. I am Mr. Cullen, and this is my wife. This is Mr. Kichline."

"I am Mr. Ito and am happy to make your acquaintance." The Japanese man took a tablet and began writing in characters Jacob didn't recognize.

"What language are you using? Is this Chinese?" he asked.

"You are observant, young man. Yes." Ito continued writing as he spoke. "This is the classical Chinese language that Japanese and Koreans also understand."

When he finished, he handed the paper to the older man, who smiled as he read. He took the pen and wrote his reply, which Mr. Ito then interpreted.

"He says, 'My name is Whang. I am not a Christian, but I am glad that you are going to Korea to help my people.'"

Something about the connection they were making warmed Jacob, who felt drawn to this old fellow in the strange get-up. He watched as the Korean waved them closer while he wrote another message.

Ito reported back. "He says he would like to teach you some Korean words and phrases if you like."

Jacob and Mrs. Cullen nodded their agreement, and the professor answered for them. "Please tell Mr. Whang we are very grateful for his generous offer, and we accept."

In a letter to his family a week later, Jacob wrote in detail about their new teacher and how he was helping them become even more familiar with the Korean language.

> I have spent a few hours each day in Mr. Whang's company, drawing from his vast vocabulary. Since he doesn't speak English, we don't have conversations, but I'm amazed at how much we manage to communicate with each other anyway. His open-air classroom provides extraordinary sights of flying fish and gray whales

while the crew goes about their duties. Always in the background are a group of other Orientals playing never-ending games of chance on their mats. Mr. Whang is a kind, patient instructor. He's helping us further understand social nuancing, which is so important to Koreans. For example, when a person is speaking with an elder, honorific language must be used, as opposed to casual expressions. Mr. Cullen had previously taught me things like not looking directly at one's elder and to not say "no," but to politely be indirect instead. When I put these principles into practice with Mr. Whang, he smiles at my efforts.

Little Harry and Iris also sit in and listen, and Mr. Whang teaches them a word a day. In fact, we adults are very much like those children since only Mr. Cullen has had any Korean language training. I like him a lot, and I'm especially touched by his spirit of humility and respect as he sits under the instruction of our new Korean friend, who is not a Christian. By now, I've written in a notebook one hundred-and-fifty words Mr. Whang has taught us. I hope to reach two hundred by the time we get to Yokohama where we'll be changing steamers. That's also where our dear new friend and our party will go our separate ways.

The ship began its docking paces, and Jacob watched with his group, eager for one last encounter with Mr. Whang. Harry and Iris bobbed up and down on tiptoes looking for the elderly Korean, holding a card they had made for him, which the Americans had all signed. Jacob had wanted to give him a present too, uncertain as to what might be meaningful to someone from such a vastly divergent culture. He'd settled on a silk scarf his grandmother had given him for Christmas. At last, with the steamer's docking whistle sounding in their ears, and the circling of gulls overhead, Mr. Whang appeared, bowing to the Americans.

Jacob stepped forward but before he could present the gift, the Korean began handing each of the couples and Jacob a motto written in his own hand. He also gave everyone red silk handkerchiefs.

"You are so kind, Mr. Whang," Cullen said. "You have given us so much."

Jacob bowed to Whang before handing him the scarf, which he took with a great smile and an answering bob. When Iris and Harry encircled and hugged his legs, the Korean kissed the tops of their heads.

Once they were ensconced on a small freighter bound for Chemulpo, a vessel far beneath the dignity of the *America Maru*, Jacob sat on his tiny bed below decks and fished out Mr. Whang's cloth motto. For the better part of two hours, he worked at translating what the dear man had inscribed: *Jeneun haeng-wiga badneun geotboda deo maneun chukbokgwa haengbogeul gajyeoda jumnida.* Jacob then spoke aloud, "The act of giving brings more happiness than receiving."

The freighter took the Americans across the Sea of Japan, Jacob entranced by the pine mountains, cascading falls, and islands. Sometimes, he spotted the curved roofs of temples almost concealed by enfolding forests and took in boat-speckled fishing villages. At sunset, they reached the last of the Japanese ports and headed west through the Korean Strait.

Jacob volunteered to stay with a frightened Harry and Iris throughout what became a storm-tossed night, succumbing twice to the urge to unload his stomach. He only snatched small pockets of sleep, vigilant to his little friends' fears and suffering, as well as their parents' abject incapacitation. When morning finally dawned, the sea had turned calmer. Dr. Davis was able to minister to his family, thanking Jacob, who cleaned himself up and went topside for a look at the port city where they would disembark.

He'd expected to see basic, plank-built dwellings. However, the appearance of industrial brick, stone, and iron-constructed buildings elbowing the others as if for supremacy took him by surprise.

"I thought we'd be in a more backward situation," he told Dennis Cullen, who joined him.

"A lot of Korea is behind our modern times, but the Japanese are transforming key port cities like this one. You'll find a lot of Japanese here, as well as people from many other nations."

Jacob intuited there would be a lot more surprises in the coming year, hopefully mostly good ones.

"Tell me, Mr. Cullen, how will we be going ashore again?"

"We'll be taking a vessel called a *sampan*. Once we disembark at Chemulpo, our emissary from the Pyongyang mission is supposed to be meeting us there."

Jacob fell silent, all at once feeling as he did when he was five years old and got separated from his mother at Bush and Bull's. He startled when Cullen kneaded his shoulder.

"I remember my first trip here, Jacob, overwhelmed by the strangeness of my surroundings. Remember how the

Lord in his goodness sent us Mr. Whang." He pointed to the distant hills. "Somewhere beyond those mountains are more men and women like him who are hungry for the eternal food we can supply."

CHAPTER EIGHTEEN

OCTOBER 1906
PYONGYANG, KOREA

Soon-hee may have been twenty-three years old, but he left the missionary complex with a youthful step and boyish grin. There was nothing like feeling well again and having the freedom to travel, especially on the Gyeongui Line, the recently-opened single-gauge railway connecting Pyongyang to Seoul.

"You seem chipper today, Mr. Oh," Clara Story said after they boarded.

"Thank you, I am." He was so absorbed in the ambience and multitude of conversations that he missed what she said next. "I do apologize, but I did not hear you just now."

"I asked if you've ever been on a train before."

A large woman squeezed next to him, thumping a cage with chickens onto the floor and narrowly missing his left foot. She excused herself, and he bowed his head to receive her apology.

"This is my first time, Miss Story. I guess you have been on many trains."

"Yes, I have, but not before I answered God's call to come to Korea."

"How does this one compare with your American trains?"

She puckered her brow, as if deciding how best to give a prudent response. "Since there's been train travel for many years in America, our passenger cars are, well, a bit fancier."

Soon-hee considered the simple wood-framed windows and hard seats. *Ah well, my Hermit Kingdom has to begin modernizing somewhere.* He changed the subject, trying to ignore the unsettled chickens kicking up dust. Most of the passengers were talking fast and gesturing in their excitement, some in Korean, others in Japanese, the rest in Chinese.

"I want to say thank you for not telling my mother about my going to Seoul and Chemulpo. I would not want her to worry, and since I will be back in less than two days, she likely will not miss me."

"Sometimes mothers overdo their concern for us." She sneezed and reached for a handkerchief.

"How do your parents feel about your being in a country so far away?"

"They've become used to the idea. Initially, they tried to talk me out of it, even arranged for me to meet a few young men they hoped would entice me to stay in Roanoke. That's in the state of Virginia where I'm from."

"I sense God's call was greater."

"Yes, Mr. Oh." She pushed back a stray piece of hair from her brown eyes. "And now here I am, and they're reconciling themselves to my becoming what we call a spinster."

"Spinster?" He tasted the strange word.

"An unmarried woman."

The train began pulling out of the station commencing the four-hour-plus excursion.

"Do you hope one day to marry?" he asked.

"I believe God may just have someone for me, and if so, we'll meet at the right time and the right place."

He recalled a handful of young American men and women who'd come to Korea single and left married. Perhaps the same would happen to Miss Story, whom he guessed to be close to him in age. Considering her strength, comeliness, and devotion, Soon-hee thought her chances at matrimony to be rather good.

He hadn't been to Seoul since before the Russo-Japanese War and found himself doing constant double-takes. The population seemed to have doubled. Ditches that used to pass for streets were now wide, clean, and dry thoroughfares teeming with people. While there were the usual oxcarts, sedan chairs, and litters, they now shared the thoroughfare with sleek electric trolleys. He couldn't wait to ride one. While he'd heard they were a fixture in American cities, trolleys had just come to Seoul three years earlier. He reached up and touched the brim of his Derby hat, pleased with his decision to wear American-style clothing today. He thought appearing in such a fashion to newly-arrived missionaries might help ease their transition while demonstrating his country's more modern visage.

The train's passengers began jostling in the aisles, grabbing packages, and clinging to the sides of their seats as the vehicle lurched to a halt.

Soon-hee raised his voice to be heard. "How far away is the hospital, Miss Story?"

"Just under three miles. Since we have overnight bags and packages, we should use the trolley rather than walk." She looked from him to the crowd, then back again. "If we get separated, meet me by the trolley stand over there." Clara pointed outside to the waiting fleet.

Soon-hee rose from his seat and squeezed through the throng and its conversational babel. Above their heads Clara Story's raised hand appeared, and he headed over to her.

The first trolley filled rapidly, and they waited with their possessions for the next, affording him a chance to catch his breath. Within a few minutes, they were able to board a second one and traveled quickly to Severance Hospital where Soon-hee openly gaped at the two-story brick building. He had never seen the likes of it in his country. Although this was his first visit, through the missionaries, he'd come to feel an association with the two-year-old hospital and its medical college. However, he hadn't anticipated Severance being this magnificent.

Clara smiled at his open admiration. "I felt the same way when I came here for the first time. This hospital is even more modern than many you'd find in the United States. I just love the Greek Revival style and those Queen Anne turrets."

He shared his thoughts. "I did not imagine it would be this impressive. So much good can take place here."

"Yes, indeed. Well, Mr. Oh, I believe you have an appointment to keep before we go to Chemulpo."

His rumbling stomach didn't escape her notice.

"I do think we both need some lunch before either of those two things." She smiled at his pinking cheeks. "A meal will give us time to take a break. Don't you just feel like we've been taken up in a whirlwind?"

Soon-hee smiled at her description. He'd done more living in the past day than in the last few months. While the trip had exhilarated him, his entire body had begun to sink into general fatigue. *I know I will feel renewed once we have a meal.*

He followed her into the lobby where a young Korean lady greeted them at a reception desk, and Clara explained who they were.

"Ah, yes, Dr. Walker told me to be on the watch for you. You may leave your bundles right here with me, and someone will take them to your rooms. Mr. Oh, you will be sleeping in the hospital's guest quarters, and Miss Story, you will stay with the new doctor and his family in an adjoining building."

"Thank you. We could both use some lunch. Where might we get food?" Clara asked.

"There's a diet kitchen just down the hall," the receptionist said. "I will show you the way."

Andrew Walker crossed his arms and smiled. Speaking in Korean he said, "Mr. Oh, I'm happy to say you're doing quite well."

His tension released. "Thank you, and thanks be to God. You may use English if you like."

"I may resort to some, but I'd like to practice my Korean if you don't mind."

"That will be fine."

"I must say, I've never seen someone who was in your condition heal so quickly. You had me pretty concerned back in Pyongyang. Normally this process takes months and for some unfortunates, is never complete." He lowered his chin. "I must caution you, however, not to overtax your system or stray from your current diet. You may have the occasional bite, but for a year at least, you need to be cautious. I also want to see you every three months for a check-up." He winked. "Do you need a letter from me to your mother?"

Soon-hee chuckled. "Perhaps when you see her again, you might remind her not to be offended when I do not eat her spicy food."

"I'll be sure to speak to her as well," Clara said.

"As for medication, I suggest you keep some on hand when you have a flare-up. Recurrences are to be expected, but we don't want them to be frequent or ongoing. In fact, this trip is strenuous, so I'd like you to be taking the medication until you get back home. Miss Story, please make sure he eats regularly." He rubbed his hands together. "I understand you'll be spending the night here with some missionaries, including a new doctor. Dr. Avison was telling me about them."

"That is correct," Soon-hee said. "One of them is a recent Princeton Seminary graduate who will work with me on translation."

"We're going to meet their boat in three hours." Clara looked at the wall clock.

"You'd best be on your way then in case there are any delays. Mr. Oh, Dr. Avison looks forward to seeing you again when you get back."

"He is a great man." He had met Severance Hospital's director on several occasions in Pyongyang and very much admired the dedicated missionary doctor.

"One more thing—on the train to Chemulpo, try to get some sleep."

"You will get no argument from me," Soon-hee said.

"When was the last time you were in Chemulpo, Mr. Oh?"

He blew out a breath, searching his memory as he surveyed the portside landscape near the station. "A long time ago, perhaps ten years. I do not recognize any of what I am seeing."

"How has the city changed?" Clara asked.

"This place used to be little more than plank houses and small shops." He moved a finger from side-to-side. "There were none of these brick and stone buildings then." *Or so many Japanese.*

"The blend of styles intrigues me," she said. "I notice Korean, of course, but also Japanese."

He stopped short of saying, "They have taken over my country in so many ways."

Korea also was becoming more modern. *But are my people growing in their walk with the Lord Jesus? Are they as eager for him as they are for new technologies?* He wondered how God would choose to answer the missionaries' many prayers to renew the people.

The train whistle announced its arrival.

"I'm glad we left Seoul when we did," Clara said. "Fortunately, the rain has stopped, and we're just on time to meet the boat. Do you think you can make a run to the dock?"

Did he have any other choice? By the time they reached the correct one, his heart was pounding. Passengers flowed down the gangplank, the atmosphere redolent of salt air and soot.

"There they are!" Clara pointed to a rumpled group of Americans, including two young children pulling at their mother's bell-shaped skirt.

He and the nurse moved closer, smiling and waving at them. When they noticed Soon-hee and Clara, they gestured back and flowed in their direction.

"Good day. You must be here from the mission," the tallest man said. When he tipped his hat, he revealed silvery blonde hair, which seemed suited to someone far older.

Soon-hee had to speak up to be heard over the concert of horns and sirens. He decided to use English in order to make them more comfortable. "Welcome to Korea." He bowed as the Americans gathered around him. "I am Soon-hee Oh, and this is Miss Clara Story."

"I'm happy to meet you both." The man shook his hand. "I'm Professor Dennis Cullen, and this is my wife Eileen. These are Dr. and Mrs. Davis, Harry and Iris."

When Iris curtsied, Soon-hee bowed at the tiny girl in a red dress with white lace, receiving in turn a coy giggle. Her brother clapped his own hands over his ears as if to shut out the harborside din.

"And this is Mr. Jacob Kichline," Cullen said.

"I'm pleased to meet you, Mr. Oh. I'm happy to know you speak English."

He stuck out his hand to the golden-thatched young man who appeared as dazed as everyone except Mr. Cullen. The professor was bouncing on his toes, as if he couldn't wait to see what there was to see, all at once.

Iris turned forlorn. "Mama, this place is so noisy. When will we get to Seoul?"

Mrs. Davis said, "Perhaps Mr. Hee can tell us."

He didn't bother to correct her misuse of his name. "We will take the train there, which lasts for two hours. Then, we will go on a brief trolley ride to the Severance Hospital."

Clara broke in, bending low to address the children. "That's where your new home is. Just think, you're almost there, and there's so much to see from the train along the way."

"Dr. and Mrs. Cullen and Mr. Kichline, you will spend the night at Severance in various guest quarters," Soon-hee added.

The professor's face shone. "And just two days from now, Mrs. Cullen and I will be in the district we've been assigned to distributing literature before joining these two gentlemen in Pyongyang."

Soon-hee noticed Eileen Cullen's wilting aspect. She needed a good rest before doing any of those activities.

Clara looked to the women. "How did you find the voyage?"

Mrs. Davis opened her mouth, seeming to search for diplomatic words but before she could say anything, little Iris spoke up.

"Most of us got sick on the ocean, but then we got better. The steamship was grand, but that thing not so much." She pulled a face and gestured at the prosaic freighter.

Clara laughed as Mrs. Davis's face colored. "Out of the mouths of babes," she said.

That night, Soon-hee stretched and yawned on the hospital cot.

"You seem as wrung out as I am," Jacob Kichline said. "I can't believe it's only nine o'clock."

"This seems to have been a rather full day for us both."

The American pulled off his dust-covered shoes and placed them under the small bed. "If you don't mind, I think I'll go to sleep now."

"Not at all. I will as well."

Adjoining the men's ward, their guest room in the hospital was a space just big enough for two small beds and a chest of drawers. When they had pulled the shade on the lone window and crawled under the crisp sheets, Soon-hee flipped the wall light switch off.

"I was surprised to see that there's electricity here," Kichline said.

Soon-hee might have taken offense but realized when a person was exhausted, prudence wasn't always at hand. "Seoul is rapidly modernizing."

"What about Pyongyang and the mission? Are they modern?"

He detected an anxious note. "We combine Western technologies with Korean customs. When you travel to outlying areas, however, you will feel you have stepped back in time." He paused. "Do you come from the country or a city?"

He yawned. "Please excuse me. I've never been this tired before. I come from a small city—Easton in the state of Pennsylvania."

"This is, I believe, on the eastern coast?"

"Yes, that's right." He yawned again. "I apologize. I don't mean to be rude."

"There is no need," Soon-hee said.

They fell asleep almost at once to sound of the nurse's feet shuffling in the ward outside their door and muffled conversations in English. Somewhere, a patient was coughing. An hour later, the two men awakened with a heart-pounding start to piercing screams.

"What in the world?" The American bolted upright.

"Someone is in distress."

"Should we try to help?"

"Let us wait." Soon-hee turned on the light, blinking against its ambush. The shrieking continued.

If the situation hadn't been so concerning, he might have burst out laughing at the geyser of blond hair shooting up from Jacob's head. His astonishingly blue eyes were wide open. Soon-hee had never seen eyes that color before and would have liked to study them further but could not without being ill-mannered.

Dr. Walker's voice carried for several moments, then laughter broke out.

"I will see what happened." Five minutes passed before Soon-hee returned grinning.

"What in the world happened?" Jacob asked.

"A boy from an outlying village was brought here for an emergency appendectomy. When he woke up, he encountered a strange face looking back at him and began screaming."

Jacob's face went ashen. "What strange face?"

"His own reflection. He had never seen a mirror before or known what he looks like."

When Soon-hee turned the light back off, he heard the new missionary murmur, "What kind of place is this?" He told himself not to make premature judgements.

CHAPTER NINETEEN

LATE OCTOBER 1906
SEOUL, KOREA

On that first night in Korea, Jacob slept erratically, flipping around like a hooked fish even when he did manage to nod off. The journey had left him completely overstimulated, and his mind struggled to catch up with this latest of his new surroundings. When daylight tiptoed into the room, he listened to the shifts changing in the ward while pondering the day ahead. After breakfast, the hospital's chief administrator, Dr. Avison, would be giving the new missionaries a tour of Severance Hospital. Then, Jacob and Soon-hee Oh would go with the Cullens to see the nearby district assigned to their care. The young couple would stay for a few days to get acquainted with the church's leaders and some of the members. When that tour concluded, Jacob and his fellow worker would return to Seoul to catch the train to Pyongyang. He breathed out, wishing they could just go to their final destination without the side trip.

He looked over at the sleeping figure across the room, assessing him without risk of being rude for gawking.

He smiled as he recalled his mother's stern admonition, drilled into him from boyhood, not to stare at people who were unusual. In the half light, Jacob surveyed the man's smooth black hair and distinct Oriental eyes. Mr. Cullen had mentioned Soon-hee's recent seminary graduation and current doctoral studies, which Jacob figured would make him roughly his own age. Yesterday at the dock, he'd expected Soon-hee to show up in Korean clothing but had been pleasantly surprised to see him in a Western suit and Derby hat similar to Jacob's own. He'd also anticipated Soon-hee to be diminutive, but when they'd stood next to each other, Jacob took him to be about Harry Flory's size. He was, however, thinner than his Lafayette pal.

Jacob also found him to be quick-witted and kind, what his sisters might call charming. On the train to Seoul, little Harry Davis had burrowed into Soon-hee's side as if they'd known each other far longer. He pictured the two of them with Soon-hee's arm enfolding the little boy, an endearing image he'd captured with his camera. And last night when the hospital ward erupted in shrieks, Soon-hee had made light of the situation when he'd discovered the reason behind the young patient's distress. "When I first saw my own reflection, I also felt like screaming."

Despite the Korean's vastly different background, Jacob thought he just might get along well with him. He started getting out of bed when he nearly jumped out of his skin at the sound of a metal object crashing to the floor just outside the room. As his heart thudded, his roommate stirred. Soon-hee opened his eyes and met Jacob's grin.

The missionaries who'd traveled together to Korea gathered for an American-style breakfast of eggs, bacon, crisp toast with butter and jam, coffee and tea. Jacob had chosen the coffee, a lot of coffee. By the time Dr. Avison began his tour at eight-thirty, Jacob was ready to take on the new day in a new world.

"As you may know, this hospital is dear to my heart, and I look forward to showing you why," Avison said as they sat in the cafeteria.

Jacob liked the affable forty-something Canadian with thinning brown hair, a full mustache, and spectacles. Oliver Avison reminded him of a mellower version of President Roosevelt, which turned Jacob's thought to Win. He wondered how his Princeton friend was coming along at Harvard. At least he'd be in his element there, not in some remote corner of Asia.

"First, I'd like to tell you how Severance Hospital got started," Avison said. "At the end of the last century, there was a coup against the royal government, and in the conflict, the queen's nephew was stabbed several times. He hovered near death, and the American missionary Horace Allen was brought in to treat the young man's wounds. His expertise and compassion helped open the door here to Western medical practices. The Korean government and some American charities got together to open a hospital here in 1885. It was called *Chejungwon*, which in English means 'House of Universal Helpfulness.'"

His eyes twinkled when little Iris Davis stifled a yawn.

"I promise not to ramble. For several years, the Korean government funded the operational expenses, and the North American Presbyterian Mission ran the hospital. Not only was modern medicine brought to this land, but Christianity was promoted as well. In the early years, there were a lot of challenges. Dr. Allen returned to the United States, and a new director, Dr. Heron, took over. Unfortunately, he died just a few years later. At the time, I was a medical professor at the University of Toronto, and I was keenly interested in Korea. When asked, I agreed to take charge of the hospital. That was back in 1893."

Jacob sat forward, rapt. The idea that someone had loved this country and been eager to come here fascinated him. Then again, didn't the Cullens and the Davises feel the same way? For Jacob, Korea had felt like a last resort.

Avison continued. "This place was in profound disarray when I got here, and I insisted on various reforms if they were going to keep me. By the next September, the Presbyterian Mission took ownership of the hospital, and they put it under my direction. Our main goal was to promote healing and evangelization."

Dennis Cullen raised his hand. "How did this come to be called Severance Hospital?"

"That's a story in itself. Just like Dr. Allen who was before me here, I wanted to open a medical school to train Koreans. However, there wasn't any money for such an enterprise. In 1899, when I returned to North America on sabbatical, I made a number of presentations in the US and Canada and always mentioned my dream. At one such meeting, a philanthropist named Louis Henry Severance donated $10,000 to fund both a new hospital and a medical school in Seoul. When I returned to Korea, we immediately set to work. We broke ground in 1902, and two years later, Severance Memorial Hospital opened its doors."

The tour broke up nearly two hours later, and Jacob said an emotional goodbye to the Davis family. They were leaving to begin getting settled in their new apartment on the hospital campus.

Mrs. Davis offered her hand. "What a pleasure to have met and traveled with you, Mr. Kichline."

"The pleasure was mine."

He choked up when misty-eyed, Iris asked, "Would you please come and visit us here?"

He bent down. "I'll do my best, and if you come to Pyongyang, you need to come see me."

She threw her arms around his neck, and he breathed in the freshness of guileless childhood. He'd never imagined he'd get this close to the missionaries and their little ones.

"Mr. Kichline, we shall keep you in our prayers," Dr. Davis said.

"Thank you." He wondered if, when they'd had prayer and Bible study on the ship, anyone beside Dr. Cullen had suspected the degree of his spiritual unrest. They were treating him as if he were their equal in maturity, and something inside him didn't want to let them down.

He watched them leave the hospital's entryway, waving at Iris and Harry when they looked back at him. He noticed the Cullens and Clara Story conferring with Dr. Avison while Soon-hee was talking to the receptionist. Jacob frowned upon noticing the subtle trembling of Soon-hee's arms as he leaned against the desk. Clara broke away from her small group and motioned to Jacob.

"Might I have a word, Mr. Kichline?"

"Yes, of course."

"I prefer to go to the courtyard for some fresh air."

He welcomed the opportunity to follow the lovely nurse outside where they sat on a bench. When she smoothed back a lock of her brown hair loosened by a gentle wind, her light brown eyes seemed to invite his confidence. Ever since he'd met her the day before at Chemulpo, he'd been drawn to her. She wasn't as pretty or dainty as Pearl, but instead conveyed a sense of strong beauty, a woman who seemed to know her own mind without putting herself forward.

"I do hope you're not too disappointed, but there's been a slight change of plans. Instead of going with Mr. and Mrs. Cullen to the village then coming back here for the train, you and Mr. Oh will be heading back to Pyongyang."

While Jacob welcomed the less arduous itinerary, he worried something might be wrong. He searched her expression for any hints of distress and found none. In fact, she was a picture of serenity.

"I don't mind, but I can't help wonder what caused the change."

"Mr. Oh was recently ill, and although he made a good recovery, I can tell this trip has been a bit much for him."

He tugged his necktie. "Is he in any danger?"

"No, not if he doesn't push himself anymore. I'd still like to stay here for a few days to help the Davises get settled, but I'll need you to look after Mr. Oh. Can you do that?"

He was willing to help, but he was no doctor. "I guess so. I don't have any medical training, though. What would I do to help him?"

"Just make sure he rests on the train and eats regularly, including a snack. I'll prepare a sack with food to take with him in case the train doesn't offer enough things he can safely have."

"Sure, I can handle that. May I ask what his illness is?" He searched her face, trying to disguise his open admiration. If he got sick in Korea, at least she'd be taking care of him.

"I don't think he'd mind your knowing. He had a bleeding ulcer, and Dr. Walker successfully treated him at the mission's hospital. Mr. Oh had a check-up yesterday, and he's in pretty good shape. It's just that the large amount of moving around on trains and trolleys and the lack of routine seem to have set him back a little. We don't want him to relapse."

"I understand." He paused, looking at his nails and realizing they required attention. "Since I'll be working closely with him, would it be okay if I called him Soon-hee? 'Mr. Oh' seems so formal, but I understand Koreans pay a lot of attention to such things. I don't want to insult him or anything."

Clara smiled. "I'm glad you asked. Back home, being on a first-name basis would make some sense, however not here, Mr. Kichline. We missionaries use formal address to show our respect for the Korean people. Every man is 'Mister,' and every woman is 'Missus.' We're laboring side-by-side with them in the Lord's vineyard. We're here to plant a Korean Church, not an American one. Many of the missionaries hold doctoral degrees, but we only refer to them as 'Mister' so we're all on a more even keel. Only the physicians are called 'Doctor,' so they can be readily identified to provide treatment. By our words and actions, we demonstrate the confidence we have in the Koreans' ability to govern their own churches once they've received sound training."

Jacob mulled this over. He'd always thought of the Koreans as inferiors, so this was going to require an attitude adjustment. "Thanks for explaining this to me."

"It's my pleasure. Believe me, Mr. Kichline, everyone who has come here has had a lot to learn, myself included. If you open your mind and your heart, though, you'll be amazed at how much you'll grow as a man and as a Christian."

Jacob took a seat on the locomotive across from Soon-hee, catching the eye of a well-dressed Oriental man across from them and two rows back. He noticed his new friend's furrowed brow when the two men exchanged glances. *I wonder what that was all about.*

When they got settled in, Soon-hee addressed Jacob. "You seem to be especially joyful, Mr. Kichline." His voice carried a hint of smokiness.

He grinned like a boy. "I like trains, and this reminds me of the ones back home."

Soon-hee smiled, and Jacob noticed dimpling, which softened his companion's appearance.

"I should think this train would feel familiar to you. The *Gyeongui Line* steam locomotives were built in your country."

"You don't say. When did they start running?"

"Just this year."

Once again, something in Soon-hee's sudden shift in manner led Jacob to believe there was more to this story.

He laughed. "I was expecting to get to Pyongyang by oxcart." As soon as the words had left his mouth, Jacob blushed. "I do apologize, Mr. Oh. Since my arrival, I've seen more industrialization in Korea than I imagined."

"There is no need to be sorry." His eyes twinkled. "You will see plenty of oxcarts today."

The train left the station a little after ten o'clock, and once they had crossed the Imjin River north of Seoul, the steady thwacking of the giant wheels lulled Jacob to sleep. An hour later, he awakened, blinking a thin crust from his eyes. He was happy to see Soon-hee reclined against the window, sound asleep.

He stretched, grateful for the spacious seat, then rose to take a stutter-stopping walk along the length of the passenger car. The travelers were mostly Korean, but some of the men and women didn't exactly look the same. He'd heard there were significant numbers of Japanese in Korea, and when he caught the eye of the man who'd nodded a greeting from across the row, Jacob's lips parted. *Maybe he's Japanese. Mr. Cullen did say there's been tension between the Japanese and Koreans since the end of the war. Maybe that's why Soon-hee grimaced.*

For the next hour, he alternately worked on a letter to his family and stared out the windows at farmlands, tiny villages, and rice paddies. When some of the workers raised their heads and hands in greeting, Jacob grinned, waving back. Next to the traditional Korean homes speckling the countryside, his Easton domicile seemed like a mansion. He began sensing someone staring at him and turned to Soon-hee, who had awakened with a smile. He seemed to smile a lot.

"I hope you slept well. Are you feeling all right?"

"Yes, thank you." Soon-hee tilted his head. "Did Miss Story tell you about my condition?"

Taken aback by his companion's directness, Jacob stammered. "I, uh, well, yes, she did say you'd been sick." He felt as if he'd been caught stealing a candy bar.

"She is such a dear woman. Tell me, Mr. Kichline, about your home. What is it like?"

Jacob sensed he didn't want to discuss his health.

"If you mean my house, my family and I live in an old stone-front two-story home."

"How old is it?"

"One-hundred and fifty-six years." His chest puffed.

"That is very young here. You will find Korea's culture goes back many thousands of years."

"Oh, yes, right. So, what kind of place will I live in at the missionary compound?" he asked.

"You will find it new and modern, including the YMCA building. That is where I live, and if there is room enough, you will have your own quarters there. If not, you will share mine. Is this agreeable to you? I live quietly and am not given to loud revels."

Jacob chuckled. "Either way suits me. I didn't bring much, mostly clothes and books, so I don't need a lot of space."

"You have left so very much to answer God's call. He will bless your sacrifices."

Jacob squirmed.

"Tell me, Mr. Kichline, who did you leave behind?"

"My family, some good friends, my church."

"I would like to know about them."

For the next ten minutes, Jacob spoke about his parents and siblings, Harry, and his Princeton friends.

He seemed to want more information.

"Is there a special woman in your life?"

Man, he's direct. There's nothing subtle about this guy. I don't want to talk about Pearl. If I had wanted to, I would have mentioned her.

As if he'd read Jacob's mind, Soon-hee expressed regret. "I can see I have made you uncomfortable, Mr. Kichline. I did not intend to do so. I have been told Koreans are more frank than Americans."

"I don't get it. You have all kinds of ways of addressing people, so you don't cause offense. The two don't seem to match."

"You are, of course, correct. I suppose all cultures have their contradictions."

Jacob no longer wanted to keep the fact of Pearl to himself. "Well, to answer your question, there was someone. I mean, maybe but not exactly." He sighed. "I'm not sure ..."

Soon-hee waved his hand as if to indicate there was no need for further details. "I also have such a person in my life. Perhaps we shall work this out together."

I think I'm going to like this guy after all.

The time to turn the tables had come. "Tell me, Mr. Oh, what's your family like?"

"Thank you for asking. They are busy with the mission. My father is one of Korea's first Presbyterian elders, and he works closely with Mr. Moffett as a Pastor's Assistant. Of course, the Moffetts, with whom I am close, are in the United States on furlough just now." He closed his eyes. "I miss him very much. He is a spiritual father and guide to me."

"When will he be back?"

"I am afraid not until next summer."

Jacob sniffed at a pungent scent wafting through the car, and Soon-hee seemed to read the situation.

"This is a strong smell, is it not?"

"It sure is. What is it?"

"This is Korean cabbage known as kimchi."

"Oh." He continued asking about his fellow traveler's family. "So, what's your mother like?"

"She also is active in ministry, mainly to the women. She teaches Bible studies at the Central Church and in the surrounding villages. She and my sister often assist Miss Story in medical missions to the outlying areas. When Mrs. Dr. Moffett is here, they help her with clinics."

Jacob's brow creased. "Mrs. Dr.?"

"Mrs. Moffett is a medical doctor. You seem surprised."

"We don't have many female physicians in the States."

"You see, Mr. Kichline, we are in some ways ahead of you." Soon-hee grinned.

Jacob laughed a little too loudly, causing heads to turn in his direction. He shook himself and focused once again on his friend. "So, you have a younger sister. Are there other siblings?"

For a long moment, Soon-hee remained silent. "I also have a younger brother who is, shall we say, the prodigal?"

Instead of following the Korean custom of being forthright, Jacob thought it best to leave well enough alone. Something in his new friend's demeanor told Jacob all he needed to know for now.

CHAPTER TWENTY

LATE OCTOBER 1906
PYONGYANG, KOREA

The day after his return from Seoul, Soon-hee awakened from a sound sleep when his new companion rattled into the room.

"I'm sorry I woke you up," Jacob said. "I was trying to be quiet." He balanced a cloth-covered tray with one hand and closed the door behind him with the other.

Soon-hee rubbed his eyes and sat up in bed as daylight trickled into the quarters they now shared. Since the YMCA was now housing a large number of boarding students, Jacob had been placed with him until additional space opened up.

The American placed the meal on a table next to Soon-hee's orderly stack of books and papers. "A woman named Mary Yoo told me to deliver this to you."

Soon-hee switched on the light, the corners of his mouth rising. "Ah, you have met our Mary Yoo. She is rather formidable, is she not?"

Jacob sat down on his bed and ran a hand through his bushy blond hair. "I never met anyone like her, and I come from a long line of German *hausfrauen*."

"I am not acquainted with this term."

"It's German, and the English translation is 'housewife.' Easton, where I'm from, was settled largely by Germans, and the women tend to be strong. Very strong." He gestured to the food. "Mary Yoo told me you were to eat now."

"And I will abide by her wishes. I do not want to get on her bad side." While he noticed Jacob's blue eyes when they'd met in Chemulpo, he hadn't realized what a remarkable shade they were, nearly purple. He was used to Westerners with blue eyes, but these were striking.

"I tried to call her 'Mrs. Yoo,'" Jacob said, "but she quickly set me straight. Do you know why?"

"When she became a Christian a few years ago, she took the name Mary in honor of our Lord's mother. Now, she prefers to be known in this way." He grinned. "She is aware of her daunting nature and believes going by 'Mary' will help gentle her spirit."

"And is this having an effect?"

"I have seen changes in her."

"Good." Jacob rubbed his hands together. "So, how are you feeling this morning? Did you sleep well? You were pretty wrung out when we got in last night, I mean tired."

"I feel much better, thank you, although I believe I should take today as a day of rest. I imagine you must also be fatigued after crossing the world to get here." He searched Jacob's face, then surveyed his unpacked trunk and a stack of clothes on his bed.

"To be honest, I could use a day off myself. I've been in constant motion for the past several weeks."

Soon-hee swung his legs over the side of his bed and lifted the cover on his breakfast tray to see what Mary Yoo had made for him. His stomach growled at the sight of a huge bowl of Korean rice porridge, and soothing pear tea.

He would have preferred something more substantial but figured there was wisdom in treating his digestion gently today.

"Have you eaten yet, Mr. Kichline?"

"I have. Mrs., uh, Mary Yoo showed me the layout of the dining room—at least she did a lot of pointing. She doesn't seem to understand much English, not like you. You have a strong command of the language."

"Thank you. I learned it at an early age from the missionaries." He placed a napkin on his lap and picked up a pair of chopsticks. "Was she serving American or Korean food this morning?"

"There was Korean food, like yours, but Mary Yoo fed me eggs, toast, and coffee."

Soon-hee smiled. "This means you have made a favorable impression upon her."

"I'm not so sure. She was scowling the entire time."

"That was not a scowl. She always looks that way. Please, there is too much food here for one person, and I would like you to try some of this. I have plates, cups, and utensils in that cabinet by the window. Will you join me?"

"Are you sure?"

"Of course. This will be a gentle introduction to Korean cuisine, which can be as you say, fiery." He went to the other side of the room and set a place for Jacob along the desk after nudging his books to the side. After he sat he asked, "Would you like to offer a prayer?"

"I, uh, well, of course."

Soon-hee thought perhaps he should have taken the initiative and not put his roommate ill at ease. He bowed his head and waited for Jacob, the scent of the food rising.

"Lord, make us truly thankful for these and all thy blessings. I ask this in Jesus' name, amen."

"Amen." Soon-hee was taken aback by the rote grace Jacob had offered, having expected something more personal and heartfelt. He filled a bowl with half of his porridge and handed it to his colleague.

As they tucked into the meal, they talked between bites.

"Say, this is pretty good," Jacob said. "It reminds me a little of the oatmeal we have back in the States."

"I am pleased to know this. Many cultures have a variation of this breakfast food." He sipped his tea and placed the cup back into the saucer. "What do you think of this beverage?"

"Well, to be honest, I can't quite wrap my palate around the taste. I've never had such a delicate tea."

Soon-hee appreciated his candor. "Please do not feel obligated to finish it." He paused between bites. "I do hope you do not mind sharing this room with me. I was hoping for your sake you might have the benefit of your own."

"This is fine." Jacob wiped a dribble of porridge from his chin. "I'm used to roommates. In fact, being in a strange place, I rather like the idea of having your company. I just hope I'm not causing you an inconvenience."

"Like you, I enjoy the fellowship." He already felt drawn to him despite his feeling that Jacob affected a superior demeanor. Underneath that layer, Soon-hee sensed there was a kind heart beating. He filled him in on the origins and purpose of the Pyongyang YMCA, including its social and evangelistic work.

Jacob grinned. "And how does Mary Yoo fit into this scenario?"

"Although I am the resident director, she is, as you may say, our mother hen or house mother. She is a widow who had no children of her own, and she has dedicated her life to this mission. She is fervent in her dedication to those under her care."

A red-hued branch tossing just outside their windows tapped against the pane.

Soon-hee put his chopsticks next to his plate after finishing his meal. “I will teach you how to use these in the coming days.”

Jacob grinned. “I’m amazed you ate porridge with those things. I’d be all thumbs.”

“All thumbs?”

“It means I’d be clumsy.”

“You do not strike me as a clumsy person. I am guessing you played sports in your country.”

Jacob smiled, seeming pleased with the assessment. “Thanks. Yes, I did, mostly baseball and football.”

He relaxed into one of two chairs in the room. “So, tell me, Mr. Kichline, how did you come to faith in the Savior?”

Jacob’s mouth hung open, then he closed his lips, appearing to take a deep breath. “I, um, I well, I was raised in a Christian home and came to believe in Jesus as a young boy.”

Soon-hee wondered why his friend was so flustered. “I did not mean to upset you.”

“Not at all, Soon-uh-Mr. Oh. America is a Christian culture. You go to church and Sunday School and make that the foundation for your life, as I have.”

“It is good you have never known a different way. You had the benefit of walking early with our Savior. When did you receive the call to become a pastor?”

Jacob looked out the window for a long moment, then back at Soon-hee. “There’s a group in America called Christian Endeavor. Have you heard of it?”

“Yes, I have, although I know little about the organization.”

“Its purpose is to encourage young people to be active in church membership and train them to become leaders.

Through this ministry, my connection to God strengthened, and during my senior year in college, I felt God calling me into the ministry. My church leaders confirmed this, and I went to Princeton to prepare."

"I see. So, you are Presbyterian?"

"I became one after I went to Princeton, but I grew up German Reformed, which is somewhat similar in theology."

Soon-hee had many questions about the Princeton Seminary, of which he had always been in a kind of awe. He would have liked to ask some of them, but Jacob changed the subject.

"Growing up in Korea, how did you happen to become a Christian, Mr. Oh?"

He stared outside at the fall scenery for a moment. Beyond the room, other residents moved about the hallway.

"When Mr. Moffett came to Korea nearly fifteen years ago, he came to my village not far from the city gates and preached the gospel. My parents were overcome with remorse for their sins and pledged to follow Jesus."

"He must've made quite an impression."

"Oh, he did. Mr. Moffett is a powerful man of God whose boldness impressed them."

"So, you heard him, too, then?

"Yes."

"How old were you?" Jacob asked.

"I was ten. Hearing Mr. Moffett open the Word of God was like emerging from deep water where one gasps to breathe. I immersed myself in the Bible and became a Catechumen. I do not know if you use this term, but here this is a person who is preparing for church membership. My father, who had once been a great sinner, became one of Korea's first Presbyterian elders and later, Mr. Moffett's Pastoral Assistant. My mother taught the Bible to our women at the new church. I believed I mentioned some of this on our journey yesterday. I will take you there, to the Central Presbyterian Church, on Sunday for services."

Jacob's eyes narrowed. "Are they in English?"

"No, Mr. Kichline. We conduct public services in Korean. The more you are exposed to my language, the faster you will grow in its use. This has been true for all of the missionaries."

"I hope so." He blew out a breath. "How big is the church?"

"If you mean its membership, about three thousand souls."

Jacob gasped. "Three thousand!"

"Yes, is not your Easton church this big?"

"Not nearly."

"I see. The churches in the surrounding countryside are not this large. All the American missionaries are involved in its leadership, but at the head is Mr. Moffett. We also have many elders and a few Pastoral Assistants, including as I said my father."

"Are many of these leaders Korean? Do they speak English? Are they even literate?"

Soon-hee grimaced at the barrage of questions, and their implications. Was Jacob Kichline that arrogant, or merely naïve? Time would tell. For now, he decided to give him the benefit of his doubts.

"Many elders are Korean, and there is a growing number of carefully trained Korean pastors. In my seminary class, there were seven others who have gone on to lead outlying churches. Most of them are either fluent in English or are learning. Our Miss Story conducts several English language classes a week."

Jacob didn't seem to know when to stop. "What I don't understand is how such simple people, except maybe for the seminary graduates, can serve as church leaders."

Soon-hee brushed back his irritation at the assumption of Korean inferiority. "Mr. Kichline, consider those whom the Lord Jesus called to be his disciples. These were not learned men, yet in his Spirit, they changed the world."

Jacob reached out to touch Soon-hee, then quickly pulled back. "I do apologize. I meant no offense. Obviously, there's a lot I don't know about this place or its people."

"I thank you."

"Are most of the leaders Presbyterians?"

"Yes, but at the mission, there is cooperation between a total of four Presbyterian denominations and the United Methodists. Other denominations serve in Korea but here, there are mostly these two."

"Just how many Protestant missionaries are in the country?"

"About two hundred I am told." He put on a smile. "After I get ready for the day, I will be happy to show you around the compound, at least where you will be working."

"I thought you wanted to rest today."

"And I shall, but I also prefer some fresh air."

"Count me in."

He couldn't help but feel pride in the small office he'd been given among those of the college and seminary professors. Soon-hee had no illusions of his workspace being up to Jacob's Princeton standards, but he was pleased with what he had.

"I like to study here as well," he said. "This office is much quieter than the energy of the YMCA." He paused. "I hope you will be comfortable here as well. I apologize that my desk is larger than the one that has been provided for you. I would be happy to switch with you."

"That's very nice of you, Mr. Oh, but I'm fine with this one."

"Very well. You are always welcome to use mine."

"Please, don't give this another thought. I'll have plenty of room, and I enjoy having a window in my workspace. I also like how close we are to the library." He edged closer to Soon-hee's full but uncluttered workspace. "I'm told the translation you do is mainly Bible-oriented, books, and tracts."

"Yes, this is true. I have done work in all of these areas, as you will."

"How do you fit this into your studies? You must be awfully busy." Jacob gazed at his colleague.

"I only do translation work for one-fourth of my time during the academic sessions. In the summer, I am fully dedicated to the work, including the distribution of materials into the surrounding countryside and some cities." He smiled at the American. "This is why we have need of your services. I understand your language skills are strong."

Jacob scratched his chin. "I used to think so—until I started learning Korean."

Soon-hee softened at his admission of a shortcoming. "Ours is a demanding tongue indeed. I am confident you will learn well here, and I will be only too happy to assist you."

"Thanks. So, what project will I be working on first?"

"We are midway through translating a most noteworthy book by an American woman. I have benefited greatly from reading it, and my mother often finds inspiration in its pages."

"What's it called?"

"Perhaps you know of this Hannah Whitall Smith who is the author of . . ."

Jacob's face blanched as he completed the sentence. "*The Christian's Secret of a Happy Life.*"

"You know this book, then?"

"My, uh, the woman I used to date ... she, uh, likes it a lot."

"Then you have strong memories attached to it."

"You might say so."

Soon-hee scrutinized his expression. "I hope you do not find this work painful."

"Same here."

He sensed a need to let this news sink in and observed a brief silence. Then Soon-hee said, "This is close to the time when I meet with some of the missionaries for prayer."

"In the daytime?"

"Oh, yes. Last summer, we had a series of meetings in which we heard messages from the Word of God pertaining to the difficulties we are facing. At the end, many of us pledged to meet daily for ongoing prayer to seek God's guidance and direction."

Jacob leaned against his desk and crossed his arms. "What are some of the challenges?"

Soon-hee hesitated, wondering how deeply he could share with this man who was, in fact, still a stranger to him. He decided to be general. "To begin, we are facing a shortage of seats at the church. Our services are packed and in poor weather, people are forced to sit outside to listen."

"Why doesn't the missions board provide money for a new or expanded church?"

"They are already most generous. You see, Mr. Kichline, we Koreans also must do our part. The missionaries are training us to manage this work on our own."

"Miss Story mentioned something like that to me. So, is that the main problem?"

"For now, in the interest of time and to put the matter simply, Korea has suffered with the takeover of our country by the Japanese. This is a deep issue with many facets. Let me just say the relations between our peoples are not always peaceful or cordial." He forced a smile. "Will you join me in prayer today, or would you like to do something else? Perhaps you need to rest."

Jacob gazed at him for a moment with a blank expression. "Thanks, but I'd prefer to wander around a bit more. Am I safe to do so?"

He winked. "The scariest person you will find on this compound is Mary Yoo."

"Believe me, I don't want to get on her bad side."

As they parted, Soon-hee turned around to watch Jacob walk away, his hands jammed into his coat pockets. He couldn't help but wonder just how spiritually sound this American was.

CHAPTER TWENTY-ONE

November 4, 1906

Pyongyang, Korea

Dear Mother and Father,

Greetings from the "Land of the Morning Calm." You can imagine how happy I was to find your letters waiting for me when I arrived on the other side of the world. That touch of home blessed me more than I can possibly say. I'm especially interested in Robert and Grace's romantic developments and am guessing as she soon will graduate from Allentown College for Women—Mae won't be far behind. Just make sure there aren't any weddings until I get back home. Please tell Teddy I'm proud of his exploits on the Easton High football team and will be cheering him on as they play our chief rival, Phillipsburg.

Since I last mailed a letter to you from Yokohama, I have a lot to tell you. My entourage and I arrived in the Korean port of Chemulpo on October 30, where we were met by an American missionary nurse and a recent Korean seminary graduate. Both are roughly my age. As you can imagine, my fellow travelers and I were utterly fatigued and fortunately only had a brief trolley ride to Seoul ahead of us. We didn't go on to Pyongyang immediately but stayed the night at the beautiful new Severance Hospital in its guest quarters.

In Seoul, I was surprised to see many modern buildings and the new, American-made, railroad. There are, of course, many traditional Korean structures. Since the end of the Russo-Japanese War, Japan is in a protectorate position governing Korea and have been updating its infrastructure.

He refreshed his pen with ink before continuing.

The next morning, after a tour of Severance, I took the train to Pyongyang with Mr. Soon-hee Oh. Nurse Story stayed in Seoul to help the Davis family get oriented and returned here just yesterday with the Cullens, who had visited their assigned churches near Seoul. Mr. Oh and I had a marvelous opportunity to get to know each other during the ten-hour train ride, and some of the time I practiced my Korean on him. He says my pronunciation is nearly flawless, but I know I have so much to learn not only about the language, but the customs here. Here's an example. As we neared Pyongyang and I exclaimed over the beautiful old city gates and the strange sedan chairs, I gestured in their direction. When I pointed to a man in traditional Korean clothing, however, Mr. Oh told me pointing is considered a rude behavior. He says people think you are blaming them for something. He was matter-of-fact about this, which spared my pride, and he taught me how to use my whole hand instead. I know you would approve, Mother.

You may be wondering about Mr. Oh. He's an interesting fellow, soft-spoken with a touch of smokiness in his accent. I'm finding that to be typical of Koreans. He's just one year my junior but has the wisdom of someone far older. Physically, he's rather tall as Koreans go and has their characteristic black hair and dark eyes in the intriguing almond shape of his race. I believe my sisters would find him handsome. He's neat and conscientious, an early-to-bed kind of person. He also spends a significant amount of time in daily prayer and Bible reading.

> He recently became one of the Presbyterian seminary's first Korean graduates and is now pursuing doctoral studies. He works part-time translating English works into his native language and oversees the young men at the YMCA. His family, including a younger sister and brother, are heavily involved with the mission. Mr. Oh's father is an elder and Pastoral Assistant while his mother and sister labor in Bible classes and do a bit of nursing in the outlying villages. I understand the brother, who's still a student at the academy, is sick a lot.
>
> One difficulty I have with adjusting is calling Soon-hee Oh "Mister." Not only do I already consider him to be a friend, we're sharing a room at the new YMCA building. There's been a record enrollment in the various schools here, so for now, there isn't an available space for me. I'm fine with this, by the way. Back to Mr. Oh ... the missionaries treat the Korean people with deep respect, which includes calling them by their titles. This may take a while for me to get used to. When he addresses me as "Mr. Kichline," I look over my shoulder to see if you're in the room, Father.

Jacob tapped his pen against his teeth, smiling over his stab at humor. He'd been the life of Lafayette and church gatherings before going to Princeton, a place where there hadn't been much levity. Maybe that unused muscle would begin to flex again here.

> The YMCA is quite modern and located in the upper right part of the mission compound, whose buildings blend Western and Korean architecture. Mr. Oh and I take our meals at an on-site dining hall overseen by an intimidating middle-aged woman named Mary Yoo. She's square-built with broad shoulders and sports a perpetually stern expression. She does most of the cooking, a blend of basic American fare and Korean food. Mr. Oh has rather delicate digestion, and by eating

some of his blander meals, I'm acclimating myself to the unusual spices. He's also teaching me to use chopsticks, which I'm just not getting the hang of yet. I usually fall back on Western utensils. On my second day here, I foolishly took a large mouthful of kimchi, which is fermented Korean cabbage. I think the steam pouring forth from my head could have powered the train from here to Seoul. Mary Yoo's expression did change ever so slightly then when she saw me gulping water.

So far, the weather has been a lot like it is at home, and the trees change colors here as well. In fact, on my first morning in Pyongyang when I looked out my window, I thought for a moment I was back on Lafayette's campus. I hadn't expected anything here to feel like home, so the familiar scenery eases my spirit as I adjust to my new surroundings.

This morning I attended my first service here, at the Central Presbyterian Church, which is the hub of the mission. The building, though newer, is in the Korean style and rather picturesque. The roof consists of clay tiles and wide, curved eaves. The sanctuary was almost full when Mr. Oh and I arrived a half hour early. I wondered where the pews were, but my friend told me everyone sits on mats so there's room for more people. Fortunately, he'd brought one for me since I didn't have my own yet. Everyone sat so close together on these woven straw mats I felt crowded. By the time the pastor, Mr. Blair, began the service, dozens of people who couldn't fit inside stood outside to catch whatever they could of the music and preaching.

The energetic service was conducted in Korean, and I recognized a few words here and there, especially when we sang some familiar hymns. The prayers were so unlike those at home, lengthier and full of ardor, as well as some tears. The singing was enough to lift the hair on the back of my neck. These people know how to worship.

He remembered when, during one of the hymns, Soon-hee grimaced in the direction of a man with a particularly booming voice. Jacob couldn't figure out the cause of his friend's ire. The man wasn't off-key, and plenty of other people were just as loud. Because Soon-hee was normally the epitome of pleasantness, the incident stayed with Jacob. He resumed writing.

> Here's something else I think you'll find astonishing. Central Presbyterian Church has about three thousand members and is growing faster than the building can accommodate. Mr. Samuel Moffett, who is in charge overall here, is currently in the States pursuing funding for an expansion and other pressing needs. Now that I'm here, I have a better understanding of how important translating materials for study, devotional, and evangelistic purposes is. The people are so hungry to learn.
>
> I shall close this letter now and go for a long walk before the evening meal. Mary Yoo takes Sundays off, and Mr. Oh has invited me to his home to dine. I plan to take lots of photographs, and when I learn how to have them developed, I'll send you some. In the meantime, I'm slipping into this envelope an assortment of postcards I picked up in Seoul, here at the mission compound, and the Pyongyang train station.
>
> Give my very best to everyone at home and keep your letters coming.
>
> I remain your loving son,
>
> Jacob Kichline
>
> P.S. I haven't seen any tigers yet, Mother, except in artwork.

Jacob had the little office to himself today, but he didn't want to be entirely alone and had left the door ajar. Outside, a Korean man in the traditional *hanbok* clothing raked leaves into enormous piles. The baggy outfit fluttered in the light wind causing Jacob to smile. So far, his own work wasn't difficult. Soon-hee had completed nearly all of *The Christian's Secret of a Happy Life* so that Jacob's job was mostly editorial. He looked for mistakes and responded to marginal notes related to correct interpretation. The hardest part was reading a book devoted to "the higher Christian life" when his own was firmly situated on its bottom rungs.

According to the author: "In order for a lump of clay to be made into a beautiful vessel, it must be entirely abandoned to the potter and must lie passive in his hands. And similarly, in order for a soul to be made into a vessel unto God's honor, 'sanctified and meet for the master's use, and prepared unto every good work,' it must be utterly abandoned to Him, and must lie passive in His hands." Back in college, Jacob had been of such a mind, a time when he'd stood strong in the faith and was in sweet fellowship with the Lord. The passage causing him the most angst this morning, however, was in the chapter related to doubts. Mrs. Smith had spared no feelings, including his own. "Spiritual conflicts! Far better would they be named spiritual rebellions! Our fight is to be a fight of faith; and the moment we let in doubts, our fight ceases, and our rebellion begins."

He got up and opened the window, breathing in the leaf-scented air. *Is that what I am—a rebel? At Princeton, wrestling with one's faith was considered almost virtuous, a necessity. Then again, look what Gresham Machen's struggles did to him until he circled back.*

A knock at the door disrupted his brooding. He turned to see earnest, bespectacled Mr. Blair, the professor who seemed most in charge of the mission while Mr. Moffett was on sabbatical.

"I say, Mr. Kichline, I hope I'm not disturbing you."

"Not at all. I was just, uh, following a line of thought. Please come in."

Blair remained near the doorway. "How's the translating coming along?"

"Mr. Oh's diligent work makes mine a lot easier."

He smiled. "That man is a treasure. Speaking of him ... I have a round-about favor to ask, also an opportunity I think would be good for you."

Jacob leaned against his desk, curious.

"I'm assigned to the care of five counties north of Pyongyang, and in that area there's a system of markets made up of five towns in a circle. Most of Korea has these. The market towns come together every fifth day, sort of like our farmers' markets back home. Do you have those where you come from?"

He grinned. "My hometown has one of the oldest farmers' markets in the country."

"Is that so? Well, I plan to go the day after tomorrow and will take Mrs. Blair with me. Miss Story and Mrs. Oh will be doing a medical clinic. Mr. Oh, that is Soon-hee not his father, usually goes with me, but he's otherwise engaged with exams. He suggested I invite you, which is a great opportunity for you to meet Koreans in the villages." He smiled as if he'd offered Jacob a new motorcar.

"Oh, I, uh, thank you." He pushed his hands in his pockets. *Thanks for nothing, roomie*. This was the last thing he'd expected or wanted to do. Why couldn't he just stay in Pyongyang? "Um, how long would we be away?"

"Just overnight."

His lips parted, then his words caught up. "Where will we stay?"

"Probably in someone's house. People open them up to travelers during market days."

"Oh." *This just keeps getting better and better.* "How far is this place, and how do we get there?" He gave a nervous chuckle. "I hope you don't mind all the questions."

"Not at all, Mr. Kichline. This isn't exactly a trip from Princeton to New York. We'll go on foot, about a day's walk. There aren't many good roads in Korea, not when you get away from the urban centers. For the most part, there are just crooked paths between low mountain passes and around rice fields." He laughed. "A while back, I got myself a red bicycle thinking it would make my trips easier. However, I kept encountering men leading huge oxen along the way, and let's just say the sight of a foreigner on a bike startled both the Koreans and their beasts. Walking is the best way to see the country and interact with the people. I find it the best way to preach the gospel."

The sound of people talking in the hallway filled a long moment, giving Jacob time to think ... and think fast. There really was no reasonable way to get out of this. Besides, at least he'd be free of the navel gazing he was doing over Hannah Whitall Smith's summons to the deeper Christian life.

"What should I bring, Mr. Blair?"

"Oh, anything that would provide for your personal comfort. We'll bring stores of food, so you needn't concern yourself with that detail." He paused, stretching his arms. "We'll meet at seven in front of Central Pres."

Jacob had always considered himself outgoing, but next to William Blair, he was a veritable recluse. Whether or not he knew the person he hailed on the road, the professor treated him like a long-lost brother. They in turn saluted him with smiles and bows.

"Don't you just love filling your lungs with this mountain air?" he asked Jacob as the group rested on a summit.

"Yes, it certainly is invigorating."

Jacob scanned the villages below and could have sworn he saw smoke from a steamer making its way across the Yellow Sea, flanked by white-sailed junks. What he could have done without was the suspension bridge they'd crossed as it swung across a menacing ravine. His mother would have had to be threatened with pain of death to have put one foot on such a span, which almost described his own condition. He considered their safe crossing in the category of miraculous.

After their break, they spent another hour on the rutted pathway steadily drawing closer to the market. They began to encounter groups of farmers with their donkeys lugging rice, firewood, and eggs, and Jacob repressed a belly laugh at the sight of one man with a live pig hanging from his back, its feet and snout trussed. The women glared at the sight, including Mrs. Oh who apparently shared the sentiments of her Western colleagues.

Mr. Blair walked up to the fellow and after they had a few words, translated their conversation. "He says the pig's mouth is bound so it can't interrupt the man's conversations."

The missionary bent closer to Jacob and said, "You never know what you're going to encounter on the road. I decided long ago no one should be a missionary if he doesn't have a good sense of humor."

One of the Koreans they met kept pace with them, and Blair asked where he was from.

He nodded at a distant mountain. “Behind,” he said in accented English. “From where do you come?”

Jacob watched the exchange, wondering if he might have an opportunity to try out his Korean.

“We live outside the West Gate at Pyongyang.”

“Why do you journey here?”

Despite the man’s distressing dental condition, Jacob liked his kind smile.

“I am an American who, along with my Korean friend here, wants to know if you have heard the story of Jesus.”

Jacob swatted a small flying insect buzzing around his right ear.

The fellow pressed his lips together before answering. “I know a little, but do not understand.”

Blair began sharing the story of God’s creation of the world and man’s special place in it, along with his fall into sin. He proceeded to outline the way the Hebrew people became God’s instrument of redemption and the coming of the Messiah. Through him, God demonstrated his great love for the world.

The man listened, bobbing his head up and down, occasionally interrupting with a question. Jacob had never heard such a spontaneous presentation of God’s redemptive history. He used to share his faith with his Lafayette classmates but never this winsomely.

“This Jesus, was he born in America?”

“He was born in Bethlehem of Judea, in the Middle East. He was Asian, like yourself.”

The man’s eyes filled as Blair told him how Jesus loved the world so much he even submitted to the piercing of his hands and feet and a death of great shame to save fallen humanity.

“*Aigo, kurus-sin-nika*?”

Jacob frowned and looked to Blair to translate.

"Yes, what I tell you is true. We would love to welcome you at the church where we worship. There you will hear all you need to know about the Lord Jesus."

When they parted ways, Jacob asked, "Do you think he'll come?"

"Koreans are direct about many things but not when it comes to invitations. Then, they're noncommittal. At least half of the time, people I talk to about Jesus will show up in church the next week."

Jacob gasped. "But Pyongyang is so far away."

"Yes, Mr. Kichline, it is, but distance is a small thing to a starving soul."

He couldn't help but wonder if this church might be able to fill his own craving void.

CHAPTER TWENTY-TWO

MID-NOVEMBER 1906
PYONGYANG, KOREA

"I shall be praying about your exam today, Soon-hee. This is your last, is it not?"

He appreciated the show of support from his friend, a second-year seminarian. The clinking of glasses, plates, and utensils permeated the dining hall.

"Yes, this will be the final one."

The young man rose with his tray. "I am confident you will do well."

Soon-hee bowed his head. "*Gamsahamnida.*"

He drained his teacup and turned to the wall clock. With only fifteen minutes left before the hall closed, Jacob was nowhere in sight. Even if he did arrive just now, Mary Yoo might not be pleased at his stretching the limits. As if he'd prophesied the event, Soon-hee sucked in a quick breath when his roommate entered the room, his hair and clothes rumpled. He watched Jacob approach the kitchen window and begin employing his hands as he spoke to Mary Yoo. Soon-hee had no doubt what her gestures meant and rose to mediate.

"Breakfast was especially tasty this morning," he said. "I so enjoy the way you prepare steamed eggs, Mary Yoo. Might there be any left for Mr. Kichline?"

Jacob's expression softened, and he mouthed a silent "Thank you."

The no-nonsense matron hitched her hands to her hips. "Mr. Kichline is late."

"Yes, but you may not be aware of what he did yesterday and the day before," Soon-hee said. Someone bumped him with a tray and apologized before leaving the scene.

"He went to the village market in the mountains with the Blairs, Mrs. Oh, and Miss Story. This was his first such visit, and he brought much joy to those he met along the way, sharing the love of Jesus. He returned very late last night, and I did not wish to wake him too early."

He wondered if she was buying what he was selling. Her eyes bored into Jacob's before turning on her heel and barking something to a member of her kitchen staff. Immediately, the young woman began filling a plate.

Jacob bowed. "Thank you, Mary Yoo. *Gamsahamnida.*"

She responded by pushing her right hand upwards.

"Thank you, Mr. Oh. Do you have time to sit with me while I have my breakfast, or do you have to leave for your exam?"

"I am able to stay for a short time."

They took their seats in the emptying space, and Jacob tucked into his meal. Soon-hee tilted his head to the right, wondering if perhaps his friend had forgotten to pray.

"How are the exams coming along?"

Soon-hee did most of the talking while Jacob ate and, once he'd finished, asked about the American's adventures. "How did you find the countryside?"

"It was unlike anything I'd ever seen before." He exhaled. "I took lots of pictures because my family would never believe some things I saw." He relaxed against the chair. "Have you ever crossed that suspension bridge?"

Soon-hee laughed. "Oh yes."

"Doesn't the height and flimsiness scare you half to death?"

"Yes, the first time, but I learned quickly to look straight ahead, never down."

"My heart pounded the entire time I went across."

"I imagine so. Where did you stay the night?"

"Mr. and Mrs. Blair took us to this inn they knew, but it was really just someone's house. While we were eating rice, I kept wondering where we were going to sleep. All I could see was the kitchen on one end and a stone-slabbed floor on the other."

Soon-hee suppressed his mirth.

"I slept in the most primitive conditions. There were about eight people stretched out on mats, smoking these long pipes, which nearly made me choke. Mr. Blair slipped the innkeeper what turned out to be ten cents for the use of his private quarters, so we all ended up sleeping in an inner room on cots we brought with us on our pack-pony. We used the rubber blankets that secured our goods as a partition between us and the women in our company. Since the house was also a kind of livery stable, I smelled barnyard odors all night long."

"Did you sleep at all?"

"A little here and a little there." Jacob raked his hair with his fingers.

"And did you enjoy the market?"

"I did. In Easton, we have a farmer's market in the center of town every Saturday, so I was reminded of those good times. I bought a few trinkets to send to my family." He broke into a grin. "There were these children who gathered around me. I suppose I was a novelty for them with my blond hair and how tall I am. When I gave them some candy from America, they treated me like Santa Claus."

"Ah, yes, the Christmas figure. Did you share with them the items you have given to me?"

"I did. Jelly beans and Barnum's Animal Crackers."

"I can imagine their glowing faces."

Jacob smiled, seeming satisfied with his goodwill gesture. "They were fascinated with my watch, but I was concerned if I removed it, I might not get it back."

Soon-hee bristled, choosing not to comment.

"Funny thing, though, after I gave a boy some animal crackers, he turned around and presented me with a paper tiger. I tried to pay him, but he refused. He had so little but was so generous."

"This is the way of my people, Mr. Kichline. Tell me, how did you find your travel companions?"

"They were great. I would never have managed without them. Miss Story is so efficient and confident, and your mother is compassionate and wonderful with the children, who were overjoyed to see her. There was this old, stooped woman who also joined them, and your mother seemed to respect her a lot and not mind her doing some of the readings."

"She was likely one of our Bible women."

He frowned. "What's that?"

"A female evangelist. Traditionally, Western male missionaries were prohibited from conversing with Korean women, so the female missionaries trained them to take the gospel to those with whom the men could not speak. Although this has changed, there are still some old Bible women around, like the one you met."

Jacob finished his meal and laid his fork aside with a chuckle. “Mr. Blair will talk to anyone and everyone—man, woman, or child. I was touched by the way he treated the lowliest beggar with the same respect he showed to the wealthy. Although I found it difficult to keep up with him at times, I was honored to be associated with him out there.”

“Yes, he is as you say.” He gazed at Jacob. “And how did you find our Miss Story?”

“She’s an amazing woman.” He rested his elbows on the table. “Tell me, what’s her background?”

“She comes from a very distinguished family in the eastern part of America. Someone has said her parents brought her out.” Soon-hee scratched his head. “I have never been sure of what this means.”

Jacob repeated, “Brought her out.” Then a light seemed to switch on. “Oh, it means her family has wealth and social position. When Miss Story reached a certain age, around eighteen, her parents introduced her to society as what’s called a debutante. This signals her availability to be married to a suitable partner.”

“Is your family like this?”

“Not really. I mean, my family is comfortable but not what I’d call wealthy. What made Miss Story give up a secure future to come here of all places?”

Soon-hee grimaced. If he didn’t find Jacob Kichline agreeable more often than not, he might not have liked him as much as he did. Underneath the conceit, he sensed vulnerability.

“A call from God is stronger than any other, and she decided there was nothing more important than to obey.”

“What did her parents think?”

He toyed with a napkin someone had left on the table. “I believe they were unhappy initially, but when they saw her determination, they gave their blessing. They have been most generous to the mission."

"That's good."

"You are interested in Miss Story?"

Jacob gave a small hop. "Oh, not especially. I just enjoy knowing the backgrounds of the people I associate with."

"Do you find her as attractive as your woman back home?" He grinned, enjoying his friend's apparent discomfort. "I see you are taken aback by my candor. I forget sometimes the reserve of Americans."

"Um, I, uh, yes, we are less forthright." He cleared his throat. "What about you? You once mentioned a female interest."

Soon-hee conjured up a picture of Jeongsook in his mind. "Yes, she is lovely. I have known her most of my life."

"Have I met her yet?"

"I am not sure of this. She assists Mrs. Dr. Moffett when she is here, also my mother and Miss Story, so she is often seen in their company." He paused. "She and her family live just outside our compound."

"Are you seeing each other?"

"Perhaps not in the way of Western rituals. We Koreans do not regard marriage or courtship as you do but are heavily influenced by Confucianism, even the Christians. I can tell by your expression you do not understand. This means there are restrictions between how men and women relate to each other."

"Oh. How do you decide who to marry?"

"Usually there is an understanding between us and our families."

"Like arranged marriages?"

"In a way, but there are distinctions that vary within families and communities."

"So, is there an understanding between your family and this woman's?"

He considered the question, ruminating over the condition of his relationship with Jeongsook, who had given him a genuine smile just a few days earlier. He didn't mind speaking about her, but he wasn't ready to discuss the problem he had with Yong-bin.

"There have been complications. We are working things out. You will find there is much in Korea that is being worked out."

"How do you mean?" Jacob pulled his chair back from the table. The dining hall was nearly empty of patrons.

Soon-hee looked to the windows, light slanting through the remaining leaves. "Korea has been in the middle of ancient tensions between its neighbors, often as a pawn between them. The missionaries have helped us to become self-sustaining, and we all had hopes after the recent war of becoming independent of foreign powers."

Someone began mopping the floor, and he knew they would soon have to leave.

Jacob sniffed. "Sounds rough."

"Yes, Mr. Kichline, you are correct. When the Americans accepted the idea of a Japanese protectorate over Korea, there was much disappointment and not a small amount of resentment. The Japanese have long treated us as their inferiors, and once again we find ourselves under their authority. The official explanation was Korea needed to be defended from hostile invaders; however, this is like putting the fox in charge of the chicken coop. Some believe we should stage an uprising, and not a few have turned away from the mission because Mr. Moffett and the others believe in staying neutral, so the gospel may take precedence."

"And where do you stand?"

"I strive to follow Mr. Moffett's godly example." He sighed. "I must confess this is sometimes a struggle, especially when I see groups of Japanese soldiers." He gazed into the distance. "He wishes to welcome the Japanese who attend our services as brothers in Christ. I do so outwardly, but inside, my spirit does not agree with my actions."

He caught Jacob's open stare, wondering if he had once again shocked the American with his honesty.

His voice turned husky when he responded. "I didn't realize, Mr. Oh. I just thought they were doing a lot to help Korea, modernizing for example. They've done all those public works, bringing your country out of the dark ages."

Soon-hee caught his eye. "Korea's is a glorious past, Mr. Kichline. Did you know my ancestors invented the first moveable type on carved wooden blocks?"

"No, I didn't." His eyelids raised. "That's impressive."

"Hundreds of years before Gutenburg, Koreans recorded the first complete set of Buddhist writings. Over a thousand years ago, in the seventh century, Koreans also constructed the Far East's first observatory. We were the first to measure and record rainfall, two hundred years ahead of the West. And before your Monitor and Merrimac, Koreans repelled Japanese invasions with armored battleships." He gazed into Jacob's intriguing blue eyes. "You see, my country is not as backward as you may think."

There was no animosity or resentment in what he told his American friend. Jacob had spoken his mind, something Soon-hee valued, and now he had responded.

The light in the dining hall flashed on and off.

"I think Mary Yoo is sending a message." His chuckle lightened any tension between them.

"We'd better get cracking then. Uh, I mean, we'd better leave."

Soon-hee grinned. "I like your funny American expressions." In fact, he liked this funny American.

CHAPTER TWENTY-THREE

MID-NOVEMBER 1906

Jacob found himself humming as he opened an enormous crate from home. Inside an array of items jammed every space—cotton damask towels, bed sheets, a down pillow, cans of pork and beans, boxes of breakfast cereal, bars of Ivory and Palmolive soaps. He laughed at the sight of several rolls of toilet paper, which he squirrelled away in a satchel under his bed. Although the missionaries used the product at the compound, what came from his family was the difference between silk and sandpaper.

Once he'd rooted through the personal stockpile, he rejoiced in finding an abundance of hymnals—one hundred to be exact—as well as schoolbooks and medical supplies. A quantity of pills, powders, empty pharmaceutical bottles, suppositories, and dressings would surely put a smile on Miss Story's face. He imagined her clapping her hands before throwing her arms around him in a celebratory hug. *Where did that come from?* He brought himself up short just as Soon-hee appeared in the doorway, his face reflecting Jacob's excitement.

"What is all of this?"

"My parents and my church sent these to the mission. Look—new hymnals." He held one out for inspection.

Soon-hee reached for the volume and ran hands over the smooth cover before looking inside. "We have needed these very badly."

"There's a lot more here for the mission."

"Mr. Blair will be so pleased." He closed his eyes and pressed his hand on his stomach.

Jacob caught his breath. "What's wrong? Are you sick?"

His roommate waved him off. "I just have a touch of my digestive distress. Please do not be concerned."

"But I am. Can I do anything to help?"

"You can pray I am able to get this under control quickly."

"When will you be seeing Dr. Walker again?"

"He will come sometime next week. Miss Story is taking good care of me."

Jacob squinted. "Then she knows about this?"

Soon-hee seemed to back-pedal. "She is aware of my condition."

"I'm talking about this time. Does she know how you feel now?"

"You are as a dog with a bone, Mr. Kichline." He hung his head. "No, she does not."

"I'll go with you to the dispensary."

"This is not necessary. You must tell Mr. Blair about this shipment."

"Only if you promise to lay down until I return. Then I'll go with you to see Miss Story."

He sighed. "I have a great deal of work to do."

"Right now, your work is to take care of yourself. The rest will just have to wait." He had a bad feeling in the pit of his own stomach.

He trudged across the campus and did a double take when he discovered Mr. Blair raking leaves, his suit jacket sleeves rolled up and tie tucked into his shirt while the young groundskeeper sat on a bench watching. Jacob had never seen such a role reversal, not at Lafayette and never at Princeton. Was he dreaming? He realized he must've made a face because when the young man saw him, he jumped up and implored Mr. Blair in rapid Korean to hand him the rake. Jacob understood him saying, "This is not right. Please."

Jacob heard the professor ask, "Are you all right now? I can always get someone else to help you."

"No, please." Embarrassment was written all over his face. He snatched the rake and got back to work.

"Oh, hello, Mr. Kichline." Blair saluted him, brushing off debris as he approached. "This is a fine day, is it not?"

"Uh, yes, Mr. Blair, very fine."

"That young chap works entirely too hard in my opinion. When I came upon him twenty minutes ago, he was nearly faint with exhaustion."

The missionary sucked in a deep breath, Jacob half expected him to do some chest pounding.

"It does a body good to do manual labor. We're so often perched behind our desks or delivering lectures that we let our bodies go slack." He moved closer. "I've seen my share of portly pastors and do not intend to become one of them."

The man was irrepressible.

"I was just coming to pay you a visit, Mr. Blair."

"Wonderful. What's on your mind, my friend?"

Jacob told him all about the parcel from home, happy to be the bearer of such good tidings.

"What marvelous news, Mr. Kichline! Your family and your church have outdone themselves in generosity. I'll get one of the college students to pick up the supplies."

"I can help. I could, uh, take the medical supplies to the dispensary." He wouldn't admit, not even to himself, his ulterior motives.

"If you can manage by yourself, fine." Blair rubbed his hands together. "Those hymnals and teaching materials will go a long way in helping us further our mission." They began walking in the direction of the academic building. "I've been meaning to ask you how you're coming along with your work."

"I'm doing well, thank you."

They saluted a group of Korean women passing by.

"And do you enjoy bunking with Mr. Oh? I'm still hoping we'll have a room open up for you before too long."

"Please don't worry about that," Jacob said. "He's quite agreeable."

"He certainly is. What about your grasp of the language?"

Jacob gave a small laugh. "You know, I'm actually beginning to think a little in Korean. When we're alone, I practice on Mr. Oh. Let's just say he's a patient teacher."

"Wonderful. I thought you two would get along famously. That man is a gem, his whole family, well ..."

Jacob wondered where Blair had been heading before stopping so quickly.

"So, tell me, since you came here, what difficulties have you faced?"

This man was as plainspoken as a Korean. Jacob considered how much to reveal of his struggles, not so much the cultural adjustments, but his faith-related ones.

These he'd kept entirely to himself since his arrival. He chose evasion, cracking a smile.

"What makes you think I'm under duress?"

"Come now, son, you'd be a freak in a side show if you weren't."

He laughed outright at the image. Maybe he would tiptoe around the one thing he constantly wrestled with.

"I do have trouble with how much the mission entrusts Bible teaching to people who seem barely literate, who haven't been part of the church for very long. Besides being backward, they don't have anywhere near the exegetical or oratorical training I, uh, you and I have had." He grimaced at the sound of his own words.

"There's no need to be ashamed of your question, Mr. Kichline. You can say anything you like in my presence about anything at all. You're correct that numerous Korean leaders are new in the faith. They didn't grow up hearing the stories of Jesus or live in a society permeated with Christian references like we did. As for oratory ..." He raised a finger. "They are naturals at delivering a sermon and teaching classes. In fact, I've taken pointers from them. Rest assured we missionaries have put the Korean leaders through rigorous training and the teaching of sound biblical interpretation and doctrine. We don't permit anyone who doesn't pass our tests to preach or teach. Sadly, we've had to let some of them go, but I'm happy to report they're being put to good use according to their other talents. One I can think of distributes Christian literature across three regions."

"They seem to accept Christianity like children. Doesn't Christian maturity only come when we wrestle?"

"Sometimes, Mr. Kichline, great learning doesn't do us any favors. I've known fellows who had their faith shipwrecked by modernist theologians with all their intricate concepts." Blair stood still beneath a nearly leafless oak tree. "There isn't a person alive who doesn't wrestle with his faith, not even those you deem naïve. The idea is to provide a firm foundation on which to rest every part of our being. Then when times of testing come, we can meet them on that holy ground."

He kept silent.

"I get the impression that when you speak of faith struggles, you aren't just referring to our Korean brothers and sisters. Tell me, Mr. Kichline, why did you come to Korea?"

He had the sensation of being trapped. "Well, I'm good at languages, and the mission board needed a translator to come here."

"I see." He gazed at Jacob. "Why didn't you take a church?"

He closed his eyes and looked down, surprising himself by what proceeded from his lips. "Because none would have me."

A bell rang signaling the changing of classes. Jacob dared lift his countenance to the professor and blurted, "Do you despise me, Mr. Blair?"

"Son, the word you just used is further from my mind than any I could think of to describe my thoughts about you. I see you as a likeable, upstanding young man who's confused about life and faith. You might be surprised by how many young men leave seminary in such a state. I find your candor refreshing. In fact, I think you're getting the hang of this place and these people."

Jacob's heaviness of spirit eased.

"Would you allow me to pray with you?"

He figured he had nothing to lose.

"All right."

He bowed his head as William Blair petitioned the Lord to guide Jacob, to help him grow in his walk with Jesus in a spirit of open-minded humility, and to use Jacob's gifts to bless the Korean people. When the missionary finished, Jacob raised his moist eyes and thanked him.

"I'll continue to pray for you, Mr. Kichline. Come to me anytime about these matters. I'll always be available."

"Thank you, sir."

"Listen closely to the Koreans, Jacob. They have a great deal to teach you that Princeton never dreamed of."

He returned to the room relieved to see that Soon-hee wasn't there. Jacob needed a quiet space to collect his thoughts and bridle his emotions after the jarring encounter. He found his mother's letter on the desk lying next to his roommate's open Bible, removed his shoes and got comfortable on his bed.

> November 5, 1906
>
> Dear Son,
>
> Greetings from Easton, Penna., where leaves are now falling in earnest, and your family and friends miss you dearly. We all pray daily for your well-being and for the work you and your fellow missionaries are doing. Often as I go about my business in church and the markets around town, people ask how you are, and I regale them with your stories. We all take great pride in what you are doing and admire you so much.

Jacob cringed, wishing he could correct his mother's mistaken notions about his honor. His eyes wandered to Soon-hee's well-used Bible realizing he'd barely touched his own since coming to Korea. He continued reading.

> The women's circle worked with the deacons, elders, and Pastor Leinbach to procure the provisions accompanying this letter. You mentioned a great need for hymnals and other teaching aides, and we trust these small offerings will offset some of the deficits. I couldn't get over how many people attend your church there and the way those membership numbers continue to grow. Reverend Leinbach says you mustn't hesitate to share the mission's needs since the Consistory takes a special interest in your Korean work.
>
> Speaking of church, you're going to find the building greatly altered when you return. The renovations have been completed, and there will be a consecration service on the eighteenth of this month. All the exterior woodwork has been painted, along with the steeple, and there were repairs to the clock face. As you enter the church from North Third Street now, there's a new, fashionable Tiffany-designed lantern, and the same designer created eye-catching cast-iron hinges on the front doors. From the narthex to the Sunday School room, new "granolithic" flooring has been laid.
>
> The altar recess has also been changed and has less of an early American appearance. The side windows within the altar recess have been covered with paneling, and there are a new altar, pulpit, baptismal font, and lectern. Most of the parishioners are thrilled to be bringing a more updated quality to the church, but I don't mind saying I miss the homier, simple elegance of the former way. Your father feels the same. I'll be curious to know your thoughts about the changes since the young people have mixed opinions.

He wasn't sure he'd like them either, having loved the church's Revolutionary War character since his childhood. Maybe modern didn't always equate with better. For some reason, he glanced again at Soon-hee's Bible and curiosity overtook him. What was his roommate reading? He got up to investigate. Since this was a Korean Bible, Jacob began reading aloud slowly, deliberately, from the first chapter of First Corinthians. "For the word of the cross is folly to those who are perishing, but to us who are being saved it is the power of God. For it is written, I will destroy the wisdom of the wise, and the discernment of the discerning I will thwart. Where is the one who is wise? Where is the scribe? Where is the debater of this age? Has not God made foolish the wisdom of the world?"

Jacob had the uncomfortable sensation of having been caught unclothed. How far he'd fallen from the sweet faith he'd known in his younger years. He found his own English Bible and finished reading the passage.

"Because the foolishness of God is wiser than men; and the weakness of God is stronger than men. For ye see your calling, brethren, how that not many wise men after the flesh, not many mighty, not many noble, are called: But God hath chosen the foolish things of the world to confound the wise; and God hath chosen the weak things of the world to confound the things which are mighty; And base things of the world, and things which are despised, hath God chosen, yea, and things which are not, to bring to nought things that are: That no flesh should glory in his presence."

He closed the Bible and scrambled in his spirit for a fig leaf to cover his shame.

CHAPTER TWENTY-FOUR

MID-NOVEMBER 1906

Soon-hee detected something besides snow in the air when he took a longer route from the YMCA building to meet with Mr. Blair in the library. He'd been spending too much time behind a desk lately and needed to feel his heart pump and his face awaken to the cold. Near the Agriculture Experiment Gardens, he sniffed the distinctive scent of American tobacco and saw smoke rising near some bushes. Curious, he turned aside from his mission, his muscles tightening at the sight of his brother and two other fellows smoking cigarettes in a huddle. He tasted a bitter tang and hurried away to his appointment.

When Soon-hee entered the building and walked over to the stairway to the second floor, he blanched upon encountering Yong-bin's teacher. *Of all the people to run into today.* He took a deep breath when the amiable instructor greeted him.

"Well, hello, Mr. Oh. How are you today?"

"I am well, thank you, and how might you be, Mr. Hamilton?" Perhaps the American would end the chance meeting with this brief acknowledgment.

The teacher smiled. "I'm enjoying this invigorating cold air."

"I am as well."

Hamilton touched his right index finger to his chin when Soon-hee started walking away. "Say, I missed Yong-bin in my class. Your sister sent word that he was home with one of his headaches."

So, he lied to her and deceived Mr. Hamilton. My brother is a reprobate. By feigning illness, he is misleading everyone around him. Am I the only one who sees the truth?

He noticed the teacher looking intently at him, as if waiting for a response and said, "I was unaware of his latest infirmity."

"Oh, that's right, you don't live at home anymore."

"I do not." *Thanks be to God.* He remembered his parents had invited him, Miss Story, and Mr. Kichline to the evening meal tomorrow. The very thought of dining in the same house as his brother nauseated him.

"Well, if you see him, please tell him I'm praying for his recovery."

"If you will excuse me, I have an appointment with Mr. Blair."

"Good day then."

He clutched at his stomach to shield himself from an ambush of pain. Gulping slowly, he was able to calm and collect himself in time to see his professor—without giving away anything being amiss. Or so he hoped.

At the prayer meeting at Westgate Church three days later, Soon-hee's arms tingled when Mr. Blair closed the gathering with undisguised tears. He'd never seen this missionary do anything but smile.

"Oh Lord, thou art the forgiver of sins, and though our sins have made us as scarlet in thy sight, thou wilt cleanse us and make us as white as snow." Blair raised his face heavenward. "We thank thee for thy presence with us and for all thou art about to do in our midst as we seek thee with expectation and humility. Make us worthy of all thou hast entrusted us weak vessels. This we ask in the name of Jesus. Amen."

The people stirred from the places where they had sat or knelt. Soon-hee had been on his knees and as he prepared to stand, he shrank at the roiling in his stomach. He'd been feeling pretty good all day, believing himself to be on a better road only to experience this latest setback. He reminded himself that Miss Story and Dr. Walker had both told him to expect a recurrence of his illness, the main thing being its duration. He wasn't sure how to categorize how he felt just now because the pain was erratic in nature, coming and going one day, absent the next, then lingering for a day or two. This week, he'd felt poorly more than not. He was doing his best to eat regular meals, avoid irritating foods, and take his medicine.

I wonder when Dr. Walker will return to Pyongyang. I need to see him soon. He knew he could get word to the physician through Clara Story, but he hesitated as if talking about it would give the ailment more power over him. He skirmished with a groundswell of discouragement.

"Mr. Oh."

He startled, turning to see the American nurse. "Hello, Miss Story." He forced a smile. "You appear all aglow."

"I keep thinking the Lord is about to do something big here, beyond what we ask or think, as the verse goes."

"I would have to agree with you." He willed the searing in his stomach to desist.

She looked from left to right. “I expected to see Mr. Kichline here today. Is he unwell?”

He attempted to appear nonchalant. “He decided not to come.”

“Do you know why?”

Soon-hee was unsure how much he wished to say about his roommate’s reluctance to attend any but the Sunday services. When he remained wordless, Miss Story gazed at him, their eyes seeming to reach an unspoken understanding.

“I see. Well, I look forward to dining with the two of you at your parents’ home tonight. This is such a special treat for me, since your mother is an amazing cook, and so is Sora.”

He’d forgotten about the invitation which could not have come at a worse time and was, in fact, upon them. “Uh, yes.” He looked at his watch. “The prayer meeting has taken much longer than I expected.”

She consulted her own timepiece on a pendant she wore. “Oh, dear. I was hoping to freshen up a bit, but if I do, I’ll be late.” She smiled at him. “May I walk with you to your home, assuming you’re headed there now?”

“Of course.” He stepped aside for a moment to shake hands and exchange a few words with Mr. Swallen.

When the room cleared, the nurse said, “Perhaps Mr. Kichline will meet us there.”

He wasn’t worried about his colleague missing this social engagement since Jacob had been talking about going to the Ohs ever since Sunday when Soon-hee’s mother had invited him after church. What did really concern Soon-hee was whether he’d be able to keep a civil tongue with his scoundrel of a brother.

"Good evening, Mrs. Oh. I brought you some gifts to thank you for having me."

Soon-hee forced a close-lipped smile. His roommate had no idea he was being rude by not having wrapped the corrugated paper box according to the Korean custom. His mother received the present with a polite bow, which Jacob Kichline returned in awkward fashion.

"*Gamsahamnida*. Please tell me, what are these objects?"

Jacob committed another gaff when he pointed to a red and yellow tin. "This is Lipton tea, the brand my mother prefers. And these are cans of pork and beans and tuna fish."

Mr. and Mrs. Oh and Sora had a look.

Mr. Oh's thick brows raised. "Americans put fish in tins?"

"Yes. This is the latest in food preservation." He seemed pleased with himself as he looked about. "Something smells wonderful."

"I hope you will like our food," Sora said, her cheeks flushing.

Soon-hee also enjoyed the familiar scents of fermented vegetables, seafood, and the coal fire that heated his childhood home.

"Do go relax, and we will soon serve the meal," Mrs. Oh said.

Soon-hee led his family's guests to the lantern-lit dining area with its low table and cushions.

"This is my first meal in a Korean home," Jacob said, "not counting the inn I stayed at a while back. Is your floor also heated underneath?"

"Yes, Mr. Kichline, you will be warm as you eat." Mr. Oh arranged his guests around the table. "I will sit here, then my wife, then you and Miss Story, Soon-hee, and Sora."

"Where is your other son?" Jacob asked.

Soon-hee's shoulders tensed. He had been wondering as well.

"Yong-bin is sick with the headache and will not be joining us for our meal."

"Oh, that's too bad." Jacob sat down hard on the cushion and laughed a little too loudly. "Woops. Your floor is closer than I thought."

When everyone was seated, Mr. Oh offered a brief prayer of thanksgiving, and his wife and daughter set to work serving, beginning with Soon-hee's father, then their guests. Soon-hee breathed easier when Jacob seemed to hesitate before lifting his spoon, chiding himself for not giving his American friend a lesson in Korean manners. These included having the younger people at the table always waiting for the oldest to take the first bite of food.

Mr. and Mrs. Oh introduced Jacob to everything from the familiar, *bap* or rice, and *guk* or soup, to *Naengmyeon* a Pyongyang signature dish of cold buckwheat noodles with pork and seasoned with kimchi. The Koreans smiled at their American guest's struggles with the short bronze chopsticks and encouraged him to use a large spoon if he was more comfortable eating that way. Once he employed the metal utensil, Jacob ate a little too fast, but Soon-hee noticed his mother grinning, probably because her carefully-prepared foods were being so well received.

Jacob exclaimed over the hotpot called *Jongol*, which Mrs. Oh cooked right at the table with slices of beef, vegetables, tofu, eggs, and clear noodles in a seasoned broth.

"This is absolutely fantastic, Mrs. Oh. I've never had anything like this before. The German-style food we eat at home is downright bland compared to this."

"This dish is my personal favorite," Clara Story said. "Mrs. Oh is a great cook."

The smile she gave Jacob wasn't lost on Soon-hee.

"Thank you very much," his mother said in careful English.

Soon-hee took very small amounts of the richer offerings, focusing on the bland rice to cushion any fiery blows to his digestion. He noted with some relief his mother had used less spice, probably in deference to the Americans. He looked forward to taking a short walk outside to use the facility and to swallow a dose of his medicine undetected.

"Soon-hee."

His mother's voice nearly made him jump out of his seat.

"You are eating very little. Sora, give your brother more kimchi. His food is weak."

He lifted his hands palms up. "I am full, *Eomeoni*. Your meal has been delicious."

"Why do you not eat more?"

"I do not eat as much as I used to." Maybe that would put her off.

She was a hound on the scent. "Why?"

Soon-hee's neck heated as he tried once again to deflect the negative attention. "I have, uh, I must still be careful."

"You are strong enough, Soon-hee," she said as if that settled the matter. "If you eat my food, you will grow even stronger."

Clara Story stepped in. "Mrs. Oh, Dr. Walker has encouraged him to take care about his food."

He waited for his mother's reaction, surprised by her sudden laugh. "No one knows a son like his mother. Soon-hee has always been my strong son."

He tasted bitterness. Yong-bin monopolized all the sympathy there was to be had in this home.

He lay on the bed pressing a wadded-up shirt against his stomach, waiting for the medicine to begin erasing the gnawing pain. He'd started to doze when the sound of the opening door roused him, and his roommate entered the darkened space.

"Oh, I'm sorry, Mr. Oh. I didn't mean to awaken you."

He was ready for the step he took next, something he'd considered for a few weeks as they grew closer. "Perhaps, Mr. Kichline, when we are in our room, you might like to call me Soon-hee."

"Thanks, I'd be honored, and please call me Jacob." He removed and hung up his coat and hat, then sat on the side of his bed to untie his shoes.

Soon-hee reached over to the lamp next to his bed and clicked on the electric switch, bathing the room in light.

"How are you feeling?"

"The medicine is helping."

"That's good." He rested his arms on his knees. "I guess your mother doesn't realize how careful you need to be."

He sighed. "She thinks I am all better, and I have not wished to worry her. She has many responsibilities."

"Yes, she sure is a busy lady. It was really nice of her to go to all that trouble to cook for us."

"She enjoys entertaining."

"I was just sorry to hear your brother wasn't feeling well enough to join us. I've only met him once, briefly in church."

"My brother is a great pretender." His bluntness shocked even himself.

"Do you mean he wasn't really sick?" Jacob stared at his roommate.

"I believe so, Mr., uh, Jacob. This morning, although he was too ill to attend his classes, I found him and two other students smoking cigarettes and laughing near the Agriculture Experiment Gardens."

"Wow. Has he done anything like that before? I mean, boys do enjoy skipping school now and then."

Soon-hee adjusted his makeshift pillow. "My brother was a frail baby, and much of his boyhood was spent with overpowering headaches. He required a good bit of attention." He wondered if Jacob might be able to read between the lines, to understand the neglect Soon-hee had experienced, much of which he had accepted as a necessity. "Yong-bin learned how to manipulate our parents."

Laughter spilled into the room from young men passing outside the door, and Soon-hee waited to see if he might have to go out and tell them to quiet down. When they moved along the hall, he returned to the conversation.

"In what way?" Jacob was asking.

"He learned to pretend illness when he wished to get out of anything he deemed unpleasant." Soon-hee spread his hands. "I do not know at this time how much is true sickness."

"The boy who cried wolf," Jacob said.

Recognizing the cultural reference, Soon-hee agreed. "Yes, this applies to my brother, though he has not met with an actual wolf."

"Are the two of you close?"

"We are not. We have been at odds since ..." He realized he wasn't ready to reveal more than he already had said. Instead he smiled. "Let us speak no further of unhappy things. You came in looking pleased. Did you enjoy speaking with Miss Story when you walked her home?"

"I certainly did. I've never met anyone like her before."

"She is strong and full of faith." He grinned. "And she is comely."

Jacob laughed. "Yes, comely she is."

"She is a fine missionary. My people like her very much and look forward to her visits."

When his roommate's mood shifted, Soon-hee investigated. "What has made you sad?"

"Oh, I'm not sad, more puzzled than anything. We were discussing your illness—I hope you don't mind—and she said being careful to eat and rest properly would help you, along with prayer."

"Why should this trouble you?" There were times he didn't understand this new friend.

"Well, she told me some stories about people she believes God has healed here."

Soon-hee leaned forward. "She is right that many have been brought back to health through prayer."

Jacob gave a sharp exhale. "Don't get me wrong. I think prayer can soothe the spirit, but the body responds to scientific methods. Through modern medicine, God has given us the means to heal ourselves."

"Why cannot both be true?"

"I suppose they can, but science must take precedence."

Soon-hee was beginning to see where his American friend was coming from. Jacob had been heavily influenced by modernist teachings.

"You believe, then, that science has the answers to our illnesses?" he asked.

"Sure. We no longer have to be superstitious about what makes people sick, or what cures them." He paused. "Miss Story and I had a friendly disagreement about this topic."

"I can imagine."

"What do you think, Soon-hee? You're a learned man."

He smiled at the compliment before quoting the Englishman Shakespeare. "As one of your great writers has said, 'There are more things in heaven and earth, Horatio, than are dreamt of in your philosophy.'"

CHAPTER TWENTY-FIVE

Late November 1906

For once, Jacob got up earlier than Soon-hee, but he was eager to begin the momentous day. He'd eat a quick breakfast and take a brisk walk before going to the print shop where his book was going to be produced today. He might not have been enamored with *The Christian's Secret of a Happy Life* but translating it into Korean had been satisfying work. He dressed quickly in the semi-darkness and noted the bounce in his step as he walked to the dining hall where just a few people had gathered.

He ate his toast with marmalade in four bites and downed two cups of green tea while ignoring the *banchan*, a collection of side dishes on his table. He knew Mary Yoo wouldn't be pleased, but far worse was the prospect of eating fermented vegetables first thing in the morning. He'd learned that particular lesson the hard way. Fortunately, her back was turned when he brought his cup and plate to the service counter, and he was out the door before she could take a survey of his table.

Judging by the way his breath formed puffy vapor outside, Jacob guessed the temperature to be around the freezing point. He fished in his coat pockets for the leather gloves his mother had sent, realizing he could have exercised in the compound's warm gymnasium. Today, however, the Taedong River drew him. He ambled down the hill, then along the city's narrow streets past the famed Water Gate to the riverfront, the air perfumed with burning coal. As he watched the ferries carrying passengers, goods, and animals against the backdrop of recently constructed bridges, his thoughts wandered back to his hometown. His grandfather had told him about the ferries that had once served as hubs between Easton and neighboring Phillipsburg, New Jersey. The old-fashioned means of transport had disappeared a hundred years ago, replaced by a covered bridge Jacob had loved crossing as a boy. He'd enjoyed the bumping of carriage wheels against the plank boards and the play of sunlight through wooden slats along the sides. Jacob recalled the way he'd start humming and how the jolting movement would bounce not only his body but his voice. That span had gone the way of the ferries ten years ago when a Lafayette professor designed a cantilever truss bridge that could accommodate modern trolley cars.

Jacob swallowed a flash of homesickness. The Delaware River, which joined the even smaller Lehigh River at "the Forks," wasn't nearly as grand as the Taedong, but those waterways meant home to him. He recalled fishing along their banks with his father and brothers, especially in the spring when the shad ran. The nippy air cut into his exposed face, motivating him to keep moving. On his way back to the compound which occupied Namson Hill, he realized he liked Pyongyang with its old-style Korean architecture against the backdrop of modern buildings. If he had his way, he'd gladly stay within the city limits for the duration of his tenure and avoid the outskirts where life was a daily struggle for most. But he could not.

He arrived in the ink-scented print shop finding Kang-min Ahn working the hand-operated press, a rather basic machine by US standards. He'd seen some of its other projects and thought it did a decent job.

"*Annyeonghaseyo.*"

The handsome printer, in his early twenties, smiled at Jacob and greeted him in English. "Good morning, Mr. Kichline. Have you come to see your book be published?"

He grinned. *My book. I wonder what Pearl would have to say about this.* He hadn't been in touch with her since coming to Korea.

"Yes, I have—that is if I'm not in the way."

Kang-min glanced about, one hand on the machine, the other feeding paper into the noisy device. "I am pleased to have you. I thought perhaps Mr. Oh might come as well."

"I got up rather earlier than he did, which I assure you is not typical. He is very conscientious."

"He is a fine man, a good man."

"Do you know him well?"

Kang-min adjusted the screw mechanism, which would apply the right among of pressure through a platen onto the inked type.

"The Oh family is rather close with my family," he said. "My sister Jeongsook often helps Mrs. Oh in her Bible studies and some medical work, and my father supports Mr. Oh in his church responsibilities."

Jacob pulled his chin, remembering something Soon-hee had told him about his interest in a young woman who worked with his mother. Might this Jeongsook be her? He'd never heard the whole story.

"They certainly are a fine family," he said. "So, about how long will printing the book take you?"

"Each sheet takes front and back passes. At two-hundred impressions for each hour, which is nearly the total number of pages, this project will be about ten hours long."

Jacob whistled. "This sounds like a two-day job. I can help if you like."

"Thank you, but I will have an assistant shortly, and together we will have this done by later today. You will come back then?"

"Yes. I'd like to see how the book turns out. Thank you for explaining the process, Mr. Ahn. I'll leave you to your work and go to mine."

Jacob didn't know just what that work would be, another book or perhaps Bible studies or tracts? He went to his office to await directions from Mr. Blair.

He was all at sixes and sevens in the office, sharpening pencils, taking out the trash, clearing out desk drawers. Mr. Blair had promised to put Jacob on a new undertaking once the book was completed, but the hardworking missionary hadn't gotten around to specifics. He glanced at his wall calendar, realizing Thanksgiving was just a few days away, on the twenty-second. Jacob hadn't given much thought to the holiday and pondered whether the missionaries observed the date and, if so, how.

He decided now would be a good time to answer a letter from his sister Grace, and if there were time, he'd write to Rand, whose own tidings had arrived a week ago. His former Princeton pal seemed happy in Connecticut, having provided details about his church's spiritual and numeric growth. He'd also hinted at a certain parishioner who'd caught his attention, and Jacob was curious to know more about her.

"Mr. Kichline."

He looked up from his desk.

"Hello, Mr. Cullen. How are you and your wife?" He was happy to see his Princeton professor.

"Just fine, and yourself? We haven't seen much of you lately."

"I've been completing my first translation work. The book is going to press as we speak."

Cullen leaned against the door frame. "So, I heard. Congratulations."

"Thank you."

"What will you work on next?"

"I'm waiting for Mr. Blair to tell me."

"If I guess correctly, he'll have you doing Bible studies, for which we have a pressing need. The Koreans are hungrier to know the Word of God than any people I've ever known." He pressed a finger to his upper lip and muttered to himself, "Maybe he won't mind if I ask." He turned his attention back to Jacob. "Actually, this is the reason for my stopping by."

Jacob perked up. "Oh?"

"Some of the Bible Women have been begging us for more literature, and I promised to take some into the nearby villages. I would love your company."

His shoulders slumped when he realized his wish to stay within Pyongyang wasn't going to be granted. They'd probably be staying at one of those primitive "inns" with their overpowering smells of pungent spices, wood and tobacco smoke, and grubby travelers. There was, however, no easy way out of going.

"Uh, sure. How long would we be gone?"

"Just an overnight if all goes according to plan."

Cullen was bouncing on his toes, an endearing gesture Jacob had noticed a few times on the journey to Korea.

"Will just you be going?"

"My wife usually travels with me, as well as Miss Story, Mrs. Oh, and her daughter, but everyone is too busy just now."

His pulse raced. "Will we have to cross one of those swinging bridges?"

Cullen laughed. "Not this time. Between you and me, I dread those."

Relaxing he asked, "When will we leave? Will we be back for Thanksgiving? I mean, do the missionaries celebrate the holiday?"

"I want to get ahead of bad weather, which can come on rather suddenly in these parts, so my goal is to leave the day after tomorrow. We'll be back in plenty of time for Thanksgiving, which I'm told is quite the event here."

Jacob's mood lifted.

On the way to the village twenty-five miles east of Pyongyang, there was plenty of time for conversation as they rode side-by-side on horseback, their saddles encumbered with Christian literature.

"I've been meaning to ask you, Mr. Cullen, about these Bible Women. I met one on my first trip to the countryside, but I only know a little about them."

"They're some of the finest people you'll ever meet," he said. "Whether young or old, each of them is completely dedicated to serving the Lord Jesus."

He ducked under a low-hanging tree limb and readjusted his hat. "They mainly minister to other women, don't they?"

"They do a number of things, but they function as evangelists and pastors. They do house-to-house visitation and care for the sick, instruct women and children in the faith, act as interpreters for the missionaries, and distribute Christian literature." He clucked his tongue. "I've been told some of them cover circuits of a hundred miles or more."

Jacob grimaced. While their intentions seemed laudable, he couldn't help but say, "But isn't that the work of an ordained pastor? What training do they have?"

"In most places in America, yes. Here the missionaries have given them special instruction for their work. Some are actually illiterate, distributing literature they can't even read." He paused. "They're truly marvelous, Mr. Kichline."

He wasn't so sure. If they didn't know how to properly interpret—or even read—the Bible, might they be doing more harm than good? He kept his thoughts to himself, but his companion seemed to read his disposition.

"Perhaps you should withhold judgment until you meet Ha-eun."

She was what Mr. Blair called "an old mother," who greeted them at the door of her single story *hanok* with tears in her eyes. Her teeth, wrinkled skin, and clothing had clearly seen better days, but she was immaculately clean. As Jacob bowed to greet her, he was struck by her radiant face, wondering how anyone living like this could be so joyful.

Dennis Cullen addressed her in Korean, and she bobbed her covered head up and down. Then she took both of Jacob's hands.

"I am happy to meet you, man of God."

"I am honored to meet you," he said in slow, deliberate Korean.

She invited them into her snug house and served tea, receiving their packages of Christian Bible studies and assorted tracts as if they were keys to a palace. Jacob didn't understand a lot of what she said, but he discerned her meaning and savored her warmth. When they left her, waving goodbye from their mounts, he was full of questions.

"Isn't she incredible, Jacob?"

"I'm still trying to understand how she can be so content when she's old, alone, and has so little."

Cullen took a while before answering. "I can always recognize among old Korean women which of them are Christians. Most of them have lived in ignorance and servitude to their husbands, who treat them as less valuable than their oxen. Their lives are full of drudgery and superstition. They get up before the sun and cook for their husbands and only get to eat after the men are fed, then just whatever is left behind. The women are mostly unloved during their lives and greatly fear death. Remember those devil's posts we passed on the way to see Ha-eun?"

Jacob shivered. "I found those disturbing."

"Yes, they are. Most Korean women, however, regard them as their only defense against the evil spirits and demons they believe dog them in life and may drag them into a hellish place when they die."

Jacob's mood took a dive.

"When such a woman hears the message of God's love and forgiveness, that he loves her to the point of giving his own Son to suffer death so she might live eternally, all the glory of it fills her soul to overflowing. His mercy shines in them like sunshine, beautifying their faces with the love of Jesus." He turned to Jacob. "And that, Mr. Kichline is something no amount of money or education can generate."

Mary Yoo and her staff had outdone themselves in creating a Thanksgiving feast. The dining hall was redolent with the scents of coffee, roasting meat, and tantalizing baked goods, each cloth-covered table hosting expectant diners. After just returning from his trip, Jacob felt as if he'd entered the hall of a great palace.

Mr. Swallen seemed to take an inordinate amount of time giving thanks to God for this bounty, taking Jacob back to his home when his father's prayers went on and on, and his mother fretted over the food going cold. Once the missionary's prayer concluded, and they began to eat, Jacob surveyed the array of American missionaries from the compound, as well as others he hadn't met from the outlying districts. Several Korean church leaders and their families were also present, everyone talking at once.

The food turned out to be rather unlike his Easton Thanksgiving table. There were no plump turkeys with giblet gravy and Pennsylvania Dutch "filling," no "chow chow," cranberry sauce, or mashed potatoes slathered with butter and gravy. Plenty of kimchi was on hand, however, as well as daikon radishes, roasted sweet potatoes, and spinach. Rather than an enormous turkey, individual chickens and pork *bulgogi* provided the meat course. Jacob surprised himself by picking at his food although his foot jiggled in anticipation of Mary Yoo's version of pumpkin pie, his favorite part of Thanksgiving meals. He briefly wondered whether his mother would allow him a slice, since he hadn't eaten all his vegetables, then closed his eyes, wondering where in the world such a thought had come from. The room had become so very hot.

One of the servers placed a piece of pie in front of him, and Jacob closed his eyes against a sensation of heat in his abdomen that radiated to his throat. A minute later, he took a large bite of the pie, barely tasting the dessert for the bile filling his esophagus.

"Mr. Kichline, are you all right?"

His eyes hazy, he turned to Soon-hee fearing what might happen if he opened his mouth. His friend started talking to Clara Story who immediately took charge.

"Mr. Kichline, Mr. Oh and I are going to help you get up. Are you able to walk?"

He rose on trembling feet, overwhelmed by an urge to use the restroom.

He awakened in the campus infirmary, his gut hollow and his mouth, dry and foul-tasting. All he could remember in his febrile state was multiple trips to the toilet to empty both ends of his body. He squinted at the sunlight-infused outer office where someone was walking around. He called out "Hello," his voice rasping.

Clara Story entered with a smile. "Well hello, Mr. Kichline. I'm happy to see you awake." She shook down a thermometer and placed the tube between his lips, pressing her fingers into his wrist.

He winced at the thought of this beautiful woman having seen him like this. Then again, she was a nurse.

She extracted the thermometer after a few minutes declaring, "One-hundred. This is a decided improvement but still rather high."

"What's wrong with me?"

"In a word, dysentery. It's a rather common condition here, and we have everything we need to help you get better. Dr. Walker has been informed, and he'll be here later to check on you."

His head tingled. "Am I going to die?" His mother might never forgive him if he died in Korea.

She smiled and patted his hand. "No, Mr. Kichline, you will not die, but you'll need a few weeks to recover. You'll also need to stay here to rest and not spread the disease."

"Soon-hee? Is he ill? Did I make anyone else sick?"

"Not that we know of. Mr. Oh is fine for now, keeping to his room as a precaution."

The good news sank in, then he moved his hand to his throat. "I'm so thirsty."

"I'll bring you some water, but you must sip it slowly."

Dr. Walker arrived a few hours later and performed a methodical checkup.

"I'd say you're in pretty good shape for the shape you're in."

Jacob grinned. "My grandmother always says that."

He draped the stethoscope around his neck. "I'll be here for at least a week, overseeing you and my other patient."

"Someone else is ill?" He thought Clara Story had said everyone else was all right so far.

"Mr. Cullen." He raised a hand. "Don't worry. Both of you are handling this as well as can be expected. You must've picked this up on your recent trip."

"May I have visitors?" he asked.

"I'm afraid not for a while. We need to isolate this so there isn't an outbreak. By God's mercy, there are just your two cases. You'll have to put up with me, Miss Story, and Miss Oh, who has volunteered her services."

"Sora Oh, Soon-hee's sister?"

"Yes." He smiled. "I'm going to see Mr. Cullen now, but before I go, please allow me to pray."

"Oh, sure, yes."

"Lord God, we give thee thanks and praise for Mr. Kichline and his love for you that brought him to this place and this time in Korea. We ask thee to draw near to him as he battles this disease, to provide thy strength and peace. We trust thee for his healing and commit him to thy tender care. Through Christ our Lord, amen."

"Amen." He smiled at the doctor through moist eyes.

By the third day, Jacob was staying awake for longer stretches, and Clara Story read to him from the Psalms and *Ben Hur*, a book he had devoured as a boy. Her lilting voice captured the various characters and set the tone for each scene, as if she were a seasoned actress. His memory took him back to Princeton and the time he'd been ill with influenza, recovering at McCosh Infirmary. While he was there, one of the seminary professors had come to see him, doing his duty as a chaplain and had spent the entire time talking about a research project. He left without praying and none too soon for the weary Jacob. Win had also visited, bringing secular magazines and Tootsie Rolls. Except for Rand, whose presence and prayer had encouraged Jacob, the others had left him comfortless. Now, he began to realize as he dozed, perhaps they'd had none to give out of the storehouses of their modernist way of thinking. Maybe, just maybe, Rand, Gresham Machen, Pearl, and these stouthearted missionaries were on to something far better than he'd been holding on to.

CHAPTER TWENTY-SIX

EARLY DECEMBER 1906

Soon-hee hadn't heard from his spiritual director since the end of summer, and he savored the new letter from Samuel Moffett for a third time. As soon as he finished reading it, he gathered his writing implements and sat down to reply. Since he'd been confined to his room at Thanksgiving, he'd positioned the desk he shared with Jacob to face outside so he didn't feel quite so isolated from those who went about their business as usual.

> December 5, 1906
>
> My Dear Mr. Moffett,
>
> With great joy, I received your letter of October 16. As you have instructed, I will send this to you at Princeton Theological Seminary. When you said that you have been accepted for a non-degree graduate program, I was concerned this meant you would be staying in America longer than anticipated. Then your reassurance of returning to Korea next summer gladdened my soul. You are very much missed here.
>
> I have read with interest your activities on behalf of Korean immigrants in California and with the New Albany Presbytery in Indiana. How busy you are and

how widely you travel! I am certain that wherever and however you and Mrs. Dr. Moffett serve, you bless many people. Thank you also for the report about baby Jamie's health and development. I shall find him very much changed when I see him again in several months and hope he will remember me.

As I write to you, snow is falling outside my window at the YMCA, and the flakes are slow and steady. I find the snow both refreshing and consoling, how the whiteness transforms all of nature. I am currently residing here by myself since my roommate Jacob Kichline took ill at the Thanksgiving feast. He has been recovering at our infirmary along with Mr. Cullen. The two of them had just returned from a brief visit to one of the villages. Dr. Walker confirmed Miss Story's initial diagnosis of dysentery and has assured all of us that both men will, by God's grace, recover sooner rather than later. Because Mr. Kichline and I share close quarters, I am confined to this space for two weeks. Mary Yoo keeps me well nourished, and I have much time to work on my courses and some Bible study translation. Without distractions, I accomplish a good deal, although I do get lonely for the company of others.

Mr. Kichline has been a very good associate. Just last month, we completed translating *The Christian's Secret of a Happy Life*, and Mr. Ahn did a fine job of printing the book, which is being distributed to surrounding churches. Mr. Blair has me working on Bible studies now, focusing on the gospel of Luke and the book of Acts. Our people are so thirsty for God's Word.

I am laboring as diligently as ever on the program you have set before me, and Mr. Blair does not allow me to spend more time translating than is good for me. This is where Mr. Kichline has been a true blessing to the work.

You inquired about my health, and I am pleased to tell you I am feeling better.

Soon-hee glanced up from the desk to watch squirrels leaving tiny tracks in the snow. He wasn't comfortable disclosing everything about his condition lest he cause Mr. Moffett undue worry.

> Dr. Walker continues to watch over me, and as long as I avoid my mother's cooking, I fare better. Thank you for your continuing prayers for me, which are much appreciated and surely effectual.

He was ready for a change of subject.

> Since the August meetings, the missionaries have continued to meet regularly in concentrated prayer, seeking a great blessing of God upon our Korean brethren. You inquired about this, as well as how the Japanese believers are advancing in the faith. These two are tied together. There remains a need for the Korean church not only to repent of its hatred for the Japanese, but to see more clearly the many ways in which we ourselves have sinned against God. As you know, many come to faith with great joy and gladness, eager to become part of the Kingdom work, without understanding the need to repent of one's sin.
>
> In addition to these concerted prayer times in which we seek to be right with our Savior, I have committed to pray at appointed times each day. The Lord Jesus does not always show me comfortable things about myself.

He swallowed hard as he continued.

> You may pray for me to overcome the resentment I feel for my brother, who continues in his prodigal condition. Then, there are sometimes uncharitable thoughts about the Japanese who are coming so gladly to the faith. I am too proud, too unforgiving.

He wished he could take back those words, but they came at the end of a page, and he didn't want to rewrite the entire section. Besides, Mr. Moffett was a man of candor and discretion, and Soon-hee believed his confession would be safe with the missionary.

> I do wish you could be here for the Pyongyang General Class for Men. This will take place during the first two weeks in January, and there is a sense of expectation regarding what our Lord might do during these meetings. I look forward to them as much as I have come to enjoy celebrating Christmas missionary-fashion. Be assured I will write to tell you how this gathering turns out.
>
> I send my highest affections to you, to Mrs. Dr. Moffett, and to Jamie and pray you to continue in good health and a robust relationship with the One whose birth we will soon observe. Though we are thousands of miles apart, I remain your devoted student,
>
> Soon-hee Oh

"I think you're ready to be sprung."

"Please excuse me?"

Andrew Walker laughed. "Me and my slang. What I mean, Mr. Oh, is that you've shown no signs of dysentery, so you're safe to be out and about."

He released a contented sigh. "This is very good news. I am very ready to enjoy some fresh air. How are Mr. Kichline and Mr. Cullen? May I visit them?"

"They're also doing nicely, though still quite weak. I think they'd enjoy seeing you." He crossed his arms behind his head and leaned back in Soon-hee's chair. "Now then, tell me how your gut is coming along. Are you having any symptoms?"

He didn't want to admit what needed to be said. "I have some tenderness."

"Where and how often?"

"In the middle, I have sometimes a burning sensation."

"How often?"

His shoulders tensed. "Every other day or so for perhaps thirty minutes, sometimes a little longer."

"What brings relief?"

"Eating and also taking the bismuth."

"Are you drinking milk as I prescribed?"

"I sometimes forget." He wasn't overly fond of the beverage the missionaries had introduced at the compound. Traditionally, Koreans did not drink cow's milk.

"I'll make sure Mary Yoo always has milk available. Are you just eating bland foods?"

"Yes." And he was plenty tired of them too.

"I know, for someone used to spicy cuisine, this must be a trial."

"I simply want to be well again."

He wondered why the physician was gazing at him and waited for him to say something.

"Mr. Oh, I have long suspected there's a connection between the mind and the body. Medicine can do marvelous healing, but our emotions also play a role in our health. I hope you don't mind my asking, but is something troubling you, something eating as it were at your spirit?"

He startled at the expression, at how much the words hit home. He took a few moments to gather his thoughts. "Yes, Dr. Walker."

"Have you been able to share what the problem is with anyone?"

He tucked his chin to his chest. "Mr. Moffett is aware."

"That's good, but he's far away and has been for some months. I do hope I've earned your trust as a physician and as a brother in Christ, Mr. Oh. I want you to feel free to speak to me not only about your stomach's health, but your spiritual health at any time."

He closed his eyes. "Thank you. I would ask just now, if you would please pray with me."

"I'll be honored." They bowed their heads. "Heavenly Father, I thank thee for my brother Soon-hee Oh and for his great love for thee, for his heart to bring in a great harvest for thy kingdom. We thank thee he didn't contract dysentery, even as we give thanks for Mr. Kichline's and Mr. Cullen's recoveries. Lord, I ask thee to bring about a complete healing of Mr. Oh's ulcer, that by thy Holy Spirit thou might do a wonderful work in him to bring relief from physical pain. Thou alone knowest the thoughts and intentions of our hearts, and I ask thee to reveal to Mr. Oh anything that might help in this healing process. Use thy means and thy methods to achieve this for his good and thy glory. I ask these things in the great name of Jesus. Amen."

"Amen."

Normally, he sat somewhere in the first four rows of Central Presbyterian, but on his inaugural Sunday back at worship, Soon-hee relegated himself to a back pew. He hadn't seen many people in two weeks, and he'd found the dining hall's activity and conversations more stimulating than usual after his confinement. Now, this gathering of over a thousand people and the energetic organ music came at him in waves. If he needed to leave, he could do so without drawing attention to himself. He waited for the prelude to begin, conversing briefly with his right-hand neighbor, the father of a seminarian. Soon-hee also noted a group of young Japanese men, their faces bright, expectant. An old

Korean man was talking with one of them, who appeared to listen with a deferential spirit. When Soon-hee's heart began to harden, he quickly turned to prayer. *Lord, grant me thy thoughts about them. Help me to love as you do and not allow bitterness to grow.*

A more peaceful mood settled over him as he looked at his father, who was assisting Mr. Swallen in worship. Despite the temperature being below twenty degrees zero, the sun's rays provided both physical and spiritual warmth as they shone through the windows.

The prelude ended, and Mr. Oh rose to call the assembly to worship.

"This is the day the Lord has made. Let us rejoice and be glad in it. Please stand for the opening hymn, 'Holy, Holy, Holy! Lord God Almighty!'"

Soon-hee's heart swelled with the soaring music, the thronging voices lifting in praise to the merciful and mighty God. He was ravenous for the preaching of the Word, having not been in church for three Sundays. When Mr. Swallen took to the pulpit, Soon-hee eagerly opened his Bible to the morning's passage.

Addressing the people in Korean, he said, "Our text today is found in Matthew, the fifth chapter, verses twenty-one to twenty-six in a passage from what is known as the Sermon on the Mount." He lifted his Bible and began to read. "'Ye have heard that it was said of them of old time, thou shalt not kill; and whosoever shall kill shall be in danger of the judgement.'"

The missionary continued reading the familiar section, Soon-hee following along. At the twenty-third verse, however, its message upended him.

"'Therefore if thou bring thy gift to the altar, and there rememberest that thy brother hath ought against thee, leave there thy gift, and go thy way; first be reconciled to thy brother, and then come offer thy gift …'"

As far as Soon-hee was concerned, Mr. Swallen had already preached his sermon.

All that afternoon, he wrestled with the Lord like the Old Testament's Jacob, wondering whether going to his brother would do any good. He'd tried once before, and Yong-bin had turned away in contempt. Might confronting him just now result in further harm to their relationship? By the end of the day, he realized that no matter how his brother might respond, for Soon-hee's own good, for his own relationship to be right with God, this thing had to be done. He went to bed reconciled to this path, slept peacefully, and the next morning after breakfast, intercepted his brother and two friends on their way to their first class.

"Good morning. May I speak with you?"

Yong-bin looked away from him, off to the side. "I cannot be late."

Soon-hee held back from retorting, "Since when has being on time ever mattered to you?" Instead, he spoke calmly. "This will take but a minute." He steered his brother away from the others and sought the shelter of a tree where clumps of dried leaves clung tenaciously to ice-covered branches.

"Yong-bin, I know you resent me for not helping you cheat on that exam when you were in need of a good grade."

Seeing the young man gaze downward, Soon-hee continued feeling emboldened.

"I know you told Jeongsook I did not care for her, that I loved someone else." He sucked in his breath. "I also have sinned in my heart by holding bitterness against you. Yong-bin, please look at me."

His brother's face upturned as if the effort pained him.

Soon-hee looked into the dark eyes. "I forgive you for what you did, and I ask you to forgive me for being full of malice toward you."

For a moment, the words hung between them as they stared at each other. Soon-hee's senses heightened as he waited for a response. Yong-bin was the first to look away before he took off like a shot in the freezing morning air.

CHAPTER TWENTY-SEVEN

DECEMBER 16, 1906

Even the mundane act of seeing Soon-hee comb his straight black hair while getting ready for church on this third Sunday of Advent brought a smile to Jacob's lips. After being confined to the infirmary for nearly three weeks, this room and the everydayness of their normal routine was a welcome change. Now, he was well enough to dine in the hall and begin a light work schedule on Monday morning. However, he wasn't fit enough to sit through one of Central Presbyterian's lengthy church services. Dr. Walker also had cautioned Jacob against large gatherings for the time being, since he was still susceptible to picking up other illnesses. He didn't mind the part about skipping services. The lack of pews, exclusive use of the Korean language, and prolonged worship left him in a stupor even on the best of days.

Soon-hee picked up his Bible after putting on his hat. "I dislike leaving you alone."

Jacob smiled at his friend's mishmash appearance, a woolen overcoat straight from a Sears catalog and, underneath, the traditional Korean *Hanbok*.

"Please don't be concerned. I'm just enjoying being back in our room again."

"I shall pay extra close attention to the sermon and share the message with you."

He almost said, "There's no need," but chose a simple "Thank you" instead.

After Soon-hee left, Jacob lay back against two pillows, his legs stretching the length of the small bed. He'd relished not only Mary Yoo's porridge and toast that morning, but the surprisingly sweet smile with which she'd greeted him. A few of the seminarians sat with him and Soon-hee, and Jacob ate slowly, having amended his habit of scarfing food. He was content to let everyone else do most of the talking, soaking up the buoyant tone in the hall.

Being at the infirmary for all those days hadn't been all bad, however—not when he'd had Miss Clara Story looking after him. He'd grown considerably fonder of her during his convalescence, appreciating her compassion and her expert medical ability. He'd never known a woman physician before this, and by all rights she wasn't one, but her skills seemed to match those of Dr. Andrew Walker. When she'd finished her rounds, she had often sat with Jacob to talk, read, and pray. He'd admired the way her nurse's cap set off her pinned-up light brown hair and eyes, and how her apron-covered dress hugged her feminine curves. He hadn't taken such an interest in a woman since meeting Pearl, a thought he found both intriguing and unsettling. *If I truly care for Pearl, how can I be attracted to Miss Story, to Clara? Maybe this means I'm not as connected to Pearl as I thought I was. Or maybe I'm just grateful to Clara for taking good care of me.*

Jacob pondered whether the nurse found him appealing. She had seemed to take a special interest in him, but then, he couldn't be sure. Had she also gone the extra mile in her treatment of Mr. Cullen or her other patients? When he'd been with her in other circumstances, he'd taken pleasure in their conversations, drawn to her easy laughter and the way she seemed comfortable with everyone she met whether high, low, or in between.

The manner in which she fell into prayer as naturally as if she were talking to a real person also intrigued him. She seemed to take God personally, expecting him to hear her and respond, the way Jacob used to be. At Princeton he had put away what he'd come to consider childish things of the faith, exchanging milk with meat, but now he wasn't sure what was juvenile and what was the child-like attitude Jesus had encouraged his disciples to cultivate. There seemed nothing sentimental or naïve about Clara Story's robust faith. In a word, her winsome qualities made for a splendid woman.

Feeling in need of some grooming, he took his clippers from his chest of drawers and started trimming his fingernails while comparing Pearl to this intriguing nurse. They also had their faith in common, although Jacob had become impatient with the way in which Pearl accepted Christianity's tenets without a need for deeper scrutiny. She wasn't exactly anti-intellectual, but she believed some things were beyond human understanding and not worth spending a lot of time mulling over. Cultivating her walk with the Lord was her focus. In his second year at Princeton, Jacob had sensed a growing distance between them when he wanted to discuss things like modernism and historical criticism. Pearl, however, had no patience with such things and had openly worried about his walk with the Lord. Clara, on the other hand, wasn't averse to having deep theological conversations. She could hold her own in discussions about modern trends and often perplexing questions about the Christian faith, including the validity of miracles.

He started jiggling his legs. He and Pearl had left each other without any commitments, just an understanding to find out what might happen over the coming year. This time apart would be a test to see whether anything remained of what they once had meant to each other. He reminded himself they both were free to pursue someone else, but he still winced at the memory of seeing Pearl and Harry standing next to each other at Jacob's going away service. Would he mind if the two of them ended up together? They'd always been good friends and more than a little compatible. He stood up and stretched his body to the right, then to the left, staring outside at the shimmering snow enfolding the grounds. Without seeking God's guidance, he decided he'd like to find out whether Clara Story might find him as desirable as he found her.

Jacob bounded into the office he shared with Soon-hee, eager to uncover the assignments Mr. Blair had set up for him. Before digging into the small pile of written instructions, he stopped to breathe in the aroma of books, old and new, and to appreciate the Korean-style prints on the walls, smiling at one of a prowling tiger. He chuckled to recall his mother's fears for him in a foreign land, including meeting up with such a wild cat. When he scanned the calendar he'd brought from home, he turned the page from November to December and saw Christmas was only a little over a week away. With a sinking spirit, he realized he hadn't made any preparations for the holiday his German heritage family celebrated with gusto. He pictured his siblings helping their mother deck their halls with pine boughs and holly, and their father procuring and setting up a tall evergreen in the parlor. As a boy, Jacob had been amused by the sight of his dignified father crouching under the tree adjusting the trunk in its metal stand, the evergreen seeming to defy any attempt at being fastened down. The fragrance of their trees always mingled with the scents of cinnamon, molasses, ginger, and nutmeg as his mother and sisters made cookies and cakes.

There would be presents on Christmas morning and an afternoon feast before the holiday culminated with the seven o'clock church service. Jacob was always last-minute about buying gifts, waiting until a day or two before the holiday. Then, he'd find himself wading through the throngs at Bush and Bull's or Laubach's, exhilarated by the festive atmosphere and amused by the harried floor walkers with their drooping boutonnieres. This wasn't Easton, Pennsylvania, however, and sending gifts to his family wouldn't take a day or two, but more like a month or more if the mails ran smoothly. He hated to think of disappointing or worrying them when no Christmas greetings arrived from Korea. He rallied at the sound of someone rapping on the door. At home he would have called out, "Come in," but not here where one greeted visitors face-to-face.

"Clara—uh, Miss Story." His face heated at his near-blunder and the sense of being caught red-handed about his recent thoughts on her behalf.

"Hello, Mr. Kichline." Her eyes twinkled. "How nice to see you back at work."

He willed himself to speak coherently, casually if at all possible. She looked every bit as pretty in her unassuming uniform as Pearl had in what she called her Gibson Girl dresses.

"Yes, I'm back in the office. It's my first time." He could have smacked himself in the head. "I, uh, was going to come by the infirmary on Wednesday as you requested."

"I know we have an appointment then, but I've been eager to see how you're feeling and to make sure you really are up to working."

The thought of her making a house call made him feel seven feet tall.

"Please come in." Thinking of appearances, he had enough sense not to close the door.

She stood just inside and began asking questions. "How are you sleeping?" "How is your appetite?" "Do you have any chills or feelings of being overly-warm?"

When he finished responding favorably, she smiled and crossed her arms. "I'd say except for rebuilding your strength, which could take a while, you're doing very well."

"This is good news."

"The temptation will be to take on too much too soon, as often happens after a lengthy illness. Just allow your body to be your guide, paying close attention to its signals. With the Christmas holidays upon us, there will be plenty of opportunities to rest and rejuvenate."

"I promise to be careful." He fidgeted, wondering if he dare ask her something more personal. Before he could stop himself, he plunged ahead. "I, uh, have a different kind of concern just now."

"Oh?" She cocked her head.

"I lost so much time at the hospital I didn't get to send my family Christmas gifts. I know anything I buy now won't arrive in time, but I'd still like to do something special for them."

"I'm sure they'll understand. You have told them about your illness, haven't you?"

He twisted his mouth. "I plan to write to them today. I wanted to make sure I could tell them in all honesty I was well again. You see, my mother worries."

She laughed, a light, pleasant sound. "I have one of those."

"The thing is I don't know what presents to get them, here I mean, because I haven't done any of that kind of shopping. I wonder if, uh, you might be able to help me know what I might give them and where to find such things."

"I'll be happy to." She looked up for a moment then back at him. "Tomorrow afternoon, I have some free time and could go with you into the shopping district. I'll also make sure you don't get overtaxed."

His head tingled. "Thank you."

"Well, then, I'd best be on my way." She clapped her hands. "I need to call on Mr. Cullen to see how he's doing."

Jacob's mouth hung open. *She didn't just come to see me after all.*

He sat at the desk in his room reliving the memories of exploring some of Pyongyang's markets with Clara Story that afternoon. The letter he was about to write to his family and enclose inside a Korean-style Christmas card would accompany the presents he'd purchased, which might possibly arrive in Easton by Twelfth Night. If not, he reasoned, receiving the gifts late would at least prolong the holiday spirit.

He glanced at Soon-hee who sat on his bed with an open Bible and notepad, his brow furrowed as he prepared for a final assignment before the end of the term. Outside the building, snow was falling at a slant. Jacob realized he'd have to write quickly if he wanted to post the letter and gifts before their mail service closed in an hour.

"Are you certain you'd not prefer using the desk, Soon-hee?" Jacob asked. He wouldn't mind writing with a large book resting on his lap.

"Thank you, I am sure," he muttered, his train of thought apparently unbroken.

Satisfied, Jacob began his letter

> Pyongyang, December 18, 1906
>
> My Dear Family,
>
> It is with a full heart I write this Christmas greeting, which you will hopefully receive before the season is over. I trust this letter finds all of you in the best of health and spirits. When I tell you some recent news, I hope you'll understand why you're not hearing from me until after December 25th and will forgive the tardiness of this note and my gifts.

Across the room, Soon-hee's pen scratched against his tablet.

> How was your Thanksgiving celebration, and how did the Lafayette-Lehigh football game turn out? I'm hoping for a good report about my former team's success and to know how Lafayette finished its season. The missionaries had a very nice holiday feast, which we ate in the YMCA's large dining hall. As you may recall, I live at the YMCA with a pleasant roommate, Soon-hee Oh. There were many Koreans among us, and although our meal didn't include turkey or filling, we did enjoy chickens, potatoes, corn, and other vegetables. Our chief cook Mary Yoo also prepared pumpkin pie, as pumpkins are grown in Korea.

He hurried to write past the mention of what had been on the menu and to tell his family about his brilliant nurse.

> Unfortunately, I had not begun to enjoy my dessert when I became feverish and sick to my stomach. Our capable

nurse Miss Clara Story intervened, and I was tucked away in the mission's infirmary with a case of dysentery. Mr. Cullen and I had just returned from a rural area where we delivered Bible literature, and we both fell ill. Dr. Andrew Walker came the next day from Severance Hospital in Seoul to examine us, and you can rest assured Mr. Cullen and I received the best medical intervention. The doctor and nurse here are very modern and very skilled. Within a few days, I was feeling much better. We stayed in the infirmary for two weeks to ensure our full recovery and to guard against any spread of the disease. My roommate and Mrs. Cullen were both isolated for two weeks because of their proximity to the professor and me, and I'm happy to report neither of them got sick.

I'm back in my office and working on Bible studies at a nice, slow pace. Miss Story, knowing how badly I wanted to send you Christmas gifts, went with me to some stores here in Pyongyang. I felt energized by the excursion and took a brief nap when I returned.

I hope you'll like the calligraphy artwork bearing images of tigers, as well as the vases, chopsticks, and Korean tea I'm sending. I'm also including several photographs I've taken of where I live and two copies of the book I helped translate, one I know you are familiar with back home. I must draw this brief letter to a close, so I don't miss today's post. I look forward to my first Korean Christmas as I look back with fondness, and not a little homesickness, at Christmases past with all of you. I send my love to you, my grandparents, aunts, uncles, and cousins.

Love,

Jacob

He wrangled a large box that had awaited him at the post office back to the Y after hastily scribbling on the parcel he was mailing to his family, “I just picked up your package. Thank you!” He hoped the message wouldn’t be erased in transit, but even so, he’d write another letter soon after opening their gifts. One of the residents opened the front door for him at the YMCA, and Jacob took his time going up the stairs to his room where he managed to rotate the doorknob and push his way inside. Soon-hee jumped up from his bed to assist.

“What a large box this is! How did you ever get it up here?”

Jacob grinned. “As you see, my strength is returning.” He wouldn’t admit how drained he was from the effort.

He craned his neck as Jacob thumped the box on his bed. “Is this from your family?”

“Yes, and I’m pretty sure this contains Christmas gifts.” He stared at the parcel, a little the worse for its expedition across the globe. “I’d love to tear into this box right now, but since my parents never let me open presents until Christmas morning, I think I’ll honor them and wait.” He paused then asked, “What Christmas traditions did you grow up with, Soon-hee?”

His dark-haired roommate smiled. “When I was a boy, one of the missionaries would dress up like your Western Santa Claus and give each child a pair of socks. We performed nativity-based plays, had lotus lantern decorations, and we decorated the first Christmas trees seen in Korea. We also feasted, but the focus was on church services and celebrating the birth of Jesus.”

“Those seem like happy memories for you.” He sat next to the package and removed his damp outwear.

“I have always loved Christmas.”

“I’m looking forward to all the activities here,” Jacob said, confused as to why his friend was frowning.

"We have always enjoyed the season here very much, a time to be more with our families apart from our labors. There was always such merriment."

Was? What does he mean by "was?"

"While you were in hospital at the beginning of Advent, the missionaries met daily to pray for revival to come to Korea. We have had such a difficult year under the Japanese protectorate." Soon-hee looked away for a moment. "With so very many reports of God's activity in various places around the world, we are seeking his presence here where we need him so desperately. The missionaries decided to give up the usual Christmas social celebrations in favor of seeking the Lord. Instead of festivities, we will gather nightly for prayers seeking repentance and unity, which are far more necessary."

Jacob rubbed the back of his neck. "Oh."

"We also will ask the Lord's favor upon the Bible studies to begin with the new year."

"Bible studies?"

"For the first two weeks of each year, Christians all around Korea gather in local churches for uninterrupted study of the Bible. Each congregation sends representatives here to study with the missionaries, and this is known as the Pyongyang General Class for Men. The Korean Presbyterians began this system some time ago, so each year would begin in prayer, Bible study, and singing."

His heart sank. Didn't the missionaries meet and study often enough as it was? Why did they have to go and ruin his first Christmas away from home?

Soon-hee continued. "I have not been told for certain, but I believe we will assist with some of the classes."

"Do you mean we'll be teaching?" Jacob pinched the skin at his throat.

"Yes, although we will not be the primary teachers but act as aides to the missionaries. Mr. Blair is scheduled to do most of the preaching, so we will likely work closely with Mr. Cullen and perhaps Mr. Bernheisel."

He tried to be interested despite his disappointment. "How many people will be coming here?"

"The past few years, attendance has averaged between eight hundred and a thousand men."

His roommate whistled. "That's a lot of people. Don't women participate?"

"Oh, yes, but they have separate meetings because the church is too small to accommodate men and women at the same time." He chuckled. "The women rather like having their privacy. Most of these people walk all the way here from places as far away as a hundred miles and at their own expense. To help defray the costs to the missionaries for their room and board, they pay a small tuition. Because of the great sacrifices made to attend this class, the local Christians are not allowed to participate. Instead, something special is done for them the following month."

"Where does everyone stay?"

"These men so crowd our campus we often have to double up on our sleeping arrangements."

Jacob's eyes narrowed. "Do you mean we might have to share our room?"

"Yes."

He blew out a breath.

"You seem dissatisfied."

"I'd be lying if I said I wasn't."

Soon-hee smiled, the dimples on his face deepening. "Something tells me we may be in for some unexpected surprises, though perhaps not the kind one can buy or sell."

CHAPTER TWENTY-EIGHT

CHRISTMAS WEEK 1906

Soon-hee grappled to know how hard he should push Jacob to attend the daily prayers, as well as what he might say to their coworkers about his absence. He was not, after all, his American brother's keeper. All he knew was, for some reason, Jacob kept making excuses. A few days earlier, his explanation about being tired from the previous day's activity had made sense to Soon-hee—the man was after all still recovering from dysentery. He sensed, however, there was more than fatigue at play. Mr. Cullen was also recovering from the same illness, yet he was taking an active part in the prayer meetings.

He cast a glance at Jacob, who sat on his bed reading another book by Soren Kierkegaard. From his own studies, Soon-hee was familiar with the Dane, whom he found confusing. He wondered what about the theologian appealed to Jacob and why Soon-hee had never seen him pick up his Bible. Something wasn't right here. Mr. Moffett would have known what to do. Soon-hee pulled on his socks and reached for his shoes, deciding he would have a word with Mr. Cullen, who had known Jacob since Princeton.

Jacob glanced up from his book. "Are you going to the prayer meeting?"

"Yes. I look forward to beginning each day in the presence of these godly men and women as we seek the Lord's face." He finished tying his shoes and rose, wondering if he'd said enough.

When Jacob's striking blue eyes met his, Soon-hee tried to read the expression. He perceived something wistful in them, as if Jacob wanted to say something but didn't know how. When he remained silent, Soon-hee shrugged into his overcoat and put on his hat and gloves. The temperature would be especially cold this morning, judging from the wind rattling the windows and the patches of ice glistening on the outside walkways.

"These meetings are not the same without your presence," he said with a thumping heart.

Jacob's Adam's apple bobbed, and he nodded his head, silent.

As the missionaries took their places, Miss Story leaned over and whispered. "I see Mr. Kichline is absent again."

"This makes me sad," Soon-hee said. "I plan to speak to Mr. Cullen today if he is available."

"I wonder if he might still be regaining his strength. Then again, there are times when a major illness causes a person to become melancholy."

He thought there might be more to the situation, but she made a good point. Jacob had been moping.

"I believe he may be sick of home."

Her brown eyes widened. "Excuse me?"

Soon-hee's cheeks colored. "Did I say this incorrectly?"

Clara Story chuckled. "I think you mean he's homesick, wishing he could be with his family in a familiar place."

He grinned. "Yes, this is what I meant to say. He received a large parcel the other day and told me about his family's German customs and how much he loves Christmas. He asked me how we will celebrate here, and I told him about our decision to focus on seeking God's presence rather than social occasions."

She snapped her fingers. "Perhaps we can arrange a little festivity on his behalf. I'll have a word with your mother. Maybe she'll agree to host a meal, with my help of course. I think Sora and Jeongsook might also help out."

This was a wonderful idea, but not without its possible complications for himself. He would need to plot a course through his mother's spicy foods, his brother's frosty demeanor, and the uncertainty of where he stood with Jeongsook. Hope rose inside when he remembered how Christmas was a season which invited the miraculous.

The American nurse leaned a bit closer and whispered. "I'll be sure to tell your mother Mr. Kichline can only eat bland foods just now, and that will also help you."

This assurance lessened at least one of his concerns.

Soon-hee loved Central Presbyterian Church's Sunday services when the voices of hundreds upon hundreds of congregants soared in prayer and song. Sometimes, he even found himself shivering when the preaching of God's Word came home to him personally and powerfully. However, something also touched him in the prayer meetings in a different, more intimate way. At those times, the few dozen missionaries and their Korean pastoral assistants weren't up on the platform but were on the floor, equals in the faith despite background, age, and educational differences. Each of them approached the Lord with humility, pleading with him to pour out his spirit on the suffering Korean Church.

Sometimes the prayers became personal, as today when Mr. Cullen asked his brothers and sisters in the faith to continue praying for his healing.

"I'm grateful to the Lord for sparing the mission from an outbreak of dysentery and for a generally healthy season when so many normally fall ill. Some of us, however, are still feeling the effects of our various infirmities."

When the prayers ended, and they were beginning to converse, Mr. Swallen spoke. "I've noticed Mr. Kichline hasn't been attending these meetings."

The top of Soon-hee's head prickled as he and Clara Story shared a side-ways look. Mrs. Cullen coughed quietly into a handkerchief.

"Is he still sick?" Swallen, known as "the Gentle Pastor," glanced about as if for an answer.

The nurse answered him. "He's much better physically, but I suspect he may be downhearted about missing his family on his first Christmas away from them."

"I'm sure he'd feel better if he were together more with his Korean family," Dennis Cullen said.

"Has he spoken to you about any of this, Mr. Oh?" Swallen turned to Soon-hee.

"He has said only a little. He is a rather private person."

"Well, let's get back into prayer for his spirit as well as his body, and I'll pay him a visit soon." Swallen bowed his head. "Our loving Father, we continue to thank thee for blessing us with thy presence. Though we cannot see thee face-to-face as your servant Moses did or fellowship with the Lord Jesus as his disciples did on the dusty hills of Galilee, thou hast given us the Holy Ghost as a promise of thy presence with us. Today as we meet, we are seeking thy wholeness, of mind, body, and spirit for Jacob Kichline, our brother in Christ. We are grateful to thee for helping both him and Mr. Cullen recover from their illnesses, for ministering to their bodies directly as well as through the expert care of Miss Story and Dr. Walker. We seek their complete healing, Lord. Use even illness and its memory for thy purposes that they may continue in rich fellowship with thee and in fruitful ministry."

Soon-hee breathed in the life-giving words, certain the Lord was listening.

"We also ask thee to intervene in Mr. Kichline's life, thanking thee for his presence and his ministry among us. Thou knowest him intimately, Lord, and we ask thee to heal not only his lingering illness but any sickness in his spirit which is known to thee, though it be a mystery to us. Please show us how to minister to him and may the plans thou hast for him in Korea be fulfilled."

Soon-hee's thoughts kept straying back to his roommate, recalling not only the way Jacob's Bible remained under a stack of other books, but how he never seemed to make time for personal prayer. Nor could Soon-hee share aspects of his own faith without receiving anything but a vacant expression in return. How had Jacob come to be a seminary student in the first place, and why was he a missionary now? Soon-hee resolved to pray for Jacob, rather than criticize. The Americans had a curious expression, something about the pot calling the kettle black.

Mr. Oh came up to his son after the prayer meeting, cupping his shoulder while the others began dispersing.

"I am sorry to hear of Mr. Kichline's ongoing illness."

"Yes." If he waited for his father to inquire about his oldest son's health, Soon-hee waited in vain.

"Perhaps he would like to come to our house on Christmas Eve for a simple meal, so he will at least be with a family."

"Miss Story and I were thinking along similar lines."

"I will speak to your mother today."

Soon-hee knew their idea would become reality. His father had said so.

When Soon-hee entered the dining room at midday, he immediately noticed Jacob sitting in a corner talking to Mr. Swallen. *How happy I am to see them together. May there be a positive outcome. May Jacob be sensitive to the leadings of the Holy Spirit.* He walked to his usual table with a lighter step not only because of this development, but because at least Jacob would have a Christmas celebration. Just before he arrived for lunch, Clara Story had come by the library to tell him that his family had agreed to host a meal.

She'd added, "Your mother promised not to serve more than one or two spicy dishes, and the rest will be easier on the digestion. I'm going to cook some American food, and Jeongsook Ahn promised to keep your mother from going too heavy on the spices."

He'd bowed his head in gratitude, his heart fluttering at the thought of Jeongsook's presence with his family. Since his illness, their interactions had been growing more frequent and friendlier, going beyond safe topics like the time of day and the weather. He had read in her eyes a certain enjoyment at being with him, but he had promised himself he would not rush her. He would let the Lord work out their relationship in his own way, in his own time.

Soon-hee finished bathing the following morning and when he returned to the room, Jacob was putting on his suit and tie.

"I'll will be going with you today," he said.

His heart swelled but as with Jeongsook, Soon-hee cautioned himself from expressing too much delight. "You must be feeling a little better."

"Yes, I suppose." He buckled his belt then combed his hair, which seemed to be fighting back.

"I am also happy you will be able to enjoy a small Christmas gathering at my home tonight. My mother, I understand, has promised to serve plain foods."

Jacob chortled. "I really do like Korean food, but just now ..."

"As you know, I understand."

"I've been so wrapped up in my own condition I've neglected to ask how you're doing."

"I am much better, thank you, as long as I follow the doctor's orders."

They walked together to the prayer meeting, and Soon-hee was going to ask Jacob to sit next to him until Mr. Swallen invited him first. The church buzzed with something like anticipation, as the missionaries took turns for the next two hours earnestly seeking the Lord to visit them in power. Soon-hee wondered whether his roommate would join in as the session grew to a close, and Jacob hadn't said anything. After William Blair prayed, there was a pocket of silence, and for a long moment, the meeting seemed to be over—until Jacob opened his mouth.

"Um, Lord, we're here to pray, to ask thee to stir us to action. We are grateful for the freedom to pray in peace on this Christmas Eve morning. Please continue to enlighten the Korean people, to bring them out of darkness and superstition. Amen."

Soon-hee opened one eye and saw Jacob was perspiring, although the church was anything but warm today. While Jacob hadn't, as the Americans might say, put his foot in his mouth, he had come close. He'd seemed to be reaching far back to a time when praying had come more naturally to him. *At least this is a start.*

He took a chance at eating a small portion of his mother's *Japchae*, which wasn't as spiced as usual, then coated his stomach with a large portion of Clara Story's roasted chicken and mashed sweet potatoes. Other things were harder for Soon-hee to swallow, including the seating arrangement. His parents had planted Jeongsook next to Yong-bin, who chattered with everyone at the table except his brother. *At least I do not have to make small talk with him.* Soon-hee breathed out, immediately confessing the renewal of his hostilities to the Lord, a step he repeated when his mother fussed over Jacob's medical condition but didn't seem to care about his own. She treated Jacob with maternal concern and paid no attention to Clara Story's protests when Mrs. Oh passed a bowl of kimchi to her oldest son. Soon-hee was about to take a small spoonful out of obligation, until the nurse caught his eye and with her lips shut tightly, shook her head.

"I am sorry, Mrs. Oh, but your son must not eat these foods just yet."

His mother gave a terse nod and glared at Soon-hee. He decided her unspoken criticism probably had more to do with his refusal to honor her by eating her food than it was for being sick. *She seems to have forgotten about my infirmity.* He might have hovered over the unpleasant thought but chose instead to think about how good he felt to see Jacob smile again.

"I wonder," the American said, "if I could take some photographs of everyone after dinner. I'd like to send them back to my family and friends in the States."

Mr. Oh spoke on behalf of his household. "We would be honored, Mr. Kichline."

Jacob appeared to be enjoying his meal, having tried most of the dishes, and he contributed to the conversation stories about his American Christmases. Jeongsook was especially interested in one tale.

"Please to tell me, Mr. Kichline, what is this bells nickel?"

Jacob smiled at her. "This is a German word, *Belsnickel.* He's a mythical character in my culture's folklore, a human-like creature dressed in shaggy furs and wearing antlers on his head. He visits children at Christmastime to make sure they've been behaving. He carries a switch to use on the bad children, but his pockets are full of candy, cakes, and nuts for those who have been good."

Soon-hee's heart melted when her beautiful eyes widened in childlike winsomeness.

"Were you a good boy, Mr. Kichline?" she asked.

He laughed. "I tried to be, especially around Christmas."

"Did you ever see this *Belsnickel*?" Yong-bin asked.

"Yes, he came around each year when I was very young."

"Did he not frighten you?" Sora Oh asked.

"He scared me silly."

Mr. Oh spoke. "Did he ever have to switch you?"

"No, sir, he did not, although I probably deserved it now and then." He paused. "*Belsnickel* was gradually replaced by the American version of St. Nicholas. We call him Santa Claus. Have you heard of him?"

Everyone said they had.

"How did the other tradition change for your people?" Mrs. Oh asked.

"Over the years, they became more American and less German. One indication was when my church went from all-German services to German and English, then just English. As for Christmas, my grandparents remember their childhood when they started setting stockings out on Christmas Eve before they went to bed in the expectation that during the night, Santa Claus would come and fill them with the same kind of treats *Belsnickel* used to distribute. I guess this doesn't happen in Korea."

Soon-hee found himself grinning. *If Belsnickel had come here, he would have no doubt used his switch on Yong-bin.*

CHAPTER TWENTY-NINE

CHRISTMAS MORNING 1906

Jacob hadn't looked forward to Christmas morning this much since he and his siblings were children. Although he was now a twenty-four-year-old man, his was the heart of a child as he awakened in the quiet darkness and reached for his alarm clock. *Seven-o-seven. Back home, it's still Christmas Eve.* He imagined his mother, grandmother, and sisters hard at work preparing the evening holiday feast, almost smelling roast goose, ham, and yeast rolls. Once everything was in the oven, the family would gather around the piano to sing carols while his sister Mae played. He wished there was some way he could speak to them, to hear their voices across a telephone line. If only such a thing were possible. *I'll send them a telegram tomorrow to wish them a Merry Christmas and let them know I received their gifts. I can also tell them they'll be receiving something from me in the coming days.* He stared up at the ceiling. *Next year, I'll be with them again, and Korea will be in the past.* Would Pearl be back in the picture, or perhaps someone else? Maybe even Clara Story?

He got up and reached for his dressing gown at the foot of the bed, pulling its hood onto his head for additional warmth. A few feet away, Soon-hee stirred. Jacob cracked open the Venetian blinds an inch and peered outside where dawn gentled the darkness with faint touches of light. Then he padded across the room, opening and closing the door softly before going to the common bathroom, which he had to himself for a change. He hurried his routine, so he could get back to the room for a headfirst dive into his family's gifts. However, sniffing breakfast aromas as they wafted upward, made him realize opening his presents might take longer than the window of time he had to arrive in the dining hall. *Ah well, making the process last longer will only bring me more joy.*

Back in the room, he bumped into something suspended from the foot of his bed and bent over to investigate. He broke into a smile at the sight of a bulging wool sock hanging from the post and turned to his roommate's side of the room.

Soon-hee had sat up and was rubbing his eyes.

"Good morning," Jacob said. "I hope I didn't disturb you."

"You did not. Happy Christmas to you."

He smiled at the strangeness of the greeting, but found he rather liked it. "Happy Christmas, Soon-hee. Um, there seems to be a stocking at the foot of my bed." He looked at his friend's bunk to see if he had one. He didn't.

"Please, do turn on the light so we may look into this."

Jacob did as he was told and pointed to the sock, quickly correctly himself. "I keep forgetting that I'm not supposed to point. Say, do you know anything about this?"

Soon-hee turned his head aside, but Jacob didn't miss the grin.

"Well, I suppose I'd better see what's inside."

He grabbed the stocking and sat on the bed waggling his legs out of excitement and to get his blood pumping in the chilly room. First, he retrieved a silk red handkerchief which had been folded expertly and secured with a ribbon.

"This is really nice. I've admired your handkerchiefs, and now, I have one of my own."

"This is very Korean. I am happy that you like it." Soon-hee wrapped a blanket around his shoulders.

Next Jacob pulled out a pen. "Nice." Then back in he went for a handful of chestnuts, a tangerine, and an apple. "I wonder how Santa Claus knew I was at the YMCA in Pyong-yang."

"I am told your Santa has magical powers, which of course he uses only for good."

"I'm just glad *Belsnickel* didn't show up." He laughed.

"I should not like to have encountered him either."

Jacob grew momentarily solemn. "I'm not sure how Santa found me here, but I'm truly grateful. *Gamsahamnida.*"

"You are most welcome. I understand he sometimes uses helpers." Soon-hee rose and slipped into his Korean dressing gown and a pair of shoes. "I am going to shower and will return shortly."

During the next few minutes, Jacob took out the box he'd been dying to open since its appearance a few days ago, untying the string and peeling back the paper carefully so as not to disturb the US stamps. He knew some of the young boys at the mission school collected them.

He breathed in ginger and molasses, his mouth watering, and dug through tissue and paper-wrapped presents held together with twine, ribbons, and seals. Being a methodical person, he took them out one-by-one and lined them up on his bed before needing to stack them on top of the desk. He didn't want to admit to himself his disappointment at not finding anything from Pearl, but then, why would she have sent him a gift?

He put a stack of cards and letters wrapped with a red and white ribbon on his pillow. By the time he emptied the container, he'd counted nearly thirty packages, excluding a dozen food items. The outpouring of generosity bewildered him. He and his family had only ever given each other one or two presents at the most for Christmas, and here he was with a Bush and Bull-worthy display right in his own room. He'd never had so many gifts at one time for any occasion and grasped just how high and wide was their love for him.

There was, however, an opposite side of this bounty. He felt badly about not having anything for Soon-hee, although Christmas gift-giving was even more understated in this culture. Jacob decided he'd share the food his family had sent, uplifted by the thought of introducing his roommate to treasured Pennsylvania German traditions. He smiled as he hefted one of the waxed paper-wrapped parcels, finding a Christmas Stollen within its folds, his all-time favorite holiday bread. *I'm going to set aside one or two gifts for Soon-hee, the least I can do after he so thoughtfully created a Christmas stocking for a homesick American.*

He unwrapped a box from his parents and discovered a pair of tan leather gloves which fit him perfectly. Next, he opened a gift from Harry, a medium-sized scrapbook filled with newspaper clippings from the Lafayette football team's 1906 season. He smiled at the thoughtful gift knowing he would relish reading the stories in the days to come. Next, his sisters had given him wool socks and a copy of *White Fang* by Jack London, and his brothers, a wool Lafayette sweater. He dug into a tin filled with molasses cookies and popped one whole into his mouth, feeling downright reckless after his bout with dysentery. As he chewed, Jacob rummaged through the remaining presents and, picking up one box, murmured, "What's this?"

"Soon-hee Oh" was inscribed on the gift tag. He discovered two more, grinning at the thought of their remembering his Korean friend. He gently shook the boxes, wondering what they might have selected for him then set them aside to review the heap of letters and cards. *I'll open them after the morning church service.*

The door to the room opened, and Soon-hee stepped inside toweling his hair dry, his eyes enlarging at the sight of all the gifts.

"This looks very much like one of your American department stores."

Jacob glowed. "I know. I've never seen so many presents in one place before."

"Then your family does not usually do such as this?"

"Never. My parents give one or two gifts at the most to me and my siblings for Christmas."

Soon-hee sat on the side of his bed, draping the towel around his neck. Footsteps along the hallway echoed in their room. "Why did they send all of this?"

"I think this is their way of saying they miss me, but they're not all from my relatives. Many came from people at my church." He cleared his throat as if preparing to make an announcement. "And not all of these presents are for me." He reached behind him and picked up one earmarked for his roommate.

Soon-hee tipped his head to the side, his mouth hanging open. "This is for me?"

Jacob handed the box to him. "Yes, for you."

"But who is this from?"

"Read the tag."

"'To Soon-hee Oh from Mr. and Mrs. Kichline.' How very kind of them."

"See what's inside."

He opened the present slowly, seeming to enjoy the process, and lifted a lid. "These are very nice." He slipped his hands into a pair of black leather gloves.

"Do they fit?"

"Oh, yes, and I have needed a new pair."

"I got some, too. I'm glad they gave us different colors, so we don't confuse them." He handed the tin of cookies to Soon-hee. "Please have one. These are made of molasses and very Pennsylvania German."

He took one, smiling with his eyes closed as he chewed. "This is delicious."

"Guess what? I found another present for you."

"I just cannot imagine this. Your family is so very kind."

"This one is from my Grandmother Kichline." He gave the box to Soon-hee.

He gazed at a handknit scarf the color of holly leaves. "I will be so very warm now."

Jacob gave a start when he glanced at his clock. "Oh boy, we'd better get down to breakfast before Mary Yoo misses us."

Soon-hee jumped up from his bed and hastened to dress. "We do not want to vex her, especially not on Christmas morning."

Except for the Korean seating arrangement and majority contingent of locals, Jacob might have been at the First Reformed Church of Easton imbibing the fragrance of wax candles and pine boughs. He closed his misting eyes at the opening strains of "Hark, the herald angels sing, glory to the newborn king!" Despite the Korean lyrics, its unmistakable melody and message encouraged his Christmas spirit. Moments later across the sanctuary and a few rows down, he saw Clara Story singing from what appeared to be the depths of her heart, her uplifted face shining. He hadn't been this joyful since coming to Korea and, if he were honest, not since his first year at Princeton. There was just something about this place and these people summoning him to go deeper.

Mr. Swallen called them to worship. "Hear the words of the Prophet Isaiah: 'The people that walked in darkness have seen a great light: they that dwell in the land of the shadow of death, upon them hath the light shined.' Let us pray. All glory to thee, great God, for the gift of thy Son, our light in the darkness and hope of all the world, the holy one of Israel sent to take away the sins of the world. Let us with the triumphant angelic choir lift our praises to thee and fill all the earth with the knowledge of our Lord and savior, Jesus Christ. Amen."

Jacob added his voice to the communal "Amen." Maybe being on the other side of the world on this holiday wasn't so bad after all.

Mr. Swallen's Christmas sermon began on an elevated note, proclaiming the good news spoken to ordinary shepherds. Then he plunged into the miraculous aspect of the God-ordained event, how God had taken on human flesh to take back his fallen creation.

"Consider the signs and wonders of Christmas." Swallen hovered over the pulpit. "We find the king of all creation born not in a palace but in a crude stable surrounded by the sounds and smells of dumb animals. He isn't heralded by members of royalty but by low-class shepherds whom polite people mostly ignored and largely distained."

Jacob reached into a pocket and pulled out a handkerchief, softly blowing his nose. Here and there, others coughed or cleared their throats.

"And then there's the matter of this baby's astounding birth. Isaiah tells us in the seventh chapter of his book, the fourteenth verse, 'Therefore the Lord himself shall give you a sign; Behold, a virgin shall conceive, and bear a son, and shall call his name Immanuel.' What are we to make of this? To many modern ears this is impossible, nonsense, barely worth considering. And yet, these are the inspired words of God, the one who breaks into our lives in the most unexpected ways, the one who asks us to seek him, not just with our minds but with our souls."

Jacob's body went rigid, his stomach roiling not unlike what had happened at Thanksgiving. A cold prickle of fear climbed his back. Why did the missionary have to go and spoil an otherwise beautiful service by bringing up a theological sticking point? At Princeton, there had been incessant discussions about the feasibility of the virgin birth. The modernists insisted it was nothing more than a metaphor while the orthodox held to its literal truth. And how had he aligned himself? He hadn't, not fully. On one hand was the faith of his fathers and mothers, the faith of his youth, a glorious, joyful, sustaining faith. On the other hand, gnawing doubt. If the modernists happened to be correct, then all the rest of Christianity fell apart, leaving nothing but another system of ethics and morals just like all the rest.

The over-packed church walls seemed to be closing in on him, and he broke into a cold sweat. As he started slumping to the left, Dr. Walker stopped his fall. The service continued as if nothing were happening to him.

"Mr. Kichline, can you hear me?"

He looked into the kind eyes, unable to focus. "I-I don't know." He felt the physician's fingers on his wrist as Walker checked Jacob's pulse.

"This may be a bit much for you just now. I'll see you to your room, so you can rest."

The doctor helped Jacob to his feet, and Jacob heard a brief exchange between Walker and Soon-hee, who remained seated.

After he'd napped for twenty minutes, Jacob sat up amidst the detritus of opened gifts and rolled his shoulders. Soon-hee was probably still at church. Dr. Walker had been like a rescuer, removing Jacob from the overstimulation of the Christmas service, as well as the troublesome message. He didn't want to revisit the sermon, so reaching for the hefty packet of letters, he thought reading his mail would restore his earlier good mood. He briefly shuffled through the envelopes, wondering where to begin. What was this? A card from Pearl. He carefully opened the envelope and drew out a greeting featuring a nativity scene and the words of Isaiah 7:14, the ones Mr. Swallen had preached on. Jacob's mouth went dry. Inside, under an innocuous printed sentiment she had written, "Merry Christmas, Jacob. Pearl." He pressed his lips together and sighed, uncertain what to make of the strange coincidence. That she had bothered about him at all gave him hope—if he wanted there to be any.

He read letters from his parents, older sister, and Harry, as well as cards from his church's ministers, past and present.

Mr. Kieffer seemed to be enjoying his new parish, although Jacob still wished he would have stayed in Easton. Then, he saw an envelope bearing a Princeton postmark and, upon closer scrutiny, saw the letter-writer was Gresham Machen. He unfolded the several sheets, marveling a man he'd known such a short time would dedicate this much effort to him. The first part informed Jacob of things happening at Princeton and in Machen's circle. The latter, Jacob read and reread in a state of wonder.

> In some ways, you remind me of my recent self, caught between opposing camps, wondering which one I was going to end up in once and for all. Things like the virgin birth really caught me in a snare. What I mean to say is, the way the modernists interpret the event naturalistically. Their arguments come across as thoughtful, rational, and sophisticated, as if believing the opposite would be to relegate a man to hayseed status. And yet, their teachings fail to satisfy the human spirit, to uplift and draw it closer to its Creator. I have found the virgin birth is indeed a doctrine upon which we can stake our soul's claims with utmost reliability, both from a historical perspective and that of biblical authority. To believe otherwise is to remain in the shadows, unable to see the Light of the World.

I don't know what to make of this coincidence. I mean, how could Machen have known this very subject would come up in church on the day I read his letter, and why even bring it up? The room seemed colder than ever, and he huddled under his warmest blanket.

CHAPTER THIRTY

LATE DECEMBER 1906

Soon-hee exchanged barely-awake greetings with a hall resident on the way back from the common bathroom, contemplating what the day might bring. Normally, he savored early mornings, but today dread hemmed him in. The day before, Japanese officials had detained a student in Yong-bin's class for insulting one of them, and Mr. Bernheisel had gone to the police station to see what might be done for the young man. *At least, my brother was not involved.*

Then again, he'd never known his brother to be politically-minded or to consider matters beyond his narrow world of sickness and tomfoolery. Yong-bin was, to borrow an English word, shallow. Soon-hee and the missionaries had turned to prayer, asking God to use this unfortunate incident for good. He wrestled against a spirit of fear, worried the episode might set off retaliatory moves against Christians.

When he got to his room, his breath caught at its prevailing darkness. The blinds were still closed, the sun making a valiant effort to penetrate the dimness, and Jacob still asleep. At this late hour, he had no reluctance about disturbing his roommate and turned on the light.

"What time is it?" Jacob groaned and flung an arm across his eyes.

"Eight thirty. We must make haste if we are to have breakfast."

He sat up as if in slow motion and scratched his chest. "Did I ever sleep."

Soon-hee went through the ritual of getting dressed. "You must have needed it. Sleep has a way of restoring both body and soul."

Jacob pivoted his long legs over the side of the bed and leaned on his elbows as if gathering courage to face the day. He looked at Soon-hee. "So, there's going to be more praying today, right?"

He detected the sour note and decided to overlook the negativity. "This morning following breakfast, I will go to the church for a time of private prayer. There will be corporate prayer for the community this evening."

Jacob rubbed his hand across his face. "That's a lot of praying, but then you told me this would happen. I don't mind saying I look forward to getting back to our translating."

He combed his hair, realizing he needed to see a barber. "Does not your church engage in prayer at the start of each year?"

"Sure, but not for two weeks. I've never seen quite this much of it anywhere else."

Soon-hee slipped his feet into his shoes. "I understand from the missionaries that we Koreans are strong intercessors." He grinned to himself. "Strong and long. We are not shy about taking our time speaking to the Lord."

"You can say that again." Jacob pulled on his bathrobe and headed for the door where he turned back. "So, what's the situation about us taking in someone else?"

Soon-hee read apprehension on his friend's face. "This is still a possibility, but the assignments have not yet been made. I hope you will not mind too much if we do get a roommate, Jacob. The fellowship we share with these men from the country churches is as you would say, priceless. Their hearts are so very tender for the Lord." He smiled. "One thing I love about the General Class for Men is when we introduce a new hymn here, soon people throughout the villages are singing the same beautiful song."

Judging from Jacob's expression, he was not impressed.

The evening's time of prayer swung wildly between waves of blessed assurances and breakers of foreboding. In a constant state of tension, Soon-hee clung to the Lord as to an anchor, determined not to let go. In the room, there were audible groans too deep for words as they all wrestled in their spirits. He pondered what the Lord might be doing among them and where this season might be heading. Not knowing seemed to bring out the best and the worst in him. He knew from the Scriptures peace could be found in quietness and trust in the sovereign Lord, but the same Lord had promised his followers would go through tribulation. *Lord, help me cling to thy promise of having overcome the world. Whatever thou might bring our way, please strengthen me in thy faith so I am found faithful rather than faithless.*

He became aware of Mrs. Bernheisel's praying with her head bowed. "Heavenly Father, thou alone knowest the thoughts and intentions of our hearts. We don't know how to pray as we ought, so may thy Spirit intercede on our behalf to accomplish thy will in us and in our ministries to the glory of Christ Jesus."

As she called upon the Lord, Soon-hee glanced at Jacob who sat across from him with his eyes open and gazing downward. His right foot pumped. How distressed Soon-hee was for his friend, whose restless spirit transferred to his own. He turned once more to silent prayer. *Lord, my concern for Jacob runs deeply. There is something terribly wrong in his walk with thee. I do not know what caused this or what gives him the most anxiety, but thou knowest the hearts of all men. Please bring him into a state of rightness in his relationship with thee and use me in this situation for Jacob's good and thy glory. If he does not know thee, may he come to true faith. If he does, please remove all that has obscured thy face in his life.* He added the other things wearing on him from within and without. *Heavenly Father, my brother also is in need of thy touch. I do not believe he truly knows thee. Bring him to repentance and salvation. And Lord, if it be thy will, transform the relationship between the Christians here and the Japanese overlords. This would not be possible without the same power that raised blessed Jesus from the dead. I thank thee that with thee all things are possible.*

The evening's prayer meeting had lasted far longer than the others, and they normally ran to three hours. Tonight, the missionaries had travailed until nearly eleven o'clock, at which time most of them exhibited dark circles under their eyes and considerably rumpled clothes. Soon-hee rose from his mat and gave a subtle stretch of his arms, noticing how the missionaries and Korean ministry leaders continued talking amongst themselves, seeming reluctant to leave. As for Jacob, he'd jumped up from the floor and fled as if pursued by a tiger when Mr. Bernheisel uttered the last "amen." The sight of Jeongsook smiling and walking in his direction turned Soon-hee's sigh into a full smile. Until Clara Story abruptly walked up to him, unaware of having interrupted the precious moment.

"I'm concerned about him," she said.

He watched Jeongsook turn away, disappointment written on her face. Soon-hee took a moment before engaging with the nurse.

"He rarely participates in our prayers and just sits there as coiled up as a spring."

"You have noticed."

Soon-hee could tell how much she shared his own heart for their suffering friend.

"Do you have any idea what's wrong with him, Mr. Oh? I can tell you that whatever his distress, this goes beyond dysentery or homesickness."

"I, too, have been considering this, Miss Story. I believe he may have had a crisis of faith at the Princeton Seminary."

"Then why on earth would he become a missionary?" She raised her hands palms up.

"This also puzzles me, and I have been burdened for him." An idea sprouted wings, one he immediately shared with her. "Perhaps in addition to my prayers, I could fast on his behalf. Many are doing so as we seek the Lord's face."

The missionary nurse closed her eyes. "Fasting is not a good plan for you at this time, but don't let that bother you, Mr. Oh. You've inspired me with a different idea."

Before she could share her thoughts, Mr. and Mrs. Cullen came over, acknowledging Clara and Soon-hee before looking to the door in tandem.

"Mr. Kichline seemed to be in a hurry tonight," the professor said.

"We've noticed how quickly he comes and goes." Eileen Cullen lowered her voice. "He almost never participates."

"At first, we thought he might be taxed physically by these lengthy meetings," her husband said, "but he seems agitated."

The three of them looked at Soon-hee.

"As I was just telling Miss Story, I have reason to believe something happened to him at the seminary to shake his foundations." He quickly added, "This is but a conjecture. He is rather private about himself."

Mr. Cullen seemed to take his time before responding. "I can tell you our friend did have a rather rough go at Princeton, like many students whose faith is shaken."

"At Princeton?" Clara's eyes widened.

"Yes, Miss Story, even at Princeton. We've had some teachers abandon their faith in favor of modernism. I believed back in the summer, as I continue to believe now, this is the perfect place for Jacob to reclaim what he has lost."

"Mr. Oh and I were just discussing how we might support him," Clara said. "I was about to suggest meeting for prayer each morning, I mean to pray for Mr. Kichline." Her brown eyes sparkled.

"Let's gather at nine tomorrow, at my home," Cullen said.

They were finishing breakfast when Soon-hee saw by the clock he had ten minutes to get to the Cullen residence. Their first morning prayer session the day before had lasted an hour, a time of seeking God's assistance to know how to help Jacob as well as the Lord's intervention. Soon-hee had sensed the Lord lingering in their midst and had left not nearly as troubled. Dennis Cullen had also shared the uplifting news he'd just received about the Korean troublemaker who'd insulted the Japanese officer. Quite unexpectedly, the young man had been released with a warning and a blistering tongue-lashing.

He drained his teacup, dabbed his lips with the cloth napkin, and got up from his chair.

"Are you going back to the room?" Jacob asked.

"Not just yet. I am going to meet some friends for prayer."

He grimaced. "Again?"

The next words seemed to pop right out of his mouth. "Would you care to join us?"

His roommate sniffed. "No, thank you. I spend enough time in prayer at church every night. I'm going to answer some letters and go for a short walk if the sun comes out."

"I shall see you later then."

Jacob lifted his hand as if to say, "Be gone."

Four days later, on January second, the church swelled with over a thousand men who'd come to Pyongyang to attend the two-week General Class for Men. Lively chatter and a good deal of bowing and smiling animated the campus, the energy pouring into the YMCA swarming with new lodgers. Mr. Blair took Soon-hee aside.

"Mr. Cullen has spoken to me about Mr. Kichline's restlessness," Blair said, "and we believe introducing a new person would be unwise. What do you think, Mr. Oh?"

"While I am inclined to agree, I am concerned we may be shirking."

Blair put his hand on Soon-hee's right shoulder. "You are definitely not shirking, but I must caution you, we still might require you to host someone if the housing situation becomes severe."

"I understand."

"How has Mr. Kichline been recently?"

“He has grown quieter. He does not often engage me in conversation but reads his books and does a good bit of writing letters.”

Blair scratched the side of his nose. “I think the Lord is at work in him. I’m happy that you, Miss Story, and the Cullens have been praying for him.”

“Although we must stop meeting now because the General Class is upon us, we continue in private prayer for him.”

“I’m believing for the best.”

Soon-hee and Jacob distributed materials for the Saturday morning session before several hundred students of all ages crammed into the YMCA’s auditorium. A handful of especially eager young men huddled in a corner praying, their heads bobbing to the rhythm of their petitions.

“You seem to be enjoying these classes,” Soon-hee said.

“I do like them. Academic environments suit me.”

“More than worship?” He glanced at Jacob, whose face blanched. Soon-hee wished he could take bake the hastily spoken words.

He didn’t answer right away. “I always did like worship before ...”

Soon-hee stood still, a stack of mimeographed papers dangling in his right hand. Something told him not to probe, and Jacob didn’t finish his sentence.

At the end of the three-hour teaching session, the men trickled out of the packed space talking amongst themselves as they headed to the church. The missionaries had decided to conduct noontime prayer meetings each day of the General Class for Men for anyone who cared to attend, and the result had astonished them. Almost everyone went, but not Jacob. As soon as class was over, he stole away, going in the opposite direction.

That night more than fifteen hundred men crammed into the Central Church to hear Mr. Blair preach on 1 Corinthians 12:17. Like the missionaries and Korean pastors who'd spoken on each of the other nights, he emphasized their need for the Holy Spirit's presence and for love and righteousness to prevail in this time of national crisis. Soon-hee sat near the front next to Jacob, both on hand to assist the leaders' needs. So far, they'd done everything from praying with the speakers to helping one of the village men find his lost pair of eyeglasses.

"The Apostle Paul has told us that since we are all members of the body of Christ," Blair preached, "if one member suffers, all the other members suffer. If a brother hates in his heart, he injures not only the whole church, he also brings pain to the Church's head, Jesus Christ."

The heat generated by the people in the crowded sanctuary staved off fiercely cold outdoor temperatures. Soon-hee coughed into his hand, his throat dry.

"Most of you are aware that shortly after I arrived in Korea, I had an accident while I was hunting, and I shot off the end of one of my fingers." Blair elevated his hand and grinned. "When the incident happened, I remembered how my head ached and my whole body suffered along with the injured finger, although it is a small member. My friends, sin is like that injury. When we commit sin, not only we suffer, but the body of Christ suffers as well. Hate is a sin, and many here have been hating the Japanese, who are also made in God's image."

Dead quiet fell over the gathering, as if each man was coming to terms with his attitude about the foreign element in their country. Soon-hee silently confessed his own resentment, which always seemed to linger just under the surface. When Blair gave the benediction, a long line formed to talk to him.

"Should we stay or leave?" Jacob asked, his eyes on the exit.

"If you would like to go home, please feel free. I will stay in case Mr. Blair requires assistance. Although he is an energetic man, preaching is vigorous, and he is bound to become weary at some point. Perhaps I may counsel or pray with some of those who seek him."

"Okay, right then. I think I'll go."

Soon-hee joined Mr. Blair and began talking and praying with some men who confessed abject hatred for the Japanese. He even shared his own resentments with the penitents, who in turn ministered to him with prayer. He'd never felt so vulnerable, but the liberation he experienced encouraged him. For the first time in his life, he embraced the liberating truth of the gospel that in Christ Jesus, there is no condemnation for those who love him.

When the last person left an hour later, Mr. Blair thanked Soon-hee for his help.

"I was happy to be of aid." An alarm went off inside when he saw the American's face turn ashen, as if all the air had gone out of him.

"Will you walk back to my home with me, Mr. Oh?"

"Yes, of course. Are you feeling well?"

"I am just tired, my friend."

They found their coats and hats and ventured into the arctic night. "You know," Blair said, "I have a feeling our prayers are being answered."

CHAPTER THIRTY-ONE

JANUARY 7, 1907

Jacob had had it up to his eyeballs with church by the end of Sunday night's service. During this General Class for Men event, he was enjoying assisting with the morning classes because they provided some intellectual stimulation. However, the incessant praying, singing and sermonizing was enough to make a drinking man out of a teetotaler. These people just didn't seem ever to get their fill of them. If this level of piousness had been required of Princeton's seminarians, he would have packed his bags, headed back to Easton, and taken a job at the silk mill. He was beginning to feel like his college frat brothers who had teased Jacob about his church-this and Christian Endeavor-that.

While he walked back to his quarters under a crescent moon, his shoes crunching in the snow, he reflected on how tonight's service at Central Pres. had been a lot more subdued than the others this week. There hadn't been as much full-throated singing or relentless praying but the event had felt to him more like what he'd experienced in his home church where people knew how to behave themselves.

Soon-hee's father had given a somewhat low-key message, which Jacob appreciated. However, he would have far preferred a sermon from a seminary-educated American. Seeing Mr. Oh preach as if he were on an equal standing with the Western missionaries went down like week-old fish. During the service, Jacob had folded his arms across his chest and promptly fallen asleep, unwilling to strain to understand words that probably had little meaning for him anyway.

There was another thing about these assemblies. Why did people have to hang around and talk for an hour or more afterwards while Jacob's tolerance was strained to its limits? Fortunately, tonight had also been different because the church emptied right away. He could give no reason for these anomalies and wasn't curious enough to search for one. Despite a weariness reaching into his very marrow, he had at least remembered his manners and sought out Mr. Oh before leaving. The middle-aged man had turned from Dennis Cullen to Jacob and smiled.

"I just wanted to say thank you for your sermon, Mr. Oh." He reached out and shook his hand.

Kyung Oh bowed. "You are most welcome, Mr. Kichline. I do hope you benefited from the hearing of God's Word."

"Yes, yes, of course." He'd avoided eye contact with Cullen.

"I'm confident that Mr. Moffett would have been very pleased," the American had said.

Oh bowed to Cullen. "I thank you for this word of encouragement."

Jacob had shoved his hands in his coat pockets. "Well, good-night then."

With their parting words echoing in his ears, Jacob had set out on his own, grateful for the few moments he had to himself. How thankful he was for not having to share their room with some country bumpkin, although Jacob would not have called his gratitude any kind of prayer. He was tired of praying.

At the end of the next morning's Bible class, he overheard Mr. Blair say something to one of the Korean leaders about a "lack of response" and how they needed to go to prayer to address the situation.

"We must cry out to God in earnest and not let go until he blesses us."

"I agree with you, Mr. Blair," the Korean said. "We must know his presence among us. I will gather the other missionaries if you like."

"Yes, please do. Let's meet at the church in one hour."

The little man was off in a hurry, and so was Jacob. He was ready to cry out all right, to be released from this ceaseless cajoling. One of the young men in the class intercepted him before he reached the door, and Jacob stood as stiff as a board facing the student.

"If you will please to excuse me, Mr. Kichline—if I may speak with you? I am needing to know how to interpret a Greek word of which you spoke. I am uncertain I understand correctly."

Oh, brother. Suddenly, Jacob considered how he might use this delay as a different means of escape from another prayer meeting.

"I am only too happy to help you," he said, steering the fellow from the classroom. "Let's talk on our way out."

He chattered as they walked down the hall past other Bible class participants, and by the time Jacob completed his complex exegesis, they had reached the stairwell.

"Does that answer your question?" he asked.

"Thank you, Mr. Kichline, you are most wise and learned."

He returned the young man's bow.

"Are you now going to the dining hall for lunch?" He regarded Jacob with expectant eyes.

"Not just yet."

"Oh, yes, you are going to join the missionaries in prayer. Please do excuse me for keeping you from such an important conference."

"I'm glad I could be of service."

They bowed to each other, and Jacob hightailed to his room before anyone else could detain him or, worse, try to walk with him to the latest prayer meeting. *Can't they see how little good they're accomplishing?*

He avoided the dining hall because he didn't want to talk to anyone or be asked why he wasn't with the other leaders. Instead, he cobbled together a small lunch from a stash of food supplies he kept in his room. If Soon-hee didn't return to their quarters before. Even if he were compelled to go, however, he remembered a method he'd once employed at Lafayette when a boring professor droned incessantly. Jacob had learned to completely shut him out while imagining himself on the baseball diamond pitching an important home game. In the daydream, Lafayette was ahead by one run at the top of ninth with two outs and men on first and third. He managed to strike out the batter on a full count, winning the contest. The crowd erupted in cheers while tossing hats into the air, his teammates thronging to him on the field. Yes, this would do nicely during the preaching. Jacob sighed. *Do I ever miss those days. How did my life get so complicated?*

He glimpsed his wall calendar and frowned. He'd only been in Korea for a few months and already couldn't wait to go home—but to what? Judging by the rejections of churches and Pearl, he wasn't ready to be a pastor or a husband, not even with a prestigious theology degree. His shirt collar seemed to grow tighter.

Soon-hee returned just before four o'clock, his face shining. "I am eager to have the evening meal and get back to the church. I am sad you missed the noon prayers, Jacob. I have rarely attended such a session in which we sought the Lord with all our hearts."

Although there was no condemnation in his friend's words, Jacob squirmed. "I needed some time alone."

"I understand. Sometimes our praying is best done in secret."

He let Soon-hee think what he would about how Jacob had spent the afternoon. As for this evening's service, he'd simply slip into his far more pleasant imaginary world.

He didn't understand the excitement in the dining hall, as if the circus had just come to town and the fellows couldn't wait to see the elephants. Jacob laughed to himself, wondering whether Koreans even knew about circuses. At least, everyone seemed in a good mood, which made his meal go down a lot easier. He even went back for seconds. After he and Soon-hee finished, they freshened up before walking to the church in the severe cold under a ceiling of stars.

Inside, the sanctuary was almost at capacity. As they walked to their places at the front, Soon-hee abruptly stopped, and Jacob bumped into him.

Soon-hee looked intently upwards, then side-to-side, seeming not to have noticed. Curious, Jacob asked, "What is it?"

"Do you not feel this?"

"Feel what?" He didn't know why, but something did seem to have shifted in the lamp-lit church.

His roommate whispered in such a hushed voice Jacob had to bend closer to hear him.

"He is here."

"Who?"

Soon-hee turned to face him. "You will see."

Jacob's skin prickled.

Mr. Blair walked over to him, his eyes shining. "Mr. Kichline, Mr. Oh, thank you for coming."

As if I had a choice. Jacob immediately looked away, ashamed of his unworthy thought.

"The other missionaries are otherwise engaged tonight with a program for the women, and Mr. Lee is depending on us to assist him."

Jacob had to come to terms with listening to yet another Korean preach. *This service could go on for hours.*

"I'm going to sit with one of the elders behind the pulpit, and I'm happy to know the two of you will be on hand in case you're needed." He rubbed his hands together. "I have a feeling about tonight."

Soon-hee smiled at the missionary, but Jacob looked away, unable to connect with whatever esoteric knowledge they seemed to possess. After taking their seats, Pastor Lee left the dais and headed in their direction.

"Good evening, Mr. Oh." Lee bowed to the men who'd risen from their mats to greet him. He turned with a smile to Jacob. "I do not believe I know this young man."

"Mr. Joon Lee, may I present Mr. Jacob Kichline, an American with the Board of Foreign Missions."

Jacob kept his hand at his side and bowed.

"He is here for a year to assist with translation work, and we are sharing a room together."

"I am most happy to meet you," Lee said. "This is a very important ministry. I pray you are richly blessed in it."

"Thank you, and I am happy to meet you, uh, Pastor Lee."

The Korean drew closer to them. "Do you also sense his presence?"

Soon-hee's eyes sparkled. "I have felt this as well."

"I will keep my sermon short. I do not wish to get in the way."

"I will be praying for you," Soon-hee said. "In fact, let us now go to the Lord and ask for his anointing to be upon you."

I hope he's speaking for himself. I can't possibly do any more praying.

Joon Lee's sermon was, as promised, brief, and Jacob anticipated the joyful prospect of an early dismissal. Maybe he'd brew a cup of tea and eat leftover Christmas cookies.

"I have shared some of God's Word with you tonight," Lee said, his clasped hands resting on the pulpit. "I would now like us to turn to a time of corporate prayer. I invite any of you who feel led to pray to do so."

Why did he have to go and do that? Jacob knew from experience Korean Christians were never in a hurry when they began expressing themselves.

Like a bolt from the blue, a Korean rose and began praying in a loud voice. Jacob tried to follow what the man was saying, but he couldn't keep up with the fast pace of his words. He watched in amazement while another man got up and prayed at the very same time, followed by many others. Although they spoke all at once, no one seemed to be competing with anyone else. Jacob turned in the direction of Soon-hee to ask him what was going on, seeing his face was glowing.

Mr. Lee began waving his hands, and the crescendo diminished to a murmur before halting altogether.

I'll bet he's going to tell them to stop before this gets out of hand.

But that wasn't what the Korean pastor said. With a huge smile, he instructed them, "If you want to pray like that, then all pray!"

This is chaotic. Whatever happened to Presbyterians doing things decently and in order?

Some men stood while the rest remained on their mats, but everyone seemed to be praying out loud, including Soon-hee and Mr. Blair. Jacob froze in shock, reminded of the Tower of Babel's aftermath with pagan people jabbering in various languages all at once. He couldn't believe Mr. Blair was going along with this madness but there he was with uplifted face praying aloud with the rest of these lunatics. He looked about, desperate for an oasis of sanity, but he found there was none. And what was this? The distinguished Princeton professor Dennis Cullen was standing across the room joining in with his hands lifted, his hands—lifted! What kind of Presbyterian minister did such a thing?

This is insane.

Something like an electric current jolted him from his seat, propelling him away from the mayhem.

I have to get out of here.

Jacob pushed his way through the supplicants who seemed too preoccupied to notice him or his headlong escape. Once outside, he gulped deep breaths as he ran full tilt across the snowy compound to the Y. He didn't care if Soon-hee or any of the missionaries reprimanded him for leaving his post. What was the worst they could do, pronounce him unfit for his assignment and send him back to America? He would be only too happy to get away from these religious fanatics, and no one back home would blame him once he'd told them what he'd witnessed.

CHAPTER THIRTY-TWO

JANUARY 7, 1907

Soon-hee could find no words to describe what was happening tonight. He was barely able to think until a verse from the second chapter of Acts brought a measure of clarity about the situation; "and suddenly there came from heaven the sound as of the rushing of a mighty wind, and it filled all the house where they were sitting." He caught his breath, his hand moving to his heart. *Are we experiencing a Korean Pentecost? Is this the Holy Spirit's visitation, what we have been praying for?*

A moment later, he thought about Jacob and how this event might be affecting him. *Perhaps this is what he needs to overcome his doubts.* He looked to his left where his roommate had been seated next to him, but Jacob wasn't there. Soon-hee craned his neck to scan the church for a sign of him across a sea of upturned faces. He drew closer to William Blair and spoke just loud enough to be heard above the growing din.

"Mr. Blair, do you know where Mr. Kichline is?"

"When this broke out, I saw him take off."

"I suppose all of this was too much for him," Soon-hee said.

"That is also my impression. We can follow up with him later, but for now, we need to focus on being of service here."

"I would agree. What do you make of this?"

Although Blair grinned, Soon-hee thought there was something else behind his expression, a kind of caution.

"I think the Holy Spirit is at work," the missionary said.

Soon-hee's breath stalled. Whatever he had hoped for in terms of being in God's presence, this wasn't part of the scenario. He looked at Mr. Lee, who had remained on the platform with his hand cradling his chin, his head bowed, and body swaying as if he were rocking an infant.

"What should we do, Mr. Blair?" he asked.

"I believe the Lord will show us how we might be of use. Just keep an eye on Mr. Lee and his assistants in case they need us."

Moments later, someone began sobbing at the center of the church, which seemed to set off an eruption of weeping. Soon-hee looked around him with widened eyes while one after the other men began crying until the torrent had engulfed the entire congregation. Nothing in his life had ever prepared him for such a display of passion. This was so unlike Koreans who highly valued group harmony and therefore were subdued about public expressions of emotion. Nor had he ever seen the American missionaries be anything but measured in their responses. However, there were Mr. Lee and Mr. Blair shedding copious tears. Emotion also welled inside Soon-hee until he too was sobbing with his head in his hands, tears filling his palms and dripping onto his shirt.

How long the crying lasted he wasn't sure, but then a middle-aged Korean man began speaking above the din.

"I confess before God and all this assembly my impure heart."

He beat his breast as if he were a figure straight out of the Old Testament.

"I have violated my marriage vows." A visceral moan tore through him. "Oh, I am a sinner!"

The man threw himself down and beat the ground with his fists, his gut-level confession seeping into Soon-hee's heart as he suffered with the man.

Another rose from across the aisle and began speaking, a man Soon-hee recognized because he cooked for Mr. Blair and his family.

Tears rolled down his cheeks. "I confess that I ... I ..."

The man rushed up to William Blair, Soon-hee watching with a pounding heart. *What is he going to do?*

"Pastor, tell me, is there any hope for me, can I be forgiven?"

Before the missionary could respond, the fellow was on the floor at his feet nearly screaming. Blair knelt by his side and put his arm around the distraught fellow speaking words Soon-hee couldn't hear through all the noise.

Another Korean lifted his voice above the bawling assembly.

"May the Lord Jesus Christ forgive me for stealing from my father. I am an unworthy son and a poor Christian." He collapsed to the ground in anguished tears.

Soon-hee didn't know how much more his overflowing spirit could take as he entered into the pain being poured forth. Following the confession, Pastor Lee motioned to the congregation from the pulpit where he had remained standing, now flanked by his pastoral assistants on either side.

"Let us pray for our brothers to be freed from their sin and guilt."

A cataract of spoken prayer ensued, and how long the series of agonized confessions lasted, Soon-hee couldn't tell. He felt himself to be the inhabitant of a dimension outside the realm of earthly time. Rather than creating mass confusion, however, the multiplicity of confessions and prayers of assurance came in benevolent waves, bearing these sons of God to his throne of grace.

Soon-hee remained at the church until three o'clock in the morning when the last people had trickled out. Back in his room, he was relieved to see that Jacob was sound asleep.

As a rule, Soon-hee needed a full night's rest to function well, more so since the commencement of his digestive issue months earlier. He was surprised, then, when he awakened at his usual six o'clock hour not only fully refreshed, but oddly aquiver from the overwhelming evening service. His first thought was more of a desire, to go to the chapel on the first floor of the Y to pray, something Jacob would likely not begin to understand. Soon-hee had felt himself in the presence of the Almighty at Central Presbyterian and craved to fellowship with him again.

He dressed and left the room quietly. At the chapel, he beheld the astonishing sight of men jamming the room, their audible prayers ascending like incense. *When did they come here? Could they have been here all night, after the church was closed?* Desiring a quieter space for his own meditation, he returned to his room. The light was on, and Jacob was gone, his bed unmade. *He never leaves without making his bed. I do hope he is all right*. The urge to pray for his wayward roommate brought Soon-hee to his knees and leaning against his own bed, tears flowing once again as his spirit stirred within him. Several times, he tried to read his Bible but couldn't see clearly and gave up the effort.

Lord Jesus Christ, guide my every thought, my every action today that I may be a suitable vessel for thy purposes. Please show me how I can help my hurting friend Jacob, and do whatever thou must to rid his spirit of all darkness and confusion. I praise thee for condescending to be with us last night and ask thee to remain with us until thou hast fully poured out thy Spirit upon us, unworthy though we may be.

As he finished praying, he gasped when he saw the time on his watch—he'd been on his knees for over an hour. He got up, smoothing his trousers before going to the dining hall where more amazements awaited him. Normally a subdued place of quiet conversation and civility, this morning the space was more like a gymnasium during an athletic contest. Soon-hee lifted his chin and surveyed the jammed tables hoping to find Jacob among the animated throng. *Where could he be? I will not be at peace until I know.*

"Mr. Oh."

He turned in the direction of the familiar voice. But what was this? Mary Yoo's face glowed, and she looked at least ten years younger.

He bowed. "Good morning, Mary Yoo. You appear radiant this morning."

"I never thought I would live to see such a day as this."

Was she excited about what was happening? Then again, wouldn't she be overworked with all the extra people she was feeding?

"Are you not overwhelmed by the amount of food preparation for all these men?"

She smiled and inclined her head to the kitchen. "Many of them are helping me. They have insisted, and so I have been able to worship with the women of the Bible Class."

Surprising even himself, Soon-hee impulsively hugged the woman, who did not seem to mind a bit. Then his thoughts circled back to his anxiety about Jacob, dispersing his previous happiness.

"Mary Yoo, have you seen Mr. Kichline?"

"He came in early, picked at his food, and left. A few men talked to him, but Mr. Kichline kept his head down. He seemed very much alone even in this busy place."

This was not good.

Soon-hee wasn't sure if, in light of the previous day's events, Mr. Cullen and Miss Story would be meeting at their appointed time to pray for Jacob. Inside, the Holy Spirit seemed to be impressing upon Soon-hee an urgency about Jacob, and he hoped they would come. He sat quietly in Cullen's office until the mantel clock chimed the tenth hour, at which time his friends entered, already deep in conversation.

"Ah, there you are, Mr. Oh. I'm happy to see you on this glorious day."

Cullen's face reminded Soon-hee of the biblical account of Moses after he'd been face-to-face with God.

"I am also pleased to see you both. I was unsure you would be coming."

The American gestured to the outside campus. "What happened last night is like a spark lighting everything around us. Mr. Lee and I will be going into the city in a bit to let people know what's going on here, although the word has been spreading through many others."

Clara was beaming. "Last night, there was also a movement of the Holy Spirit among the women, a time of confession and weeping such as I've never seen before."

She wiped a sudden tear from her cheek. "You should've seen the joy on Mary Yoo's face. Oh, but I delighted to see her in such a state of peace."

The sudden presence of a fourth person alerted Soon-hee, and his scalp prickled at the sight of Jacob Kichline, his form casting shadows in the doorway. Unlike Mary Yoo, there was no contentment on his reddened face.

Cullen greeted him a little too cheerfully. "Mr. Kichline, do come in."

When Soon-hee caught Jacob's eye, the darkness he encountered chilled him.

He remained right where he was, his fists clenched. "How could you allow this, this travesty?"

A trickle of spittle accompanied the fighting words.

Cullen frowned. "Travesty?"

"That, that thing that happened last night at the church, at *church*." Jacob's face was the shade of rage. "That is a sacred space, but Mr. Lee turned it into a ... a pagan revel."

Soon-hee could barely move. His friends opened their mouths to speak, but Jacob overrode them, not having fully vented his temper.

"I can understand unlearned Koreans behaving in such a way, but you know better." He thrusted a trembling index finger in Cullen's direction. "You should have put a stop to that yammering." His throat made an odd noise. "I fault you and Mr. Blair for what happened, Mr. Cullen. I may not have met Mr. Moffett, but from what I've heard about him, he wouldn't have allowed such an outrage to take place. I can tell you I will not set foot in that church again or attend your ceaseless prayer meetings until you and the other missionaries—I mean the American and Canadian missionaries, not these pretend Korean pastors—stop this, this *thing*. I came to Korea to do translation work, not to be part of a spectacle. If you don't like it, you can send me right back to America."

Cullen reached out to the agitated fellow. "Mr. Kichline ..."

"I have said my piece."

He turned on his heel and took off, a sour stench trailing behind him. Soon-hee could barely breathe for the crushing weight in his chest. The trio remained silent for several moments, then Clara Story spoke.

"Anyone kicking against the goads like Jacob Kichline may very well be on his own road to Damascus."

Soon-hee was cheek-to-jowl at the front of the church for the evening meeting, which had begun on the previous night's high note. Hundreds more, including women to whom they'd opened the services, had squeezed into the building with more just outside in the freezing cold. On the platform, several of the Korean elders, including his father, sat behind the pulpit monitoring those who came forward to confess their sin. The declarations of guilty souls stunned Soon-hee as they recounted every imaginable transgression, bribery, hatred, assault, theft, adultery, arson, even murder. Each time a penitent unloaded his burden, the congregation broke out in weeping, including Soon-hee, who could not seem to help himself.

At one point, he gazed in open-mouthed wonder when he saw his brother go to the pulpit. Yong-bin was an image of misery, and not over some sham headache.

With a shaky voice the young man said, "I confess to you my sin of pretending to be ill in order to have my own way and of deceiving my family. I also confess my hatred for my brother Soon-hee. He would not help me cheat on an assignment, and I was vindictive. I did my best to turn the one he loves against him by telling her things he never said."

The hair on the back of Soon-hee's neck stiffened, his throat as dry as week-old rice. *Am I dreaming this? This could only be the work of Almighty God in my brother.*

Yong-bin wailed as he raised his hands and looked into Soon-hee's eyes. "Please forgive me, my brother, and please forgive me, God. Cast me not away forever!"

Mr. Blair squeezed Soon-hee's shoulder as he rose to meet Yong-bin in the aisle. The two brothers embraced, sobbing, and were soon joined by their father, shedding his own abundant tears.

"Oh, my sons, my sons!"

Soon-hee trembled as he confessed, "I, too, have sinned. My heart has been so hard against you, Yong-bin. How deeply I have resented you." He wept aloud. "Oh, God, free me from my own sin!"

After some moments, he knew not how many, Soon-hee sat down next to his brother and their father. Mr. Kim, an official who oversaw some of the men's missionary work, got up from where he sat with the church elders and went to the pulpit, which he clutched with trembling hands.

"I have been guilty of fighting against God. Though I am an elder in the church, I have been guilty of hating Kang You-moon."

Soon-hee's jaw dropped. This Mr. Kang was Mr. Blair's distinguished assistant at the North Pyongyang Church, a man roundly admired.

"I have been guilty of hating not only him," he continued, "but also Pang Mok-sa."

William Blair's face turned pale. Soon-hee gasped when Mr. Kim made a direct reference to Blair, whose Korean name was Pang Mok-sa. *What could possibly have gone wrong between these two godly men?* Soon-hee didn't have to wait to get an answer.

Mr. Kim looked in Blair's direction. "A year ago, during a school field-day exercise, you were in a hurry and spoke brusquely to me. I thought you had treated me in a shabby manner, and since then, I have not been able to forgive you. Can you forgive me? Can you pray for me?"

Soon-hee had a sensation of the roof lifting and the Spirit of God coming down in an avalanche of power. While Blair went to meet Mr. Kim and embrace him near the front of the sanctuary, hundreds of men stood with their arms outstretched to heaven. Hundreds more lay prostrate. Each of them pleading aloud in their distress. A wall of sound.

William Blair returned to his original place and motioned for Soon-hee and his father. "I think we best gather for a consultation with the other leaders," he said. "I don't want this to get out of hand."

"I must agree," Mr. Oh said.

Soon-hee gave his own consent, and they plodded through the dense crowd, leaving Yong-bin to his own earnest prayers. Once on the platform, the leaders met in a huddle at the back.

"What shall we do?" Dennis Cullen asked. "If we let them go on like this, I'm afraid some will go crazy."

Pastor Lee, who'd preached the night before, addressed his concern. "While I understand your concern, I do not think we should interfere with what God is doing here. We prayed to him for an outpouring of his Spirit upon Korea, and I believe he is responding."

"I think you're right," William Swallen said. "I suggest we separate and try to comfort those who are in the most distress. We must tell them that despite their sins, whatever they may be, God will forgive them. When the Spirit of God calls upon guilty souls, there must be heart-rending confession, and when it happens, no power on earth can stop it."

Chapter Thirty-Three

January 8, 1907

After fleeing from William Cullen's office, Jacob needed to work off his negative energy. He considered a brisk walk to the river, but this was January, in Korea. A heavy snow was falling, and the cutting wind sliced right through his outerwear. Besides, he'd overheard some men saying the upheaval at the mission compound had spilled into the city. There seemed no avoiding the hullabaloo. Everywhere he turned, someone was in a flap about what they claimed was God's visitation. Clearly, lunacy had overtaken the entire Christian community including those who should have taken authority over it.

He decided to return to his room knowing Soon-hee wouldn't be there. His roommate was probably handling the General Class's teaching alone. Jacob bore a dullness in his chest as he not only considered letting Soon-hee down, but when he replayed the recent scene with him, the professor, and Clara Story. *What must they think of me? I've never spoken like that to anyone before for any reason.* Maybe they wouldn't want anything more to do with him, a prospect which left him bereft. He'd already been distancing himself, but the thought of having no one to turn to depressed him. Why was he constantly out-of-step when he'd always had so many friends? Recent encounters and faces flashed before him—church pulpit committees, Pearl, Harry, the Christian Endeavor group he'd alienated. The wind stung his moistening eyes.

Part of him believed he was just sticking to his principles, which sometimes leads to rejection. Just look at what had happened to Jesus. Then again, people could bring misery upon themselves. He groaned as he wrestled to know which of these categories he was occupying. What made him think he knew better than these seasoned missionaries, even if he had gone to Princeton? Was he so full of spiritual insight as to judge their response to this so-called visitation of God? Hadn't he left the seminary more confused than certain anyway? But how could anyone with eyes to see not realize how fanatical this was? He remembered snippets of accounts he'd heard at Princeton as well as through Pearl of revivals breaking out around the world in the past couple of years. Was it possible they were legitimate? Might he be the one out of step with God? He swallowed hard and set his face against the storm.

He entered the dining hall encased in snow, needing a cup of hot tea.

Mary Yoo caught sight of him and rushed over to his side.

"Mr. Kichline, you are frozen."

"I know. I could use some tea."

"Remove your coat. I will take care of you."

He found her unusually amiable, wondering why she was in such a good mood.

Within minutes, she returned to the table where he sat rubbing his hands against his arms to warm them both. He sipped the hot liquid so as not to burn his tongue. What was this? Mary Yoo had sat across from him, leaving her kitchen staff. He'd never seen her sit before this.

She tilted her head to the side. "Are you unwell, Mr. Kichline?"

Her concern softened his own edges. "What's happening here makes me uneasy."

Why in the world did I tell her such a thing? Am I so desperate I'll reveal my innermost thoughts to a cafeteria worker? He almost despised himself for having such unworthy thoughts.

Mary Yoo stared at him. "When God speaks to us, we are not supposed to be at our ease."

He sighed. "How can you be so sure he is speaking to you?"

"I will tell you. When I first came here, I was a Christian, but some of the old ways stayed in here." She pointed to her heart. "More than a few times, I took money for the food and kept some for myself because I thought I deserved to have it." Her eyes misted.

Jacob gave a start, speechless.

Her dark eyes seared into his. "We are all guilty of something, and God is baring our sins. Repentance has given me peace. Let him say what you need to hear. He forgives." Her face was beaming.

She patted his shoulder and returned to the kitchen, her voice rising above the others as she gave orders. Jacob's pulse raced. How could this little woman be so sure about God when his ways baffled the greatest minds of this age? He drank the tea and left.

He went to the room long enough to change into dry clothes, then escaped to the office. He hoped to find a measure of stability on the firm ground of academic pursuit and fished out the next translation project on the schedule. Within the hour, Jacob looked up from his work, his heart thudding at the sight of Soon-hee and Clara standing at the door, concern etched on their faces.

"We've been looking all over for you," the nurse said.

He couldn't face either of them after the way he'd treated them.

"Are you all right?" Soon-hee asked.

"What do you, think, Mr. Oh?" Why had he used the more formal address? Why was he pushing them away, again? What is wrong with me? Somewhere along the way, he'd lost himself, a thought more chilling than the current weather.

He missed the look they exchanged.

"Is there anything we can do to help?" Clara Story asked. "We're concerned."

"Please, don't be. I prefer to be alone." Now he was lying.

He didn't hear their whispered words and only looked in their direction when he was certain they had left. Jacob put his head in his hands.

He holed up there the entire day with the door shut. He often paced, trying to sort out what was happening at the mission and within himself. Buoyed by an inspiration, he decided to write to the one person he thought would understand him, Gresham Machen. After filling three pages detailing the disturbing scenes in the church, he supplied his own commentary.

> I never dreamed people could behave and think so irrationally, Mr. Machen. When I was at Princeton, there

> were occasional mentions about revivals in various places, like Los Angeles, Kentucky, and Wales, but I never gave them much thought. To me, they were anomalies, just a bunch of misguided people trying to imitate the early Apostles. I can't imagine, however, that the First Century Christians at Pentecost behaved as wildly as I've seen in Pyongyang. Men writhed and pounded the floor, grown men wept with abandon. I heard people saying God had come, but all I felt was a compulsion to leave what struck me as a spiritual bacchanalia.
>
> At this point, I don't know what my future here holds. I even think there's a possibility I may be asked to leave because I'm not falling in line. Believe me, I would welcome the opportunity to be in a sane place among sane people again.

Jacob filled more pages until his right hand cramped. Then he put the pen down and massaged his fingers, calmed by sharing his thoughts with Machen who seemed to him the soul of wisdom. Jacob wished he could see down the road, to know how everything was going to turn out, but the best he could do was put one foot in front of the other.

Since Jacob didn't have Gresham Machen's address at the office, he went back to his room at the Y finding the blinds closed. Soon-hee was lying on top of his bed, one arm reposed above his head, apparently napping. Jacob moved as quietly as possible to avoid rousing him and quickly found the box he was looking for. He sat down close to the window to draw from the available light and saw Machen's letter with its return address next to a photograph of Pearl. He gazed at her likeness, her expression seeming to say, "I care about you, Jacob. I'm believing the best for you."

Shaken, he put the picture back, wrote Machen's Princeton address on an envelope, and stuffed the letter inside.

His own bed looked mighty good, and for some reason he couldn't explain, Jacob didn't feel an immediate need to escape. He laid down and pulled the Hudson's Bay blanket his parents had sent up to his chin. Pouring his heart out to Machen had released some of his pressure. He recalled something the young Princeton professor had told him just before Jacob left for Korea.

"I encourage you not to be discouraged or ashamed of your wrestling. If you contend in a spirit of receptivity rather than rebellion, the risen Lord will have vital communion with you."

His shoulders rose and fell on a sigh. *I'm not ashamed of questioning my early faith, but I haven't exactly been receptive to anything else God might want to say to me.* He sighed. *That God gets involved in our lives at all is one of my main doubts, which has made praying difficult. Am I rebellious? I don't think so. The people here have lost their collective minds, so I don't call opposing them "rebellion." Isn't discernment more like it?*

Jacob's thoughts started breaking into incoherent bits and pieces, and he drifted off to sleep. An hour later, he awakened and, orienting himself, saw Soon-hee sitting on his bed with his back to the wall, reading. He'd cracked open the blinds about halfway.

"Hello, Jacob." Soon-hee's voice was soft.

"Hello."

"If I am in your way, I will leave."

"No, you're not." Jacob sat up and smoothed back his rumpled hair. "Soon-hee, I regret speaking harshly to you."

"Thank you. I know you are having difficulties." He closed his book. "Please forgive me for causing you offense."

"You've done nothing to offend me." He stood to his feet and reached for his drying coat and hat. "If you'll excuse me, I need to mail a letter."

After going to the post office, he decided to go to Dennis Cullen's house. Jacob needed to try to see him, unable to carry his burden alone. The wind had eased up as he walked across the frozen campus and soon found himself at the man's residence shivering.

Mrs. Cullen opened the door, her face upturned. "Mr. Kichline, come in from the cold."

"I hope I'm not intruding. I just came to see if Mr. Cullen was in."

"I regret to say he isn't. There are special meetings taking place in all the churches today, and he's leading one." She lifted her hands, palms up. "I don't know when he'll be back."

If she wondered why Jacob wasn't with them, she didn't say anything. All at once, two little girls sprang into view and pounced on him like eager puppies.

"Well, hello there." Jacob returned their hugs, rather enjoying the feeling of being on someone's good side.

Eileen Cullen laughed. "Girls, give him some room to breathe. These two belong to the Swallens, and I'm watching them for a few hours. Mr. Kichline, I just put the kettle on. Please stay for tea, and we can catch up while the children play." Her raised eyebrows brought them under immediate control.

Her invitation calmed him, and the girls' unabashed joy breached Jacob's wall of isolation. While Mrs. Cullen prepared the tea, he sat on the floor with the children, helping them build a house of colorful blocks. For the moment, he forgot the millstone around his neck. Right after Mrs. Cullen called him to the table and said a prayer, the front door opened, and her husband appeared.

"Well, hello, Jacob. This is a pleasant surprise," he said.

Cullen strode over to him and shook Jacob's hand before removing his outer garments.

"We're just about to have tea, dear. Jacob came by hoping to see you, and I still have the Swallens' little girls. You're back earlier than I thought."

"The Koreans were so eager to spread the word of what's been happening we curtailed the meeting, so they could be on their way rejoicing as it were." He sat across from Jacob. "How are you?"

"I, uh, I'm okay."

Cullen gazed at him for a moment until his attention swung to his wife who gave him her cup and saucer. "You appear to be leaving us, my dear. Won't you stay?"

"Jacob came to see you. Besides, I can keep the children occupied." She turned to her visitor. "I'm so happy to see you. You're always welcome here."

"Thank you, Mrs. Cullen."

The professor sipped his tea. "My, but that tastes good on such a bitterly cold day." He gazed at Jacob. "What's on your mind, my friend?"

He called me his friend. Jacob put the cup and saucer on the table, his hand shaking.

"Mr. Cullen, I'm sorry I skipped the General Class today."

"I see. Actually, we dismissed early because most of the participants had gone to their homes, eager to spread the tidings."

"Oh, okay. I still should have checked in with you." He blew out a breath. "I'm profoundly ill-at-ease with what's going on here. All this weeping, shouting, and pounding on the floor. I can begin to understand why Koreans carry on in such a way because they haven't been Christians for very long. But to see well-educated Americans going along with this ..." He stared at the floor. "I know I shouldn't have lost my temper with my friends."

Cullen seemed to study him while the girls' laughter floated from the next room. "To be honest with you, I've had my own misgivings about the emotional nature of this event."

This was unexpected. "You have?"

"Yes, and so has Mr. Blair, Mr. Swallen, Mr. Bernheisel, and not a few Korean leaders. None of us have ever seen anything like this, so we've all been caught off guard by the intensity. Furthermore, in all the places this story is being told, in the city as well as the villages, similar outbreaks are occurring." He drained the tea and jangled the cup onto the saucer. "We even thought about putting a stop to the service last night when the confessions became emotionally fervent again. Then, Mr. Blair reminded us we've been praying for an outpouring of God's Spirit upon the people, and we don't get to dictate our terms to him. We did our best to comfort the most distressed among the men, reminding them no matter what they may have done, God would forgive them. They experienced great peace then."

Jacob's voice was a whisper. "I couldn't wait to get out of there."

"I don't entirely blame you. I'm thrilled God is among us, but I would be just fine never again to witness what I saw last night unless he deemed it absolutely necessary." He heaved a sigh. "Each of us has our own ideas about whether or not public confession of sin is desirable, but when the Spirit of God falls upon a guilty soul, nothing can stop his confession."

Jacob pressed his hands together, considering this. "Perhaps you may be right, Mr. Cullen."

"Tell me something, Jacob, how has your spirit been since coming to Korea? Are you finding any answers to the faith questions you brought with you?"

"I still feel unsettled, and if anything, I have more questions, especially since this happened."

"I can be perfectly candid with you, or I can put a temporary bandage on what hurts. Which do you prefer?"

Jacob gave him a small smile. "I'll try to hear what you have to say."

"That's a good fellow. I know all about Princeton Seminary. I was educated there and have taught there, so I know how the sausage is made. One thing I've learned is often scholars make the simplest concepts way too complicated. There's a tendency to believe a person has to be complex to be considered profound. The heart of profundity, however, is simplicity." He gazed at Jacob. "Jesus said unless we become as a little child, we cannot enter the kingdom of God."

"This makes sense, but I thought we were supposed to put away childish things as we got older."

"I understand this to mean we need to grow beyond the milk phase in order to feast on the rich meat of God's word. Jacob, education is a good thing, but when our learning becomes greater than our obedience, we become like self-righteous Pharisees. The Lord's redemptive plan is simple enough for the most unlearned to grasp." He laughed. "Those two little Swallen girls probably have a better grasp of salvation, and certainly have a closer walk with God, than some professors I knew at Princeton. You know the ones—they've troubled your soul and caused it nothing but grief. Furthermore, many of the Koreans I've met, toothless and living in what we consider shacks, have the most inspiring faith you'll ever encounter. They have learned the secret of contentment in Christ. Given a choice, I'd much rather be in their shoes." He paused. "I hope you won't take offense, but there's something I believe I must say to you."

Jacob bit his lip.

"In First Corinthians, Paul said God chooses people and things that humans consider foolish in order to shame the so-called wise. Jacob, you have put yourself in the place of a truly foolish man." Cullen's eyes misted. "I beg you not to stay there, not at the peril of your soul."

CHAPTER THIRTY-FOUR

JANUARY 9, 1907

Soon-hee collapsed onto his bed at eleven o'clock, worn-out from the elevated emotion and frenetic activity of the past few days. Most of the General Class attendees had left by now, keen to spread the glad tidings in all the places they lived while the Holy Spirit continued to move on campus. He was still coming to terms not only with the outpouring itself, but with Yong-bin's unexpected public declaration of guilt and the joyful renewal of their relationship. He wondered what his mother had been told and how she would process her youngest son's life of dishonesty. As usual, Jeongsook was not far from his mind. He hoped in the light of Yong-bin's full disclosure, they might now fully rekindle their former attachment. Through it all, he had never stopped loving her.

Breathing out, he turned off the light and settled into the warmth of his bed. Outside the wind whistled around the window, lulling him to the edges of slumber. He wasn't sure how long he'd been asleep when the sound of their squeaking door awakened him.

"Jacob?"

"I'm sorry I woke you up. I was trying to be quiet."

The door clicked shut behind Jacob, who removed his coat, hat, and boots, then sat on the side of his bed.

"Are you good, Jacob?"

"I suppose. I've been with Mr. and Mrs. Cullen."

Soon-hee realized this might be all his friend chose to reveal.

After some moments, Jacob spoke again. "There's something I'd like to say to you, that is, if you're not too tired."

He was about to turn on the light, but something held him back. "I am not." He sat up in bed.

"I want to apologize for the sharp way I spoke to you. I was out of line."

He wanted to give his absolution but detected there might be more his roommate wished to say.

"In fact, Soon-hee, I've been arrogant with you ever since I came to Korea." His voice hitched. "I'm truly sorry and ask your forgiveness."

Soon-hee clicked on the light and saw tears streaking down his friend's cheeks.

"I do forgive you." He shook Jacob's hand, Western-style, then brushed moisture from his own cheeks. "My cup is overflowing."

Jacob wiped his face with a handkerchief. "How so?"

"My brother confessed to the entire church how he had feigned illness many times and how he disrupted my relationship with Jeongsook after I refused to help him cheat on an assignment."

"Wow."

"You express my sentiments well."

"I'm really happy for you."

"Tomorrow, my entire family will go into Chunghwa to conduct a service." He looked down, blushing. "Jeongsook is coming with us."

Jacob wet his lips. "Is this the place where Mr. Cullen and Miss Story are also going?"

"Yes." He waited before asking, "Might you wish to come as well?"

Jacob climbed into his bed without responding, and Soon-hee decided not to pursue the matter. He turned off the light and lay back onto his pillow.

"Soon-hee?"

"Yes?"

"Thanks for inviting me. I'll go too."

The Oh household busied itself with preparations for the trip to the Presbyterian church twelve miles south of Pyongyang. For once in his life, Soon-hee took pleasure in his brother's company, marveling at the transformation in Yong-bin's radiant face. The only person who said very little was Mr. Oh, who kept mainly to himself and communicated with a succession of grunts and gestures. When they finished and ventured into the cold, they caught up with Dennis Cullen and Clara Story outside the infirmary. There, they paused for a brief prayer before setting out on horseback. As he petitioned the Lord, the steam on Cullen's breath seemed to perform a waltz.

The sun glistened against the previous night's snowfall, the ice clinging to bare branches heralding them on their way. During the three-hour journey, Soon-hee naturally paired off with Jacob, often casting glances at Jeongsook, who rode with Sora. He wondered whether something else might be wrong between them when Jeongsook seemed to avoid him. When he found himself next to her at the end of their trip, he chattered about the beautiful day and the group's plans. She responded only briefly, then withdrew. Just before they reached their destination, Jeongsook lifted her warm brown eyes to his.

"I have something on my heart that I must speak to you."

His heart raced, grateful no one seemed to be taking note of their intimate moment as they conversed among themselves.

"I will listen." He looked straight ahead, as the horse plodded underneath him.

"I am truly sorry for believing what Yong-bin told me about, about ..." Her chin lowered. "I was wrong for thinking ill of you. Can you forgive me?"

Soon-hee broke into a smile. "Yes, Jeongsook, of course I forgive you."

She exhaled. "Do you think we can be as we once were?"

"I would like nothing more."

The road to his future seemed all at once as clear as the blue sky.

The church was packed to beyond capacity with men, women, and children elbow-to-elbow. Cullen and Oh senior led the service while the rest of them were scattered throughout the sanctuary ministering to penitents who couldn't seem to confess their sins fast enough—some petty, others downright criminal. Their combined transgressions were enough to make the angels weep, but their rejoicing in being released from bondage was far greater.

After praying with a young boy who had stolen a neighbor's chicken, Soon-hee scanned the crowd for a glimpse of his friend, finding Jacob across the room, bent over an old woman. With him, Clara Story had rested a hand on the lady's stooped shoulder. They appeared to be praying. So did Soon-hee—that the Lord would use this experience to take Jacob to a much better place in his faith.

He didn't think anything was unusual when his father went up to the pulpit an hour into the service.

"The Spirit of the Lord is moving us to repent of our sins and to receive his forgiveness," Kyung Oh said. "You must know that your spiritual leaders are also men of flesh and blood, subjected to the same temptations as every other man." He cleared his throat.

Yong-bin stepped next to his brother, his eyes bright and wide open. "What is happening?"

"Maybe he has an instruction for us." A fluttering in his chest told him otherwise.

"In the hearing of everyone in this place, I wish to confess the sin of treating my wife with harshness." Oh's voice broke.

Soon-hee pressed his palms to his cheeks. *Surely I am dreaming.* He and his brother gaped at each other.

Their father went on. "I have treated her as little more than a servant and not the helpmeet the Lord so generously blessed me with."

What was this? Their mother joined him on the platform with tears in her shining eyes, and he caressed her shoulder. Then he said, "I have not treated all of my children with the love of the Lord Jesus either. I have favored one above the others."

Soon-hee's knees seemed to buckle, then, he felt Jacob's presence standing next to him.

"Are you okay?"

"The Lord seems to be renewing my entire family," Soon-hee said. "And he is renewing me. The resentment I clung to is disappearing from my spirit." He gave a laugh. "I feel both weak and strong."

Sora joined them and embraced her brothers, all of them in tears.

After their father's confession, he made another startling announcement.

"There are some men who asked for permission to speak, and it has been granted to them. I hope you will listen to and accept them as I have done."

Soon-hee began to think he might just have to pick up his jaw from the floor if the surprises continued. Coming to the platform and standing before the Korean congregation, four Japanese soldiers faced those who had hated them. Each of the men took a turn speaking, confessing their contempt for the Korean people and apologizing for inflicting insults large and small.

The final one to address them said, "I speak for us all in seeking your forgiveness and asking if we too might know Jesus Christ."

Soon-hee immediately went forward to help his father and Mr. Cullen set up the baptismal font. After filling the cold basin, he bowed to the Japanese men.

"I have resented your people, and I ask for your pardon. From this moment, you are my brothers in the faith."

Soon-hee and Jacob were finishing their breakfast the following morning when William Blair approached them, his breath labored and cheeks pink from the cold.

"There you are. I was so hoping to find you here." He put his hands on his thighs, bending over.

"Are you okay?" Jacob asked. He pulled out the chair beside him.

The missionary raised an index finger as he huffed. "I ran across the campus at a sprint. I've had a request from one of the Christian schools just to the north to do a special service this afternoon. According to reports Mr. Swallen and I have received, the students are in such a state over this revival the administrators have had to cancel classes. I know you got in late last night from Chunghwa, but I wonder if you might be willing to go with me."

Soon-hee looked to his roommate, eager to answer this call but wondering if Jacob would be so amenable. They didn't have any public obligations today, but Jacob had been subdued since yesterday's gathering. Soon-hee considered how not everyone needed to be caught up in a frenzy of weeping over his sins to become right with God, but was Jacob in such a place?

"Yes, Mr. Blair, I'll go."

The missionary rubbed his hands together. "Thanks, Jacob."

"I also would like to help," Soon-hee said.

"Let's meet here at eleven o'clock for an early lunch so we can get there by noon." He laughed. "Let's hope Mary Yoo doesn't mind."

Fervent young people swarmed the school's chapel along with a strong adult contingent from the community. The headmaster had told the Pyongyang delegation they were unable to keep the townspeople away entirely.

"They are so eager to receive what God is pouring out."

William Blair began the service with a welcome, prayer, and the hymn "Nearer, My God, To Thee," followed by a brief account of what had been happening the past few days at Central Presbyterian Church and around the area.

"Many of you are also eager to have an encounter with God," he said, "to confess your sins and get right with him. My colleagues and I are here to invite you to share your burdens with us and to receive God's wondrous gift of salvation and freedom from all that binds your spirit."

Before he'd uttered the last word, students stampeded to the front where they unloaded every sin encumbering them. Soon-hee stood at the bottom of the platform with Jacob to maintain a sense of order as one-by-one children went to the pulpit, bowed their heads, and made a clean breast of their transgressions.

Soon-hee lost track of time as the Spirit of the Lord took precedence over all other matters. Despite his aching feet and back, he had never felt stronger. All at once he realized his stomach didn't hurt anymore, hadn't in fact, bothered him since the start of the revival. He recalled how at breakfast, he'd carelessly spooned kimchi over his eggs without suffering a single pang of discomfort afterwards. Just as God was renewing multitudes of Koreans, he had healed Soon-hee.

CHAPTER THIRTY-FIVE

February 15, 1907
Pyongyang, Korea

Dear Mr. Machen,

I greet you in the name of our Lord and Savior Jesus Christ and pray that this finds you in good health and strong of spirit. Please excuse me for not responding sooner to your letter. However, when I tell you what's been happening here, I think you'll understand why.

I'll begin with the Christmas holidays, which were rather unusual for me. The missionaries and their Korean associates had been in earnest prayer for much of the past year, seeking a special blessing from God for the Korean Church. They were fervent for the kind of revival that has broken out in several other places these past few years. The leaders decided to forego the usual Yuletide festivities in favor of concentrated times of worship and communal prayer. I must confess to you, I found their decision disappointing. In a spirit of further candor, I was rather tired of constantly being in church. Letters and gifts from home, as well as a holiday meal in a Korean home offset my homesickness.

At the start of each new year, the missionaries welcome men from the furthest villages to Pyongyang for intensive Bible study, and of course, prayer. Many brought their

> wives and children, who also received instruction. Along with my roommate Soon-hee Oh, a Pyongyang Theological Seminary graduate who's now pursuing a doctorate, we helped Mr. William Blair teach a men's Bible class. This was for me a welcome opportunity for more scholarly pursuits. I'd been rather ill at the end of the fall with dysentery, and I used lingering weakness as an excuse to avoid most of the prayer meetings.
>
> On the second night during the worship service, a Mr. Lee was preaching, and after a brief sermon, invited the congregants to pray. I thought he was going to, but instead men began standing up and praying aloud in a disorderly way. I found this unseemly and watched as the situation soon got out of hand. Several Koreans went up to the pulpit, with Mr. Lee's blessing, and began confessing sin. This led to an outbreak of weeping all around the church. When a few men near me fell to the ground, pounding on it with their fists and wailing, I left in a hurry. I was thoroughly disgusted by the violation of Presbyterian teachings about upholding decency and order. Similar scenes repeated the following night. The entire campus was in an uproar, convinced that God brought revival to Korea, but I wanted nothing to do with it. I even accused Soon-hee, Dennis Cullen, and another missionary of lawlessness. When they responded with love and concern, I hardened my heart.

Jacob paused to dip his pen in the inkwell. Soon-hee was sitting on his bed pouring over a Greek New Testament and glanced at him with a smile. Outside, oil lamps gleamed in the sparkling winter darkness, illuminating a fresh coating of snow.

> Although I stood against what was happening, inwardly I was in turmoil. As I once told you, I was raised in the Church and came to believe in the Lord Jesus at an early age. The things of faith came easily for me. You also may

recall from our last conversation at Princeton how much I struggled there to reconcile my youthful beliefs with modernism. I didn't want to let go of what had been so dear to me, but I didn't know how to continue in such faith when great scholars masterfully argued against it. That inner wrestling became a fully-blown faith crisis during January's outpouring.

In my distress, I went to see Dennis Cullen at his home, first to apologize for my offensive behavior, and also to pour out my embattled spirit. I find it difficult to put into words what he told me, let alone succinctly. Suffice it to say, I realized how proud and arrogant I had become at Princeton. I had come to believe no one without a seminary education had a correct interpretation of the Scriptures. I'd become just like the Pharisee in Luke 18 who thanked God that he wasn't like other men. Not that being of such a mind had benefited me, except to puff me up.

That night and throughout the next day, my heart began to soften. I confessed my arrogance to those I'd hurt and started experiencing joy in prayer and worship. Someday perhaps, I can fill out the details with you in person, for they are well worth telling.

Since the start of revival in early January, special services have been ongoing. The local schools have also paused to focus on seeking the Lord, and I've had the privilege of providing leadership at some of them. Each time a young soul repents, either for the first time or to receive a deeper visitation of the Lord, I've rejoiced with the angels in Heaven.

Whereas I once couldn't wait to go home to America and leave what I had considered a God-forsaken place, I now look forward to completing my year here. I'm not only doing translation work, but along with Soon-hee am conducting in-depth Bible studies for the boys and young men. I've gone on several trips to outlying churches and witnessed how the Spirit continues to move among the Koreans. When people weep over their sins, I no longer shrink in disgust but embrace them in tears. I've been astonished to see these churches empowered in numbers and in spirit.

There are stories too numerous to mention in this already lengthy letter, but I'll share just one more. Mr. Cullen, Soon-hee, and I had been asked to stop by a church with a few tepid Christians in a goldmining camp on a trip to the outlying areas. We were, however, behind schedule and stopped just long enough to promise those who came to greet us a longer visit in the near future. Soon-hee offered to say a prayer and as he began, a spirit of repentance fell upon them. Most miners live the coarsest of existences, but there they were weeping as they received new life. I'm eager to return to them to see how the Lord has been working since we left.

Well, Mr. Machen, I think you'll understand how my hand is beginning to cramp! I'm reminded of John who said Jesus had done many more works than could be recorded. Perhaps someday, one or several of the missionaries will write books about the revival that began in Pyongyang in the opening days of 1907. I'm going to hold dear these stories for the rest of my life.

May the same Spirit that raised Jesus from the dead be in you.

Jacob Kichline

Jacob took a break from his letter-writing to go with one of the mission's Korean workers into the city. The middle-aged man had a long-ago sin he wanted to confess to a Chinese merchant and needed Jacob's support, which he was happy to give. When they got to the shop, the formidable owner didn't even seem to recognize the Korean.

Jacob could see his friend trembling and prayed the encounter would go well.

"Many years ago," the Korean said, "I unjustly charged you for certain goods and kept what was extra for myself." He then emptied his pockets of a good bit of money and laid it on the counter.

As he accepted the offering, the Chinese man's eyes widened. He seemed more astonished by the restitution being made than the confession itself.

"I do not understand. I never knew you had cheated me, so you did not have to come to me. Why have you done this?"

"Because I have given my heart to the Lord Jesus, and he requires of me a pure heart," the Korean man said.

"Then I must know this Jesus too!"

Jacob stepped forward and prayed with the Chinaman to become a Christian. Before they left the store, he invited the man to a service. The Korean's transparency touched Jacob so deeply. He wrote to Harry expressing his remorse for being insolent with the Christian Endeavor and included a message for his friend to read to the group. Jacob also confessed his pride to his pastor and church elders, as well as the leaders of pulpit committees with whom he'd interviewed. Although the confessions were difficult to write, by swallowing his arrogance, he experienced greater freedom in Christ.

He saved his final letter for Pearl, determined to be straightforward without inviting her response or asking for another chance. He withdrew the needle work motto she had gifted him from a drawer with its assurance that God would complete the good work he'd begun in Jacob. While this gave him the hope of a good future, he didn't know if he and Pearl had anything left but the past.

Then, there was his admiration for Clara Story, who had become even dearer and closer to him during the last incredible month. Jacob had no idea how God might be leading him regarding these two women, but he wanted to be in the Lord's will, whatever it was.

"Mr. Kichline, I am so very happy you are my teacher."

When the ten-year-old boy hugged him, Jacob returned the gesture. He took the smiling fellow by the shoulders and surveyed him at arms' length.

"And I am very happy you're my student."

He smiled as he watched the youth leave the classroom with his compatriots. Jacob never dreamed when he came to Korea he would cherish instructing young boys in the faith. His heart gave a small leap at the sight of Clara Story coming through the door.

"Well, hello, Mr. Kichline."

"Hello, Miss Story. To what do I owe this pleasant surprise?" He stacked his Bible and notebooks on the desk.

"I just saw a first-grader with tummy upset and thought I'd see if you were still here."

"I'm glad you stopped by." He nodded at her outdoor attire. "Are you heading back to the infirmary?"

"Actually, I'm going home."

"May I walk with you?" he asked. "I just finished teaching for the day."

"Yes, I'd like that."

He pulled on his scarf and coat, worked his hands into his gloves, and popped on his hat before stepping aside to let her pass through the door. Outside, they speculated about when the first signs of spring might arrive, then she became more personal.

"I'm filled with joy at the change in you."

His face warmed. "And I'm grateful for the way you put up with me in my former state."

"You're not alone, you know."

A group of chattering girls passed them, calling out welcomes.

"How do you mean?" he asked.

"Everyone struggles to come to terms with his sin."

He took a deep breath. "When did you?" He realized he'd never heard this part of Clara's story before.

"About midway through college, I found myself questioning everything." She looked at him. "Maybe that's why I wasn't terribly offended when you blew up at me that day."

He could tell she was teasing him and took the remark in stride.

"Fortunately, my struggle only lasted for one semester." They walked in a momentary silence. "So, Jacob Kichline, what does the future look like for you now? Might you be teaching elementary-aged boys?"

He laughed. "The thought has crossed my mind, but I keep coming back to my earlier calling of pastoral ministry. I'll just need to make sure my church has a robust Sunday School in which I'm personally involved."

"Will you be leaving Korea at the end of your appointed year?"

Why was she asking him? She sounded casual enough, but might there be a deeper meaning behind her words? He wanted to know her plans too without sounding like he was announcing his affection for her.

"Yes, I'll go back to my hometown and begin looking for a church to serve. How about you? Will you be returning to the States any time soon?" His heart pounded.

She let out a sigh. "Whereas Korea is a step along God's journey for you, this place is my calling and my home now."

He tripped on a rock and quickly steadied himself. He was going to miss his very dear friend Clara Story.

March 15, 1907
Bethlehem, PA

My Dear Jacob,

Your recent letter has been a source of endless thanksgiving since I read it for the first time. The visitation of God upon the Korean people fills me with joy, and I've been sharing the glad tidings with everyone who will listen. How amazing to think that in this modern age, God continues to work miracles of redemption and revival.

Most of all, I thank him for bringing you out of the fog you've lived in since you went to Princeton. I sensed you slipping away and never stopped praying that even though you might stumble, you would not fall, except at his feet in surrender. How I praise him for his work in your life!

May the rest of your sojourn in the Land of the Morning Calm be a time of blessings more abundant than you can ask or imagine. When you return, I'll want to hear all your stories. I haven't nearly such dramatic accounts to relate, but I've seen the Lord working at my church and through Christian Endeavor. I think he's doing a new thing in this old and fallen, though vastly beautiful, world of his creation.

In closing, I would remind you of the verse I stitched in the embroidery I made for you. "He which hath begun a good work in you will perform it until the day of Jesus Christ."

Perhaps, just perhaps, he'll also continue a work in us.

Faithfully yours,
Pearl

Sitting at his desk, Jacob found himself immersed in light when the sun broke through the clouds.

EPILOGUE

OCTOBER 19, 1907
NAZARETH, PENNSYLVANIA

Alfred Sime, chairman of the Drylands Presbyterian Church pulpit committee leaned back in his seat, surveying the room with a pleased expression. "That was an excellent sermon, Mr. Kichline," he said, "so relatable. When your pastor told us you were back from Korea, we hoped you might be willing to give us another try."

The tension around Jacob's temples eased, replaced by the joy he sensed in the voices of parishioners as they chatted and drank coffee in the fellowship hall. "Thank you, Mr. Sime. When I found out you were still looking for a pastor, I hoped you might give me another chance."

Judging by the relaxed expressions of the other men involved with the search, Jacob had a feeling this situation might turn out well for all of them. The same men had been all stiff handshakes and pasted on smiles the last time he'd candidated here.

"Your year abroad has changed you," Sime said, looking Jacob over.

"Yes, sir, it has. I went to Korea in a confused and, I'm sorry to say, rather arrogant condition."

"What happened?" a balding elder asked.

Jacob noticed the way late-morning sunlight played on the wall of the vacant minister's office. "In a word, God got hold of me. The revival that broke out in Pyongyang affected countless lives, including mine." He smoothed an imaginary crease on his right trouser leg. "I'm grateful for the way the Lord restored the years that the locusts had eaten while I was at Princeton."

Alfred Sime pressed his palms against his thighs. "Well, I personally believe the Lord has had Drylands wait to fill our pulpit until you were ready, Mr. Kichline."

Jacob held his breath when the committee chairman paused.

Sime looked around at the other men before resting his gaze on Jacob. "We are all of one accord and would like to extend a call for you to become our next pastor."

He lowered his head before responding. "You do me a great honor, and I am grateful. I do accept your call." Jacob smiled to himself over the way his word choice reminded him of Soon-hee. He couldn't wait to share his news with his dear Korean friend. He couldn't wait to tell Pearl.

TO MY READERS

Thank you for reading *Land of the Morning Calm*. If you enjoyed this novel, please consider leaving a review on Amazon or your favorite book site—your feedback helps more readers discover this moving story. You can also follow me on social media for updates, behind-the-scenes content, and news about future projects. Connect with me at www.rebeccapricejanney.com, Instagram, Facebook, X, and MeWe.

Rebecca Price Janney

ABOUT THE AUTHOR

Rebecca Price Janney is the multi-award-winning author of twenty-eight published books, including multi-award-winning *East of the Sun* and her beloved Easton Series. A historian and popular speaker, she lives with her husband, son, and Cavalier King Charles Spaniel in Pennsylvania's Lehigh Valley.

MORE BOOKS BY REBECCA PRICE JANNEY

EASTON SERIES

- *Easton at the Forks*
- *Easton in the Valley*
- *Easton at the Crossroads*
- *Easton at the Pass*
- *Easton at Christmastide*
- *Easton at Sunset*

MORNING IN AMERICA SERIES

- *Morning Glory*
- *Sweet Sweet Spirit*

HEIRS OF FREEDOM SERIES

- *East of the Sun*
- *Land of the Morning Calm*

www.ingramcontent.com/pod-product-compliance
Lightning Source LLC
LaVergne TN
LVHW020522100826
845148LV00010B/1310

* 9 7 9 8 8 9 1 3 4 5 2 0 1 *